Also by
JOAN JOHNSTON

Hawk's Way titles

The Substitute Groom
The Unforgiving Bride
The Headstrong Bride
The Disobedient Bride
The Cowboy Takes a Wife
The Wrangler and the Rich Girl
The Cowboy and the Princess
The Rancher and the Runaway Bride

Other titles

Sisters Found
Honey and the Hired Hand
A Little Time in Texas
A Wolf in Sheep's Clothing
Never Tease a Wolf
Marriage by the Book
Fit to Be Tied

JOAN JOHNSTON

Hawk's Way
REBELS

HQN™

Recycling programs
for this product may
not exist in your area.

ISBN-13: 978-0-373-77560-6

HAWK'S WAY: REBELS

Copyright © 2011 by Harlequin Books S.A.

The publisher acknowledges the copyright holder
of the individual works as follows:

THE TEMPORARY GROOM
Copyright © 1996 by Joan Mertens Johnston

THE VIRGIN GROOM
Copyright © 1997 by Joan Mertens Johnston

www.HQNBooks.com

Printed in U.S.A.

CONTENTS

THE TEMPORARY GROOM

CHAPTER ONE

CHERRY WHITELAW was in trouble. Again. She simply couldn't live up to the high expectations of her adoptive parents, Zach and Rebecca Whitelaw. She had been a Whitelaw for three years, ever since her fifteenth birthday, and it was getting harder and harder to face the looks of disappointment on her parents' faces each time they learned of her latest escapade.

This time it was really serious. This was about the worst thing that could happen to a high school girl. Well, the second worst. At least she wasn't pregnant.

Cherry had been caught spiking the punch at the senior prom this evening by the principal, Mr. Cornwell, and expelled on the spot. The worst of it was, she wasn't even guilty! Not that anyone was going to believe her. Because most of the time she was.

Her best friend, Tessa Ramos, had brought the pint bottle of whiskey to the dance. Cherry had been trying to talk Tessa out of spiking the punch—had just taken the bottle from Tessa's hand—when Mr. Cornwell caught her with it.

He had snatched it away with a look of dismay and said, "I'm ashamed of you, young lady. It's bad enough when your behavior disrupts class. An irresponsible act like this has farther-reaching ramifications."

"But, Mr. Cornwell, I was only—"

"You're obviously incorrigible, Ms. Whitelaw."

Cherry hated being called that. *Incorrigible.* Being *incorrigible* meant no one wanted her because she was too much trouble. Except Zach and Rebecca had. They had loved her no matter what she did. They would believe in her this time, too. But that didn't change the fact she had let them down. Again.

"You're expelled," Mr. Cornwell had said, his rotund face nearly as red as Cherry's hair, but not quite, because nothing could ever be quite that red. "You will leave this dance at once. I'll be in touch with your parents tomorrow."

No amount of argument about her innocence had done any good, because she had been unwilling to name her best friend as the real culprit. She might be a trouble-maker, but she was no rat.

Mr. Cornwell's pronouncement had been final. She was out. She wasn't going to graduate with the rest of her class. She would have to come back for summer school.

Rebecca was going to cry when she found out. And Zach was going to get that grim-lipped look that meant he was really upset.

Cherry felt a little like crying herself. She had no idea why she was so often driven to wild behavior. She only knew she couldn't seem to stop. And it wasn't going to do any good to protest her innocence this time. She had been guilty too often in the past.

"Hey, Cherry! You gonna sit there mopin' all night, or what?"

Cherry glanced at her prom date, Ray Estes. He lay sprawled on the grass beside her at the stock pond on the farthest edge of Hawk's Pride, her father's ranch, where she had retreated in defeat. Her full-length, pale green chiffon prom dress, which had made her feel like a fairy princess earlier in the evening, was stained with dirt and grass.

Ray's tuxedo was missing the jacket, bow tie, and cummerbund, and his shirt was unbuttoned halfway to his waist. He was guzzling the fourth can of a six-pack of beer he had been slowly but surely consuming since they had arrived at the pond an hour ago.

Cherry sat beside him holding the fifth can, but it was still nearly full. Somehow she didn't feel much like getting drunk. She had to face her parents sometime tonight, and that would only be adding insult to injury.

"C'mon, Cherry, give us a li'l kiss," Ray said, dragging himself upright with difficulty and leaning toward her.

She braced a palm in the smooth center of his chest to keep him from falling onto her. "You're drunk, Ray."

Ray grinned. "Shhure am. How 'bout that kiss, Cher-ry?"

"No, Ray."

"Aww, why not?"

"I got thrown out of school tonight, Ray. I don't feel like kissing anybody."

"Not even me?" Ray said.

Cherry laughed at the woeful, hangdog look on his face and shook her head. "Not even you." Ray was good fun most of the time. He drank a little too much, and he drove a little too fast, and his grades hadn't been too good. But she hadn't been in a position to be too picky.

She had dreamed sometimes of what it might be like to be one of the "good girls" and have "nice boys" calling her up to ask for dates. It hadn't happened. She was the kind of trouble nice boys stayed away from.

"C'mon, Cher-ry," Ray said. "Gimme li'l kiss."

He teetered forward, and the sheer weight of him forced her backward so she was lying flat on the ground. Cherry was five-eleven in her stocking feet and could run fast enough to make the girls' track team—if she hadn't always been in too much trouble to qualify. But Ray was four inches taller and forty pounds heavier. She turned her head away to avoid his slobbery, seeking lips, which landed on her cheeks and chin.

"I said no, Ray. Get off!" She shoved uselessly at his heavy body, a sense of panic growing inside her.

"Aww, Cher-ry," he slurred drunkenly. "You know you want it." His hand closed around her breast.

"Ray! No!" she cried. She grabbed his wrist and yanked it away and heard the chiffon rip as his grasping fingers held fast to the cloth. "Ray, please!" she pleaded.

Then she felt his hand on her bare flesh. "No, Ray. No!"

"Gonna have you, Cher-ry," Ray muttered. "Always wanted to. Know you want it, too."

Cherry suddenly realized she might be in even worse trouble than she'd thought.

BILLY STONECREEK was in trouble. Again. His former mother-in-law, Penelope Trask, was furious because he had gotten into a little fight in a bar in town and spent the night in jail—for the third time in a year.

He had a live-in housekeeper to stay with his daughters, so they were never alone. He figured he'd been a pretty damned good single parent to his six-year-old twins, Raejean and Annie, ever since their mother's death a year ago. But you'd never know it to hear Penelope talk.

Hell, a young man of twenty-five who worked hard on his ranch from dawn to dusk all week deserved to sow a few wild oats at week's end. His ears rang with the memory of their confrontation in his living room earlier that evening.

"You're a drunken half-breed," Penelope snapped, "not fit to raise my grandchildren. And if I have anything to say about it, you won't have them for much longer!"

Billy felt a burning rage that Penelope should say such a thing while Raejean and Annie were standing right there listening. Especially since he hadn't been the least bit drunk. He'd been looking for a fight, all right, and he'd found it in a bar, but that was all.

There was no hope his daughters hadn't heard Penelope. Their Nintendo game continued on the living room TV, but both girls were staring wide-eyed at him. "Raejean. Annie. Go upstairs while I talk to Nana."

"But, Daddy—" Raejean began. She was the twin who took control of every situation.

"Not a word," he said in a firm voice. "Go."

Annie's dark brown eyes welled with tears. She was the twin with the soft heart.

He wanted to pick them both up and hug them, but he forced himself to point an authoritative finger toward the doorway. "Upstairs and get your baths and get ready

for bed. Mrs. Motherwell will be up to help in a minute."
He had hired the elderly woman on the spot when he
heard her name. She had proven equal to it.

Raejean shot him a reproachful look, took Annie's
hand, and stomped out of the room with Annie trailing
behind her.

Once they were gone, Billy turned his attention back
to his nemesis. "What is it this time, Penelope?"

"This time! What is it every time? You drove my
Laura to kill herself, and now you're neglecting my
grandchildren. I've had it. I went to see a lawyer today.
I've filed for custody of my granddaughters."

A chill of foreboding crawled down Billy's spine.
"You've done what?"

"You heard me. I want custody of Raejean and
Annie."

"Those are my children you're talking about."

"They'll have a better life with me than they will
with a half-breed like you."

"Being part Comanche isn't a crime, Penelope. Lots
of people in America are part something. Hell, you're
probably part Irish or English or French yourself."

"Your kind has a reputation for not being able to hold
their liquor. Obviously, it's a problem for you, too. I don't
intend to let my grandchildren suffer for it."

A flush rose on Billy's high, sharp cheekbones. He
refused to defend himself. It was none of Penelope's
business whether he drank or not. But he didn't. He
went looking for a fight when the pain built up inside,
and he needed a release for it. But he chose men able
to defend themselves, he fought clean, and he willingly
paid the damages afterward.

He hated the idea of kowtowing to Penelope, but he didn't want a court battle with her, either. She and her husband, Harvey Trask, were wealthy; he was not. In fact, the Trasks had given this ranch—an edge carved from the larger Trask ranching empire—as a wedding present to their daughter, Laura, thereby ensuring that the newlyweds would stay close to home.

He had resented their generosity at first, but he had grown to love the land, and now he was no more willing to give up the Stonecreek Ranch than he was to relinquish his children.

But his behavior over the past year couldn't stand much scrutiny. He supposed the reason he had started those few barroom brawls wouldn't matter to a judge. And he could never have revealed to anyone the personal pain that had led to such behavior. So he had no excuses to offer Penelope—or a family court judge, either.

"Look, Penelope, I'm sorry. What if I promise—"

"Don't waste your breath. I never wanted my daughter to marry a man like you in the first place. My granddaughters deserve to be raised in a wholesome household where they won't be exposed to your kind."

"What kind is that?" Billy asked pointedly.

"The kind that doesn't have any self-respect, and therefore can't pass it on to their children."

Billy felt his stomach roll. It was a toss-up whether he felt more humiliated or furious at her accusation. "I have plenty of self-respect."

"Could have fooled me!" Penelope retorted.

"I'm not letting you take my kids away from me."

"You can't stop me." She didn't argue with him further, simply headed for the front door—she never used the back, as most people in this part of Texas did. "I'll see you in court, Billy."

Then she was gone.

Billy stood in the middle of the toy-strewn living room, furnished with the formal satin-covered couches and chairs Laura had chosen, feeling helpless. Moments later he was headed for the back door. He paused long enough to yell up the stairs, "I'm going out, Mrs. Motherwell. Good night, Raejean. Good night, Annie."

"Good night, Daddy!" the two of them yelled back from the bathtub in unison.

Mrs. Motherwell appeared at the top of the stairs. "Don't forget this is my last week, Mr. Stonecreek. You'll need to find someone else starting Monday morning."

"I know, Mrs. Motherwell," Billy said with a sigh. He had Penelope to thank for that, too. She had filled Mrs. Motherwell's head with stories about him being a dangerous savage. His granite-hewn features, his untrimmed black hair, his broad shoulders and immense height, and a pair of dark, brooding eyes did nothing to dispel the image. But he couldn't help how he looked. "Don't worry, Mrs. Motherwell. I'll find someone to replace you."

He was the one who was worried. How was he going to find someone as capable as Mrs. Motherwell in a week? It had taken him a month to find her.

He let the kitchen screen door slam and gunned the engine in his black pickup as he drove away. But he couldn't escape his frenetic thoughts.

I'll be damned if I let Penelope take my kids away from me. Who does she think she is? How dare she threaten to steal my children!

He knew his girls needed a mother. Sometimes he missed Laura so much it made his gut ache. But no other woman could ever take her place. He had hired a series of good housekeeper/nannies one after another—it was hard to get help to stay at his isolated ranch—and he and his girls had managed fine.

Or they would, if Penelope and Harvey Trask would leave them alone.

Unfortunately, Penelope blamed him for Laura's death. She had been killed instantly in a car accident that had looked a whole lot like a suicide. Billy had tried telling Penelope that Laura hadn't killed herself, but his mother-in-law hadn't believed him. Penelope Trask had said she would see that he was punished for making Laura so miserable she had taken her own life. Now she was threatening to take his children from him.

He couldn't bear to lose Raejean and Annie. They were the light of his life and all he had left of Laura. God, how he had loved her!

Billy pounded his fist on the steering wheel of his pickup. How could he have been so stupid as to give Penelope the ammunition she needed to shoot him down in court?

It was too late to do anything about his wild reputation. But he could change his behavior. He could stop brawling in bars. If only there were some way he could show the judge he had turned over a new leaf....

Billy didn't drive in any particular direction, yet he eventually found himself at the stock pond he shared with Zach Whitelaw's ranch. The light from the rising moon and stars made a silvery reflection on the center of the pond and revealed the shadows of several pin oaks that surrounded it. He had always found the sounds of the bullfrogs and the crickets and the lapping water soothing to his inner turmoil. He had gone there often to think in the year since Laura had died.

His truck headlights revealed someone else had discovered his sanctuary. He smiled wistfully when he realized a couple was lying together on the grass. He felt a stab of envy. He and Laura had spent their share of stolen moments on the banks of this stock pond when the land had belonged to her father.

He almost turned the truck around, because he wanted to be alone, but there was something about the movements of the couple on the ground that struck him as odd. It took him a moment to realize they weren't struggling in the throes of passion. The woman was trying to fight the man off!

He hit the brakes, shoved open his truck door, and headed for them on the run. He hadn't quite reached the girl when he heard her scream of outrage.

He grabbed hold of the boy by his shoulders and yanked him upright. The tall, heavyset kid came around swinging.

That was a mistake.

Billy ducked and came up underneath with a hard fist to the belly that dropped the kid to his knees. A second later the boy toppled face-forward with a groan.

Billy made a sound of disgust that the kid hadn't put up more of a fight and hurried to help the girl. She had curled in on herself, her body rigid with tension. When he put a hand on her shoulder, she tried scrambling away.

"He's not going to hurt you anymore," he said in

the calm, quiet voice he used when he was gentling horses. He turned her over so she could see she was safe from the boy, that he was there to help. Her torn bodice exposed half of a small, well-formed breast. He made himself look away, but his body tightened responsively. Her whole body began to tremble.

"Shh. It's all right. I'm here now."

She looked up at him with eyes full of pain.

"Are you hurt?" he asked, his hands doing a quick once-over for some sign of injury.

She slapped at him ineffectually with one hand while holding the torn chiffon against her nakedness with the other. "No. I'm fine. Just...just..."

Her eyes—he couldn't tell what color they were in the dark—filled with tears and, despite her desperate attempts to blink the moisture away, one sparkling teardrop spilled onto her cheek. It was then he realized the pain he had seen wasn't physical, but came from inside.

He understood that kind of pain all too well.

"Hey," he said gently. "It's going to be all right."

"Easy for you to say," she snapped, rubbing at the tears and swiping them across her cheeks. "I—"

A car engine revved, and they both looked toward the sound in time to see a pair of headlights come on.

"Wait!" the girl cried, surging to her feet.

The dress slipped, and Billy got an unwelcome look at a single, luscious breast. He swore under his breath as his body hardened.

The girl obviously wasn't used to long dresses, because the length of it caught under her knees and trapped her on the ground. By the time she made it to her feet, the car she had come in, and the boy she had come with, were gone.

He took one look at her face in the moonlight and saw a kind of desolation he hadn't often seen before.

Except perhaps in his own face in the mirror.

It made his throat ache. It might have brought him to tears, if he had been the kind of man who could cry. He wasn't. He thought maybe his Comanche heritage had something to do with it. Or maybe it was simply a lack of feeling in him. He didn't know. He didn't want to know.

As he watched, the girl sank to the ground and dropped her face into her hands. Her shoulders rocked with soundless, shuddering sobs.

He settled beside her, not speaking, not touching, merely a comforting presence, there if she needed him. Occasionally he heard a sniffling sound, but otherwise he was aware of the silence. And finally, the sounds he had come to hear. The bullfrogs. The crickets. The water lapping in the pond.

He didn't know how long he had been sitting beside her when she finally spoke.

"Thank you," she said.

Her voice was husky from crying, and rasped over him, raising the hairs on his neck. He looked at her again and saw liquid, shining eyes in a pretty face. He couldn't keep his gaze from dropping to the flesh revealed by her tightened grip on the torn fabric. Hell, he was a man, not a saint.

"Are you all right?" he asked.

She shook her head, gave a halfhearted laugh, and

said, "Sure." The sarcasm in her voice made it plain she was anything but.

"Can I help?"

"I'd need a miracle to get me out of the mess I'm in." She shrugged, a surprisingly sad gesture. "I can't seem to stay out of trouble."

He smiled sympathetically. *I have the same problem.* He thought the words, but he didn't say them. He didn't want to frighten her. "Things happen," he said instead.

She reached out hesitantly to touch a recent cut above his eye. "Did Ray do this?"

He edged back from her touch. It felt too good. "No. That's from—" *Another fight.* He didn't finish that thought aloud, either. "Something else."

He had gotten a whiff of her perfume. Something light and flowery. Something definitely female. It reminded him he hadn't been with a woman since Laura's death. And that he found the young woman sitting beside him infinitely desirable.

He tamped down his raging hormones. She needed his help. She didn't need another male lusting after her.

She reached for an open can of beer sitting in the grass nearby and lifted it to her lips.

Before it got there, he took it from her. "Aren't you a little young for this?"

"What difference does it make now? My life is ruined."

He smiled indulgently. "Just because your boyfriend—"

"Ray's not my boyfriend. And he's the least of my problems."

He raised a questioning brow. "Oh?"

He watched her grasp her full lower lip in her teeth—and wished he were doing it himself. He forced his gaze upward to meet with hers.

"I'm a disappointment to my parents," she said in a whispery, haunted voice.

How could such a beautiful—he had been looking at her long enough to realize she was more than pretty—young woman be a disappointment to anybody? "Who are your parents?"

"I'm Cherry Whitelaw."

She said it defiantly, defensively. And he knew why. She had been the talk of the neighborhood—the "juvenile delinquent" the Whitelaws had taken into their home four years ago, the most recently adopted child of their eight adopted children.

"If you're trying to scare me off, it won't work." He grinned and said, "I'm Billy Stonecreek."

The smile grew slowly on her face. He saw the moment when she relaxed and held out her hand. "It's nice to meet you, Mr. Stonecreek. I used to see you in church with your—" She cut herself off.

"It's all right to mention my wife," he said. But he knew why she had hesitated. Penelope's tongue had been wagging, telling anyone who would listen how he had caused Laura to kill herself. Cherry's lowered eyes made it obvious she had heard the stories. He didn't know why he felt the urge to defend himself to her when he hadn't to anyone else.

"I had nothing to do with Laura's death. It was simply a tragic accident." Then, before he could stop himself, "I miss her."

Cherry laid a hand on his forearm, and he felt the muscles tense beneath her soothing touch. She waited for him to look at her before she spoke. "I'm sorry about your wife, Mr. Stonecreek. It must be awful to lose someone you love."

"Call me Billy," he said, unsure how to handle her sympathy.

"Then you have to call me Cherry," she said with the beginnings of a smile. She held out her hand. "Deal?"

"Deal." He took her hand and held it a moment too long. Long enough to realize he didn't want to let go. He forced himself to sit back. He raised the beer can he had taken from her to his lips, but she took it from him before he could tip it up.

"I don't think this will solve your problems, either," she said with a cheeky grin.

He laughed. "You're right."

They smiled at each other.

Until Billy realized he wanted to kiss her about as bad as he had ever wanted anything in his life. His smile faded. He saw the growing recognition in her eyes and turned away. He was there to rescue the girl, not to ravish her.

He picked a stem of sweet grass and twirled it between his fingertips. "Would you like to talk about what you've done that's going to disappoint your parents?"

She shrugged. "Hell. Why not?"

The profanity surprised him. Until he remembered she hadn't been a Whitelaw for very long. "I'm listening."

Her eyes remained focused on her tightly laced fingers. "I got expelled from high school tonight."

He let out a breath he hadn't realized he'd been holding. "That's pretty bad, all right. What did you do?"

"Nothing! Not that I'm innocent all that often, but this time I was. Just because I had a whiskey bottle in my hand doesn't mean I was going to pour it in the punch at the prom."

He raised a skeptical brow.

"I was keeping a friend of mine from pouring it in the punch," she explained. "Not that anyone will believe me."

"As alibis go, I've heard better," he said.

"Anyway, I've been expelled and I won't graduate with my class and I'll have to go to summer school to finish. I'd rather run away from home than face Zach and Rebecca and tell them what I've done. In fact, the more I think about it, the better that idea sounds. I won't go home. I'll...I'll..."

"Go where?"

"I don't know. Somewhere."

"Dressed like that?"

She looked down at herself and back up at him, her eyes brimming with tears. "My dress is ruined. Just like my life."

Billy didn't resist the urge to lift her into his lap, and for whatever reason, she didn't resist his efforts to comfort her. She wrapped her arms around his neck and clung to him.

"I feel so lost and alone," she said, her breath moist against his skin. "I don't belong anywhere."

Billy tightened his arms around her protectively, wishing there was something more he could do to help. He crooned to her in Comanche, telling her she was safe, that he would find a way to help her, that she wasn't alone.

"What am I going to do?" she murmured in an anguished voice. "Where can I go?"

Billy swallowed over the knot in his throat. "You're going to think I'm crazy," he said. "But I've got an idea if you'd like to hear it."

"What is it?" she asked.

"You could come and live with me."

CHAPTER TWO

CHERRY HAD FELT SAFE and secure in Billy Stonecreek's arms, that is, until he made his insane suggestion. She lifted her head from Billy's shoulder and stared at him wide-eyed. "What did you say?"

"Don't reject the idea before you hear me out."

"I'm listening." In fact, Cherry was fascinated.

He focused his dark-eyed gaze on her, pinning her in place. "The older lady who's been taking care of my kids is quitting on Monday. How would you like to work for me? The job comes with room and board." He smiled. "In fact, I'm including room and board because I can't afford to pay much."

"You're offering me a job?"

"And a place to live. I could be at home evenings to watch the girls while you go to night school over the summer and earn your high school diploma. What do you say?"

Cherry edged herself off Billy's lap, wondering how he had coaxed her into remaining there so long. Perversely, she missed the warmth of his embrace once it was gone. She pulled her knees up to her chest and wrapped her arms around the yards of pale green chiffon.

"Cherry?"

Her first reaction was to say yes. His offer was the

simple solution to all her problems. She wouldn't have to go home. She wouldn't have to face her parents with the truth.

But she hadn't lived with Zach and Rebecca Whitelaw for four years and not learned how they felt about certain subjects. "My dad would never allow it."

"A minute ago you were going to run away from home. How is this different?"

"You obviously don't know Zach Whitelaw very well," she said with a rueful twist of her lips. "If he knew I was working so close, he'd expect me to live at home."

"Not if you were indispensible to me."

"Would I be?" she asked, intrigued.

"I can't manage the ranch and my six-year-old twin daughters all by myself. I'm up and working before dawn. Somebody has to make sure Annie and Raejean get dressed for school and feed them breakfast and be there when they get off the school bus in the afternoon." Billy shrugged. "You need a place to stay. I need help in a hurry. It's a match made in heaven."

Cherry shook her head. "It wouldn't work."

"Why not?"

"Can I be blunt?"

Billy smiled, and her stomach did a queer flip-flop. "By all means," he said.

"It's bad enough that you're single—"

"I wouldn't need the help if I had a wife," Billy interrupted.

Cherry frowned him into silence. "You're a widower. I'm only eighteen. It's a toss-up which of us has the worse reputation for getting into trouble. Can you imagine what people would say—about us—if I moved in with you?" Cherry's lips curled in an impish grin. "Eyebrows would hit hairlines all over the county."

Billy shook his head and laughed. "I hadn't thought about what people would think. We're two of a kind, all right." His features sobered. "Just not the right kind."

Cherry laid her hand on his arm in comfort. "I know what you're feeling, Billy."

"I doubt it."

Cherry felt bereft as he pulled free. He was wrong. She understood exactly what he was feeling. The words spilled out before she could stop them.

"Nobody wants anything to do with you, because you're different," she said in a quiet voice that carried in the dark. "To prove it doesn't matter what anyone else thinks, you break their rules. When they look down their noses at you, you spit in their eyes. And all the time, your heart is aching. Because you want them to like you. And respect you. But they don't."

Billy eyed her speculatively. "I guess you do understand."

For a moment Cherry thought he was going to put his arm around her. But he didn't.

She turned to stare at the pond, so he wouldn't see how much she regretted his decision to keep his distance. "I've always hated being different," she said. "I was always taller than everyone else, thanks to my giant of a father, Big Mike Murphy." When she was a child, her father's size had always made her feel safe. But he hadn't kept her safe. He had let her be stolen away from him.

"And I don't know another person with hair as

godawful fire-engine red as mine. I have Big Mike to thank for that, too." Cherry noticed Billy didn't contradict her evaluation of her hair.

"And your mother?" Billy asked. "What did you get from her?"

"Nothing, so far as I can tell," Cherry said curtly. "She walked out on Big Mike when I was five. That's when he started drinking. Eventually someone reported to social services that he was leaving me alone at night. They took me away from him when I was eight. He fell from a high scaffolding at work the next week and was killed. I think he wanted to die. I was in and out of the system for six years before the Whitelaws took me in."

"I'm sorry."

"It doesn't matter now."

"Doesn't it?" Billy asked.

Cherry shrugged. "It's in the past. You learn to protect yourself."

"Yeah," Billy said. "You do."

Billy had inherited his six-foot-four height and dark brown eyes from his Scots father. His straight black hair and burnished skin came from his Comanche mother. They had been killed in a car wreck when he was ten. He had developed his rebellious streak in a series of foster homes that treated him like he was less than human because he wasn't all white.

He opened his mouth to share his common experiences with Cherry and closed it again. It was really none of her business.

"Too bad you aren't looking for a wife," Cherry mused. "That would solve your problem. But I guess after what happened, you don't want to get married again."

"No, I don't," Billy said flatly.

"I certainly wasn't volunteering for the job," Cherry retorted. Everyone knew Billy Stonecreek had made his first wife so unhappy she had killed herself. At least, that was the story Penelope Trask had been spreading. On the other hand, Billy Stonecreek had been nothing but nice to her. She couldn't help wondering whether Billy was really as villainous as his mother-in-law had painted him.

They sat in silence. Cherry wished there was some way she could have helped Billy. But she knew Zach Whitelaw too well to believe he would allow his daughter to move in with a single man—even if she was his housekeeper. Not that Zach could have stopped her if she wanted to do it. But knowing Zach, he would find a way to make sure Billy changed his mind about needing her. And she didn't want to cause that kind of trouble for anybody.

"Having you come to work for me wouldn't really solve my biggest problem, anyway," Billy said, picking up the beer can again.

Cherry took it out of his hand, set it down, and asked, "What problem is that?"

He hesitated so long she wasn't sure he was going to speak. At last he said, "My former mother-in-law is taking me to court to try and get custody of my daughters. Penelope says I'm not a fit parent. She's determined to take Raejean and Annie away from me."

"Oh, no!" It was Cherry's worst nightmare come to life. She had suffered terribly when she had been taken from her father as a child. "You can't let her do that! Kids belong with their parents."

Cherry was passionate about the subject. She had often wondered where her birth mother was and why she had walked away and left Cherry and Big Mike behind. Cherry had died inside when the social worker came to take her away, and she realized she was never going to see Big Mike again. It was outrageous to think someone could go to court and wrench two little girls away from their natural father.

"You've got to stop Mrs. Trask!" Cherry said. "You can't let her take your kids!"

"I'm not *letting* her do anything!" Billy cried in frustration. His hands clenched into fists. "But I'm not sure I can stop her. Over the past year I haven't exactly been a model citizen. And I haven't been able to keep a steady housekeeper. Especially once Penelope fills their ears with wild stories about me."

Billy made an angry sound in his throat. "If Laura hadn't died... Having a wife would certainly make my case as a responsible parent stronger in court."

"Isn't there somebody you could marry?"

"What woman would want a half-breed, with a ready-made family of half-breed kids?" Billy said bitterly.

Cherry gasped. "You talk like there's something wrong with you because you're part Comanche. I'm sure you have lots of redeeming qualities."

Billy eyed her sideways. "Like what?"

"I don't know. I'm sure there must be some." She paused and asked, "Aren't there?"

Billy snorted. "I've been in jail for fighting three times over the past year."

Cherry met his gaze evenly and said, "Nobody says you have to fight."

"True," Billy conceded. "But sometimes…"

"Sometimes you feel like if you don't hit something you'll explode?"

Billy nodded. "Yeah."

"I've felt that way sometimes myself."

"You're a girl," Billy protested. "Girls don't—"

"What makes you think girls don't get angry?" Cherry interrupted.

"I guess I never really thought much about it. What do you do when you feel like that?"

"Cause mischief," Cherry admitted with a grin. Her grin faded as she said, "Think, Billy. Isn't there some woman you could ask to marry you?"

Billy shook his head. "I haven't gone out much since Laura died. When I haven't been working on the ranch, I've spent my time with Raejean and Annie. Besides, I don't know too many women around here who'd think I was much of a catch."

Cherry sat silently beside Billy. Her heart went out to his two daughters. She knew what was coming for them. She felt genuinely sorry for them. For the first time in a long time she regretted her past behavior, because it meant she couldn't be a help to them.

"I wish we'd met sooner. And that I had less of a reputation for being a troublemaker," Cherry said. "If things were different, I might volunteer to help you out. But I'm not the kind of person you'd want as a mother for your kids."

Billy's head jerked around, and he stared intently at her.

Cherry was a little frightened by the fierce look on his face. "Billy? What are you thinking?"

"Why not?" he muttered. "Why the hell not?"

"Why not what?"

"Why can't you marry me?" Billy said.

Cherry clutched at her torn bodice as she surged to her feet. "You can't be serious!"

Billy rose and grabbed her by the shoulders, which was all that kept her from running. "More serious than I've ever been in my life. My kids' lives depend on me making the right choices now."

"And you think marriage to me is the right choice?" Cherry asked incredulously. "We're practically strangers! I barely know you. You don't know me at all."

"I know plenty about you. You understand what it feels like to be different. What it feels like to lose your parents. What it feels like to need a parent's love. You'd be good for my kids. And you could really help me out."

"Why me?"

"I'm desperate," Billy said. "I thought you were, too."

Cherry grimaced. Why else would a man choose her except because he was desperate? And why else would a woman accept such a proposal, unless she were desperate, too?

"Are you ready to go home and face your parents and tell them you got expelled and that you aren't going to graduate?" Billy demanded.

"When you put it that way, I... No. But marriage? That seems like such a big step. Make that a *huge* step."

"It doesn't have to be a real marriage. It can be strictly a business arrangement. We can stay married long enough for you to finish the high school credits you need and maybe take some courses at the junior college. When you figure out what you want to do with the rest of your life, we could go our separate ways."

"Couldn't I just be your housekeeper?"

Billy shook his head. "You've said yourself why that wouldn't work."

"But marriage is so…permanent."

"It would be if it were for real. Ours wouldn't be."

"Are you suggesting we tell people we're married but not really go through with it?"

He considered a moment. "No, we'd have to get married, and as far as I'm concerned, the sooner the better."

Cherry's heart bounced around inside her like a frightened rabbit. She pressed a fistful of chiffon hard against her chest, as though she could hold her heart still, but it kept right on jumping. "You want to get married right away? This week?"

"As soon as we can. We could fly to Las Vegas tonight."

"Fly?"

"I've got a pilot's license. We can charter a small private plane for the trip. Would you mind?"

"I guess not," Cherry said, overwhelmed by the speed at which things were moving.

"The more I think about it, the more I like the whole idea. Getting married would certainly spike Penelope's guns."

Cherry gnawed on her lower lip. "If you're looking for someone who'd be an asset in court, maybe you ought to reconsider taking me as your wife. My reputation's almost as bad as yours."

"You're a Whitelaw," Billy said. "That means something around this part of Texas."

"An adopted Whitelaw," Cherry reminded him. "And I'm not so sure my parents wouldn't change their minds if they had the chance."

Billy smiled. "I think we can make this arrangement work for both of us. How about it, Cherry? Will you marry me?"

If Cherry had been anybody except who she was, she would have said no. Any rational person would have. It didn't make sense to marry a virtual stranger, one who had reportedly made his previous wife miserable. But Cherry wasn't thinking about Billy or even about herself. She was thinking about his two innocent little girls. If marrying Billy would give them a better chance of staying with their father, she really didn't think she had any other choice.

"All right, Billy," she said. "I'll marry you."

Billy gave a whoop of joy, swept her up into his arms, and whirled her in a dizzying circle, sending chiffon flying around her.

"Put me down, Billy," she said, laughing.

He immediately set her on her feet. When she swayed dizzily, he reached out to steady her.

The feel of his strong, callused hands on her bare shoulders sent an unexpected quiver skittering down her spine. She knew she ought to step away, but Billy's dark eyes held her spellbound.

"Okay now?" he asked, his voice rasping over her.

"I'm fine." She shivered, belying her words.

"You must be getting chilly." He slipped an arm around her shoulder that was warm and supportive... and possessive.

She shivered again as he began walking her toward his pickup. Only this time she realized it had nothing to do with the cold.

As Billy held open the pickup door she said as casually as she could, "This will be a marriage in name only, right?"

He closed the door behind her, slid over the hood, got into the cab, and started the pickup before he answered, "That's right."

She gave a gusty sigh of relief as the engine roared to life. "Good."

"We don't even have to sleep in the same bed," Billy said as he headed back toward the main road. "You can have the room my housekeeper will be vacating. If I feel the urge for some feminine comfort, I can get what I need from a woman in town."

"Wait a minute," Cherry said. "I don't think I'm going to want my husband satisfying his lustful urges in town."

"I won't really be your husband," Billy reminded her.

"As far as my parents and neighbors and friends are concerned, you will be."

Billy eyed her cautiously. "What do you suggest?"

"Couldn't you just...not do it."

"I'm a man, not a monk," Billy said.

Cherry pursed her lips thoughtfully. "Then I suppose I'd rather you come to me than go to some other woman."

"This is starting to sound like a real marriage," Billy said suspiciously. "I was looking for a temporary solution to both our problems."

"Oh, you don't have to worry about me falling in love with you or anything," Cherry reassured him. "I don't believe in happily-ever-after."

"You don't?"

Cherry shook her head. "Except for the Whitelaws, I've never met any married couples who really loved each other. But I can see where it would be unfair to expect you to give up sex for who knows how long. Only, if you don't mind, I'd rather we had a chance to get to know each other a little better before...you know..."

"Maybe this marriage thing isn't such a good idea, after all," Billy said. "You're just a kid, and—"

"I may be only eighteen," Cherry interrupted, "but I've lived a lifetime since my father died. You don't have to worry about me. I've been in and out of a dozen foster homes. I've spent time in juvenile detention. I've survived the past four years in a house with seven other adopted brothers and sisters. I've come through it all with a pretty good idea of what I want from life. I'm plenty old enough to know exactly what I'm doing."

"I doubt that," Billy said. Maybe if he hadn't been so panicked at the thought of losing Annie and Raejean, he would have taken more time to think the matter over. But marriage to Cherry Whitelaw would solve so many problems all at once, he accepted her statement at face value.

"All right, Cherry. We'll do this your way. I won't go looking for comfort in town, and you'll provide for my needs at home."

"After we get to know one another," Cherry qualified.

"After we get to know one another," Billy agreed.

He turned onto the main highway and headed for the airport. "Will your parents worry if you don't show up at home tonight?"

"It's prom night. I was supposed to be staying out all night with some friends of mine and have breakfast with them tomorrow. In fact, if you'll stop by my friend's house, I've got an overnight bag there with a change of clothes."

"Good. That'll leave us about twelve hours to get to Las Vegas and tie the knot before we have to face your parents."

Cherry pictured that meeting in her mind. *Good grief*, she thought. *The fur is going to fly.*

CHAPTER THREE°

THE WEDDING CHAPEL in Las Vegas was brightly lit, even at 3:00 a.m. To Cherry's amazement, they weren't the only couple getting married at such an ungodly hour. She and Billy had to wait ten minutes for an elderly couple to complete their vows before it was their turn. The longer they waited, the more second thoughts she had. What had she been thinking? Zach was going to be furious. Rebecca was going to cry.

The image she conjured of two identical cherubic six-year-old faces was all that kept her from running for a phone to call Zach and Rebecca to come get her. She tried to recall what Billy's twins looked like from the last time she had seen them at church. All she could remember were large dark eyes—like Billy's, she realized now—in small, round faces.

What qualities had they gotten from their mother? Cherry tried to remember how Laura Trask had looked the few times she had seen her. Did the twins have delicate noses like hers? Determined chins? Bowed lips? Had they remained petite like their mother, or become tall and raw-boned like their father?

"If you keep chewing on your lip like that, you're going to gnaw it right off."

Startled, Cherry let go of her lower lip and turned to find Billy behind her.

"Here," he said, handing her a bouquet of gardenias. "I got them from a vendor out in front of the chapel. I thought you might like to carry some flowers."

"Thank you, Billy." Cherry took the bouquet with a hand that shook. "I guess I'm a little nervous."

"Me, too," he admitted.

Cherry wished he would smile. He didn't.

"The bouquet was a lovely thought." She raised it to her nose and sniffed. And sneezed. And sneezed again. "I must be—*achoo!*"

"Allergic," Billy finished, the smile appearing as he retrieved the bouquet from her and set it on an empty folding chair. "Forget the flowers. There are blooms enough in your cheeks for me."

"You mean the freckles," Cherry said, covering her cheeks with her hands. "I know they're awful, but—"

Billy took her hands in his and kissed her gently on each cheek. "They're tasty bits of brown sugar. Didn't anyone ever tell you that?"

Cherry froze as a memory of long ago came to mind. She was sitting on Big Mike's lap at the supper table. He was alternately taking bites of vanilla ice cream and giving her ice-cold kisses across her nose and cheeks, making yummy sounds in his throat and saying, "Your freckles sure taste sweet, baby."

Her throat tightened with emotion, and she looked up, half expecting to see Big Mike standing in front of her.

But it was Billy, his brow furrowed as his dark eyes took in the pallor beneath her freckles. "Are you all right? You look like you're about to faint."

Cherry stiffened knees that were threatening to

buckle. "I've never fainted in my life. I don't expect to start now."

"Are you folks ready?" the minister asked.

"Last chance to back out," Billy whispered to Cherry.

The sound tickled her ear, but she managed to stifle the inappropriate giggle that sought voice. This ridiculous wedding ceremony was serious business. "I'm not backing out. But if you've changed your mind—"

"I haven't," Billy interrupted her.

He tightened his grip on one of her hands and released the other, leading her down the aisle to the makeshift pulpit at the front of the room.

Throughout the ceremony, Cherry kept repeating two things over and over.

Those little girls need me. And, *This is the last time I'll be disappointing Zach and Rebecca. Once I'm married, I won't be their responsibility anymore.*

She was concentrating so hard on convincing herself she was doing the right thing that she had to be prompted to respond when the time came.

"Cherry?"

She turned and found Billy's eyes on her. Worried again. *And I won't be a burden to Billy Stonecreek, either,* she added for good measure. "What is it, Billy?"

"Your turn to say I do."

Cherry gave Billy a tremulous smile and said, "I do." It was more of a croak, actually, but when Billy smiled back, she knew it was all right.

"Rings?" the minister asked.

"We don't have any," Billy replied.

The minister pulled open a drawer in a credenza

behind him, and she heard a tinny clatter. To Cherry's amazement, the drawer was full of fake gold rings.

"Help yourself," the minister said.

Cherry watched Billy select a plain yellow band and try it on her finger. Too small. The next was too big. The third was also a little loose, but because she wanted the awkward moment over with she said, "This one's fine, Billy."

"That'll be ten dollars extra," the minister said.

She saw the annoyed look that crossed Billy's face and pulled the ring off. "I don't need a ring."

Billy caught it before it could drop into the drawer and put it back on her finger. He caught her chin and lifted it so she was forced to look at him. "I'm sorry, Cherry. I should have thought of getting you a ring. This is so…"

Cheap? Tawdry? Vulgar? Cherry knew what he was thinking, but couldn't bring herself to say it, either. "Don't worry about it, Billy. It doesn't matter."

"You deserve better."

"It's not a real marriage. I don't need a real ring," Cherry said quietly so the minister wouldn't overhear.

Billy let go of her chin. He opened his mouth as though to speak and closed it again. Finally he said, "I guess you're right. This one will have to do. Shall we get this over with?"

They turned back to the minister, and he finished the ceremony. "You may kiss the bride," the minister said at last.

It wasn't a real wedding, so Cherry wasn't expecting a real kiss. To her surprise, Billy put his hands on either side of her face and murmured, "The ring is phony, but at least this can be real."

Cherry had done her share of kissing. Experimenting with sex was an age-old method of teenage rebellion. She thought she knew everything there was to know about kissing and sex. It was no big deal. Boys seemed to like it a lot, but she didn't understand what all the fuss was about.

Something odd happened when Billy Stonecreek's lips feathered across hers. An unexpected curl of desire flitted across her belly and shot up to her breasts. Her hands clutched fistfuls of his Western shirt as his mouth settled firmly over hers. His tongue traced the seam of her closed lips, causing them to tingle. She opened her mouth, and his tongue slipped inside for a quick taste of her.

She made a sound in her throat somewhere between confusion and protest.

His hand slid around to capture her nape and keep her from escaping.

Cherry wasn't going anywhere. She was enthralled by what Billy was doing with his lips and teeth and tongue. She had never felt anything remotely like it. Before she was ready, the kiss ended.

She stared, bemused, into Billy's hooded eyes. His lips were still damp from hers, and she didn't resist the impulse to reach out and touch.

His hand clamped around her wrist like a vise as her fingertips caressed his lips. "Don't." His voice was harsh, and his lips pressed flat in irritation.

Cherry realized her reaction, her naive curiosity, must have embarrassed him. The kiss had merely been a token of thanks from Billy. He didn't want anything from her in return.

She had told him she didn't want to be touched until they knew each other better. But she had touched him. She had set the ground rules, and then she hadn't followed them.

It wasn't a real marriage. She had to remember that.

There were papers to sign and collect before they could leave. The minister was in a hurry, because two more couples had arrived and were awaiting their turns. Minutes after the ceremony ended, she and Billy were back in the rental car they had picked up at the airport.

Billy finally broke the uncomfortable silence that had fallen between them. "I don't know about you, but I could use a few hours of sleep before we fly back. We have the time. Your parents won't start missing you until noon."

"I must admit I feel exhausted," Cherry said. But she wasn't sure whether it was fatigue or a delayed reaction to their strange wedding. She had never wanted to get married, but that didn't mean she hadn't fantasized about having a grand wedding. She had imagined wearing a white satin gown with a train twenty feet long, having at least three bridesmaids, and hearing the wedding processional played on an immense pipe organ. This ceremony had fallen far short of the fantasy.

"Regrets?" Billy asked.

Cherry stared at him, surprised at his intuitiveness. "Were my thoughts that transparent?"

"I can't imagine any woman wanting to get married

the way we did. But drastic situations sometimes require drastic solutions. In this case I believe the end—we're now legally husband and wife—justifies the means."

Cherry hoped Zach would see the logic in such an argument.

The hotel Billy chose was outlined in pink and white neon and advertised a honeymoon suite in the center of a pink neon heart. "At least we're sure they've got a honeymoon suite here," Billy said with a cheeky grin.

Cherry laughed breathlessly. "Why would we need a honeymoon suite?"

"It's probably going to have a bigger bed than the other rooms," Billy said. "It'll be more comfortable for someone my size."

"Oh," Cherry said.

"That almost sounded like disappointment," Billy said. "I agreed to wait until you're ready to make it a real marriage. Are you telling me you're ready?"

"No, Billy. I'm not."

He didn't say anything.

"Are you disappointed?" Cherry asked.

"I guess grooms have fantasies about their wedding nights the way brides have fantasies about their weddings," Billy conceded with a grin. "Yeah. I suppose I am. But I'll survive."

Cherry wondered if Billy was remembering his first wedding night. She knew she looked nothing like Laura Trask. She wasn't the least bit petite. Her hair wasn't golden blond, and she didn't move with stately grace. She had a million freckles that speckled her milk-white skin and frizzy hair that changed color depending on the way the sun struck it. She had a small bosom that had

no freckles at all and absolutely no intention of letting
the groom find that out for himself tonight. No, this was
not a night for fulfilling fantasies.

She followed Billy inside the hotel with the overnight bag she had picked up at her friend's house, so
they weren't entirely without luggage. She pressed the
ring tight against her fourth finger with her thumb so
it wouldn't slip off. She stood at Billy's shoulder while
he registered and got a key card for the door.

They took the elevator to the top floor and found the
honeymoon suite at the end of the hall. Billy used the
key card to open the door.

Before she could say anything, Billy picked her up
and carried her over the threshold. She was wearing the
jeans and T-shirt she had put on to replace the torn chiffon dress and she could feel the heat of him everywhere
his body touched hers.

Her arm automatically clutched at his shoulder to help
him support her weight, but she realized when she felt
the corded muscles there, that he didn't need any help.
He carried her over to the bed and let her drop.

She bounced a couple of times and came to rest.
"Good grief," she said, staring at the heart-shaped bed.
"How do they expect two people to sleep on something
shaped like this?"

He wiggled his eyebrows. "I don't think they expect
you to sleep, if you know what I mean." He dropped
onto the bed beside her and stretched out on his back
with his hands behind his head on one of the pillows.
"It's nowhere near as big as it looked in neon, either."

Cherry scooted as far from him as she could, but
although there was plenty of room for two pillows at the

top of the bed, the bottom narrowed so their feet ended up nearly touching.

Billy toed off one cowboy boot, then used his stock-inged foot to shove off the other boot. He reached for the phone beside the bed. "I'll ask for an eight o'clock wake-up call," he said. "That'll give us time to fly back before noon."

Cherry was wearing tennis shoes, and she reached down and tugged them off with her hands and dropped them on the floor. She lay back on the pillow with her legs as far on her side of the bed as she could get them, which was a few bare inches from Billy's feet.

Billy reached over and turned out the lamp beside the bed. It should have been dark in the room, but the neon lights outside bathed the room in a romantic pink glow.

"Do you want me to close the curtains?" Billy asked. "It's kind of pretty."

Which might make a difference if they wanted to watch each other while they made love, Cherry thought, but wasn't going to matter much when they closed their eyes to sleep. But she noticed Billy didn't get up to close the curtains.

"Good night, Cherry," Billy said, turning on his side away from her. "Thanks again."

"Good night, Billy," Cherry said, turning on her side away from him. "You're welcome."

She lay there in uncomfortable silence for perhaps five minutes before she whispered, "Are you asleep, Billy?"

Cherry felt the bed dip as he turned back toward her.

"I thought you were tired," he said.

"I am. But I'm too excited to sleep. It's not every day a girl gets married."

She stiffened when she felt one of his hands touch her shoulder and slide down to the small of her back.

"Don't get skittish on me, woman. I'm just going to rub your back a little to help you relax."

His thumb hit her somewhere in the center of her back, and his hand wrapped around her side.

Cherry gave a luxuriant sigh as he massaged her tense muscles.

"Feel better?"

"Yes." She was impressed again by his strength. And his gentleness. And wondered how his hand would feel caressing other places on her body.

Cherry sought a subject they could discuss that would get her mind off the direction it seemed to be headed. "Could you tell me a little bit about your daughters?"

"Raejean and Annie are just finishing the first grade. Their teacher has had a devil of a time telling them apart."

"Do they look that much alike?" Cherry asked.

Billy chuckled. "Sometimes they try to fool me. But it isn't hard to tell them apart once you get to know them. Raejean carries herself differently, more confidently. She looks at you more directly and talks back more often. Annie is kinder, sweeter, more thoughtful. She follows Raejean's lead. When the two of them team up, they can be a handful."

"Have you had a lot of trouble with them?"

His hand paused for a moment, then resumed its disturbing massage. "A little. Just lately. I think they're missing Laura as much as I am."

He rubbed a little harder, as though he had admitted something he wished he hadn't.

"Were you expecting twins when they were born?"

Cherry felt his hand tighten uncomfortably on her flesh. She hissed in a breath, and his hand soothed the hurt.

"The twins were a complete surprise. They came early, and for a while it was touch and go whether Laura and the girls would all make it. They did, but there were complications. The doctor said Laura couldn't have any more children."

"You wanted more?"

"I didn't care one way or the other. But Laura did."

Abruptly his hand left her back, and he rolled away from her. "Go to sleep, Cherry."

Apparently their conversation was over, leaving her with a great deal of food for thought.

The twins missed their mother. Like he did.

Cherry could do something to replace the loss in the twins' lives. She could be a mother to Billy's little girls. Of more concern was the temptation she felt to ease Billy's sorrow. There were dangers in such an undertaking. She had to remember this was a temporary marriage. It was safer to let Billy cope with his loss on his own.

On the other hand, Cherry never had chosen the safe path. As she closed her eyes again, she saw the four of them smiling at one another...one happy family.

BILLY STARED AT THE neon outside the window, willing himself to sleep. But he couldn't stop thinking about his new wife.

The wedding kiss had surprised him. In the fluorescent light of the wedding chapel, Cherry Whitelaw had looked like anything but a radiant bride. Her blue eyes had been wide with fright and her skin pale beneath a mass of orange freckles. He'd had significant second thoughts about the marriage. And third and fourth thoughts, as well. All his thoughts came back to the same thing. She needed his help. And he needed hers.

He had been proud of her for getting through that awful ceremony—including the last-minute search for a ring that would fit—with so much dignity. That was why he had offered her the kiss, not because he had been wondering what her lips would taste like. When she had reached out to him afterward, he had stopped her because that wasn't part of their deal, not because he had been shocked at the way his body had gone rock-hard at her touch. Just thinking about it caused the same reaction all over again.

Billy swore.

"Billy? Is something wrong?"

"Nothing's wrong, Cherry. Go to sleep."

He closed his eyes, determined to get some rest, but a picture of her breast half revealed by the torn chiffon bodice appeared behind his eyelids.

He opened his eyes and stared at the neon again. Who would have thought he would find a freckle-faced redhead so erotically exciting? Or that his new wife would be off-limits for heaven knew how long? Billy heaved a long-suffering sigh. It was going to be one hell of a marriage.

His eyes slid closed again as sleep claimed his exhausted body.

BILLY WAS HAVING a really spectacular dream. He had a handful of soft female breast, which just happened to belong to his new wife. Her eyes were closed in passion, and as he flicked his thumb across her nipple, he heard a moan that made his loins tighten. He lowered his head to take her nipple in his mouth. It was covered by a thin layer of cotton. He sucked on her through the damp cloth and felt her body arch toward him. Her hands threaded into his hair...and yanked on it—

Billy came awake with a jerk. "What the hell?"

Cherry was sitting bolt upright in bed with her hands crossed defensively under her breasts. A damp spot on her T-shirt revealed that he hadn't been dreaming.

It shouldn't have surprised him. His last thoughts before drifting to sleep had been about Cherry. No wonder his body had been drawn to hers during the night. He shoved a hand through hair that was standing on end and groaned. "God, Cherry, I'm sorry. I was dreaming."

She eyed him suspiciously.

"I swear I didn't know what I was doing."

That made her look crestfallen.

"Not that it isn't exactly what I'd like to be doing at this moment," he said.

She gave a hitching breath that was almost a sob. "We agreed to wait."

"Yeah, I know," Billy said. "I don't suppose you've changed your mind."

She hesitated so long he thought maybe she had. Until she shook her head no.

Billy looked at the clock. It was only six. But he didn't

trust himself to lie back down beside her. "I can't sleep anymore. How about if we head for the airport?"

"All right," she said.

He started pulling on his boots and felt her hand on his shoulder. He froze.

She cleared her throat and said, "I liked what you were doing, Billy. It felt…good. I wanted you to know that. It's just…"

He shoved his foot down into the boot and stood. He had to get away from her or he was going to turn around and lay her flat on the bed and do something he would be sorry for later. "I know," he said. "We agreed to wait."

She had a brave smile on her face. And looked every bit her youthful age.

What on earth had possessed him to marry her?

It was a silent flight from Las Vegas to the airport in Amarillo. And an even more silent truck ride to the Stonecreek Ranch. Billy pulled up to the back door of a large, two-story white clapboard house and killed the engine. The blue morning glories he had planted for Laura were soaking up the midday sun on a trellis along the eastern edge of the porch.

"We're home," Billy said. His throat tightened painfully. They were the same words he had spoken to Laura—how many years ago?—when they had moved into this house.

Suddenly he realized he couldn't go back into Laura's house right now with a new wife. It was still too full of Laura. He needed a little time to accept the fact that she really was gone forever.

"Look, why don't you go inside and introduce yourself

to Mrs. Motherwell, my housekeeper. I just realized I was supposed to pick up a load of feed in town this morning. I'll be back in an hour or so."

Cherry was staring at him as if he had grown a second head. "You want me to go in there without you?" she asked.

"Just tell Mrs. Motherwell you've come to replace her. I'll explain everything to the kids when I get back." When Cherry continued sitting there staring at him, he snapped, "Changed your mind already?"

His new wife looked sober and thoughtful. There were shadows of fatigue beneath her eyes. "No. I'm determined to see this through." She gave him one last anxious look before she left the truck. "Don't be gone long."

"I won't."

Billy resisted the urge to gun the engine as he backed away from the house. Once he hit paved road he headed the truck toward town. He hadn't gone two miles when he saw flashing red and blue lights behind him. He glanced down at the speedometer and swore. He swerved off the road and braked hard enough to raise a cloud of dust.

He was out of the truck and reaching for his wallet to get his driver's license when he saw the highway patrolman had a gun in his hand that was pointed at him.

"Freeze, Stonecreek, or I'll blow your head off."

Billy froze. "What the hell's the matter with you?"

"Put your hands up. You're under arrest."

"Arrest? For what?"

"Kidnapping."

It took a full second for the charge to register. *Kid-*

napping? Then he realized what must have happened and groaned. "Look, Officer, I can explain everything."

"You have the right to remain silent," the officer began.

Billy's lips pressed flat. He had married Cherry Whitelaw in the hope of solving his problems. Instead he had jumped right out of the frying pan into the fire.

CHAPTER FOUR

CHERRY STARED at the back door of Billy's house—now her home, too—trying to work up the courage to go inside, wondering, absurdly, if she should knock first.

She turned and stole a glance at Billy's rugged profile as he drove away, pondering what it was about him she had found so beguiling. He had rescued her, listened to her troubles, and shared his in return. She had felt his desperation and responded to it. Now he was her husband. She twisted the cheap gold ring that confirmed it wasn't all a dream, that she was, indeed, Mrs. Billy Stonecreek.

Good grief. What had she done?

Cherry had gone off half-cocked in the past, but the enormity of this escapade was finally sinking in. Surely it would have been better to face Zach and Rebecca and explain the truth of what had happened at the dance. How was she going to justify this latest lapse of common sense?

She felt a surge of anger at Billy for abandoning her at the door. It wouldn't have taken long to introduce her to Mrs. Motherwell and explain the situation. So why hadn't he done it?

Maybe because he's having the same second thoughts as you are. Maybe in the cold light of day he's thinking he made a bad bargain. Maybe he's trying to figure out a way right now to get out of it.

If the back door hadn't opened at that precise moment, Cherry would have turned and headed for Hawk's Pride.

But it did. And Cherry found herself face-to-face with Penelope Trask.

"I saw you standing out here," Mrs. Trask said. "Is there something I can do for you?"

"I, uh… Is Mrs. Motherwell here?"

"She packed her bags and left this morning."

Cherry stood with her jaw agape, speechless for perhaps the first time in her life. Had Mrs. Trask already managed to gain legal custody of Billy's children? Had their marriage been for naught? She wished Billy were here.

"Don't I know you? Aren't you one of those Whitelaw Bra—" Mrs. Trask cut herself off.

Cherry knew what she had been about to say. The eight adopted Whitelaw kids were known around this part of Texas as the Whitelaw Brats, just like Zach and his siblings before them, and Grandpa Garth and his siblings before that. Cherry had done her share to help earn the nickname. She was proud to be one of them.

She met the older woman's disdainful look with defiance. "Yes, I'm a Whitelaw Brat. You have a problem with that?"

"None at all. But if you're looking for your missing sister, she isn't here. I have no idea what my no-account excuse for a son-in-law has done with her." She started to close the door in Cherry's face.

Cherry stuck her foot in the door. "Wait! What are you talking about?"

A flare of recognition lit Mrs. Trask's eyes. "Oh, my God. You're the girl, aren't you? The one Billy kidnapped." She stuck her head out the screen door and looked around. "Where is he? I have a few things to say to him."

"Kidnapped?" Cherry gasped. "I wasn't kidnapped!"

"Your parents reported you missing late last night."

"Why would they think I was with Billy?"

"Your date wrapped his car around a telephone pole, and when he kept mumbling your name the police called your parents, thinking maybe you'd been thrown from the car. At the hospital, the boy told your father that he'd left you at the stock pond with Billy, after my son-in-law ran him off with his fists.

"Your father couldn't find you at the stock pond, and when he came looking for you here in a rage, Mrs. Motherwell called me. Your father seemed bent on strangling someone before the night was out."

Probably me, Cherry thought morosely.

"Of course I came right over," Mrs. Trask said. "All I could tell your father was that I wouldn't put it past my reckless son-in-law to kidnap an innocent young woman."

"Mrs. Trask, I wasn't kidnapped."

"I suggest you go home and tell that to your father. He told the police Billy must have kidnapped you, because you'd never go off on your own like that." Mrs. Trask smirked. "Of course, that was before he found out you'd been expelled from school earlier in the evening."

Cherry groaned.

"You're in an awful lot of trouble, young lady. Where have you been? And where's Billy?"

Cherry put a hand to her throbbing temple. Zach and Rebecca must be frantic with worry. And disappointed beyond belief. She didn't want to think about how angry they were going to be when they heard what she had done.

"May I please use your phone?" It was her phone now, so she shouldn't have to ask. Except, this didn't seem the right moment to announce that she and Billy had run off to Las Vegas to get married.

Mrs. Trask hesitated, then pushed the screen door open wide. "Come on in, if you must."

As soon as Cherry's eyes adjusted to the dim light in the kitchen, she saw Raejean and Annie standing together near the table.

They wore their straight black hair in adorable, be-ribboned pigtails, and stared at her with dark, serious brown eyes. Their noses were small and their chins dainty, like their mother, but they had high, sharp cheekbones that reminded her of Billy. They were tall for six-year-olds and dressed exactly alike in collared blouses tucked into denim coveralls and white tennis shoes.

"Hello, Raejean," she said, addressing the child who had her arm wrapped comfortingly around the other's shoulder.

The child's eyes widened in surprise at being recognized. Then she said, "I'm not Raejean, I'm Annie."

The other twin's mouth dropped open, and she glanced at her sister. Then she turned to Cherry, pointed to her chest with her thumb, and said, "I'm Raejean."

"I see," Cherry said. They were both missing the

exact same front tooth. No help there telling them apart. Billy had said Raejean was the confident one, so Cherry had assumed it was Raejean who was giving comfort to her sister. But maybe she had been wrong.

"I need to use your phone," she said, moving toward where it hung on the kitchen wall.

Cherry felt the girls watching her while she dialed.

"We don't need another housekeeper," the twin who had identified herself as Annie said. "We're going to stay at Nana's house until Daddy gets home."

Cherry felt her heart miss a beat. She turned to Mrs. Trask and said, "Billy went into town for supplies. He should be back any time now. There's no need to take the girls anywhere."

"I'll be the best judge of that," Mrs. Trask said. "Go upstairs, girls, and finish packing."

The twins turned and ran. Cherry heard their footsteps pounding on the stairs as the ringing phone was answered by her sister, Jewel. Of her seven Whitelaw siblings, Jewel was the sister closest to her in age. Jewel had been adopted by Zach and Rebecca when she was five—the first of the current generation of Whitelaw Brats.

It had taken Cherry a while to straighten them all out, but now she could recite their names and ages with ease. Rolleen was 21, Jewel was 19, she was 18, Avery was 17, Jake was 16, Frannie was 13, Rabbit was 12, and Colt was 11.

Of course Rabbit's name wasn't really Rabbit, it was Louis, but nobody called him that. Jewel had given him the nickname Rabbit when he was little, because he ate so many carrots, and the name had stuck. Colt was the only one of them who had been adopted as a baby. The rest of them had all known at least one other parent before being abandoned, orphaned, or fostered out.

"Is anybody there?" Jewel asked breathlessly. "If this is the kidnapper, we'll pay whatever you ask."

"It's me, Jewel."

"Cherry! Where are you? Are you all right? Are you hurt?"

"I'm fine. I'm at Billy Stonecreek's ranch."

"So he did kidnap you! I'll send Daddy to get you right away."

"No! I mean..." Cherry had turned her back to Mrs. Trask and kept her voice low thus far, but she figured there was no sense postponing the inevitable. "Billy didn't kidnap me. Last night we flew to Las Vegas and got married."

She was met with stunned silence on the other end of the line. Which was a good thing, because Mrs. Trask gave an outraged shriek that brought the two little girls back downstairs on the run.

"Nana! Nana! What's wrong?"

"I have to go now, Jewel," Cherry said. "Tell Zach and Rebecca I'm okay, and that I'll come to see them soon and explain everything."

"Cherry, don't—"

Cherry hung up the phone in time to turn and greet the twins a second time. Again, she identified the twin taking the lead as Raejean, which meant the one standing slightly behind her was Annie. "Hello, Raejean. Hello, Annie."

"I'm Annie," Raejean contradicted.

Before Annie could misidentify herself as Raejean,

Mrs. Trask snapped, "Don't bother trying to tell them apart. They're identical, you know."

"But—" From Billy's descriptions of them it was so obvious to her which twin was which. Couldn't Mrs. Trask see the difference?

"What's wrong, Nana?" Raejean asked. "Why did you scream?"

Mrs. Trask's face looked more like a beet or a turnip than a human head, she was so flushed. It was clear she wasn't sure exactly what to say.

"Your grandmother was just excited about some news she heard," Cherry said.

"What news?" Annie asked.

"It's a surprise I think your Daddy will want to tell you about himself when he gets home," Cherry said.

"We're not going to be here that long," Mrs. Trask retorted. "The girls and I are leaving."

"Not until Billy gets back," Cherry said firmly. "I'm sure Raejean and Annie want to wait and say goodbye to their father." Cherry turned to the girls and asked, "Don't you?"

Raejean eyed her consideringly, but Annie piped up, "I want to wait for Daddy."

Mrs. Trask made an angry sound in her throat. "I hope you're happy now," she said to Cherry. "My grandchildren have had a difficult enough time over the past year, without adding someone like you to the picture."

Cherry reminded herself that Mrs. Trask was always going to be Raejean and Annie's grandmother. Throwing barbs now, however satisfying it might be, would only cause problems later. Zach and Rebecca would have been astounded at her tact when she spoke.

"I'm sorry we surprised you like this, Mrs. Trask. I know Billy will want to explain everything to you himself. Won't you consider waiting until he returns before you leave?"

"No."

Of course, there were times when being blunt worked best. Cherry crossed to stand beside the twins. "I'm sorry you have to leave, Mrs. Trask. The girls and I will have Billy give you a call when he gets home."

Cherry saw the moment when Mrs. Trask realized that she had been outmaneuvered. She wasn't going to make a quick and easy escape with Billy's children. Cherry was there to stand in her way.

Billy chose that moment to pull open the screen door and step into the kitchen.

Annie and Raejean gave shrieks of joy and raced into his wide open arms. He lifted them both, one in each arm, and gave them each a smacking kiss. "How are my girls?" he asked.

Raejean answered for both of them.

"Some man got mad at Mrs. Motherwell because she didn't know where you were and Nana came and Mrs. Motherwell packed her bags and left and Nana said we should pack, too, and go live with her until you came back home, only this lady came a little while ago and said you were coming home really soon and we had to wait for you because you have a surprise for us. What's our surprise, Daddy? Can we have it now?"

Cherry had watched Billy's narrowed gaze flicker from his daughter to Mrs. Trask and back again as Raejean made her breathless recital. When Raejean got to the part about a surprise, his gaze shot to her, and she thought she saw both panic and resignation.

"What are you doing back here so soon?" Mrs. Trask said. "I was told you were going into town for supplies."

"I got stopped by the police long before I got there and arrested for kidnapping," Billy said.

"Then why aren't you in jail?" Mrs. Trask demanded.

Billy's lips curled. "I showed them my marriage license."

"Who got kidnapped, Daddy?" Annie asked.

"Nobody, sweetheart," Billy replied. "It was all a big mistake."

"Then, can we have our surprise now?" Annie asked.

He knelt down and set them back on their feet. Keeping an arm around each of them, he said, "The surprise is that you have a new mother."

Annie's brow furrowed. "A new mother?"

Raejean frowned. "Our mother is in heaven."

"I know that," Billy said in a sandpaper-rough voice that made Cherry's throat swell with emotion. "I've married someone else who's going to be your mother from now on."

Raejean and Annie looked at each other, then turned as one to stare with shocked, suspicious eyes at Cherry.

Raejean's head shot around to confront her father. "Her?"

Billy nodded.

Raejean jerked free and shouted, "I don't want another mother! Make her go away!" Then she ran from the room.

Annie's eyes had filled with tears and one spilled over as she stared at Raejean's fleeing form. Cherry willed the softhearted child to accept her, but Annie paused only another moment before she turned and ran after her sister.

Cherry met Billy's stricken gaze. She felt sick to her stomach. The two charming and innocent little girls she had married Billy to save from harm, didn't want anything to do with her.

"You're a fool, Billy," Mrs. Trask said, grabbing her purse from the kitchen counter. "I don't know what you hoped to accomplish with this charade, but it won't work. I'm more convinced than ever that my grandchildren belong with me." She gave Cherry a look down her nose. "I'll see you both in court."

She made a grand exit through the doorway that led to the front of the house. Cherry and Billy stood unmoving until they heard the front door slam behind her.

"She's right," Billy said. "I always intend to do the right thing, but somehow it turns out wrong."

"This wasn't wrong, Billy. If I hadn't gotten here when I did, Mrs. Trask would have taken the children and been gone before you returned. At least Raejean and Annie are still here."

"And angry and unhappy."

"We can change that with time."

"I hope so. It won't help much to argue in court that I've got a wife to take care of my children, if my children hate her guts."

"We have a more immediate problem," Cherry said.

"What's that?"

"Zach Whitelaw."

"What about him?"

"He's going to kill you on sight."

Billy gave a relieved laugh. "Is that all? I thought it was something serious."

"Don't joke," Cherry said. "This is serious. Three years ago a boy tried to force himself on Jewel at a Fourth of July picnic. I'll never forget the look in Zach's eyes when Jewel stood crying in his arms, her face bruised and her dress torn. He took a horsewhip to the boy and nearly flayed him alive. Both families kept it quiet, but you know how that sort of thing gets around. None of us girls has ever had any problems with boys since then.

"That's why it surprised me when Ray... If Ray hadn't been drunk, he would never have done what he did."

"And we wouldn't be where we are today," Billy said. "I won't let any man whip me, Cherry. If your father tries—"

"I'm only telling you all this so you'll understand why I have to go home and explain all of this to him by myself. Once he understands I was willing and—"

Billy shook his head. "We go together, or you don't go at all."

"Zach's going to be furious with me."

"All the more reason for us to go together. You may have been his daughter yesterday, but you're my wife today. No man is going to threaten my wife. Not even her father."

Cherry stared wide-eyed at Billy. She supposed she should have told him that no matter how angry Zach got with her, he would never raise a hand to her. In the past she had been sent to her room without supper, or been forced to spend a day alone thinking about the wisdom of a course of action. But the Whitelaws had always used reason, rather than force, to teach their children right from wrong.

Billy wouldn't have to defend her, but she reveled in the thought that he was willing to do so. Of more concern to her was the possibility that the two men might provoke one another to violence. She already knew that Billy liked to fight. Zach would be more than willing to give him one.

"I'll let you come with me on one condition," she said.

"What's that?"

"We bring the girls with us."

Billy frowned. "What purpose would that serve?"

"Zach won't be able to fight with you—or yell at me—if he's busy meeting his new grandchildren."

"Raejean and Annie don't even like you. What makes you think they'll take to your father?"

"Trust me. Zach Whitelaw could sell snow in Alaska. He'll have Raejean and Annie eating out of his hand in no time. Besides, we have no choice but to take them with us. Mrs. Motherwell is gone."

"I forgot about that," Billy said as he headed toward the door that led upstairs. "Damn. All right. Let me go get them. We might as well get this meeting over with."

"Billy," Cherry called after him. When he stopped and turned to her, she said, "We can still call the whole thing off."

He walked the few steps back to her and lifted her chin with his finger. "Buck up, kid. You're doing great."

Cherry felt tears prickle her eyes and blinked to keep them from forming.

Billy leaned down and kissed her mouth. His touch was gentle, intended to comfort. "I'm sorry, Cherry. I shouldn't have left you here alone and driven away. It's not easy to admit it, but I was scared."

Cherry searched his eyes. If he had once been afraid, the fear was gone now. If he had regrets, he wasn't letting her see them. She wished she knew him better as a person. Could she rely on him? Would he be there for her when the going got rough?

When he pulled her into his arms and hugged her, she felt safe and secure. She knew that was an illusion. Her father had made her feel safe, too. But they had been torn from each other. It was better not to try and make more of this relationship than it was.

Before she could edge herself away from Billy, the screen door was flung open. Billy threw her aside to confront whatever danger threatened them.

Zach Whitelaw stood in the doorway.

CHAPTER FIVE

"DADDY, DON'T!" Cherry cried as Zach took a step toward Billy, his hands tightened into angry knots.

Zach froze, his eyes wide with shock.

It took Cherry a second to realize she had called him "Daddy" instead of "Zach," something she had never done before. She felt confused, unsure why she had blurted it out like that, especially now, when she wasn't going to be his daughter anymore, but someone else's wife.

"Please don't fight," she said.

"Stay out of this, Cherry," Billy said, his hands curling into fists as menacing as Zach's.

"How did you get here so quickly?" Cherry said to her father. "I just got off the phone with Jewel."

"The police called me when they picked up Billy. A phony marriage license isn't going to save you from me," he snarled at Billy.

"We really are married," Cherry said, taking a step to put herself between the two men. Temporarily, it kept them from throwing punches.

Zach snorted. "In a Las Vegas ceremony? That's no kind of wedding."

"It's legal," Billy said coldly.

There was nothing Zach could say to counter that except, "Come home, Cherry. I know the situation last night must have upset you, but Rebecca and I want you to know we're on your side. We believe there must be some reasonable explanation for what happened. We can fix this problem."

"It's too late for that. Billy and I are married. I'm staying with him."

Zach glared at Billy. "You should be ashamed of yourself, taking advantage of a vulnerable child to—"

"She's no child," Billy said quietly. "She's a woman. And my wife." His hands slid around Cherry's waist from behind, and he pulled her back against the length of his body.

Cherry saw the inference Zach drew from Billy's words and actions that the two of them had done what husbands and wives do on their wedding night. By the time her father's gaze skipped to her face, she bore a flush high on her cheekbones that seemed to confirm what he was thinking. There was no way she was going to admit the truth.

She saw the wounded look in Zach's eyes before he hid it behind lowered lids.

"I didn't mean to hurt you or Rebecca," she forced past the lump in her throat.

"Why, Cherry?" he asked. "Why couldn't you trust us to be on your side? I thought..."

They were good parents. They had done everything they could to make her feel loved and appreciated, safe and secure. But they expected her to believe parents could protect their children from the evils of the world. She knew from experience that simply wasn't true. She could never trust them completely. She would never trust anybody that much again.

"I'm sorry, Zach." She saw his gaze flicker at her reversion to the less familiar, less personal title. "Please tell Rebecca—"

Zach cut her off. "You explain this to your mother. I couldn't find the words." He turned and left as abruptly as he had come.

Cherry felt her nose burning, felt the tears threaten and fought them back. She had chosen to travel this road. She had no one to blame but herself for her predicament. Crying over spilled milk wasn't going to accomplish anything.

"Thanks for sticking by me," Billy said against her ear.

"I'm your wife."

"Sometimes that doesn't mean much when parents enter the picture," Billy said bitterly.

Cherry turned in his embrace and put her arms around him to hug him, laying her cheek against his shoulder. "I'll try to be a good wife, Billy." She raised her face to his, only to find herself unexpectedly kissed.

There was as much desperation as there was hunger in Billy's kiss. Something inside Cherry responded to both emotions, and she found herself kissing Billy back.

"Hey! What are you doing to my dad?"

Cherry pulled free of Billy's grasp and turned to the child who had spoken. Behind her stood the other twin, her face less belligerent, more perplexed.

"Uh…" Cherry began. She had no idea where to go from there. She expected Billy to make some sort of explanation, but he gave her a helpless one-shouldered shrug. Cherry turned back to the twins and said to the one who had spoken, "Your dad and I were kissing, Raejean. That's what married people do."

"I'm Annie," Raejean said.

"I'm Raejean," Annie dutifully added.

"Hey, you two," Billy said. "What's the big idea trying to fool Cherry?"

Raejean's chin jutted. "I don't know why you're so mad, Daddy. She isn't fooled at all." She turned to Cherry, her brow furrowed. "How do you do that, anyway? No one but Mommy and Daddy has ever been able to tell us apart."

Cherry said, "There's nothing magic about it. You're as different from your sister as night from day."

"We're twins," Raejean protested. "We're *exactly* alike."

"You look alike on the outside," Cherry conceded, "but inside here—" Cherry touched her head. "And here—" She touched her heart. "You're very different."

"I'm glad you can tell us apart," Annie said. "I don't like fooling people."

"I don't care if you can tell us apart," Raejean said. "I'm not going to like you."

"Isn't it a little soon to make up your mind about that?" Cherry asked. "You hardly know me."

"I know you want to be my mother. I don't want another mother. My mother's in heaven!" Raejean turned and headed for the stairs. She hadn't gone very far before she realized Annie hadn't automatically followed her. She turned and said, "Come on, Annie."

Annie hesitated briefly before she turned and followed her sister.

Cherry whirled on Billy the instant they were gone.

"I can't do this all by myself, Billy. You're going to have to help."

"You can't blame them for being confused, Cherry. After all, the only woman they've ever seen me kissing is their mother."

"Then maybe we shouldn't let the girls see us kissing. Maybe you should keep your distance when they're around."

Billy thought about it for a moment, then shook his head. "I don't want to do that for two reasons. Penelope would be sure to notice if we never touched each other. It would be a dead giveaway that there's something fishy about our marriage."

"And the second reason?"

"I don't want my daughters to see me ignoring the woman they believe is my wife. It would give them the wrong impression of what marriage is all about."

"I see." What she saw was that Billy had all sorts of reasons for kissing and hugging her that had nothing whatsoever to do with actually loving her. But loving hadn't been a part of their bargain. She had to remind herself of the rules of this game. *Help each other out. Don't get involved. Don't start to care.* That way lay heartache.

"All right, Billy," Cherry said. "I'll play along with you where the kissing and touching is concerned. So long as we both know it's only an act, I suppose neither of us can be hurt. Now that we have that settled, I believe you need to get to town for those supplies, and I'd better get some lunch started."

Cherry turned her back on Billy, but she hadn't taken two steps toward the sink before his arms slid around her from behind again, circling her waist. Her treacherous body melted against him. She forced herself to stiffen in his embrace. "Don't, Billy," she said in a quiet voice.

"You're my wife, Cherry."

"In name only," Cherry reminded him. "We can pretend for everybody else, but I think it's best if we're honest with each other. We aren't in love, Billy. We never will be."

Billy's hands dropped away, but he didn't move. She felt the heat of his body along the entire length of her back. Her eyes slid closed, and she held herself rigid to keep from leaning back into his fiery warmth.

"If we're being honest," Billy said in a husky voice, "I think you should know I'm more than a little attracted to you, Cherry. I have been since the moment I first laid eyes on you." Billy took her by the shoulders and turned her to face him. "That's the truth."

She lifted her eyes to meet his. "That's lust, Billy. Not love."

His dark eyes narrowed, and his hands dropped away from her shoulders. "There's nothing wrong with desiring your wife in bed."

"I'm not your wi—"

"Dammit, Cherry!"

When Billy took a step back and shoved his hands into his jeans pockets, Cherry had the distinct impression he did it to keep himself from reaching for her again.

"You *are* my wife," he said through gritted teeth. "Not forever. Not even for very long. But we most definitely are married. I suggest you start thinking that way!"

Before she could contradict him, he was gone, the screen door slamming behind him.

BILLY COULDN'T REMEMBER a time when he had been more frustrated. Even when he had been arguing with Laura about whether or not she should try to get pregnant again when the doctor had advised her against it, he hadn't felt so much like he was butting his head against a stone wall. Deep down, he knew Cherry was right. It would be better for both of them if he kept his distance from her.

He had made up his mind to try.

Of course, that was before he stepped into Cherry's bedroom the morning after their wedding. He had expected her to be up and dressed, since he had helped her set the alarm for 5:30 a.m. the previous evening. Apparently, she had turned it off.

He found her sleeping beneath tousled sheets, one long, exquisite leg exposed all the way to her hip, one rosy nipple peeking at him, her lips slightly parted, her silky red curls spread across the pillow, waiting for a lover's hands to gather them up.

He cleared his throat noisily, hoping that would be enough to wake her. All she did was roll over, rearranging the sheet, exposing an entire milky white breast.

He swallowed hard and averted his eyes. He sat down beside her, thinking maybe the dip in the mattress would make her aware of his presence.

She slept on.

His gaze returned to rest on her face. Close as he was, he could see the dark shadows under her eyes. She must not have slept very well. He could understand that.

He hadn't slept too well himself. He had resorted to a desperate act—marriage—to solve one problem and had created a host of others in the process. Not the least of which was the fact he wanted to have carnal knowledge of his new wife.

He debated whether he ought to kiss her awake. But he wasn't Prince Charming. And Sleeping Beauty had never had such a freckled face. Nevertheless, his body responded to the mere thought of pressing his lips against hers, of tasting the hot, sweet wetness of her mouth.

Billy swore viciously.

And Cherry woke with a start.

It took her a second to realize how exposed she was, and she grabbed at the sheet as she sat up and drew her knees to her chest. Her blue eyes were wide and wary. "What are you doing in here?"

"I came to wake you up. You overslept."

She glanced at the clock, then dropped her forehead to her knees and groaned. "I must have turned off the alarm."

"I figured as much when you didn't show up in the kitchen. I've already had my breakfast. I left some coffee perking for you. The kids'll be up in a little while. You probably have time for a quick shower."

Thinking about her naked in the shower had about the same effect as contemplating kissing her. Billy needed to leave, but he was too aware of what Cherry would see if he stood right now. So he went right on sitting where he was.

Unfortunately, she now had the sheet flattened against herself, and he could see the darker outline of her nipples beneath the soft cotton. He found that every bit as erotic as seeing her naked.

"Hell," Billy muttered, shifting uncomfortably on the edge of the bed.

"What's the matter?"

Billy's lip curled wryly. "I'm not used to looking at a woman in bed without being able to touch."

"Oh." She clutched the sheet tighter, exposing the fact that her nipples had become hard nubs.

Billy bolted to his feet and saw her gaze lock on the bulge beneath his zipper. He froze where he was, his body aching, his mouth dry.

He watched her until she lifted her eyes to his face. Her pupils were enormous, her lips full, as though he had been kissing her. She was aroused, and he hadn't even touched her.

"Tell me to go, Cherry." He wanted to consume her in a hurry, like ice cream on a hot day. He wanted to take his time and sip at her slow and easy, like a cool mint julep on a lazy summer afternoon.

She licked her lips, and he felt his body harden like stone.

"The girls will be up soon," Cherry reminded him. "I need to get dressed."

Heaven help him, he had forgotten all about his daughters. He shoved a distracted hand through his hair and huffed out a breath of air. "I'll be working on the range today. If you need anything…"

Cherry smiled. "Don't worry about us, Billy. We'll manage fine."

"All right. So long."

He was almost out the door when she called him back.

"Billy?"

He turned and found her standing beside the bed with the sheet draped around her in a way that revealed as much as it covered. "What?" he asked, his voice hoarse from the sudden rush of desire he felt.

"You didn't kiss me goodbye."

He shook his head. "I don't think that would be a good idea, Cherry."

Before he realized what she had in mind, she closed the few steps between them and lifted her face to him. "I thought a lot about our situation last night, when I couldn't sleep," she said earnestly. "And I realized that if we're going to convince Mrs. Trask that this is a real marriage, we're going to have to act as much like a happily married couple as possible.

"Zach always gives Rebecca a kiss goodbye in the morning." She gave him a winsome smile. "So, pucker up, Mr. Stonecreek, and give me a kiss."

She didn't give him much of a choice. She raised herself on tiptoe and leaned forward and pressed her lips against his.

Billy gathered her in his arms and pulled her close as his mouth opened over hers, taking what he had denied himself only moments before. His hands slid down her naked back, shoving the sheet out of his way. Then he held her buttocks tight against his arousal with one hand while the other caught her nape and slid up to grasp a handful of her hair.

He took his time kissing her, his tongue thrusting hard and deep, and then slowing for several soft, probing forays, seeking the honey within. She made a moaning sound deep in her throat, and he gave an answering growl of passion.

When he let her go at last, she gave him a dazed look through half-closed lids, then grabbed at the sheet that had slid down to her waist and pulled it back up to cover herself. He grinned and said, "That was a good idea. I think we'll keep it up."

It took all the willpower he had to turn and walk out the bedroom door.

Cherry watched Billy go this time without calling him back. She was still quivering from his kiss. She forced her wobbly legs to take one step, and then another, as she headed for the bentwood rocker where she had thrown her robe. She slipped it on and let the sheet drop to the floor.

She was tying her terry-cloth robe closed when she heard a knock on the door. She hurried to open it and found Billy standing there with his hat on, his hip cocked, and his thumbs in his front pockets.

"Did you forget something?" she asked.

Not a thing, Billy realized. He remembered exactly how she had looked in bed. *And you look as delicious in that robe as you did in bed.* He couldn't very well tell her he had come back just to look at her again. So he said, "I forgot to say good morning." He smiled and tipped his hat. "Mornin', ma'am."

Cherry laughed.

And then, because he was looking for an excuse to spend more time with her, he said, "I wondered if you'd like to join me for a cup of coffee before I leave."

"I should get dressed," Cherry said, tightening the belt on her robe. "The girls will be up soon."

"You're right about that." Billy searched for something else to say, because otherwise he would have no excuse to linger.

"By the way, I never got around to telling you, but you'll need to go grocery shopping today. The ranch has an account at the store in town. I think Harvey Mills already knows we're married—I doubt there's anyone in the county who doesn't know by now—but just in case, I'll give him a call and tell him to put your name on the account. Feel free to get anything you think we'll need."

It was more than Cherry had heard Billy say at one time since she had met him at the pond. But the words had nothing to do with what he was saying with his eyes. His eyes were eating her alive. Her heart was pumping hard. Her breasts felt full. Her mouth felt dry.

She cleared her throat and said, "Shopping. Got it. Anything else?"

"Not unless you'd like that cup of coffee."

Cherry slowly shook her head. She had to send him away or she was going to invite him into her room. "I need to shower and dress before the girls wake up. Have a nice day, Billy."

"Yeah. I'll do that."

When he didn't leave, she raised a brow and said, "Is there something else, Billy?"

"If you want, I can go with you later today to see your family…to explain things."

Cherry felt a sense of relief. "Thanks, Billy. I'd like that."

"Well. I guess I'd better get started."

It took him another moment or two before he moved

away from the door. She watched his sexy, loose-limbed amble until he was gone from sight, then scurried up the stairs to the shower.

However, when she reached the bathroom, it was locked. She would have to wait her turn. She leaned against the wall, a towel over her arm, one bare foot perched atop the other and waited. And waited. The door never opened.

She leaned her ear against the door, but there was no sound coming from inside. She knocked and said, "Is someone in there?"

No answer.

"Raejean? Annie?"

Nothing.

She walked down the hall to the girls' bedroom. Their unmade twin beds were empty. She checked the other doors along the hall and found an office and Billy's bedroom, but no sign of the children.

"Raejean!" she called loudly. "Annie! If you're hiding somewhere up here, I want you to come out right now!"

Nothing.

She crossed back to the bathroom door and listened intently. She thought she heard whispers. She banged on the door. "I know you two are in there. I want you to come out right now."

Nothing.

She grabbed the doorknob and yanked on it, then slammed her shoulder against the door as though to break it open. "Open up!"

Nothing.

Cherry leaned back against the wall and sighed

heavily. She hadn't counted on this sort of misbehavior when she had nobly volunteered to rescue Billy's daughters from their grandmother's clutches. Right now, Mrs. Trask was more than welcome to the two of them!

Cherry smiled. Actually, she had pulled the same trick on one of her foster parents. She had spent almost two days in the bathroom before hunger finally forced her out. Which gave her an idea.

"All right, fine, stay in there. But you're going to get awfully hungry before the day is out. I'm going downstairs to make myself some blueberry pancakes with whipped cream on top and scrambled eggs and sausage and wash it all down with some hot chocolate with marshmallows."

Loud, agitated whispers.

The bathroom door opened and one of the twins stuck her head out. "Whipped cream on pancakes?"

Cherry nodded.

An identical face appeared and asked, "Big marshmallows? Or little ones?"

"Which do you prefer?"

"Little ones. Mrs. Motherwell only bought the big ones."

"Then we'll cut them into little pieces," Cherry suggested.

"All right." Annie shot out of the bathroom before Raejean could stop her and took Cherry by the hand. "Let's go."

Cherry waited to see what Raejean would do. The twin obviously wasn't happy to see rebellion in the ranks. She seemed unsure whether to stay where she was or abandon the fort. Her stomach growled and settled the matter. Raejean left the bathroom and headed down the hall toward the stairs, ignoring the hand Cherry held out to her.

Cherry realized as she followed Raejean down the stairs, Annie chattering excitedly beside her, that she might have won this battle, but the war had just begun.

CHAPTER SIX

BREAKFAST WAS A HUGE success. Cherry sat at the kitchen table giving herself a pat on the back for having pleased both girls so well. Two plates had been licked clean. Annie must have eaten almost as many additional marshmallows as the two of them had cut up together for her hot chocolate. Raejean had devoured the entire batch of whipped cream. The kitchen was a mess, but Cherry would have time to clean it once the twins were at school.

"Uh-oh," Annie said.

"Daddy's going to be *really* mad," Raejean said.

Cherry followed the direction of the girls' gazes out the kitchen window and saw the school bus at the end of the lane. It paused momentarily, honked, and when no one appeared, continued on its way.

"Oh, no!" Cherry raced to the back door, yanked it open and shouted to the bus driver. "Wait!"

He didn't hear her, which was just as well, because when she turned back to the kitchen she realized the girls weren't dressed and their hair wasn't combed.

Billy hadn't asked much of her—only that she feed his children breakfast and get them to school and be there when they got home in the afternoon. She couldn't even manage that.

She looked at the clock. Seven-thirty in the morning

and she was already a failure as a stepmother. Before despair could take hold, it dawned on her that elementary school surely couldn't start this early. Maybe she could still get the girls there on time.

"When do classes start?" she asked Raejean.

"Eight o'clock sharp," Raejean answered. "Mrs. Winslow gets *really* mad if we're late."

"You still have time to get there if we move like lightning," Cherry said.

She hurried the girls upstairs, but the more urgency she felt, the slower they both seemed to move. She ended up accidentally yanking Annie's hair as she shoved the hairbrush through a knot.

"Ouch!" Annie cried. "That hurt."

Cherry was instantly contrite. She had too much experience of her own with substitute parents who were in too much of a hurry to be gentle with her. She went down on one knee in the bathroom beside Annie and said, "I'm sorry, Annie. I should have been more careful. I guess I'm worried that I won't get you to school on time."

"Yeah. And Daddy will be *really* mad," Raejean reminded her through a mouthful of toothpaste.

"Spit and rinse," Cherry ordered Raejean as she finished putting Annie's hair into pigtails. "I'll get to you next."

For a moment Raejean seemed to consider putting up a fight, but she stood still while Cherry pulled the brush through her tangled hair.

"My mom always put ribbons in our hair," Raejean said.

Cherry heard the wistful longing in the complaint,

but there wasn't time to fulfill any wishes this morning. "Tonight we'll see what we can find and have them ready for tomorrow morning," she promised.

It wasn't until she had dressed herself and was ushering the girls out the back door that she realized she had no idea what they were going to use for transportation. There had to be some vehicle available, because Billy had suggested she go shopping during the day. But the only thing on four wheels she saw was a rusted-out pickup near the barn.

A set of hooks inside the back door held a key attached to a rabbit's foot. She grabbed the key, shoved the girls out the door, and prayed the truck had an automatic transmission.

It didn't.

"Don't you know how to drive?" Annie asked, concern etched in her young brow.

"I can drive. I have the license to prove it."

"Then why aren't we moving?" Annie asked.

Cherry stared helplessly at the stick shift on the floor of the pickup. "I'm not sure how to get this thing into gear." She tried moving the stick, and it made an ominous grinding sound.

"If you break Daddy's truck, he's going to be *really* mad," Raejean said.

Cherry was getting the picture. If she didn't figure out something soon, she was going to be dealing with a seriously annoyed teacher when she got the girls to school and a fierce, wild-eyed beast of a man when Billy got home.

She crossed her arms on the steering wheel and leaned her head down to think. She could call her sister

Jewel to come rescue her, but that was so mortifying a prospect she immediately rejected it. She felt a small hand tapping her shoulder.

"I can show you how to do it," Annie volunteered.

Cherry lifted her head and stared suspiciously at the six-year-old. "You know how to drive a stick shift?"

"Sure," Annie said. "Daddy lets us do it all the time."

Since there wasn't anyone else to show her how, Cherry said, "All right. Go ahead and show me what to do."

"Put your foot on that pedal down there first," Annie said. "Turn the key, and then move this thing here."

Cherry pushed down the clutch, turned on the ignition, and reached for the black gearshift knob. To her amazement the gearshift moved easily without making a sound. However, she ended up in third gear, didn't give the truck enough gas, and let the clutch go too fast. The pickup stalled.

"You have to follow the numbers," Raejean chided, pointing to the black gearshift knob. "See? One, two, three, four, and R."

"R isn't a number," Cherry pointed out.

"R is for Reverse," Annie piped up.

Maybe Billy did let them drive, Cherry thought. At least they knew more about a stick shift than she did. "All right. Here goes."

It was touch and go at first, but she managed to get the truck into second gear, and they chugged down the lane headed for the highway. She stalled a couple of times and ground the gears more than once before she got the hang of it. But she felt proud of herself when she finally pulled into the school parking lot and killed the engine.

"We made it," she said, glancing at her wristwatch. "With five minutes to spare."

"You forgot our lunches," Raejean said.

"What lunches?"

"Mrs. Motherwell always made us a sack lunch. We're going to starve," Annie said.

"Daddy's going to be *really* mad," Raejean said.

"Maybe you could buy your lunches today," Cherry suggested.

"I guess we could," Raejean conceded.

Annie and Raejean held out their hands for money.

Cherry realized she hadn't brought her purse with her. She checked both her jeans pockets and came up empty. "Look, I'll go home and make lunches for you and bring them back to school. How would that be?"

"Okay, I guess," Raejean said.

"I don't feel so good," Annie said, her hand on her stomach.

"Probably all the excitement this morning," Cherry said sympathetically. "You'll feel better once you're settled in class. Have a nice day, Raejean. Enjoy yourself, Annie."

She watched the two girls make their way inside, Raejean skipping and Annie holding on to her stomach.

To be honest, her own stomach was churning. It had been a hectic morning. And it wasn't over yet. She had to get home, make lunches and get back, then get the kitchen and the house cleaned up before the girls got home in the afternoon.

It was a lot of responsibility for someone whose biggest problem before today was whether she could figure out her calculus homework or get the formulas right in chemistry class. The entire responsibility for the house and two lively children now rested on her shoulders. It was an awesome burden.

She should have thought of that sooner. Now that she had made the commitment, she was determined to see it through. There were bound to be a few glitches at first. The important thing was to keep on trying until she succeeded.

Of course, she wasn't going anywhere until she figured out how to get the pickup into Reverse. No matter how many times she put the gearshift where she thought R ought to be, she couldn't get the truck to back up. When the final tardy bell rang, she was still sitting there.

She was going to have to call Jewel after all.

"Hey, Cherry, what's the matter?"

Cherry looked up into the sapphire blue eyes of her eleven-year-old brother, Colt. A black curl had slipped from his ponytail and curled around his ear. He was wearing tight jeans instead of the frumpy ones currently in style, and a white T-shirt and cowboy boots reminiscent of James Dean. Colt truly was the rebel in the family. But he somehow convinced everybody that doing things his way was their idea.

Cherry glanced at the empty schoolyard and said, "You're late, Colt."

He grinned. "Yeah. Looks that way."

"You don't seem too concerned about it. Zach will be—" Cherry stopped herself when she realized she was about to echo Raejean and say "*really* mad."

"Dad knows I'm late," Colt said. "Things were a little crazy this morning because of you disappearing and all. You really did it this time, Cherry. Mom went ballistic when she heard what you did, and Dad hasn't come down off the ceiling since he got back from the Stonecreek Ranch. Are you really married to Billy Stonecreek?"

"Uh-huh."

"Neat. He really knows how to use his fists to defend himself." Colt shrugged his book bag off and did some shadow boxing. He was tall for his age, his body lean, his movements graceful. "Billy's been in three fights this year," he said. "Do you think he'd show me a few punches?"

"Absolutely not! And where did you find out all this information about Billy?" Cherry asked.

"I heard Mom and Dad talking. They're worried that Billy's a bad influence on you. They said he's gonna undo all the hard work they've done, and you're gonna end up back in trouble again."

Cherry felt her face heating. Not that she didn't appreciate what Zach and Rebecca had done for her. But she had come a long way since the days when she had habitually cut school and been ready to fight the world.

"You'd better get inside," she told Colt.

"It's all right. Mom called and told them I'd be late," Colt replied. "What are you doing here?"

"I drove Raejean and Annie Stonecreek to school."

"Why didn't they take the bus?"

"They missed the bus."

Colt grinned. "Overslept, huh? You never were very good at getting up in the morning."

"Not that it's any of your business, but I didn't over-sleep. I merely lost track of the time."

"Same difference," Colt said. "So why aren't you headed back home?"

"I can't figure out how to get this damn truck into Reverse."

Colt laughed. "It's easy. Press the stick down and over."

"Press down? You have to press *down* on the stick before you move it?"

"Sure."

Cherry tried it, gave the truck a little gas, and felt it move backward. "Good grief," she muttered. "Thanks, Colt. I owe you one."

"Will you ask Billy if he'll show me a few punches?"

"I'll think about it," she replied as she backed out of the parking lot. "Tell Rebecca I'll come see her tonight," she called out the window as she drove away.

It was the coward's way out to have Colt relay her message. She should have called Rebecca and told her she was coming. But she didn't want to be forced into explaining things to her mother over the phone, and she knew Rebecca must be anxious for some sort of explanation for what she had done. The truth was, she needed the rest of the day to think of one.

By the time she made it back to the ranch she was a pro at shifting gears. She parked the truck behind the house, stepped inside the kitchen, and realized it looked like a tornado had been through. What if Billy came back home for some reason and saw it looking like this?

But she didn't want to stop and clean it right now and

take a chance on being late with the girls' lunches. The mess was even worse by the time she finished making sandwiches. She vowed to clean up the kitchen as soon as she returned. She was out the door half an hour later, sack lunches in hand.

When she arrived at the principal's office, Cherry was surprised to be told that Annie still wasn't feeling well. Her teacher had asked the office to call the house and have someone come and pick her up.

"I was concerned when I couldn't reach anyone at the ranch," the principal said, "so I called Mrs. Trask."

"Oh, no," Cherry groaned. "Call her back, please, and tell her it isn't necessary to come. I'll take Annie home."

"I'll try," the principal said. "But she's probably already on her way."

Cherry's only thought was to get Annie and leave as quickly as possible.

"I'm Cherry Whitelaw, Mrs. Winslow," she said when she arrived at Annie's classroom. Cherry flushed. "Except it's Stonecreek now. My name, I mean. I'm here for Annie."

"She's lying on a cot at the back of the room, Mrs. Stonecreek. Raejean insisted on sitting with her."

It felt strange to be called by her married name. Only she really was Mrs. Stonecreek, and responsible for the twins' welfare. She sat on a chair beside the cot and brushed the bangs away from Annie's forehead. "How are you, sweetheart?"

Annie moaned. "My stomach hurts."

"She ate too many marshmallows," Raejean said from her perch beside her sister.

"Marshmallows?" Mrs. Winslow asked.

"Annie had a few marshmallows with her hot chocolate this morning," Cherry said.

"How many is a few?" Mrs. Winslow asked.

Cherry hadn't counted. "Too many, I guess. Can you walk, Annie? Or do I need to carry you?"

Annie sat up, holding her stomach. "I don't feel so good."

Cherry picked her up in her arms.

"Where are you taking her?" Raejean demanded.

"Home," Cherry said.

"I'm going, too," Raejean said.

"There's no reason for you to miss a day of school," Cherry said reasonably. "I'll take good care of Annie."

"How do I know that?" Raejean demanded. "You're practically a stranger!"

"Raejean," Mrs. Winslow said. "Mrs. Stonecreek is right. There's no reason for you to leave."

"I'm going with Annie," Raejean said to Mrs. Winslow, her face flushed. "I'm not staying here alone."

"You won't be alone," Mrs. Winslow soothed. "You'll—"

"I'm going with Annie!" Raejean cried.

"Raejean—" Cherry began.

"I'm going with Annie!" she screeched hysterically.

Cherry knew the dangers of giving in to a tantrum. But in her mind's eye she saw Mrs. Trask arriving to find a scene like this and knew she was over a barrel. "All right, Raejean, you can come. I'm sorry for the trouble, Mrs. Winslow."

She turned and headed for the door with Annie in

her arms and Raejean a half step behind her. She was almost out the door when Mrs. Trask showed up.

"What's the matter with my granddaughter? What have you done to her?" she demanded.

"Annie is fine, Mrs. Trask." Cherry kept moving down the hall toward the front door of the school, still hoping to escape without a major confrontation.

"Annie's sick because she ate too many marshmallows," Raejean volunteered.

"Marshmallows?" Mrs. Trask said as though what she was really saying was "Poison?"

"Annie will be fine, Mrs. Trask."

"I was afraid of something like this. You're not responsible enough to be left in charge of two little girls."

Cherry didn't want to admit Mrs. Trask might be right. She had misjudged the situation this morning, but that didn't mean she couldn't do better. She would learn. After all, nobody had practice being a parent before they actually became one.

"Thank you for coming, Mrs. Trask, but as you can see, I have the situation well in hand."

"I'm coming home with you," Mrs. Trask said.

"I don't believe that's necessary," Cherry countered. "I—"

"What's going on here?"

Cherry stopped in her tracks.

It was Billy. He didn't look *really* mad, as Raejean had promised. He looked frantic, his brow furrowed, his sweat-stained work shirt pulled out of his jeans and hanging open, revealing a hairy chest covered with a damp sheen of sweat. He was still wearing his buckskin work gloves, but he was missing his hat. He had obviously shoved an agitated hand through his dark hair more than once, leaving it awry. He looked virile and strong...and very worried.

"I stopped by the house for some tools and found you gone and a message on the answering machine that Annie wasn't feeling well. Is she all right?"

"I'm sick, Daddy," Annie cried.

For a moment Cherry thought Billy would take Annie from her. Instead he asked, "Do you need any help with her?"

"I can manage if you'll get the door to the pickup."

"I knew something like this would happen," Mrs. Trask said to Billy as they all headed outside to the rusted pickup.

"Something like what, Penelope?" Billy said.

"Something awful."

"Kids get stomachaches, Penelope," Billy said.

"Not if parents are careful and watch what they eat."

"Look, Penelope, I appreciate you coming, but Cherry and I can handle things now."

"How can you trust that woman—"

Billy turned on his former mother-in-law, and for the first time Cherry saw the anger Raejean had threatened. "*That woman* is my wife. And I have the utmost trust in her to take the very best care possible of Raejean and Annie."

"Well, I don't."

"You don't have anything to say about it, Penelope."

"We'll see about that! The day is coming—"

Billy cut her off again. "You'll have your day in court,

Penelope. Until then, I can manage my family just fine without any help from you."

Cherry was impressed by Billy's support of her. She had done nothing to deserve his trust, and yet he had given it to her. She wanted very much to prove his faith in her was well-founded. She was simply going to have to try a little harder to be responsible.

"I'll follow you back to the house," Billy said to her as he buckled Raejean into her seat belt. "Maybe we can figure out what made Annie sick."

"She ate too many marshmallows," Raejean volunteered.

"What the hell was she doing eating marshmallows at breakfast?" Billy demanded of Cherry.

"I gave them to her," Cherry confessed. "With her hot chocolate. I guess I gave her a few too many."

Billy opened his mouth and snapped it shut on whatever criticism was caught in his throat. "We'll discuss this when we get home." He turned and marched to the other truck, a pickup in much better shape than the one she was driving.

The ride home was silent except for an occasional moan from Annie. When they arrived home, Billy carried Annie inside with Raejean trailing behind him. Billy breezed through the chaos in the kitchen without a pause and headed for the stairs. Cherry followed them, feeling as unwelcome as red ants at a picnic.

She stood at the bedroom door watching as Billy tucked Annie into bed and settled Raejean at a small desk with a coloring book and some crayons. She was amazed at his patience with his daughters. Amazed at his calm, quiet voice as he talked to them. The longer she watched, the worse she felt.

Billy had needed someone to help him out. All she had done was cause more trouble. Maybe he would want out of the marriage now. Maybe that's what he wanted to discuss with her.

When he rose at last and came toward her, he indicated with a nod that she should precede him down the stairs. Cherry felt the tension mounting as she headed into the kitchen, where the peanut butter jar stood open and blobs of jelly lay smeared on the counter. A pan bearing the scraped remnants of scrambled eggs sat in the sink, along with one lined with scalded milk.

She turned to face Billy. "I can explain everything," she said.

That was when he started laughing.

CHAPTER SEVEN

"WHAT'S SO FUNNY?" Cherry demanded.

"Annie eating all those marshmallows. She probably begged you for more."

"How did you know?"

"Laura and I let the twins eat too much ice cream the first time they tried it. It's hard to deny them anything when you see how much they're enjoying it. You'll learn." His expression sobered as he added, "That's what parents have to do, Cherry. They have to set limits and stand by them, for the sake of the kids."

"I'll try to do better, Billy," she replied.

Rather than say more, he merely scooped her into his arms, gave her a hug and said, "I've got to get back to mending fence. See you at supper."

It wasn't until he was out the door and gone that she realized he hadn't said a word about the sorry state of the kitchen. Cherry took a look around. There was no way he hadn't noticed. She blessed him for not criticizing, and decided to reward him with a sparkling kitchen when he next saw it.

Of course, that was before she knew what the afternoon held in store.

Grocery shopping was out of the question because Annie was in bed sick, so she took some hamburger out of the freezer to defrost for meatloaf while she cleaned up the kitchen. When she went to check on the twins, she found Annie sound asleep.

Raejean was gone.

She searched the entire house, high and low, without finding her. "She couldn't have left the house. I would have seen her," Cherry muttered to herself.

Unless she went out the front door.

Cherry found the front door open a crack.

"Oh, no, Raejean."

She was afraid to leave Annie alone in the house while she searched, but she knew she had to find Raejean before Billy came home. It was one thing to let a child overeat; it was quite another to lose one entirely. She had no choice but to call for help.

"Jewel, can you come over here?"

"What's wrong, Cherry? Should I get Mom and Dad?"

"No! I'm sure I can handle this. Would you please just come over?"

When she was home from college, Jewel helped run Camp Littlehawk, a retreat that Rebecca had started years ago at Hawk's Pride for kids with cancer. Summer sessions hadn't yet begun, so Jewel was free to come and go as she pleased.

"I'll be there in thirty minutes," Jewel said. "Is that soon enough?"

"No. But I guess it'll have to do."

"It sounds serious, Cherry. Are you sure—"

"I'm sure I can handle it with your help, Jewel. Please hurry."

The next thirty minutes were the longest of Cherry's life. Billy had shown a tremendous amount of trust in her, and she had already let him down once. She had to find Raejean before anything happened to her.

"How can I help?" Jewel asked the instant she came through the kitchen door.

With that single question, Jewel proved what a gem of a sister she was and why she was Cherry's favorite sibling. Jewel gave a thousand percent to whatever she did and never asked for anything in return.

She walked with a slight limp, a result of the car wreck that had orphaned her, and her face bore faint, criss-crossing scars from the same accident. She had mud-brown eyes and dishwater-blond curls, and looked so ordinary you wouldn't see her in a crowd. But she had a heart so big it made her an extraordinary human being.

"I'm in way over my head, Jewel," Cherry confessed. "I thought taking care of two little girls was going to be a breeze. It isn't."

"What's the problem?" Jewel asked.

"Annie's upstairs in bed sick, and Raejean's missing. I need you to watch Annie while I hunt for Raejean."

"I'll be glad to do that. Are you sure you don't want some more help hunting down Raejean?"

"I'd rather try to find her myself first. With any luck, she's hiding somewhere close to the house."

Cherry looked in the barn, which was the most obvious place for the little girl to hide. It was dark and cool and smelled of hay and leather and manure. A search of the stalls turned up two geldings and a litter of kittens, but no little girl.

She climbed the ladder that led to the loft and gave it a quick look, but there was nothing but hay bales and feed sacks, so she climbed down again. As she turned to leave the barn, she heard a sound in the loft. Several pieces of straw wafted through the air and landed on the cement floor in front of her.

"I know you're up there, Raejean," she said. "Please come down. I've been very worried about you."

Footsteps sounded on the wooden floor above her before Raejean said, "You have not! I'm not coming down till my Daddy gets home."

Cherry climbed the ladder to the loft and followed the sounds of a sobbing child to the feed sacks in the corner. Raejean was huddled there, her knees wrapped up in her arms, her stubborn jaw outthrust as she glared at her new stepmother.

Cherry sat on the scattered straw across from Raejean. "I know what it feels like to lose your mother, Raejean. I know what it feels like to have a stranger try to boss you around. I'm sorry your mother died. I'm sorry she isn't here right now. I know I can never replace her. But your Daddy asked me to take care of you and Annie for him while he works every day. Won't you let me help him?"

Raejean's tear-drenched eyes lowered as she picked at a loose thread on the knee of her coveralls. "I miss my mommy. I want my nana."

Cherry's heart climbed to her throat. She could understand Raejean's need for the familiar. In the ordinary course of things, it would have been wonderful to have the girls' grandmother take care of them temporarily. But Mrs. Trask wanted to wrench them away from their father permanently. Cherry wasn't willing to worry Raejean with that possibility, but she wasn't going to encourage Raejean's desire to run to her grandmother for solace, either.

"I'm sure your daddy will take you to visit your grandmother soon. Right now we need to go back inside and check on Annie. I invited my sister, Jewel, to stay with her while I looked for you, but I think Annie needs us."

"She doesn't need you!" Raejean retorted.

"Maybe not. But she needs you. Will you come back inside with me?"

Cherry's heart sank when the little girl said nothing. What was she supposed to do now? She couldn't very well drag Raejean down the ladder. And while she could probably let her sit up here until Billy came home, it wasn't a particularly safe place for a six-year-old.

She put a comforting hand on Raejean's shoulder, but the child shrugged it off. "Please, Raejean? I need your help with Annie."

"Oh, all right," Raejean said. "But I'm coming inside for Annie. Not for you."

Her face remained sullen as she followed Cherry inside, and she glowered when she discovered that Annie was still asleep.

"Maybe while Annie's sleeping you could help me make supper," Cherry cajoled.

"I don't know how to cook," Raejean said. "Mrs. Motherwell wouldn't let us in the kitchen, and Nana has a lady to do all her cooking."

"Would you like to learn?"

Reluctantly Raejean nodded her head.

"Let's give it a try, shall we?"

"If the emergency is over, I've got some chores I need to do this afternoon," Jewel said.

"I'll walk you to your car," Cherry said. "I'll be back in a few minutes, Raejean. Then we can get started on supper."

"When will I see you again?" Jewel asked as they headed downstairs.

"I told Colt I was going to bring the girls and Billy to meet Zach and Rebecca this evening, but I think I'd better revise that plan. Will you tell Rebecca that Annie's not well, and that we'll come visit as soon as we can?"

"Why don't you call her yourself?" Jewel urged as Cherry walked her out to her car. "I know she wants to talk to you."

"I can't face her, Jewel. Not after the way I disappointed her again."

"You know Mom and Dad are proud of you."

"Most of the time."

"You're their daughter. They love you."

"I don't know why," Cherry said with a sigh.

Jewel shook her head. "There's no rhyme or reason to loving someone. You should know that by now." She gave Cherry a hug. "Take care, Mrs. Stonecreek."

"Please don't call me that, Jewel."

"Why not? You're married, aren't you?"

"Yes." *Temporarily.* "It feels strange, that's all. It's a marriage of convenience," she confessed. "Billy needed someone to take care of his girls, and I—I couldn't face Zach and Rebecca after what happened at the prom."

"I figured it might be something like that."

Cherry could tell Jewel was curious, but Jewel didn't

ask questions. She merely smiled and gave Cherry another hug. "Call me if you need me, okay?"

As Jewel drove away, Cherry turned back to the house, to perhaps the biggest challenge of her life—being a mother to two little girls who didn't want one.

BILLY ENTERED THE KITCHEN at dusk, after a long, discouraging day that had included a visit to a lawyer, to find utter chaos.

The open peanut butter and jelly jars were gone from the counter, replaced by catsup and a round container of oatmeal. Dirty dishes no longer sat in the sink; it was filled with potato peels. The kitchen smelled like something good was cooking in the oven. But instead of a table set for supper, he found three flour-dusted faces standing on a flour-dusted floor, laboring over a flour-dusted table.

"Hi, Daddy!" Raejean's face bore perhaps the biggest smile Billy had seen there since Laura's death. She held a rolling pin in her small hands and was mashing it across some dough spread on the table. "We're cooking."

"Hi, Daddy!" Annie's grin was equally large. She held up two flour-dusted hands, one of which held a hunk of half-eaten dough. "We're making an apple pie for you, because it's your favorite!"

Billy finally let his gaze come to rest on Cherry. She had been in his thoughts too often during the day. She had a panicked look on her face as she glanced around at the mess in the kitchen. She pointed to the dough in Annie's hand and said, "I only let her have this little bit. It's not enough to make her sick."

"I see," Billy said.

What Billy saw was Cherry reassuring him that she had learned her lesson. That she was willing to take responsibility for being the adult when she was barely one herself.

"We're running a little late," Cherry said, rubbing her hands across the front of her jeans and leaving them flour-dusted, as well. "After we got the meatloaf and mashed potatoes prepared, there was still time before we expected you back, so we decided to make a pie."

"I see."

What Billy saw was something he had never seen when Laura was alive, and likely never would have seen, even if she had lived. Laura had never learned to cook, and she didn't pretend to be any good at it or take any joy in it. The only apple pie she had ever made for him had come from a frozen food box. Culinary expertise hadn't been high on Billy's list of requirements for a wife, so he had never minded.

Now he realized what he had been missing. To see the three of them working together to make something especially for him touched a place deep inside of him. It fed a hunger for the sort of hearth and home that he imagined others experienced, but which had been lost to him since his parents' deaths. It was an added bonus to see Raejean and Annie so happy.

A different man might have seen only the mess and not the loving gesture that had been the source of it. Billy merely said, "Would you mind if I take a quick shower before I join you? I'm a little rank after a day on the range."

Cherry looked relieved. "That'll be fine. It'll give us time to finish up here."

He started for the hall but turned around before he got there and returned to the table. He saw the wariness in Cherry's eyes, the vulnerable look that said, "What have I done wrong now?"

He brushed a patch of flour from her cheek with his thumb before he lowered his mouth to touch hers. The shock was electric. When he could breathe again, he said, "Thanks, Cherry. Homemade apple pie will be a real treat."

"I helped," Raejean said.

"Me, too," Annie added.

Billy gave each of them a quick kiss on the nose. "I can tell," he said with a smile. "You two need a shower almost as bad as I do."

He made himself leave them and go shower, even though he was tempted to stay. He had to remind himself that Cherry was only there for a little while. Long enough to keep Penelope at bay. Long enough to make sure he kept custody of his kids.

By the time he got back downstairs, the pie was in the oven and the kitchen had undergone a partial transformation. The sink was stacked high with everything that had been on the table, but the floor was swept clear, and Cherry and his daughters no longer sported a liberal dusting of flour on their faces and clothes.

"I set the table," Raejean said proudly.

"It looks great," Billy said as he eyed the knife and fork on a folded paper napkin beside his plate.

"I picked the flowers," Annie said.

A collection of blue morning glories with tiny, half-inch stems floated in a bowl of water.

"They're beautiful," Billy said as he sat down and joined them at the kitchen table. "Your mother…" His throat closed suddenly. The swell of emotion surprised him. He had thought he had finished grieving. But the senseless tragedy of Laura's death was there with him again, as though it hadn't happened a full year in the past, but only yesterday.

The two girls looked at him expectantly, waiting for him to finish. He swallowed back the lump in his throat and managed to say, "Your mother would have loved to see them there."

"It was Cherry's idea," Annie volunteered. "She said they would be pretty."

"They are," Billy agreed softly. He let his gaze slip to Cherry for the first time since he had come to the table. "Morning glories were Laura's favorite flower," he said.

"I didn't know," she replied. "I can take them off the table, if you like."

"No. Leave them there. It's all right." He had to keep on living. He had to go on despite the fact Laura was no longer with him. He fought back the anger at Laura for leaving him alone to raise their two girls. It didn't help to feel angry. Better not to feel anything.

Only, that wasn't possible anymore. Not with Cherry living in the same house. Just looking at her made him feel way too much. He wanted her. And felt guilty because of it, even though he knew that was foolish. He was still alive. He still had needs. And she was his wife.

Temporarily. And only as a matter of convenience.

That didn't seem to matter to his body. It thrummed with excitement every time he looked at her. He wondered how her breasts would feel in his hands. He wondered whether she had freckles everywhere. He wanted to see her blue eyes darken with passion for him.

He was damned glad she couldn't read his mind.

After supper, the two little girls who had enjoyed making pie were less willing to clean up the results of their handiwork.

"Mrs. Motherwell always did the dishes by herself," Raejean protested.

"Yeah," Annie added.

"Maybe so, but she isn't here anymore," Cherry said. "Now everybody helps in the kitchen."

Raejean's eyes narrowed as though gauging whether she had to obey this dictum. She glanced at her father, still sitting at the table finishing up his second slice of pie, and asked, "Even Daddy?"

Billy had been listening to the byplay between Cherry and his daughters, a little surprised that she expected the twins to help. There was nothing wrong with them learning to do their share of the chores. Of course, he hadn't expected to be included. Dishes were women's work.

Now what, smart guy? Are you going to act like a male chauvinist pig? Or are you going to provide a good example to your children and pitch in to help?

Billy rose and carried his plate to the sink. "All of us have to do our part," he said. "Even me."

It was fun.

He had never done dishes as a family project, but there were definite advantages to doing the work as a team. Like having the girls tease him with the sprayer in the sink as they stood on a chair and rinsed off the dishes before Cherry loaded them in the dishwasher. And tickling Cherry, who turned out to be the most ticklish person he had ever known.

In the past, jobs at the ranch had been divided into *his* and *hers*. Cherry made everything *ours*.

"Where did you learn all these communal work ethics?" Billy asked as they each toweled off one of the twins after their bath.

"When there are eight kids in a household, everyone has to chip in and do their part," Cherry said. "And knowing there was at least one extra pair of hands to help made every job easier."

"And more fun," Billy said, as he picked up the twins, one in each arm, and headed toward their bedroom.

"And more fun," Cherry agreed as she turned down the twins' beds.

Billy set each twin on her bed and then sat down cross-legged on the floor between them. Cherry stood against the wall, her arms crossed around herself, watching them.

"Tell us a story," Raejean begged.

"Please, Daddy," Annie wheedled.

When the twins were younger and having children was still a novelty, Billy had often told them bedtime stories. As they had gotten older and his responsibilities on the ranch had become more pressing, Laura had been the one to put the girls to bed at night. He'd had to be satisfied with looking in on them after they were already asleep. Over the past year he had allowed a series of housekeepers to enjoy this precious time with his daughters.

Billy realized that he would probably be working on the bookkeeping right now if Cherry hadn't made everything so much fun that he had wanted to stay with them rather than retire to his office to work. He was grateful to her, but he couldn't tell her why without admitting he had been lax as a parent.

It shocked him to realize that maybe Penelope was right about him. Maybe he hadn't been a very good parent for his daughters over the past year. Maybe it was time to acknowledge that being a father meant more than planting the seeds in a woman that grew into children and earning the money that put food in their mouths, a roof over their heads, and clothes on their backs.

When he finished the story and his giggling girls were tucked in and kissed on their noses, he turned at last to find Cherry and realized that sometime during the reading of the bedtime story she had left the room.

"Good night, girls," he said as he turned out the light. "Sleep tight."

"Don't let the bedbugs bite!" they recited in chorus.

Billy headed downstairs in search of Cherry, anxious to thank her for making him aware of the priceless moments he had been missing with his daughters.

He knocked on the door to her room, but she wasn't there. He searched the house and finally found her sitting in one of the two rockers on the front porch. It was dark outside, and when he turned on the front porch light she said, "Please leave it off."

"All right," he said as he settled in the second rocker. "What are you doing sitting out here in the dark?"

"Thinking."

"About what?"

"About us. About why we got married." She pulled her feet up onto the rocker seat, circled her legs with her arms, and set her chin on her knees as she stared into the darkness. "We shouldn't have done it, Billy," she said softly.

"I disagree, Cherry. Especially after today."

She lifted her head and turned to stare at him. "I would think, if anything, today proved what a rotten mother I am. I wasn't going to tell you, but Annie and Raejean missed the bus this morning, so I had to take them there and I didn't know how to drive a stick shift and I forgot to make them lunches and then I let Annie eat too many marshmallows and then Mrs. Trask showed up at school because I wasn't here to get the call from the principal, and then Raejean ran off and the kitchen was a mess and supper wasn't ready and—"

Billy stood abruptly and lifted her out of the rocker and settled her in his lap as he sat back down. He felt the tension in her body and wanted desperately to ease the misery he had heard in her voice.

"So maybe you don't have the mechanics down. But you know everything about being a mother that really counts."

"Like what?" she said, her voice muffled because she had her mouth pressed against his throat.

"Like wanting them to be happy. Like caring what happens to them. Teaching them to do their share. Showing them the pleasure of doing something nice for somebody else. And showing me how much I've been missing by letting someone else try to be both parents, instead of doing my part."

He felt her relax against him, felt her hand curl up behind his neck and thread into his hair. He liked the feel of her in his arms, liked the way she leaned on him.

"Thanks, Billy," she murmured. "I want to be a help-mate for you."

She sounded tired, half asleep. After the day she had described to him, it was no wonder. "You are, Cherry," he said, pulling her close. "You are."

He only meant to give her a kiss of comfort. His intent wasn't the least bit amorous. He tipped her chin up with his forefinger and pressed soothing kisses on her closed eyelids, her freckled cheeks, and her nose. And one last kiss on her mouth.

Only he let himself linger a bit too long.

And Cherry returned the kiss. Her tongue made a long, lazy foray into his mouth.

His body reacted instantly, turning rock-hard. He groaned, almost in pain. He wanted her. Desperately. But he had agreed to wait.

"Cherry, please," he begged.

She didn't answer him one way or the other. He had to touch her, needed to touch her. He slid his hand up under her T-shirt and let his fingertips roam the silky flesh across her belly. His thumb caught under her breast.

He reached for the center clasp of her bra, holding his breath, hoping she wouldn't ask him to stop. He felt the clasp come free and huffed out a breath all at the same time.

She made a carnal sound as his hand closed over the

warmth of her breast and gasped as his thumb flicked across the rigid nipple.

His mouth covered hers, and his tongue mimicked the sexual act as his hand palmed her flesh and then slid down between her legs. He cupped her and felt the heat and heard her moan.

His mouth slid down to her throat, sucking hard at the flesh as his thumb caressed her through a thin layer of denim, making her writhe in his arms.

"Billy, no!"

He froze, his breath rasping out through his open mouth, his body aching. He didn't try to stop her when she stumbled from his lap and grabbed at one of the porch pillars to hold herself upright. Her whole body was trembling with desire—or fear, he wasn't sure which.

"I'm sorry," she said. "I can't. I'm sorry."

Then she was gone.

CHAPTER EIGHT

CHERRY SPENT THE FIRST month of her marriage trying desperately to win Raejean's and Annie's trust. And trying desperately not to think about how close she had come those first few days to making love with Billy.

She had felt warm and safe and secure in his arms. She had felt desired and cherished. She had felt the beginnings of passion—and torn herself from his embrace.

It was fear that had kept her from surrendering. Fear that she would begin to care too much. Fear that what she felt for him was illusion. Fear that what he felt for her was too ephemeral to last. If she gave herself to him body and soul, she would be lost. And when the marriage was over, she would die inside.

It was safer to keep her distance. That was the hard lesson she had learned as a child. She knew better than to trust anyone with her heart. If she gave it up to Billy, he would only break it.

But she wasn't strong enough to deny herself his touch entirely. She liked his kisses. She liked his caresses. And they were a necessary part of the charade she and Billy were playing out for the benefit of Mrs. Trask.

Of course, Mrs. Trask wasn't there each morning when Billy slipped up behind her while she was making coffee and nuzzled her neck and said in a husky voice, "Good morning, Cherry."

Mrs. Trask wasn't there when she turned and pressed herself against him, sieved her fingers into his thick, silky hair, and waited for his morning kiss.

Mrs. Trask wasn't there when Billy lowered his head and took her lips in a kiss as tender as anything Cherry had ever experienced, or when that same kiss grew into something so terrifyingly overwhelming that it left her breathless.

If Billy had asked her to yield entirely, she would likely have stopped allowing the kisses. But he seemed to be satisfied with what she was willing to give him. It wasn't until a month had passed that it dawned on Cherry that each morning Billy asked for a little more. And each morning she gave it to him.

A hand cupping her breast. The feel of his arousal against her belly. Drugging kisses that left her knees ready to buckle. Her hand pressed to the front of his fly to feel the length and the hardness of him. His mouth on her throat. Her robe eased aside, and his mouth on her naked breast.

The feelings were exquisite. Irresistible. Like Billy himself.

If physical seduction had been his only allure, she might have resisted him more successfully. But not only was she attracted to Billy physically, she liked and admired him, as well. He was a good father, a hard worker, a considerate helpmate. Cherry knew she was sliding down a slippery slope. She was in serious danger of complete surrender.

She tried not to think about Billy during the day.

It was easy for great stretches of time to involve herself with Raejean and Annie and housekeeping and the chores in the barn she had taken over for Billy. And she had started night school to earn her high school diploma, and there was always homework to be finished. Her life was full and busy, and she felt useful and satisfied.

Most of the time.

But she could feel Billy's eyes on her in the evening after supper when they spent time with the children and gave them their baths. Watching her. Waiting for her to want him the way he wanted her.

The sexual tension between them had grown palpable. Her skin tingled at the mere thought of him touching her. Her breasts ached for the feel of his callused hands. Her blood raced when she saw him come through the door each evening, his washboard belly visible through his open shirt, his sinewy arms bared by rolled-up shirtsleeves, his muscular body fatigued from a day of hard labor.

And her heart went out to him when she saw his face, his dark eyes haunted by the stress of an imminent showdown in court with Mrs. Trask. Was it any wonder she wanted to hold out her arms to him and offer comfort?

As he shoved open the kitchen screen door, her thoughts became reality. Their eyes met and held for an instant, and Cherry knew that tonight she would give herself to him. Tonight she would offer him solace, even if it meant giving up her own peace of mind.

"Hi, Daddy," Raejean said as Billy settled his Stetson on a hat rack by the kitchen door.

"Hi, Daddy," Annie echoed.

Cherry felt a tightness in her chest as she saw the smile form on his face when he lifted the girls up into his arms and gave each of them a kiss on the nose. He loved them so very much. And there was a very real danger that he would lose them.

"How are my girls?" he asked. "What are you doing to keep busy now that school's over?"

"Cherry made us work!" Raejean said.

Billy raised his eyebrows. "Oh?"

"We had to help dig a garden behind the house."

"A garden?"

Cherry met Billy's surprised look and explained, "I thought it would be nice to have some fresh vegetables." Then she realized how presumptuous it was to assume she would still be around in the fall to harvest them.

"We had to plant flowers around the edge of the garden when we were done digging," Annie said.

"What kind of flowers?" Billy asked.

"Marigolds," Annie chirped. "It was fun, Daddy."

"Did you have fun, too, Raejean?" Billy asked.

"Maybe," Raejean conceded. "A little."

Cherry knew it had been an adjustment for Raejean and Annie to find themselves suddenly responsible for chores appropriate to their ages. Before Laura's death they had been too young, and the series of housekeepers had found it easier to do the work themselves than to involve the children. Cherry had explained to Billy that she wasn't there as a housekeeper, she was there as a surrogate mother. And she could best teach the girls the things they would need to know to manage a ranching household by involving them in every aspect of what she did.

It wasn't until she had come to live with Rebecca and Zach that Cherry had been included in precisely that way in the running of a household. In previous foster homes she had been more like a maid-of-all-work. In the Whitelaw home she had been part of a family in which each member did his or her part. She had learned the satisfaction to be had from contributing her fair share.

The more she put to good use the lessons Rebecca had taught her, the more she realized how much she had learned from her, the more grateful she felt for having been adopted into the Whitelaw family, and the more guilty she felt for having run away and married Billy instead of coming home and facing Zach and Rebecca the night she had been expelled.

There was no doubt she had been a difficult child to parent. The longer she was a stepparent, the more understanding she had of the other side of the fence. And the more appreciation she had for Zach and Rebecca's endless patience and love.

She knew she ought to tell them so.

But she couldn't face them and say on the one hand how much she appreciated all the things they had taught her, while on the other she was perpetrating the deceit involved in her temporary marriage to Billy Stonecreek.

So she had found excuses to avoid visiting them and reasons to keep her family from visiting her. Except for Jewel, who knew everything, and was quick to point out that Cherry was acting like an idiot and should simply call Zach and Rebecca and confess everything.

"They'll understand," Jewel had said. "And they'll forgive. And they'll still love you as much as ever. That's what parents do."

Cherry was finding that out for herself. Raejean still resented her and complained about nearly everything Cherry asked her to do, although she would eventually do it. Annie hadn't surrendered her trust to Cherry in loyalty to Raejean.

If her marriage to Billy had been a permanent thing, Cherry would have said time was on her side. It had taken more than a year for her barriers to come down with Zach and Rebecca, but in the face of all that love, they *had* come down. She needed to win Raejean's and Annie's trust before the court hearing—a matter of weeks. A great deal depended on her finding a way to break through the little girls' stubborn resistance.

They had long since broken through hers. She loved them both dearly, enough to know it was going to hurt a great deal when she was no longer a part of their lives.

"You got a letter today," she told Billy as he set the girls back on their feet. "It looks official."

Billy's face was grim as he went to the kitchen counter where she always left the mail and sorted through it. He picked up the envelope, looked at it, and set it back down again. "It can wait until after the kids are in bed."

Cherry understood why he was postponing the inevitable. But she knew he was as aware of it sitting there all evening as she was.

He hugged the girls so hard at bedtime that Annie protested, "I can't breathe, Daddy."

She knew he was afraid of losing them. So was she.

She walked ahead of him down the stairs and instead

of heading for the porch rockers to relax for a few minutes before going back to work, she headed for the kitchen. Billy followed her.

She went directly to the stack of mail, found the letter she wanted, and handed it to him. "Read it."

He tore it open viciously, his teeth clenched tight enough to make a muscle in his jaw jerk. He read silently. Without a word, he handed the official-looking letter to her. "Read it."

She read quickly. The court date had been set for July 15. Billy was asked to appear and explain certain accusations that had been made against him that he was not a fit custodian for his children.

"Three weeks," he said bitterly. "Three lousy weeks before I have to appear in court and prove I'm a fit father. How the hell am I going to do that, Cherry? Tell me that? I can't make those nights in jail go away. And you can bet Penelope will make sure the judge knows that the mother I've provided for my children is an eighteen-year-old girl who used to be a juvenile delinquent."

Cherry went white around the mouth. She hadn't expected his attack. It was useless to point out that he was the one who had suggested marriage. It didn't change the facts. "What do you want to do, Billy? Do you want to annul the marriage? Would that help, do you think?"

"Oh, God, no!" His arms closed tight around her. "I'm sorry, Cherry. I didn't mean to suggest that any of this is your fault, or that you aren't a wonderful mother. You are. Raejean and Annie are lucky to have you. Only…"

"Only I have been a juvenile delinquent."

"And I've spent a few nights in jail," Billy said. "Nobody's perfect, Cherry. We simply have to convince the judge that all that behavior is in the past. That right now we're the best possible parents for two little girls who've lost their mother, and whose grandmother is a bit misguided."

"Is that what she is?" Cherry asked, her lips twisting wryly.

"She misses her daughter, Cherry. She's still grieving. But that doesn't mean I'm going to give her my children to replace the one she lost," Billy said, his voice hard, his eyes flinty.

"Raejean still doesn't like me," Cherry pointed out. "What is the judge going to make of that?"

Billy's brow furrowed between his eyes. "I don't know, Cherry. He'll have to understand that we're all still making adjustments. He'll have to see that you're doing the best you can."

She took a deep breath and said, "I couldn't bear to see you lose them, Billy."

"I won't. I can't." He paused at the realization that the court had the power to take his children away from him before repeating, "I won't."

His arms tightened painfully around her, and she knew he was holding on to her because he was afraid of losing them. When his mouth came seeking hers—seeking solace, as she had known he would—she gave it to him.

"I need you," he said in a guttural voice. "I need you, Cherry."

"I'm yours, Billy," she answered him. "I'm all yours."

He picked her up and carried her to her room, shoving

open the bedroom door with his hip and laying her on the bed. He turned on the bedside lamp and sat down beside her.

"I want to see you. I want to feel your flesh against mine," he said as he tore off her T-shirt and threw it across the room. He had her bra unclasped a second later and it was gone, leaving her bared to him from the waist up.

He stopped to look at what he had. "No freckles here," he mused as a callused finger circled her breast. "Just this rosy crest," he finished as his mouth closed on her.

Her hands tangled in his hair and held him as he suckled her. Her body arched with pleasure as his hand slipped down between her legs to hold the heat and the heart of her.

Cherry had endured weeks of teasing foreplay. Now she wanted what had been denied her. "Please, Billy. Please." She shoved at his shirt, wanting to feel his flesh against her fingertips. She reached for his belt buckle and undid it with trembling fingers and then undid the button and slid down the zipper on his jeans. Billy copied everything she did.

When her hand slid beneath his briefs to reach for him, his did the same beneath her panties.

They stopped and looked at each other and grinned.

"Gotcha," Billy said as he slid a finger deep inside her. She was wet and slick, and he added another finger to the first.

Cherry groaned.

Her gaze trailed down to where her hand disappeared

inside Billy's briefs. She tightened her grasp and slid her hand up and down the hard length of him.

Billy groaned.

Their mouths merged, their tongues mimicking the sexual act as their hands kept up their teasing titillation.

Suddenly it wasn't enough. Cherry wasn't sure which of them shoved at the other's jeans first, but it wasn't long before both of them were naked. A moment after that, Billy was inside her.

They both went still.

It felt like she had found her other half. Now she was whole.

Cherry looked up into Billy's dark eyes and saw a wealth of emotion. Too many feelings. More than were safe. She closed her eyes against them.

"Look at me, Cherry," Billy said.

She slowly raised her lids and gazed at him with wonder.

He loves me, she thought. *I never dreamed...I never imagined...*

She waited for the words, but he never said them.

And she knew why. She didn't love him back. She wouldn't allow herself to love him. He knew the rules. It was to be a safe, temporary marriage.

Her eyes slid closed again as his mouth covered hers, hungry, needy. For the first time in her life she was grateful for her height, which made them fit together so perfectly that they could be joined at the hip and their mouths still meet for a soul-searching kiss. She felt the passion rise, felt her body shiver and shudder under the onslaught of his desire.

His body moved slowly at first, the tension building equally slowly, until it was unbearable, until she writhed beneath him, desperate for release.

"Please, Billy," she cried. "Please!"

She heard a savage sound deep in his throat as his body surged against hers, as he fought the inevitable climax, wanting to prolong the pleasure.

She felt her body tensing, thrusting against his, seeking the heaven he promised, until they found it, his seed spilling into her at last.

His weight was welcome, comforting, as he lowered his exhausted, sweat-slick body onto hers, their chests still heaving to gather breath to support their labored bodies, their heartbeats still pounding to carry blood to straining vessels.

Eventually, as their breathing slowed and their hearts returned to normal, Billy slid to her side and spooned her bottom against his groin. His hand curled around her breast as though it were the most natural place in the world for it to be. "Thanks, Cherry. I needed that. You," he amended.

It was more than she was willing to admit, so she remained mute. She was content to lie in his arms, saying nothing, enjoying the closeness.

It was during this quiet aftermath that she realized they had used no protection. They both knew better. Under the circumstances, a pregnancy could be disastrous. "Billy," she murmured.

"Hmm."

"We didn't use anything."

"Hmm?"

"To keep me from getting pregnant."

His stiffening body revealed his distress. "I should have asked. I should have—"

She turned in his arms and put her fingertips against his lips. "It's the wrong time of the month, I think."

"You think?"

"If there is a safe time," she amended, "this is probably it."

"Thank God," he said.

Even though she knew rationally that it was in both of their interests for her not to get pregnant, it was still irksome to see the amount of relief on Billy's face. "I guess you don't want any more children," she said.

"It isn't that," he said. "I always wanted more kids. But Laura..."

She remembered that Laura couldn't have any more. Only, that wasn't what Billy said next.

"Laura wasn't supposed to get pregnant because it was dangerous."

She felt him shudder and a thought occurred to her. "Are you saying she got pregnant anyway?"

He paused so long she didn't think he was going to answer her. At last he said, "Yes."

"What happened? To the baby, I mean?"

"She miscarried. Twice."

He pulled her close so his chin rested on her head, and she couldn't see his eyes. But she could feel him trembling and hear his convulsive swallow.

"The second time it happened I told her that if she didn't stop trying to get pregnant, I'd refuse to sleep with her anymore. I didn't want to take the chance of losing her. She meant too much to me, more than any baby ever could."

Another swallow.

"She was furious with me. She said she had promised me a houseful of kids, and she knew I couldn't be happy with just the twins. I told her the twins were enough. But she didn't believe me.

"The truth was, she had this insane idea that a woman who couldn't have kids wasn't a real woman. She refused to stop trying to get pregnant, despite the risk to her health. So I told her I was through arguing. I wasn't going to sleep with her again until she changed her mind and agreed to be sensible."

He shuddered.

"She went stomping out of the house, furiously angry, and got into the car. And...and she was killed."

"Oh, my God," Cherry breathed. "And you're not really sure whether it was an accident, or whether she killed herself on purpose, is that it?"

"She wouldn't kill herself. Not because of something like that. She wouldn't. It was an accident."

Cherry wasn't sure who he was trying to convince, himself or her.

"All Penelope saw the year before she died was Laura's despondency over the first miscarriage," Billy continued. "Penelope knew we'd been arguing a lot around the time of Laura's death, although she didn't know what we'd been arguing about. Laura didn't tell her about the miscarriage—probably because she knew her mother would be on my side."

"Why didn't you tell Mrs. Trask what had happened?" Cherry asked.

"It was none of her business!" Billy retorted. "It was between me and my wife."

"Maybe if she understood why—"

"It's over and done with now."

"Perhaps if you explained—"

"Laura's dead. There's no bringing her back."

And he wasn't sure he wasn't to blame, Cherry realized. No wonder he had gotten into so many fights in the year since Laura's death. He had been in pain, with no way of easing it. Because he would never know for sure what had happened.

"It wasn't your fault she died," Cherry said quietly.

"How do you know that?" he snarled.

"You were right. It wasn't safe for her to continue getting pregnant. You had to take a stand."

"I should have found some other way to say no."

"Hindsight is always better. You did the best you could at the time."

"That's supposed to make me feel better?"

She leaned back to look into his troubled eyes and saw the need in him to strike out against the pain. There were other ways of easing it. She laid her hand against his cheek and said, "You're a good man, Billy. You never meant for her to be hurt. Whether it was an accident... or not...Laura was responsible for what happened."

"I want to believe that," he said. "I try to believe that. But..."

"Believe it," she whispered as her lips sought his.

His arms surrounded her like iron bands, and his mouth sought hers like a thirsting man who finds an oasis in the desert. He was inside her moments later, needing the closeness, needing the comfort she offered, the surcease from endless pain.

She held him in her arms as he loved her and crooned

to him that everything would be all right. That he was a good man and a good father and he shouldn't blame himself anymore for what wasn't his fault.

He spilled himself inside her with a cry that was almost anguish. He slipped to the side and pulled her to him, holding her close with strong arms that promised always to keep her safe.

She knew it was wrong to trust in him. He would betray her in the end. Unfortunately, the heart doesn't always obey the dictates of the more reasonable head.

I love him, she thought. And then, *I can't love him. I shouldn't love him. I'd be a fool to love him.*

They fell asleep, their bodies entangled, their souls enmeshed, their hearts confused.

CHAPTER NINE

OVER THE NEXT three weeks the twins sensed the growing tension in Billy, and their behavior grew worse instead of better. Cherry tried to be understanding, but she was under a great deal of pressure, as well, since she had to study for night school finals, which she couldn't afford to fail.

Things came to a head the day before the court hearing, when Cherry asked Raejean for the third time to take her cookie and juice snack back to the kitchen to eat it.

"I don't have to do what you say," Raejean said. "You're not my mother!"

"I'm the one in charge," Cherry replied, using her last ounce of patience to keep her voice level. "And I say you have to get that juice out of the living room. If it spills in here, it'll ruin the furniture."

Cherry couldn't imagine what had possessed Laura to put silk and satin fabrics in a ranch living room. It wasn't a place to look at; they actually lived in it. If it had been up to her, she would have put protective covers on the furniture long ago to save the delicate fabrics from everyday wear and tear. When she had broached the subject to Billy, he had said, "We live here. If the furniture gets dirty, it gets dirty."

Cherry didn't figure that included spilling grape juice

on white satin. So she insisted, "Take that juice into the kitchen, Raejean. Now!"

"Oh, all right!" Raejean huffed. "Come on, Annie. Let's go."

"I'm watching Sesame Street," Annie protested from her seat beside Raejean on the couch.

Raejean pinched her. "Come on. If I have to go, you have to go."

"Raejean," Cherry warned. "Leave Annie be. Take your glass and go."

Raejean shot Cherry a mutinous look as she snatched at the glass on the end table, accidentally knocking it over—right onto the arm of the couch.

The two of them stared, horrified, as the grape juice soaked into the white satin, leaving a huge purple blotch.

"Oh, no!" Cherry cried. She looked for something to sop up the mess, but there was nothing handy. And by then the couch had soaked up the juice like a sponge.

"It's all your fault," Raejean cried, tears welling in her eyes. "If you hadn't been yelling at me, I wouldn't have spilled it."

"Daddy's going to be *really* mad," Annie whispered as she abandoned Sesame Street to ogle the growing stain.

"Go to your room," Cherry said. "Both of you!"

"I didn't do anything," Annie protested.

"We don't have to do what you say!" Raejean said. "Do we, Annie?"

Annie looked uncertain, and Raejean pinched her again.

"Ow!" she said. "Stop it, Raejean."

"Stop it, both of you!" Cherry cried. She knew she had lost control, but she wasn't sure how to get it back. "Apologize to your sister, Raejean."

"I don't have to. Tell her, Annie. Tell her Nana's going to be taking care of us from now on, so we don't have to do what Cherry says anymore."

Cherry couldn't believe what she was hearing. "Who said your grandmother's going to be taking care of you from now on?"

"Nana did."

"When?" Cherry said.

"When she called on the phone."

"When was that?" Cherry demanded.

"This morning, when you were in the shower. She said that after tomorrow she's going to be taking care of us, and we'll get to play in her pool and Grampa's buying us a new dollhouse and we won't have to do chores anymore, either," she announced.

Cherry stared at Raejean, aghast. She didn't know what to say. The little girl had no idea what Mrs. Trask really intended. She didn't seem to realize that going to live with her grandmother meant leaving her father for good. And Cherry had no intention of frightening her by explaining it.

She was furious with Mrs. Trask but resisted the urge to criticize her in front of her granddaughters. She was way out of her depth and drowning fast. She needed help.

To Cherry's surprise, the name and face that came to mind wasn't Billy's. Or even Jewel's. It was Rebecca's.

She wanted her mother.

"Let's go," she said suddenly.

"Go where?" Raejean asked suspiciously.

"To see your other grandmother."

Both girls stared at her with wide eyes.

"We have another grandmother?" Annie said.

"Uh-huh. You sure do."

"Who is she?" Raejean asked. "Where does she live?"

"Her name is Rebecca Whitelaw, and she lives on a ranch called Hawk's Pride. It isn't far from here. Shall we go? It's either that, or go to your room. You choose."

There was no contest, and Cherry wasted no time getting the girls into the pickup and driving to the adobe ranch house at Hawk's Pride that she had called home for the previous four years. Since Camp Littlehawk was under way, she knew where to look for Rebecca. Sure enough, she found her working with the novice riders at the corral. Raejean and Annie raced ahead of her to stand gaping at the lucky horseback riders.

"That's good, Jamie," Rebecca encouraged, one foot perched on the lowest rung of the wooden corral. "Let the pony know who's boss."

"I suppose that's good advice for parents dealing with children, too," Cherry said as she joined Rebecca.

"Cherry! What a wonderful surprise! Ted, would you watch the children for a few minutes while I speak with my daughter?"

Cherry noticed that Ted was on crutches. That didn't surprise her. Rebecca often found people in need and offered them a helping hand. Cherry was sure Ted was great with kids or horses or both. It always worked out that way. Rebecca's faith in people had never been proven wrong. It was that same goodheartedness that had led Rebecca to rescue a rebellious fourteen-year-old juvenile delinquent and adopt her as her own.

"I'd like you to meet your new granddaughters," Cherry said as Rebecca took the few steps to reach the twins. They were standing on the bottom rail of the corral with their arms hanging over the top.

"Raejean, Annie, I'd like you to meet your Grandma 'Becca." 'Becca was what Jewel had called Rebecca when Jewel was a child. It was also a fond nickname Zach used when he was teasing her. And it was the first thing that came to mind when Cherry searched for a name the little girls could use to address their new grandmother.

Raejean and Annie turned lively black eyes on Rebecca.

"Are you really our grandmother?" Raejean asked.

"Yes," Rebecca said with a smile.

"Are you going to give us cookies and milk, like Nana?" Annie asked.

"I'll even help you bake the cookies, if you like," Rebecca said. "If you'll tell me which one of you is which."

"I'm Annie," Raejean said. "And this is Raejean," she said, pointing to her shyer twin.

"Raejean," Cherry warned.

"Aw, Cherry." She hesitated before admitting, "I'm really Raejean, and this is really Annie."

"Pleased to meet you both," Rebecca said. "It's going to be fun having grandchildren come to visit."

"Will you let us ride horses, too?" Raejean asked, eyeing the children on horseback enviously.

"Would you like to ride one now?"

Raejean's and Annie's faces lit up as though they had been given the key to heaven. "Oh, yes!" they said in unison.

It didn't take long to get ponies saddled and send the girls into the ring with the other children to be supervised by Ted.

As soon as the twins were settled, Rebecca said, "All right, Cherry. Spit it out. What's wrong?"

"Everything," Cherry admitted. She felt like crying suddenly. The whole weight of the world had been on her shoulders for the past seven weeks, and it was as though with that one admission she had shifted the burden to her mother.

"Tell me about it," Rebecca said.

And Cherry did. About why she and Billy had married and the awful wedding and the twins' resentment, how Mrs. Trask was manipulating the children's feelings, and how scared she was that Billy would lose his children.

"What about you? Would it hurt you to lose them?"

Cherry hadn't even let herself think about the possibility. When she did, she felt a terrible ache in her chest. "Yes. Oh, yes. I'd miss them terribly. As much trouble as they are, I love them dearly."

Rebecca smiled. "So what can I do to help?"

Cherry shoved a hand through her tumble of red curls and let out a gusty sigh. "I'm not sure. Could you and Zach just be there in court tomorrow? Would that be possible?"

"Oh, darling, of course we'll be there. Is that all? Are you sure there isn't something else I could do to help?"

"I think you've already done it," Cherry said.

"Done what?"

"Taught me to believe in love again."

"Oh, darling..."

Cherry saw the tears in her mother's eyes and felt her throat tighten until it hurt. "I owe you so much... Mother." She gave a sobbing laugh and said, "There, I said it. Mother. Oh, God, why did I wait so long?"

It had taken being a mother herself to understand the tremendous gift Zach and Rebecca had given her. She could hardly see Rebecca through the blur of tears, and when she blinked, she realized Rebecca had her arms open wide. She grasped her around the waist and held on tight.

Cherry refused her mother's invitation to stay for dinner. "Billy and Zach—Daddy—aren't comfortable enough around each other yet. I'd rather give them time to get to know each other better before we show up for supper."

"All right. Whatever you think best. You can count on us to be in court tomorrow to support you both."

"Thanks, Mother. That means a lot."

"I wasn't sure before that you were ready for marriage and all its responsibilities," Rebecca said. "This visit has reassured me."

"That I'm ready for marriage?"

"That you're ready for whatever life offers. Be happy, Cherry. That's all I can ask."

Cherry smiled. "I'll try, Mom."

"Mom. I like that," Rebecca said. "Mom feels even better than Mother."

"Yeah, Mom," Cherry agreed with a cheeky grin. "It does."

CHERRY SPENT THE REST of the afternoon floating on air. She had never felt so confident. She had never been so certain that everything would turn out all right. Her youthful optimism remained firmly in place until Billy was late arriving home for supper. She waited an hour for him before she finally fed the girls and sent them upstairs to play.

She put a plate of food in the oven to stay warm while she cleaned up the kitchen. She still wasn't worried. Billy had been late once or twice before when some work had needed to be finished before dark.

But sundown came and went without any sign of Billy.

Cherry told herself, as she bathed the twins, that there was probably some good reason for the delay. Maybe he was working hard to make up for the fact he would be in court all day tomorrow. Maybe the truck had broken down and he had needed to walk home.

Maybe he had an accident. Maybe he's lying hurt or dying somewhere while you've been blithely assuming everything is fine.

Cherry silenced the voice that told her disaster had struck. Nothing could have happened to Billy. He was strong and had quick reflexes, and he knew the dangers of the kind of work he did. He was fine.

But he was very late.

Cherry read the girls two bedtime stories, thinking he would show up at any minute to tease and tickle them and kiss them good-night.

"Where's Daddy?" Raejean asked when Cherry said it was time to turn out the light.

"Isn't he coming home?" Annie asked.

"Of course he's coming home. He just had some errands to run. As soon as he arrives, he'll come and kiss you good-night. Go to sleep now."

She turned out the light and was almost out of the room when Raejean whispered, "Is Daddy going away?"

Cherry turned the light back on. Both Raejean and Annie stared back at her with frightened eyes. *Damn Mrs. Trask and her phone calls,* Cherry thought. She crossed and sat beside Raejean and brushed the bangs away and kissed her forehead reassuringly.

"Your daddy isn't going anywhere. He'll be right here when you wake up in the morning."

"Nana said Daddy might be going away," Raejean confessed." I don't want him to leave."

"Neither do I," Annie whimpered.

"Oh, my dear ones," Cherry said. She lifted a sobbing Raejean into her arms and carried her over to Annie's bed, then slid an arm around each girl and rocked them against her. "Don't worry. Everything's going to be fine. Your Daddy's not going anywhere. And neither am I."

"Are you going to be our mother forever?" Annie asked.

Cherry was struck dumb by the question. She realized the folly of her promise that she wasn't going anywhere. She and Billy had a temporary marriage. She had no right to presume he would want it to continue any longer than necessary to convince the court to let him keep his children.

She was forced to admit the truth to herself.

She didn't want the marriage to end. She wanted to stay married to Billy. She wanted to be the twins' mother forever. All she had to do was convince Billy to let her stay.

When he showed up. If he ever did.

"Why don't we ask your daddy when he comes home if it's all right with him for me to be your mother forever," she answered Annie at last. "Would that be all right?"

"I guess," Annie said. "If you're sure he's coming home."

"I'm sure," Cherry said.

That seemed to assuage the worst of their fear, and she managed to get them tucked in again. As she was turning out the light, Raejean said, "Cherry?"

"What is it, Raejean?"

"I don't want you to leave, either."

Cherry smiled. "Thanks, Raejean. That means a lot to me."

She rose up on one elbow and said, "I'm sorry about spilling grape juice on the couch. You don't think Daddy came home and saw it while we were gone and got *really* mad, do you?"

Her heart went out to the child. "No, Raejean, I don't think it's anything you did that's making your father late getting home. I'm sure he's been delayed by business. Go to sleep now. Before you know it, he'll be waking you up to kiss you good-night."

As she was closing the door, Cherry heard Annie whisper, "That's silly. Why is Daddy going to wake us up to kiss us good-night?"

"So we'll know he's home, dummy," Raejean explained scornfully.

"Oh," Annie whispered back. "All right."

Cherry headed downstairs hoping that Billy would arrive to fulfill her promise and waken the twins with a kiss.

As the night passed and he didn't return, she began to worry in earnest. The worst thing was, she had no idea where he might have gone. She made up her mind to wait until midnight before she called the police to report him missing. That's when the bars in town closed.

Not that she believed for one second that he had gone to a bar. Not with everything on the line the way it was. Not with everything he did subject to intense scrutiny in the courtroom. Not as determined as he was to keep custody of his children in the face of his mother-in-law's clutching grasp for them.

She sat in the dark on the front porch step, waiting for him to come home. At five minutes before midnight she saw a pair of headlights coming down the dirt road that led to the house. Her heart began to pound.

Surely it was Billy. Surely it was him and not someone coming to tell her he had been hurt.

The vehicle was headed for the back of the house, moving too fast for safety. She ran through the house, turned on the back porch light and slammed her way out the back door. She was there when the pickup skidded to a stop.

When she saw it was Billy's truck, she released a breath of air she hadn't realized she had been holding. The relief turned quickly to anger when Billy stepped out of the truck and she saw his face. One eye was swollen almost closed and his lip had a cut on one side.

"You've been fighting!" She gasped as he began to

weave his way unsteadily toward her. "You're drunk!" she accused. "How could you, Billy? How could you?"

"I'm not drunk!" he said. "I've just got a couple of cracked ribs that are giving me hell."

She quickly moved to support him. "What happened? Where have you been? Who did this to you?"

She felt him slump against her. "Aw, Cherry, I don't believe I let this happen. Not the day before I have to go to court. The judge'll never understand."

"Forget the judge. Explain this to me."

"I went to town to get some supplies at the hardware store and ran into that Ray character, the one who took you to the prom."

"Ray did this to you?" she asked incredulously.

"Him and three of his friends."

"But why?"

"It doesn't matter why. Or it won't to the judge. All he'll see is that I've been fighting again. Lord, Cherry, I hurt. Inside and out."

"Come on in to the kitchen and let me bind your ribs," Cherry said. "Maybe I can get the swelling down in your eye, so it won't look so bad tomorrow."

"Maybe I can say I'm sick and get a postponement," Billy suggested.

"Is it possible the Trasks won't find out about the fight? Did the police come?" she asked.

"They were there," Billy said.

"But you weren't arrested?" Cherry said. "That must mean something. I mean, that you weren't at fault."

"I wanted to fight, all right," Billy said flatly. "And I'd do it again."

"Don't say things like that. You can't keep getting

into fights, Billy. Not if you want to keep custody of your girls. What could be so important it was worth risking your girls to fight about?" she demanded.

He didn't answer her, but that could have been because he was too busy hissing in a breath as she administered antiseptic to the cuts on his face. She eased the torn shirt off his shoulders and saw the bruises on his ribs. They must have kicked him when he was down.

"Where have you been all night, if you weren't in a bar somewhere drinking?" Cherry asked.

"I went to the stock pond to sit and think," he said.

"While you were thinking, did it occur to you that I'd be worried," Cherry asked archly.

"I'm sorry, Cherry. I lost track of the time."

He sat stoically while she strapped his ribs. But the light had gone out of his eyes. He had already given up. He had already conceded the battle to Penelope.

"You aren't going to lose tomorrow," she said to him. "You can tell the judge a bull stomped you, or—"

Billy snorted. "Stomped on my eye? Forget it, Cherry. You know as well as I do that my fight with Penelope is over before it's begun."

"I refuse to accept that!" Cherry snapped back. "You're a good father. You love your children, and you provide a stable home for them."

"That isn't enough."

"What more can the judge ask?" Cherry demanded.

Billy reached up gingerly and brushed his hair out of his eyes. "I don't know. You can believe there'll be something Penelope can offer that I can't."

"There's *nothing* she can give them that you can't,"

Cherry said fiercely. "And there's something you can give them that no one else can."

"What?"

"Love. A parent's love. Don't discount it, Billy. It's a powerful thing."

She saw the doubt in his eyes. He wanted to believe her, but he was afraid to let his hopes get too high. She lowered her lips to his, tender, as gentle as she had ever been. She brushed at the hank of hair that had fallen once more on his forehead. "You're going to win, Billy. Believe it."

He took her hand and pressed her palm against his lips. "Thanks, Cherry. I needed to hear that."

But she saw he didn't completely believe it. He believed this was the beginning of the end. He believed he was going to lose his children. That he was going to lose her. She could feel it in the way he clung to her hand.

She pulled herself free, unwilling to indulge in his despair.

"The girls were worried about you," she said as she scurried around fixing an ice pack for his eye. "I promised them you would wake them up to kiss them goodnight so they would know you got home all right."

"I'll go do that now," he said, groaning as he got to his feet, the ice pack pressed against his eye.

"Don't fall coming back downstairs," she said.

He turned and looked at her. He was in no condition to make love to her, and for a second she thought he was going to refuse to come back downstairs and join her in bed. But he nodded his head in acquiescence.

"I'll be down in a few minutes."

Cherry hurried to finish her ablutions and ready herself for bed before Billy came to her room. The sexiest nightgown she owned was a football jersey, and she quickly slipped it over her head. She was naked underneath it.

She pulled the covers down and slipped under them to wait for him. She left the light burning, because she knew he liked to watch her as they made love.

It didn't take her long to realize, once Billy entered her room and began undressing himself, that he needed help. She got out of bed and came to him, sick at heart at this reminder of the fight that might cost him his children.

She took her time undressing him, kissing his flesh as she exposed it. Shoulders. Chest. Belly. She sat him down and pulled off his boots and socks and made him stand again so she could unbuckle his belt and unzip his jeans and pull them off. By the time he was naked, he was also obviously aroused.

"Lie down," she coaxed. "You're hurt. Let me do all the work."

She had never said she loved Billy in words. But she showed him with her mouth and hands and body. She eased herself down on his shaft, and when he arched his body into hers, said, "Lie still. I'll move for both of us."

She did, riding him like a stallion, never giving him a rest, until both of them were breathing hard and slick with sweat. She pushed him to the brink, brought him back, and took him there again. Until at last she rode him home.

He was already asleep, his breathing deep and even,

by the time she slipped to his side, reached over to turn out the light, and snuggled against him.

"You'll win, Billy," she whispered into the darkness. "You have to win. Because I love you and Raejean and Annie. And I can't bear to give you up."

She felt his arm tighten around her.

At first she was terrified because she thought he must have heard her. Then she realized it was a reflexive move. He had reached for her in his sleep and pulled her close.

"You're not going to lose me, Billy," she murmured against his throat. "I'm not going anywhere."

His body relaxed, and she closed her eyes to sleep.

CHAPTER TEN

THE DAY OF THE HEARING dawned fly-buzzing hot, as though to deny the cloud of disaster that loomed over their heads. In the bright sunshine Billy's face looked even worse than it had the night before. His left eye was swollen nearly shut, and the myriad bruises had taken on a rainbow of colors—pink, yellow and purple. He walked stiffly up the courthouse steps, like an old man, an occasional wince revealing what even that effort cost him in pain.

Cherry had put on a simple, flowered cotton dress with a Peter Pan collar she often wore to church. It made her look every bit as young as she was. Billy was dressed in a dark suit that fit his broad shoulders like a glove and made him into a dangerous, imposing stranger.

The twins bounced along beside them in matching dresses and pigtails, chattering like magpies, excited by the prospect of going on a picnic after the court hearing was over. Cherry chattered back at them, putting on a cheery false front to prove she wasn't as frightened as she was.

She and Billy had exchanged very few words since waking that morning, but their eyes had met often, communicating a wealth of information.

I feel awful.

I can see that. You look like you got stomped by something mean.

What if I say something wrong? What if I can't convince the judge to let me keep my kids?

Everything will be all right.

What if it isn't? What will I do?

I'm here for you, Billy.

I'm scared, Cherry.

So am I.

I'm glad you're here with me.

He reached out to take her hand, clutching it so tightly it hurt, as they entered the courtroom. The instant the twins saw their grandparents sitting at a table at the front of the courtroom with two men dressed in expensive suits, they went racing down the aisle to greet them.

"Hi, Nana," Raejean said, giving her grandmother a hug. Mrs. Trask wore a sleek designer suit that shouted wealth, her short-cropped, silvery-white hair perfectly coiffed.

"Hi, Grandpa," Annie said, getting a sound hug from her grandfather. Mr. Trask sported a double-breasted wool blend suit, his pale blond hair cut short on top and trimmed high over his ears.

The adults exchanged not a word, but their eyes spoke volumes.

Animosity from Mrs. Trask.

Antagonism from Billy.

Anguish from Cherry.

"Raejean. Annie. Come sit over here," Billy ordered.

Reluctantly the girls left their grandparents and came to sit beside Billy and Cherry across the courtroom.

Billy's attorney had already suggested that Billy

compromise with Mr. and Mrs. Trask and give them partial custody of the children. The lawyer had warned that with their duo of legal experts, the Trasks would very likely win full custody if Billy insisted on fighting them in court.

"Are you ready, Mr. Stonecreek?" Billy's lawyer asked as Billy and Cherry joined him.

"I'm ready." Billy knew his lawyer believed they were fighting a lost cause. But he wasn't willing to give up his children without clawing for them tooth and nail.

Billy turned to find the source of a small commotion at the back of the courtroom. "Cherry, look."

Cherry looked and felt tears prickle behind her eyes. Her whole family was trooping into the courtroom. Zach and Rebecca, Rolleen, Jewel, Avery, Jake, Frannie, Rabbit, and Colt. She knew what it meant at that moment to be part of a family. They were there for her.

"Thank you," she mouthed.

Her mother smiled encouragement. Zach nodded. Colt grinned and gave her a thumbs-up, while Jewel mouthed back, "We're with you, Cherry."

At that moment the judge entered the courtroom, and the bailiff called, "All rise."

Cherry stood and reached for Billy's hand as he reached for hers. They stood grim-lipped, stark-eyed, waiting for the worst, hoping for the best.

"In the interest of keeping this hearing as open and frank as we can get it," the judge began, "I think the minor children should wait outside. Is there someone who can take care of them?"

Jewel popped up in back. "I will, Your Honor."

"Very well. The children will leave the courtroom and remain outside until I call for them."

"Why do we have to leave, Daddy?" Raejean asked, her brow furrowed.

"Because the judge said so," Billy answered.

"I don't want to go," Annie said, clinging to Cherry's skirt.

"It's all right, Annie," Cherry said. "It's only for a little while. We'll all be together again soon."

She hoped.

Cherry prayed that the girls wouldn't make a scene in front of the judge, proving Cherry and Billy couldn't control their children. To her immense relief, they allowed Jewel to take their hands and lead them from the courtroom.

"This is a hearing to decide whether Mr. Stonecreek's two minor children should be taken away from him and given to their grandparents," the judge began solemnly. "I would like the petitioners to explain in their own words why they are seeking custody of their grandchildren."

"It's simple, Your Honor," Mrs. Trask said as she rose to her feet. "Billy Stonecreek is an inadequate and irresponsible parent who is doing irreparable harm to my grandchildren by neglecting them. He also happens to be a drunken brawler without an ounce of self-respect. It's a well-known fact that his kind can't hold their liquor."

"His kind?" the judge inquired.

"Billy Stonecreek's mother was an Indian, Your Honor," Mrs. Trask replied disdainfully.

The judge's brows arrowed down between his eyes, but all he said was, "Please continue."

"My former son-in-law has instigated several free-for-alls over the past year since my daughter's death, for which he has been repeatedly jailed. As you can plainly see from the condition of his face, he hasn't reformed his behavior over time.

"He has subjected my granddaughters to a series of housekeepers who come and go. His latest act of idiocy was to marry an eighteen-year-old high school dropout, who was a juvenile delinquent herself."

Billy had remained silent during Penelope's attack on him. When she started on Cherry, he couldn't sit still for it. "Wait one damn minute—"

"Sit down, Mr. Stonecreek," the judge admonished. "You'll have a chance to speak your piece."

Penelope shot Billy a smug smile and continued. "This pitiful excuse for a father doesn't have the time, money, or inclination to give his children the things they need. On the other hand, Mr. Trask and I are ready, willing, and able to provide a secure and stable home for our grandchildren."

"Is there anything else?" the judge asked.

Mrs. Trask hesitated before she said, "I believe Billy Stonecreek is responsible for my daughter, Laura's, death, Your Honor."

The judge raised a disbelieving brow.

"He didn't kill her with his bare hands," Mrs. Trask said. "But he made her so unhappy that...that she took her own life."

Cherry bounced up and said, "That's not true, Your Honor!"

The judge made a disgruntled sound. "Young lady—"

"Please, Your Honor. You have to let me speak," Cherry pleaded.

The judge turned to Mrs. Trask and said, "Are you finished, Mrs. Trask?"

"I am, Your Honor." She sat down as regally as a queen reclaiming her throne.

"Very well, then. Proceed, Mrs. Stonecreek."

"It simply isn't true that Billy is responsible for Laura's death."

"Cherry, don't," Billy muttered.

Cherry looked Billy in the eye and said, "I have to tell them, Billy. It's the only way."

When he lowered his gaze, she turned to face the judge. "Laura Stonecreek didn't commit suicide, Your Honor. She was involved in a tragic automobile accident. She was unhappy, all right—because she wanted to have more children, but wasn't medically able to carry another child to term. On the day she had her fatal accident, Laura miscarried a child for the second time."

An audible gasp could be heard from the other table.

"Billy didn't want her to take the risk of getting pregnant anymore. When Laura left the house that day she was despondent, but not because Billy didn't love her enough. It was because he loved her too much to take the chance of losing her by getting her pregnant again.

"Billy Stonecreek is the most gentle, most kind, and considerate man I know. He's a wonderful father to his girls, and they love him dearly. If you could only see him with them, giving them a bath, reading a story to them, kissing them good-night. They trust him to take care of them always. It would be a travesty to separate them."

"What you say is all to the good, Mrs. Stonecreek," the judge said. "But I'm concerned about your husband's propensity to physical violence. I'm especially concerned to see his condition today. I would think he would have avoided this sort of behavior, when he knew he would be appearing before this court."

Cherry felt miserable. Billy had refused to tell her why he had gotten into another fight. And he had said he would do it again. She could understand the judge's point. There was nothing she could say to defend Billy, except, "He's a good man, Your Honor. He loves his children. Please don't take them away from him."

"Excuse me, Your Honor."

Cherry turned at the sound of her father's voice. Zach was standing, waiting to be recognized by the judge.

"What is it, Zach?"

Cherry was surprised to hear the judge call her father by his first name until she remembered what Billy had said when he married her. The Whitelaws were well known around this part of Texas. It appeared Zach had a personal acquaintance with the judge.

"I can explain the cause of Billy's most recent altercation, if the court will allow it."

The two lawyers conferred hastily at the Trasks' table before one rose to say, "I object, Your Honor. Mr. Whitelaw has no standing to get involved in this case."

"I'm the grandfather of those little girls, too, Your Honor," Zach said. "My daughter hasn't adopted them yet, but that's only a formality. I know she loves them as though they were already her own."

Cherry's throat thickened with emotion.

"I see no reason why I shouldn't allow Mr. White-law to make his point, Counsel," the judge said. "Especially in light of the consequences if I rule against Mr. Stonecreek. I'd like to hear an explanation for this most recent fight—if there is one. Go ahead, Zach."

"First let me say that I did not initially approve of my daughter's marriage. I thought she was too young, and I knew Billy Stonecreek's reputation for getting into trouble. I thought he would be a bad influence on her."

Cherry felt her heart sinking. Nothing her father had said so far was the least bit helpful to Billy. In fact, it was as though he had dug the hole deeper.

"However," Zach said, "I've since changed my mind. I did enough checking to find out that my son-in-law is a hardworking, church-going man who spends most of his free time with his children. With three notable exceptions—all occurring since his wife's tragic death—he has been an outstanding citizen of this community.

"Although my son-in-law chose to start those three fights over the past year in bars, no one I talked to has ever seen him the least bit drunk. He has never hurt anyone seriously, and he has always paid for whatever damages there were. I know that doesn't excuse him entirely."

"Or at all," the judge interjected. "What I'd like to know is why Mr. Stonecreek started those fights."

"Only Billy himself knows the answer to that question. If I were guessing, I'd say he was a young man in a lot of pain and looking for a way to ease it."

"Then he chose the wrong way," the judge said. "All

this is very interesting, but it doesn't explain why he was fighting within days of this hearing."

"To defend his wife's honor," Zach said.

Cherry's glance shot to Billy. He lowered his gaze to avoid hers, and a flush spread high on his cheekbones.

"I'm listening," the judge said.

"I was in Estes's Hardware Store yesterday when Billy came in. He picked up what he needed and went to the counter to pay. Ray Estes stood at the register and began making abusive, slanderous comments about my daughter, Cherry, in front of several other men, friends of Ray's, who were also waiting for service.

"Billy asked Ray to stop, but Ray continued provoking him, saying things to sully my daughter's reputation that no man could stand by and let another man say about his wife. Even then, Billy didn't throw the first punch.

"He told Ray he didn't want to fight, that he knew Ray was only mad because of what had happened the night Billy had kept him from assaulting Cherry. Billy said he would forget the insults if Ray would say he was sorry and hadn't meant what he'd said. Billy wanted the words taken back.

"Ray called Billy a coward, said he only fought men who were drunk. Even then, Your Honor, Billy kept his hands to himself. His fists were white-knuckled, but he didn't launch a blow.

"That's when Ray shoved him backward, and one of Ray's friends tripped him so he fell. Ray came over the counter and kicked him hard, while he was down. That was when Billy came up swinging. Ray's friends held his arms, so Ray could go at him. That's when he got the black eye.

"To tell you the truth, Your Honor, I took a few swings at those fellows myself. So you see, Billy tried to avoid a fight. He only got involved when it was a clear matter of self-defense."

Cherry gave her father a grateful look as he sat down, then met Billy's dark-eyed gaze. She reached for his hand under the table and clasped it tight. "Oh, Billy," she whispered. "Why didn't you tell me?"

"I shouldn't have let Ray provoke me," Billy muttered. "But I couldn't let him get away with saying those ugly things about you. I couldn't, Cherry."

She squeezed his hand. "It's all right, Billy. Surely the judge won't blame you now that he's heard the truth."

"I'll concede Mr. Stonecreek may have been provoked beyond endurance in this case," the judge said, confirming Cherry's hope. "The courts have conceded there are such things as 'fighting words' to which a man may respond justifiably with violence. And I'll take into consideration your suggestion that Mr. Stonecreek's other forays into fisticuffs may have been motivated by something other than drunkenness," the judge said.

"However," he continued, "I am concerned by several of Mrs. Trask's other accusations. Especially those concerning Mrs. Stonecreek's past behavior and her ability to function as a capable mother to two little girls."

"I'd like to speak on my wife's behalf, if I may," Billy said, rising to face the judge.

"Very well, Mr. Stonecreek," the judge replied.

"My daughters are lucky to have someone as wonderful as Cherry to be their mother," Billy said. "I feel myself fortunate to have her for my wife. Cherry was expelled from school for something she didn't do. Since then, she's taken care of Raejean and Annie during the day and gone to school every night to make up the classes she needs for graduation. I have every confidence that she'll complete her education with high marks and receive her diploma."

"I wasn't questioning your wife's intelligence," the judge said gently. "I'm more concerned about her maturity, her sense of responsibility, the example she'll set for the children."

Cherry saw Billy's Adam's apple bob as he swallowed hard. She wished she had led a different life. What could he say to defend her? She had been a troublemaker all her life. There was some truth in everything Mrs. Trask had said about her.

"I think Cherry's actions speak for themselves. My daughters are happy, healthy, and well-adjusted. Cherry treats them as though they were her own flesh and blood. You see, Your Honor, she knows what it feels like to lose your parents at a young age. She knows how important it is to make a child feel safe and secure and loved. That's what Cherry offers my children. Unconditional love. There's nothing more important to a child than knowing they're loved, is there, Your Honor?"

The judge cleared his throat. "Yes, well, that's true, of course."

"But, Your Honor," Mrs. Trask protested, seeing the tide shifting. "The same young woman whose merits Billy is extolling spent time in a juvenile detention facility. The fact remains, she was expelled from school. And she's only eighteen years old!"

"I will take all of that into consideration, Mrs. Trask," the judge promised. "Does anyone have anything further to say? Very well. I will need some time in chambers to deliberate this matter. I'll have a decision for you shortly. Court is recessed."

"All rise," the bailiff commanded.

Cherry rose on shaky legs and grabbed hold of Billy's hand for support. They had done all they could—which seemed precious little—to convince the judge they would be good parents. But was it enough?

One thing had become clear to Cherry. It wasn't only the children she was afraid to lose. She was afraid of losing Billy, too.

He had only married her temporarily to have a mother for his children. What role would there be for her in his life if his children were taken from him? Would she only be a painful reminder of what he had lost?

Cherry looked into Billy's eyes, all her fears naked for him to see. *Do you love me, Billy? If it weren't for the children, would you still want me for your wife?*

And found the reassurance she sought.

His love was visible in the reassuring warmth of his gaze, in the way he held firmly, supportively, to her hand, in the way he had defended her in court.

Without a word, Billy rose and pulled her into his embrace. His arms closed tight around her. "Don't leave me, Cherry," he whispered in her ear.

"I'm not going anywhere," she promised.

"I want us to be together forever."

"Forever? But—"

"No matter what happens here today, I want you with me. I love you, Cherry."

"I love you, too, Billy."

They held each other tight, offering strength and solace, parting only as the twins came hurtling down the aisle to greet them. Raejean leapt into Billy's arms, while Cherry scooped up Annie.

"Jewel says we have lots of aunts and uncles and cousins," Raejean announced. "Zillions of them!"

Cherry laughed. "Not quite that many."

"How many?" Annie asked.

"I don't know, exactly," Cherry said. "But lots."

"Can we go on a picnic now?" Raejean asked.

"Not yet," Billy said. "Soon."

"We have to go home first and change our clothes," Cherry reminded her.

"Can we leave now?" Annie asked. "Is the judge all done?"

"Almost," Cherry said. "He wants to think about things a little while before he makes up his mind."

"Makes up his mind about what?" Raejean asked.

Cherry and Billy exchanged a tormented glance.

Makes up his mind about whether to take you away from us.

Billy's heart had been thundering in his chest ever since the hearing began. He felt himself on the verge of panic, and the only thing he had to hang on to was Cherry's hand. So far, he had protected his daughters from knowing about the desperate courtroom struggle that would decide their future.

This morning, as he and Cherry had sipped coffee together at dawn, he had decided that even if the Trasks won custody, he would do his best to make the transition as amicable as possible. Surely the judge wouldn't deny him visitation rights, and he would continue to have a strong and loving relationship with his children.

Only, if there was one thing Billy had learned in this life, it was that there were no guarantees. He was terrified the judge would rule against him. He was terrified the Trasks would try to bar him from all contact with his children.

Right now he felt like taking Raejean and Annie and Cherry and running as far and as fast as he could. Fortunately, Cherry's family came to the rail that separated the spectators from the litigants, all of them talking at once, making escape impossible, even if he had succumbed to the urge.

He felt a hand on his shoulder and turned to find Zach Whitelaw standing behind him.

"I want to thank you for your words of support, sir," Billy said.

"It was my pleasure, son. I never had a chance to congratulate you on your wedding. I expect you to take good care of my daughter."

Billy would have answered if his jaw hadn't been clenched to keep his chin from quivering with emotion. Instead, he gave a jerky nod.

"The judge is coming back already, Dad," Colt said. "Wasn't it supposed to take longer?"

It had already been too long, as far as Billy was concerned, although he realized it had only been a matter of minutes since the judge had left the courtroom.

"We'd better get back to our seats," Zach said.

Billy was afraid to send his daughters away, afraid they weren't going to be his when he saw them again.

"All rise," the bailiff said.

Jewel was leading the children out of the courtroom when the judge said, "The children can stay."

Billy exchanged a quick look with Cherry and quickly gathered Raejean and Annie into the circle of his arms in front of him.

Cherry gave him a quavery smile. "Surely it's a good sign that the judge let them stay," she whispered as she slipped her arm around his waist. It was questionable who was supporting whom.

When the judge sat, Billy and Cherry sat, each of them holding one of the twins on their laps. They could hear the clock ticking as the judge shuffled papers.

Finally he looked up and said, "The circumstances of this case are unique. The grandparents of these children have a great deal to offer them, not the least of which is the experience to be gained with age. The children's father has shown a lack of judgment on occasion that makes his suitability as a parent questionable."

Billy's heart felt like it was going to pound right out of his chest. *He's going to give them to Penelope. I'm going to lose my children.*

"However," the judge continued, "the law favors the natural parents of a child over any other custodian. And there are other factors evident here that I believe have to be considered in my decision."

What is your decision, dammit? Billy raged inwardly.

"I've decided to leave custody of the minor children with their father," the judge announced.

Shouts of joy and clapping erupted behind Billy.

"I want quiet in the court," the judge said, pounding his gavel.

Billy was too stunned to move, his throat too tight to

speak. He saw Cherry through a blurred haze of tears. She was laughing and crying at the same time.

"We won, Billy. We won!" Cherry sobbed.

"What did we win, Daddy?" Raejean said.

"Did we get a prize?" Annie asked.

"Quiet in the court," the judge repeated.

"Shh," Billy said to the girls. "Let's listen to the judge."

He was more than willing to listen, now that he knew his children were his to keep.

"There will be those who question my decision in light of the evidence heard here today about the actions of the children's father and stepmother. They have made mistakes in the past. However, they both seem dedicated to rectifying their behavior.

"So I have based my decision not on what either of them might have done in the past, but on what I saw here in this courtroom today that bodes well for the future.

"Seldom have I seen two individuals more supportive of each other, or more apparently devoted to each other. These children will have what too few children have these days—two parents who love and respect one another. I am convinced that these two young people are capable of providing a stable, healthy and happy home for the two minor children. Good luck to you both. Court is dismissed."

"All rise," the bailiff ordered.

Billy's knees were rubbery when he stood, and he slipped an arm around Cherry to keep himself upright. He realized he was grinning as he accepted the congratulatory slaps of the Whitelaws.

"Can we go on a picnic now?" Raejean asked.

"Soon," Cherry promised with a hiccuping laugh that was choked by tears of joy.

"Can Nana and Grampa Trask come, too?" Annie asked.

Billy looked across the room at the bitter face of Mrs. Trask and realized he only felt sorry for her. She had lost her daughter. Now she had lost her grandchildren, too. Because it would be a cold day in hell before he let her near his children again.

He felt Cherry's hand on his arm.

"The girls need their grandparents, Billy," she said. "And Mr. and Mrs. Trask need their grandchildren."

Billy struggled to be generous. He was still angry. And still afraid that the Trasks might yet find some way to take his children from him. But Cherry was right. Raejean and Annie loved their grandparents. It would be cruel to take them away. For their sakes, he had to forgive what the Trasks had tried to do.

"Why don't you go ask Nana and Grampa Trask if they'd like to come on our picnic with us?" Billy said to Raejean and Annie.

Billy pulled Cherry close against him as they watched the girls skip across the room to invite Penelope and Harvey Trask to join their picnic. Billy met Penelope's startled glance when she heard what the girls had to say. He saw her hesitate, then shake her head no and say something to the children.

Moments later the girls returned and Raejean said, "Nana says maybe next time."

Billy exchanged one last poignant look with Penelope before she turned away. Then he glanced down at Raejean and ruffled her hair. "Next time," Billy said.

Cherry met his eyes, her gaze proud and supportive, and said, "Next time for sure."

"Let's go home," Billy said as he reached for Cherry's hand. She reached out for Annie, and he reached out for Raejean. They walked out of the courtroom hand in hand in hand in hand, a family at last.

* * * * *

* * *

THE VIRGIN GROOM

This book is dedicated to my son, Blake.
May you always strive to be the best you can be.

CHAPTER ONE

SWEAT STREAMING FROM HIS TEMPLES, strong hands clenched tight on the parallel bars that supported him, Mac Macready put his full weight on his left leg. He felt a sharp pain, but the leg held. He gritted his teeth to keep from groaning. So far, so good.

Mac kept his eyes focused on the area between the bars in front of him, willing his leg to work. He took an easy step with his right leg, then called on the left again. The pain was less sharp the second time he put his weight on the restructured limb. He could handle the pain. More important, the leg had stayed under him. He glanced across the room at his friend and agent, Andy Dennison, and grinned.

Mac Macready could walk again.

"You did it, Mac," Andy said, crossing the room to slap him on the back. "It's great to see you back on your feet."

"About time," Mac said. "I've spent the better part of two years trying to get this damned leg of mine back into shape." A sharp pain seared up his leg, but he refused to sit down, not now, when he had just made it back onto his feet. He took more of his weight on his arms and kept walking. A bead of sweat trickled between his shoulder blades before it caught on his sleeveless T-shirt. He summoned another smile. "Give me a couple of months, and I'll be ready to start catching passes again for the Tornadoes."

Mac caught the skeptical look on Andy's face before his agent said, "Sure, Mac. Whatever you say."

He understood Andy's skepticism. Mac had said the same thing after every operation. Who would have suspected a broken leg—all right, so maybe it had been shattered—would be so difficult to mend? But his body had rejected the pins they had used to put things back together again at ankle and hip. They had finally had to invent something especially for him.

Then the long bones in his leg hadn't grown straight and had needed to be broken and set again. He had fought complications caused by infection. Finally, when he had pushed too hard to get well, he had ended up back in a cast.

The football injury had been devastating, coming as it had at the end of Mac's first phenomenal season with the Texas Tornadoes. His future couldn't have been brighter. He was a star receiver, with more touchdown catches than any other rookie in the league. His team was headed for the Super Bowl. With one crushing tackle, everything had fallen apart. The sportscasters had called it a career-ending injury. Mac wasn't willing to concede the issue.

"Good work, Mac," the physical therapist said, reaching out to help him into the wheelchair waiting for him at the end of the parallel bars. "Put your arm around me."

He flashed the young woman a killer grin, inwardly cursing the fact that after six measly steps he was on the verge of collapse. "Better watch out, Hartwell. Now that I'm back on my feet, I'm going to give your fiancé some serious competition."

Diane Hartwell blushed. Most women did when Mac turned on the charm. He had the kind of blond-haired, blue-eyed good looks that made female heads swivel to take a second look. Mac wondered what she would think if she knew the truth about him.

Diane answered wryly, "I'm sure George would gladly trade me to you for an autographed football."

"Done," Mac said brightly, biting back a grimace as Diane bent his injured leg and placed his foot on the wheelchair footrest.

"I was only kidding," Diane said.

"I wasn't," Mac said, smiling up at her. "Tell your fiancé I'll be glad to autograph that football for him anytime."

"Thanks, Mac," Diane said. "I appreciate it."

"Think nothing of it, Hartwell. And tell George to hang on to that ball. Someday it'll be worth something."

Once Mac resumed his career, he would break every record in the book. He had that kind of determination. And he had been that good. Of course, that was before the accident. Everybody—except himself—questioned whether he would ever be that good again.

It had been touch and go for a while whether he would even walk. But Mac had known he would walk again, and without the aid of a brace. He had done it today. It seemed he was the only one who wasn't surprised.

He had known he would succeed, because he had beaten the odds before. When he was eight, he had suffered from acute myelocytic leukemia. It should have killed him. He had recovered from the childhood disease and gone on to win the Heisman Trophy and be drafted in the first round by the Texas Tornadoes. Mac had no intention of giving up his dreams of a future in football.

Andy wheeled him down the hospital corridor to his room. "When do you get out of here?" his agent asked.

"The doctor said once I could stand on my leg, he would release me. I guess that means I can get out of here anytime now."

"The press will want a statement," Andy said as he stopped the wheelchair beside Mac's hospital bed. "Do you want to talk to them? Or do you want me to do it?"

Mac thought of facing a dozen TV cameras from a wheelchair. Or standing with crutches. Or wavering on his own two feet. "Tell them I'll be back next season."

"Maybe that's not such a good—"

"Tell them I'll be back," Mac said, staring Andy in the eye.

Andy had once been a defensive lineman and wore a coveted Super Bowl ring on his right hand. He understood what it meant to play football. And what it meant to stop. He straightened the tie at his bull neck, shrugged his broad shoulders and smoothed the tie over his burgeoning belly, before he said, "You got it, Mac."

"Thanks, Andy. I am coming back, you know."

"Sure, Mac," Andy said.

Mac could see his agent didn't believe him any more than the doctors and nurses who had treated him over the past two years. Even Hartwell, though she encouraged him, didn't believe he would achieve the kind of mobility he needed to play in the pros. Mac needed to get away somewhere and heal himself. He knew he could do it. After all, he had done it once before.

"Where can I get in touch with you?" Andy asked.

"I'm headed to a ranch in northwest Texas owned by some friends of mine. I have an open invitation to visit, and I'm going to take them up on it. I'll call you when I get there and give you a number where I can be reached."

"Good enough. Take care, Mac. Don't—"

"Don't finish that sentence, Andy. Not if you're going to warn me not to get my hopes up."

Andy shook his head. "I was going to say don't be a fool and kill yourself trying to get well too fast."

"I'm going to get my job back from the kid who took over for me," Mac said in a steely voice. "And I'm going to do it this year."

Andy didn't argue further, just shook Mac's hand and left him alone in the hospital room.

Mac looked around at the sterile walls, the white sheets, the chrome rails on the bed, listened to the muffled sounds that weren't quite silence and inhaled the overwhelming antiseptic smell that made him want to gag. He had spent too much of his life in hospital beds—more than any human being ought to have to. He wanted out of here, the sooner the better.

He could hardly wait to get to the wide open spaces of Zach and Rebecca Whitelaw's ranch, Hawk's Pride. More than Zach or Rebecca or the land, he had a yearning to see their daughter Jewel again. Jewel was the first of eight kids who had been adopted by the Whitelaws, and she had returned to Hawk's Pride after college to manage Camp LittleHawk, the camp for kids with cancer that Rebecca had started years ago.

Mac remembered his first impressions of Jewel—huge Mississippi-mud-brown eyes, shoulder-length dirt-brown hair and an even dirtier looking white T-shirt and jeans. She had been five years old to his eight, and she had been leaning against the corral at Camp LittleHawk watching him venture onto horseback for the first time.

"Don't be scared," Jewel had said.

"I'm not," he'd retorted, glancing around at the other five kids in the corral with him. The horses were stopped in a circle, and the wrangler was working with a little boy who was even more scared than he was.

"Buttercup wouldn't hurt a fly," Jewel reassured him.

He remembered feeling mortified at the thought of riding a horse named Buttercup. And terrified that Buttercup would throw him off her broad back and trample him underfoot. Even though he'd been dying of cancer, he'd been afraid of getting killed. Life, he had learned, was precious.

"I'm not scared," he lied. He wished he could reach up and tug his baseball cap down tighter over his bald head, but he was afraid to let go of his two-handed grip on the saddle horn.

Jewel scooted under the bottom rail of the corral on her hands and knees, which explained how she had gotten so dirty, and walked right up to the horse—all right, it was only a pony, but it was still big—without fear. He sat frozen as she patted Buttercup's graying jaw and crooned to her.

"What are you saying?" he demanded.

"I'm telling Buttercup to be good. I'm telling her you're sick and—"

"I'm dying," he blurted out. "I'll be dead by Christmas." It was June. He was currently in remission, but the last time he'd been sick, he'd heard the doctors figuring he had about six months to live. He knew it was only a matter of time before the disease came back. It always did.

"My momma died and my daddy and my brother," Jewel said. "I thought I was gonna die, too, but I didn't." She reached up and touched the crisscrossing pink scars on her face. "I had to stay in the hospital till I got well."

"Then you know it's a rotten place to be," he said.

She nodded. "Zach and 'Becca came and took me away. I never want to go back."

"Yeah, well I don't have much choice."

"Why not?" she asked.

"Because that's where you go when you're sick."

"But you're well now," she said, looking up at him with serious brown eyes. "Except you don't have any hair yet. But don't worry. 'Becca says it'll grow back."

He flushed and risked letting go of the horn to tug the cap down. It was one of the many humiliations he had endured—losing his hair…along with his privacy…and his childhood. He had always wanted to go to camp like his sister, Sadie, but he had been too sick. Then some lady had opened this place. He had jumped at the chance to get away from home. Away from the hospital.

"Your hair doesn't grow back till you stop getting sick," he pointed out to the fearless kid standing with her cheek next to the pony's.

"So, don't get sick again," she said.

He snickered. "Yeah. Right. It doesn't work like that."

"Just believe you can stay well, and you will," she said.

The circle of horses began to move again, and she headed back toward the fence. It was then he noticed her limp. "Hey!" he shouted after her. "What happened to your leg?"

"It got broken," she said matter-of-factly.

Mac hadn't thought much about it then, but now he knew the pain she must have endured to walk again. Jewel would know what he was feeling as he got out of the hospital for what he hoped would be the last time. Jewel would understand.

After that first meeting, he and Jewel had encountered each other often over the next several years. He had beaten the leukemia and returned as a teenager to become a counselor at Camp LittleHawk. That was when Jewel had become his best friend. Not his *girlfriend*. His *best friend*.

He already had a girlfriend back home in Dallas. Her name was Louise and he called her Lou and was violently in love with her. He had met Lou when she came to the junior-senior prom with another guy. She had only been in the eighth grade. By the time he was a senior and Lou was a freshman, they were going steady.

He told Jewel all about the agonies of being in love, and though she hadn't yet taken the plunge, she was all sympathetic ears. Jewel was the best buddy a guy could have, a confidante, a pal. A soul mate. He could tell her anything and, in fact, had told her some amazingly private things.

Like how he had cried the first time he had endured a procedure called a back-stick, where they stuck a needle in your back to figure out your blood count. How he had wet the bed once in the hospital rather than ask for a bedpan. And how humiliating it had been when the nurse treated him like a baby and put the thermometer into an orifice other than his mouth.

It was astonishing to think he could have been so frank with Jewel. But Jewel didn't only listen to his woes, she shared her own. So he knew how jealous and angry she had been when Zach and Rebecca adopted another little girl two years older than her named Rolleen. And how she had learned to accept each new child a little more willingly, until the youngest, Colt, had come along, and he had felt like her own flesh-and-blood baby brother.

Mac had also been there at the worst moment of her life. He had lost a good friend that fateful Fourth of July. And Jewel... Jewel had lost much more. After that hot, horrible summer day, she had refused to see him again. So far, he had respected her wish to be left alone. But there was an empty place inside him she had once helped to fill.

He had received an invitation to her wedding the previous spring. It was hard to say what his feelings had been. Joy for her, because he knew how hard it must have been for her to move past what had happened to her. And sadness, too, because he knew the closeness they had enjoyed in the past would be transferred to her husband.

Then had come the announcement, a few weeks before the wedding, that it had been canceled. He had wondered what had gone wrong, wondered which of them had called it off and worried about what she must be feeling. He would never pry, but he was curious. After all, he and Jewel had once known everything there was to know about each other. He had picked up the phone to call her, but put it down. Too many years had passed.

Mac had never had another woman friend like Jewel. Sex always got in the way. Or rather, the woman's expectations. And his inability to fulfill them.

What kind of man is still a virgin at twenty-five? Mac mused.

An angry man. A onetime romantic fool who waited through college for his high school sweetheart to grow up, only to be left for another guy.

It hadn't seemed like such a terrible sacrifice remaining faithful to Louise all those years, turning down girls who showed up at his dorm room in T-shirts and not much else, girls who wanted to make it with a college football hero, girls who were attracted by his calendar-stud good looks. He had loved Lou and had his whole life with her ahead of him.

Until she had jilted him her senior year for Harry Warnecke, who had a bright future running his father's bowling alley.

Lou had been gentle but firm in her rejection of him. "I don't love you anymore, Mac. I love Harry. I'm pregnant, and we're going to be married."

Mac had been livid with fury. He had never touched

her, had respected her wish to remain a virgin until she graduated from high school and they could marry, and she was pregnant with some guy named Harry's kid and wanted to marry him.

It had taken every ounce of self-control he had not to reach out and throttle her. "Have a nice life," he had managed to say.

His anger had prodded him to hunt up the first available woman and get laid. But his pain had sent him back to his dorm room to nurse his broken heart. How could he make love to another woman when he still loved Lou? If all he had wanted was to get screwed, he could have been doing that all along. His dad had always told him that sex felt good, but making love felt better. He had wanted it to be making love the first time.

His final year of college, after he broke up with Lou, he went through a lot of women. Dating them, that is. Kissing them and touching them and learning what made them respond to a man. But he never put himself inside one of them. He was looking for something more than sex in the relationship. What he found were women who admired his body, or his talent with a football, or his financial prospects. Not one of them wanted him.

It wasn't until he had been drafted by the pros and began traveling with the Tornadoes that he met Elizabeth Kale. She was a female TV sports commentator, a woman who felt comfortable with jocks and could banter with the best of them. She had taken his breath away. She had shiny brown hair and warm brown eyes and a smile that wouldn't quit. He had fallen faster than a wrestled steer in a rodeo.

She hadn't been impressed by his statistics—personal

or football or financial. It had not been easy to get her to go out with him. She didn't want to get involved. She had her career, and marriage wasn't in the picture.

Mac didn't give up when he wanted something—and he'd wanted to marry Elizabeth. As the season progressed, they began to see each other when they were both in town. Elizabeth was a city girl, so they did city things—when they could both fit it into their busy schedules. Mac wooed her with every romantic gesture he could think of, and she responded. And when he proposed marriage, she accepted. Elizabeth made what time she could for him, and they exchanged a lot of passionate kisses at airports where their paths crossed.

He had carefully planned her seduction. He knew when and where it was going to happen. He was nervous and eager and restless. By a certain age—and Mac had already reached it—a woman expected a man to know all the right moves. Mac had been to the goal line plenty of times, but he had never scored a touchdown. He was ready and willing to take the plunge—figuratively speaking—but now that he had waited so long, the idea of making it with a woman for the first time was a little unnerving. Especially with Elizabeth, who meant so much to him.

What if he did it wrong? What if he couldn't please her? What if he left her unsatisfied? He read books. And planned. And postponed the moment.

Then he broke his leg. *Shattered his leg.*

Mac tasted bile in his throat, remembering what had happened next. Elizabeth had come to the hospital to see him, flashbulbs popping around her, as much in the news as his girlfriend as she was as a famous newscaster. She listened at his bedside to the prognosis.

His football career was over. He would be lucky if he ever walked again. He would always need a brace on his leg. Maybe he could manage with a cane.

He had seen it in her eyes before she spoke a word. The fear. And the determination. She said nothing until the doctors had left them alone.

"I can't—I won't—I can't do it, Mac."

"Do what, Elizabeth?" he asked in a bitter voice that revealed he knew exactly what she meant, though he pretended ignorance.

"I won't marry a man who can't walk." She slipped her widespread fingers slowly through the hair that fell forward on her face, carefully settling it back in place. He had always thought it a charming gesture, but now it only made her seem vain.

"I can't go through this with you," she said. "I mean, I...I hate hospitals and sick people and I can't...I can't be there for you, Mac."

He had known it was coming, but it hurt just the same. "Get out, Elizabeth."

She stood there waiting for...what?...for him to tell her it was all right? It wasn't, by God, all right! It was a hell of a thing to tell a man you couldn't stand by him in times of trouble. *For better or for worse.* It told him plenty about just how deep her feelings for him ran. Thin as sheet ice on a Texas pond.

"I said get out!" He was shouting by then, and she flinched and backed away. "Get out!"

She turned and ran.

His throat hurt from shouting and his leg throbbed

and his eyes and nose burned with unshed tears. He shouted at the nurse when she tried to come in, but he couldn't even turn over and bury his head in a pillow because they had his leg so strapped up.

Mac forced his mind away from the painful memories. There had been no seductions during the past two years, though he had spent a great deal of time in bed. He had been too busy trying to get well. Now he was well. And he was going to have to face that zero on the scoreboard and do something about it.

He could find a woman who knew the ropes—there were certainly enough volunteers even now—and get it over with. But he found that a little cold and calculating. The first time ought to be with a special woman. Not that he would ever be stupid enough to fall in love again. After all, twice burned, thrice chary. But he wanted to like and respect and admire the woman he chose as his first sexual partner.

Lately his dreams had been unbelievably erotic. *Hot, sweat-slick bodies entwined in twisted sheets. Long female legs wrapped around his waist. A woman's hair draped across his chest. His mouth on her—* He shook off the vision. Now that he was finally healthy— meaning he could get out of bed as easily as he could fall into it—it was time he took care of unfinished business.

Jewel's face appeared in his mind's eye. He saw the faint, crisscrossing scars from the car accident that had left her an orphan and had never quite faded away. Her smile, winsome and mischievous. Heard the distressed sound of her voice when she admitted her breasts kept growing and growing like two balloons. And her laughter when he had offered to pop them for her.

With Jewel he wouldn't have to be afraid of making a fool of himself in bed. Jewel would understand his predicament. But she was the last person he could ever have sex with. Not after what had happened to her.

He was sure she would see the humor in the current situation. Jewel had a great sense of humor. At least, once upon a time she had. He could hardly believe six years had passed since they had last seen each other. They had both been through a great deal since then.

Mac hoped Jewel wouldn't mind him intruding on her this way. But he was coming, like it or not.

CHAPTER TWO

PETER "MAC" MACREADY WAS THE last person Jewel
Whitelaw wanted to see back at Hawk's Pride, because
he was the one person besides her counselor who knew
her deepest, darkest secret. She should have told someone else long ago—her parents, one of her three sisters
or four brothers, her fiancé—but she had never been
able to admit the truth to anyone. Only Mac knew. And
now he was coming back.

If she could have left home while he was visiting, she
would have done so. But Camp LittleHawk was sche-
duled to open in two weeks, and she had too much to
do to get ready for the summer season to be able to pick
up and leave. All she could do was avoid Mac as much
as possible.

As she emerged from a steamy shower, draped herself
in a floor-length white terry cloth robe and wrapped her
long brown hair in a towel, she learned just how impossible that was going to be.

"Hi."

He was standing at the open bathroom door dressed
in worn Levi's, a Tornadoes T-shirt and Nikes, leaning
on a cane. He didn't even have the grace to look embarrassed. A grin split his face from ear to ear, creating two
masculine dimples in his cheeks, while his vivid blue

eyes gazed at her with the warmth of an August day in Texas.

"Hi," she said back. In spite of not wanting him here, she felt her lips curve in an answering smile. Her gaze skipped to the knotty-looking hickory cane he leaned on and back to his face. "I see you're standing on your own."

"Almost," he said. "Sorry about intruding. Your mom said to make myself comfortable." He gestured to the bedroom behind him, on the other side of the bathroom, where his suitcase sat on the double bed. "Looks like we'll be sharing a bath."

Jewel groaned inwardly. The new camp counselors' cottages had been built to match the single-story Spanish style of the main ranch house, with whitewashed adobe walls and a red barrel-tile roof. Each had two bedrooms, but shared a bath, living room and kitchen. As the camp manager, she should have had this cottage all to herself. "I thought you'd be staying at the house," she said.

"Your mom gave me a choice." He shrugged. "This seemed more private."

"I see." Her mother had asked her if she minded, since Jewel and Mac were such old friends, if she gave Mac a choice of staying at the cottage or in the house. Jewel hadn't objected, because she hadn't been able to think up a good reason to say no that wouldn't sound suspicious. As far as her parents knew, she and Mac still were good friends. And they were.

Only, Jewel had expected Mac to keep his distance, as he had for the past six years. And he had not.

Mac's brow furrowed in a way that was achingly

familiar. "I can tell Rebecca I've changed my mind, if you don't want me here."

Jewel struggled between the desire to escape Mac's scrutiny and the yearning to have back the camaraderie they had once enjoyed. Maybe it would be all right. Maybe the subject wouldn't come up. *Yeah, and maybe horses come in green and pink.* "I…"

He started to turn away. "I'll get my bag."

"Wait."

He turned back. "I don't want to make you uncomfortable, Jewel. I won't talk about it. I won't even bring up the subject." His lips curled wryly. "Of course, I just brought up the subject to say I won't bring it up, but I promise it'll be off-limits. I need a place to rest and get better, and I thought you might not mind if I stayed here."

His eyes looked wounded, and her heart went out to him. She crossed to him, because that seemed easier than making him walk to her with the cane. His arms opened to her and she walked right into them and they hugged tightly.

"God, I've missed you," he said, his deep voice rumbling in her ear.

"This feels good," she admitted. "It's been too long, Mac."

There was nothing sexual in the embrace, just two old friends, two very good friends, reconnecting after a long separation. Except Jewel was aware of the strength in his arms, the way her breasts felt crushed against his muscular chest and the feel of his thighs pressed against her own. She stiffened, then forced herself to relax.

"You're taller than I remember," he said, tucking her towel-covered head under his chin.

"I've grown three inches since... I've grown," she said, realizing how difficult it was going to be avoiding the subject she wanted to avoid. "It's a good thing, or I'd get a crick in my neck looking up at you."

He had to be four inches over six feet. She remembered him being tall at nineteen, but he must have grown an inch or two since then, and of course his shoulders were broader, his angular features more mature. He was a man now, not a boy.

He was big. He was strong. He could physically overwhelm her. But she had known Mac forever. He would never hurt her. She reminded herself to relax.

The towel slipped off, and her hair cascaded to her waist.

"Good Lord," Mac said, his fingers tangling in the length of it. "Your hair was never this long, either."

"I like it long." She could drape it forward over her shoulders to help cover her Enormous Endowments.

"I think I'm going to like it, too," he said, smiling down at her with a teasing glint in his eyes.

She gave him an arch look. "Are you flirting with me, Mr. Macready?"

"Who, me? Naw. Wouldn't think of it, Ruby."

Jewel grinned. In the old days, he had often called her by the names of different precious gems—"Because you're a Jewel, get it?"—and the return to such familiarity made her feel even more comfortable with him. "Get out of here so I can get dressed," she said, stepping back from his embrace.

The robe gaped momentarily, and his glance slipped

downward appreciatively. She self-consciously pulled the cloth over her breasts to cover them completely.

"Looks like they've grown, too," he quipped, leering at her comically.

She should have laughed. It was what she would have done six years ago, before disaster had struck. But she couldn't joke with him anymore about her overgenerous breasts. She blamed the size of them for what had happened to her. "Don't, Mac," she said quietly.

He sobered instantly. "I'm sorry, Jewel."

She managed a smile. "It's no big deal. Just get out of here and let me get dressed."

He backed up, and for the first time she saw how much he needed the cane. His face turned white around the mouth with pain, and he swore under his breath.

"Are you all right?" she asked.

"No problem," he said. "Leg's almost as good as new. Figure I'll start jogging tomorrow."

"Jogging?"

He gave her a sheepish look. "So maybe I'll start out walking. Want to go with me?"

She daintily pointed the toe of her once-injured leg in his direction. "Walking isn't my forte. How about a horseback ride?"

He shook his head. "Gotta walk. Need the exercise to get back into shape. Come with me. My limp is worse than yours, so you won't have any trouble keeping up. Besides, it would give us a chance to catch up on what we've both been doing the past six years. Please come."

She wrinkled her nose.

"Pretty please with sugar on it?"

It was something she had taught him to say if he really wanted a woman to do something. She gave in to the smile and let her lips curve with the delight she felt. "All right, you hopeless romantic. I'll walk with you, but it'll have to be early because I've got a lot of work to do tomorrow."

"Figured I'd go early to beat the heat," he said. "Six-thirty?"

"Make it six, and you've got a deal." She reached out a hand, and Mac shook it.

The electric shock that raced up her arm was disturbing. It took an effort to keep the frown from her face. This wasn't supposed to happen. She wasn't supposed to be physically attracted to Mac Macready. They were just good friends. *Yeah, and horses come in purple and orange.*

She closed the bathroom door and sank onto the edge of the tub. She had always thought Mac was cute, but he had matured into a genuine hunk. No problem. She would handle the attraction the way she had from the beginning, by thinking of him as a brother.

But he wasn't her brother. He was a very attractive, very available man. Who once had been—still was?— her best friend.

She clung to that thought, which made it easier to keep their relationship in perspective. It was much more important to have a friend like Mac than a boyfriend.

JEWEL REPEATED THAT SENTENCE like a litany the next morning at 5:55 when Mac showed up in the kitchen dressed in Nikes and black running shorts and nothing else. The kitchen door was open and through the screen she was aware of flies buzzing and the lowing of cattle. A steady, squeaking sound meant that her youngest brother, Colt, hadn't gotten around to oiling the windmill beside the stock pond. But those distractions weren't enough to keep her from ogling Mac's body.

A wedge of golden hair on his chest became a line of soft down as it reached his navel and disappeared beneath his shorts. She consciously forced her gaze upward.

Mac's tousled, collar-length hair was a sun-kissed blond, and his eyes were as bright as the morning sky. He hadn't shaved, and the overnight beard made him look both dangerous and sexy.

Without the concealing T-shirt and jeans, she could see the sinewy muscles in his shoulders and arms, the washboard belly and the horrible mishmash of scars on his left leg. He leaned heavily on the cane.

She poured him a bowl of cornflakes and doused them with milk. "Eat. You're running late."

"Oh, that I were running," he said. "I'm afraid walking is the best I can do." He hobbled across the redbrick tile floor to the small wooden table, settled himself in the ladderback chair opposite her and began consuming cereal at an alarming rate.

"What's that you're wearing?" he asked.

She tugged at her bulky, short-sleeved sweatshirt, dusted off her cutoff jeans and readjusted her hair over her shoulders. "Some old things."

"Gonna be hot in that," he said between bites.

But the sweatshirt disguised her Bountiful Bosom, which was more important than comfort. "Hungry?" she inquired, her chin resting on her hand as she watched him eat ravenously.

"I missed supper last night."

She had checked his bedroom and found him asleep at suppertime and hadn't disturbed him. He had slept all through the afternoon and evening. "You must have been tired."

"I was. Completely exhausted. Not that I'd admit that to anyone but you." He poured himself another bowl of cereal, doused it with the milk she had left on the table and began eating again.

"Nothing wrong with your appetite," she observed.

He made a sound, but his mouth was too full to answer.

She watched him eat four bowls of cereal. That was about right—two for dinner and two for breakfast. "Ready to go walking now?" she asked.

"Sure." He took his dish to the sink and reached back for hers, which she handed to him.

Seeing the difficulty he was having trying to do everything one-handed, so he could hang on to his cane, she said, "I can do that for you."

"I'm not a cripple!" When he turned to snap at her, he lost his one-handed grip on the dishes. His cane fell as he lurched to catch the bowls with both hands. Without the cane, his left leg crumpled under him.

"Look out!" Jewel cried.

The dishes crashed into the sink as Mac grabbed hold of the counter to keep from falling backward.

"Damn it all to hell!" he raged.

Jewel reached out to comfort him, but he snarled, "Don't touch me. Leave me alone."

Jewel had whirled to leave, when he bit out, "Don't go."

She stopped where she was, but she wanted to run. She didn't want to see his pain. It reminded her too much of her own.

He stared out the window over the sink at the endless reaches of Hawk's Pride, with its vast, grassy plains and the jagged outcroppings of rock that marked the entrance to the canyons in the distance.

"It must be awful," she whispered, "to lose so much."

His eyes slid closed, and she watched his Adam's apple bob as he swallowed hard. He slowly opened his eyes and turned to look at her over his shoulder. "This... the way I am... It's just temporary. I'll be back as good as new next season."

"Will you?"

He met her gaze steadily. "Bet on it."

She knew him too well. Well enough to hear the sheer bravado in his answer and to see the unspoken fear in his eyes that his football career was over. They had always been deeply attuned to one another. He was vulnerable again, in a way he once had been as a youth—this time not to death itself, but to the death of his dreams.

"What can I do, Mac?"

He managed a smile. "Hand me my cane, will you?"

It was easier to do as he asked than to probe the painful issues that he was refusing to address. She crossed to pick up his cane and watched as he eased his weight off his hands and onto his leg with the cane's support.

"Are you sure it isn't too soon to be doing so much?" she asked as he hissed in a breath.

He headed determinedly for the screen door. "The only way my leg can get stronger is if I walk on it."

She followed after him, as she had for nearly a dozen years in their youth. "All right, cowboy. Head 'em up, and move 'em out."

He flashed her his killer grin, and she smiled back, letting the screen door slam behind her.

It was easier to pretend nothing was wrong. But she could already see that things were different between them. They had both been through a great deal in the years since they had last seen each other. She knew as well as he did what it felt like to live with fear, and with disappointment.

She had worked hard to put behind her what had happened the summer she was sixteen and Harvey Barnes had attacked her at the Fourth of July picnic. But even now the memory of that day haunted her.

She had been excited when Harvey, a senior who ran with the in crowd, asked her to the annual county-wide Fourth of July celebration. She'd had a crush on him for a long time, but he hadn't given her a second glance. During the previous year, her breasts had blossomed and given her a figure most movie stars would have paid good dollars to have. A lot of boys stared, including Harvey.

She had suspected why Harvey had asked her out, but she hadn't cared. She had just been so glad to be asked, she had accepted his invitation on the spot.

"Why would you want to go out with a guy who's so full of himself?" Mac asked after she introduced him to Harvey. "I'd be glad to take you." As he had previously, every year he'd been at Hawk's Pride.

"I might as well go with one of my brothers as go

with you," she replied. "Harvey's cool. He's a hunk. He's—"

"Yeah, yeah, yeah. I get the message," he said, then teased in a singsong voice, "Pearl's got a boyfriend, Pearl's got a boyfriend."

She aimed a playful fist at his stomach to shut him up, but the truth was, she was hoping the picnic date with Harvey, their first, would lead to a steady relationship.

Mac caught her wrist to protect his belly and said, "All right, go with Harvey Barnes and have a good time. Forget all about me—"

Jewel laughed and said, "That mournful face isn't going to make any difference. I'm still going with Harvey. I'll see you at the picnic. We just won't spend as much time together."

Mac looked down at her, his brow furrowed. He opened his mouth to say something and shut it again.

"What is it?" she asked, seeing how troubled he looked.

"Just don't let him... If he does anything... If you think he's going to..."

"What?" she asked in exasperation.

He let go of her hands to shove both of his through his hair. "If you need help, just yell, and I'll be there."

He had already turned to walk away when she grabbed his arm and turned him back around. "What is it you think Harvey's going to do to me that's so terrible?"

"He's going to want to kiss you," Mac said.

"I want to kiss him back. So what's the problem?"

"Kissing's not the problem," Mac pointed out. "It's what comes after that. The touching and...and the rest.

Sometimes it's not easy for a guy to stop. Not that I'm saying he'd try anything on a first date, but some guys… And with a body like yours…"

Her face felt heated from all the blood rushing to it. Over the years they had managed not to talk seriously about such intimate subjects. Mac never brought them up except in fun, and until recently she hadn't been that interested in boys. She searched his face and found he looked as confused and awkward discussing the subject as she felt.

"How would you know?" she asked. "I mean, about it being hard to stop. Have you done it with Lou?"

His flush deepened. "You know I wouldn't tell you that, even if I had."

"Have you?" she persisted.

He tousled her hair like a brother and said, "Wouldn't you like to know!"

In the days before the picnic, Mac teased her mercilessly about her plan to wear a dress, since she only wore jeans and a T-shirt around the ranch.

Her eldest sister, Rolleen, had agreed to make a pink gingham dress for her, copying a spaghetti-strapped dress pattern that Jewel loved, but which she couldn't wear because her large breasts needed the support of a heavy-duty bra. Rolleen created essentially the same fitted-bodice, bare-shouldered, full-skirted dress, but made the shoulder straps an inch wide so they would hide her bra straps.

On the day of the picnic, Jewel donned the dress and tied up her shoulder-length hair in a ponytail with a pink gingham bow. Her newest Whitelaw sibling, fifteen-year-old Cherry, insisted that she needed pink lipstick on her lips, which Cherry applied for her with the expertise of one who had been wearing lipstick since she was twelve.

Then Jewel headed out the kitchen door to find Mac, who was driving her to the picnic grounds to meet Harvey.

"Wow!" Mac said when he saw her. "Wow!"

Jewel found it hard to believe the admiration she saw in Mac's eyes. She had long ago accepted the fact she wasn't pretty. She had sun-streaked brown hair and plain brown eyes and extraordinarily ordinary features. Her body was fit and healthy, but faint, crisscrossing scars laced her face, and she had a distinctive permanent limp.

The look in Mac's eyes made her feel radiantly beautiful.

She held out the gingham dress and twirled around for him. "Do you think Harvey will like it?"

"Harvey's gonna love it!" he assured her. "You look good enough to eat. I hope this Harvey character knows how lucky he is." The furrow reappeared on his brow. "He better not—"

She put a finger on the wrinkles in his forehead to smooth them out. "You worry too much, Mac. Nothing bad is going to happen."

Looking back now, Jewel wished she had listened to Mac. She wished she hadn't tried to look so pretty for Harvey Barnes. She wished...

Jewel had gotten counseling in college to help her deal with what had happened that day. The counselor had urged her to tell her parents, and when she had met

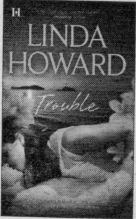

REQUEST YOUR FREE BOOKS!

2 FREE NOVELS
FROM THE ROMANCE COLLECTION
PLUS 2 FREE GIFTS!

YES! Please send me 2 FREE novels from the Romance Collection and my 2 FREE gifts (gifts are worth about $10). After receiving them, if I don't wish to receive any more books, I can return the shipping statement marked "cancel." If I don't cancel, I will receive 4 brand-new novels every month and be billed just $5.74 per book in the U.S. or $6.24 per book in Canada. That's a saving of at least 28% off the cover price. It's quite a bargain! Shipping and handling is just 50¢ per book in the U.S. and 75¢ per book in Canada.* I understand that accepting the 2 free books and gifts places me under no obligation to buy anything. I can always return a shipment and cancel at any time. Even if I never buy another book, the two free books and gifts are mine to keep forever.

194/394 MDN FDC5

Name	(PLEASE PRINT)	
Address		Apt. #
City	State/Prov.	Zip/Postal Code

Signature (if under 18, a parent or guardian must sign)

Mail to the **Reader Service:**
IN U.S.A.: P.O. Box 1867, Buffalo, NY 14240-1867
IN CANADA: P.O. Box 609, Fort Erie, Ontario L2A 5X3

Not valid for current subscribers to the Romance Collection
or the Romance/Suspense Collection.

Want to try two free books from another line?
Call 1-800-873-8635 or visit www.ReaderService.com.

* Terms and prices subject to change without notice. Prices do not include applicable taxes. Sales tax applicable in N.Y. Canadian residents will be charged applicable taxes. Offer not valid in Quebec. This offer is limited to one order per household. All orders subject to credit approval. Credit or debit balances in a customer's account(s) may be offset by any other outstanding balance owed by or to the customer. Please allow 4 to 6 weeks for delivery. Offer available while quantities last.

Your Privacy—The Reader Service is committed to protecting your privacy. Our Privacy Policy is available online at www.ReaderService.com or upon request from the Reader Service.

We make a portion of our mailing list available to reputable third parties that offer products we believe may interest you. If you prefer that we not exchange your name with third parties, or if you wish to clarify or modify your communication preferences, please visit us at www.ReaderService.com/consumerschoice or write to us at Reader Service Preference Service, P.O. Box 9062, Buffalo, NY 14269. Include your complete name and address.

MROM11

Try these Healthy and Delicious Spring Rolls!

INGREDIENTS

2 packages rice-paper spring roll wrappers (20 wrappers)

1 cup grated carrot

¼ cup bean sprouts

1 cucumber, julienned

1 red bell pepper, without stem and seeds, julienned

4 green onions finely chopped— use only the green part

DIRECTIONS

1. Soak one rice-paper wrapper in a large bowl of hot water until softened.

2. Place a pinch each of carrots, sprouts, cucumber, bell pepper and green onion on the wrapper toward the bottom third of the rice paper.

3. Fold ends in and roll tightly to enclose filling.

4. Repeat with remaining wrappers. Chill before serving.

Find this and many more delectable recipes
including the perfect dipping sauce in

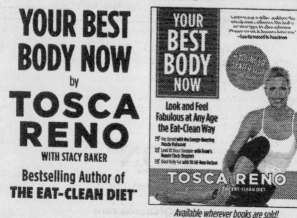

JOAN JOHNSTON

77478	HAWK'S WAY: CALLEN & ZACH	___ $7.99 U.S.	___ $9.99 CAN.
77380	HAWK'S WAY: CARTER & FALCON	___ $6.99 U.S.	___ $6.99 CAN.
77526	HAWK'S WAY GROOMS	___ $7.99 U.S.	___ $9.99 CAN.
77329	SISTERS FOUND	___ $7.99 U.S.	___ $7.99 CAN.
77509	HAWK'S WAY: FARON & GARTH	___ $7.99 U.S.	___ $9.99 CAN.

(limited quantities available)

TOTAL AMOUNT	$ _____
POSTAGE & HANDLING	$ _____
($1.00 FOR 1 BOOK, 50¢ for each additional)	
APPLICABLE TAXES*	$ _____
TOTAL PAYABLE	$ _____

(check or money order—please do not send cash)

To order, complete this form and send it, along with a check or money order for the total above, payable to HQN Books, to: **In the U.S.:** 3010 Walden Avenue, P.O. Box 9077, Buffalo, NY 14269-9077; **In Canada:** P.O. Box 636, Fort Erie, Ontario, L2A 5X3.

Name: _____
Address: _____ City: _____
State/Prov.: _____ Zip/Postal Code: _____
Account Number (if applicable): _____

075 CSAS

*New York residents remit applicable sales taxes.
*Canadian residents remit applicable GST and provincial taxes.

HQN™

We *are* romance™

www.HQNBooks.com

Jerry Cain and fallen in love with him her junior year at Baylor, the counselor had urged her to tell Jerry, too.

She just couldn't.

Jerry had been a graduate student, years older than she was, and more mature than the other college boys she had met. He had figured out right away that she was self-conscious about the size of her breasts, and it was his consideration for her feelings that had first attracted her to him. It had been easy to fall in love with him. It had been more difficult—impossible—to trust him with her secret.

Jerry had been more patient with her than she had any right to expect. She had loved kissing him. Been more anxious—but finally accepting—of his caresses. They were engaged before he pressed her to sleep with him. They had already sent out the wedding invitations by the time she did.

It had been a disaster.

They had called off the wedding.

That was a year ago. Jewel had decided that if she couldn't marry and have kids of her own, she could at least work with children who needed her.

So she had come back to Camp LittleHawk.

"Hey. You look like you're a million miles away."

Jewel glanced around and realized she could hardly see the white adobe ranch buildings, they had walked so far. "Oh. I was thinking."

"To tell you the truth, I enjoyed the quiet company." Sweat beaded Mac's forehead and his upper lip. He winced every time he took a step.

"Haven't we gone far enough?" she asked.

"The doctor said I can do as much as I can stand."

"You look like you're there already," she said.

"Just a little bit farther."

That attitude explained why Mac had become the best at what he did, but Jewel worried about him all the same. "Just don't expect me to carry you back," she joked.

Mac shot her one of his dimpled smiles and said, "Tell me what you've been doing with yourself lately."

"I've been figuring out the daily schedule for Camp LittleHawk."

"Need any help?"

She gave him a surprised look. "I'd love some. Do you have the time?"

He shrugged. "Don't have anything else planned. What kinds of things are you having the kids do these days?"

She told him, unable to keep the excitement from her voice. "Horseback riding, picnics and hayrides, of course. And handicrafts, naturally.

"But I've come up with something really exciting this year. We're going to have art sessions at the site of those primitive drawings on the canyon wall here at Hawk's Pride. Once the kids have copied down all the various symbols, we're going to send them off to an archaeologist at the state university for interpretation.

"When her findings are available, I'll forward a copy of them to the kids, wherever they are. It'll remind them what fun they had at camp even after they've gone."

"And maybe take their minds off their illness, if they're back in the hospital," Mac noted quietly.

Jewel sat silently watching Mac stare into the distance and knew he was remembering how it had been in the beginning, how they had provided solace to each other, a needed word of encouragement and a shoulder to lean on. She knew he had come back because she was here, a friend when he needed one.

"I can remember being fascinated by those drawings myself as a kid," Mac mused.

"Didn't you want to be an archaeologist once upon a time?"

"Paleontologist," he corrected.

"What's the difference?"

"An archaeologist studies the past by looking at what people have left behind. A paleontologist studies fossils to recreate a picture of life in the past."

"What happened to those plans?" she asked.

"It got harder and harder to focus on the past when I realized I was going to have a future."

"What college degree did you finally end up getting?"

He laughed self-consciously. "Business. I figured I'd need to know how to handle all the money I'd make playing football."

But his career had been cut short.

He turned abruptly and headed back toward the ranch without another word to her.

Jewel figured the distance they had come at about a mile. She looked at her watch. Six-thirty. Not very far or very fast for a man who depended on his speed for a living.

About a quarter of a mile from the house, Mac was using his hand to help move his left leg. Jewel stepped to his side and slipped her arm around his waist to help support his weight.

"Don't argue," she said, when he opened his mouth to protest. "If you want my company, you have to take the concern that comes along with it."

"Thanks, Opal," he said.

"Think nothing of it, Pete."

She hadn't called him Pete since he had started high school and acquired the nickname "Mac" from his football teammates. It brought back memories of better times for both of them. They were content to walk in silence the rest of the way back to the house.

Jewel had forgotten how good it felt to have a friend with whom you could communicate without saying a word. She knew what Mac was feeling right now as though he had spoken the words aloud. She understood his frustration. And his fear. She empathized with his drive to succeed, despite the obstacles he had to overcome. She understood his reluctance to accept her help and his willingness to do so.

It was as though the intervening years had never been.

Except, something else had been added to the mix between them. Something unexpected. Something as unwelcome as it was undeniable.

No *friend* should have felt the frisson of excitement Jewel had felt with her body snuggled up next to Mac's. No *friend* should have gotten the chill she got down her spine when Mac's warm breath feathered over her temple. No *friend's* heart would have started beating faster, as hers had, when Mac's arm circled her waist in return, his fingers closing on her flesh beneath the sweatshirt.

She would have to hide what she felt from him. Oth-

erwise it would spoil everything. Friendship had always
been enough in the past. Because of what had happened,
because she was in no position to ask for—or accept—
more, friendship was all they could ever have between
them now.

As they reached the kitchen door, she smiled up at
Mac, and he smiled back.

"Home again, home again, jiggety jog," she said.

"Same time tomorrow?"

She started to refuse. It would be easier if she kept
her distance from him. But it was foolish to deny herself
his friendship because she felt more than that for him.

She gave him a cheery smile and said, "Sure. Same
time tomorrow." She breathed a sigh of relief that
she wouldn't have to face him again for twenty-four
hours.

"As soon as I shower, we can go to work planning all
those activities for the kids," he said.

Jewel gave him a startled look.

"Changed your mind about wanting my help?"

She had forgotten all about it. "No. I...uh..."

He tousled her hair. "You can make up your mind
while I shower. I'll be here if you need me."

A moment later he had disappeared into the house.
It was only then she realized he was going to use up all
the hot water.

"Hey!" she yelled, yanking the screen door open to
follow after him. "I get the shower first!"

He leaned his head out of the bathroom door. She
saw a length of naked flank and stopped in her tracks.

"You can have it first tomorrow," he said. His eyes
twinkled as he added, "Unless you'd like to share?"

She put her hand flat on his bare chest, feeling the crisp, sweat-dampened curls under her palm, and shoved him back inside. "Go get cleaned up, stinky," she said, wrinkling her nose. "We've got work to do."

He saluted her and stepped back inside.

It was the right response. Just enough teasing and playful camaraderie to disguise her shiver of delight—and the sudden quiver of fear—at being invited to share Mac's shower.

CHAPTER THREE

"WOW! MAC MACREADY IN THE FLESH!"

Mac felt embarrassed and humbled at the look of admiration—almost adulation—in Colt Whitelaw's eyes. Mac had just shoved open the kitchen screen door to admire the sunrise on his third day at Hawk's Pride when he encountered Jewel's fourteen-year-old brother on the back steps. He had known the boy since Colt came to the Whitelaw household as an infant, the only one of the eight Whitelaw kids who had known no other parents than Zach and Rebecca. "Hi there, kid."

Colt was wearing a white T-shirt cut off at the waist to expose his concave belly and ribs and with the arms ripped out to reveal sinewy biceps. Levi's covered his long, lanky legs. He was tossing a football from hand to hand as he shifted from foot to booted foot. With the soft black down of adolescence growing on his upper lip, he looked every bit the eager and excited teenager he was.

"Mom said you were coming, but I didn't really believe her. I mean, now that you're famous and all, I didn't think you'd ever come back here. I wanted to come over as soon as you got here, but Mom said you needed time to settle in without all of us bothering you, so I stayed away a whole extra day. I'm not bothering you, am I?"

Mac resisted the urge to ruffle Colt's shaggy, shoulder-length black hair. The kid wouldn't appreciate it. Mac knew from his own experience that a boy of fourteen considered himself pretty much grown up. Colt was six feet tall, but his shoulders were still almost as narrow as his hips. His blue eyes were filled with wonder and hope, without the cynicism and disappointment that appeared as you grew older and learned that life threw a lot of uncatchable balls your way.

"Sit down and tell me what you've been doing with yourself," Mac invited. He eased himself into one of the two slatted white wooden chairs situated on the flagstone patio at the back of the cottage. Colt perched on the wide arm of the other chair.

The patio was arbored, and purple bougainvillea woven within a white lattice framework provided shade to keep the early morning sun off their heads and a pleasant floral fragrance.

Mac was aware of Colt's scrutiny as he gently picked up his wounded leg and set the ankle on the opposite knee. When he was done, he laid his cane down on the flagstone and leaned back comfortably in the chair.

"I was watching the game on TV when your leg got busted," Colt said. "It looked pretty bad."

"It was," Mac agreed.

"I heard them say you'd never walk again," Colt blurted.

Mac managed a smile. "Looks like they were wrong."

"When you didn't come back after a whole year, they said you'd never play football again."

"It's taken me a while to get back on my feet, but I expect to be back on the football field in the fall as good as new and better than ever."

"Really?" Colt asked.

Mac was fresh out of the shower after his second morning of walking with Jewel, and wished now he had put on jeans and boots instead of shorts and Nikes. The kid was gawking at his scarred leg like he was a mutant from the latest horror movie.

Mac figured it was time to change the subject, or he'd end up crying his woes to the teenager. He gestured to the football in Colt's hands and said, "Are you on the football team at school?"

Colt made a disparaging face and mumbled, "Yeah. I'm the quarterback."

Most boys, especially in Texas, would have been ecstatic at the thought of being quarterback. "It sounds as if you don't care much for football."

"It's all right. It's just…" Colt slid off the arm backward into the slatted wooden chair, with his legs dangling over the arm, the football cradled in the notch of his elbow. "Did you always know what you wanted to do with your life?"

Mac nodded. He had always known he wanted to play football. He just hadn't been sure his body would give him the chance. "How about you?"

"I know exactly what I want to do," Colt said. "I just don't think I'm going to get the chance to do it."

"Why not?"

"Dad expects me to stay here and be a rancher."

"Is that so bad?"

"It is when I'd rather be doing something else."

Mac stared at Colt's troubled face. "Anything you'd like to talk about?"

Colt shrugged. "Naw. I guess not." He settled his feet

on the ground and rose with an ease that Mac envied. "Guess I'd better get going. Now that school's out for the summer, I've got a lot of chores to do."

Mac turned his eyes in the direction of the squealing windmill.

Colt laughed. "I'll get to it right away. Hope it hasn't been keeping you awake."

"I've slept fine." Like the dead. He had slept straight through the afternoon and evening of his first day here, and yesterday he had been exhausted after a day spent mostly sitting down, working out a crafts program for the camp with Jewel. He knew his body needed rest to heal, but he was tired of being tired. He wanted to be well again.

Colt began loping away, then suddenly turned and threw the football in Mac's direction. Instinctively, Mac reached out to catch it. His fingertips settled on the well-thrown ball with remembered ease, and he drew it in.

Colt came loping back, a wide grin splitting his face. "Guess you haven't lost your touch." He held out his hand for the ball.

Mac looked up at the kid, an idea forming in his head. "How would you like to throw a few to me over the next couple of weeks, after I get a little more mobile?"

Colt's eyes went wide with wonder. "You mean it? Really? Hot damn, that would be great! I mean, golly, that would be great!" he quickly corrected himself, looking over his shoulder to see if any of his family had heard him. "Just say when and where."

"Let's say two weeks from today," Mac said. "I'll come and find you."

Colt eyed Mac's injured leg. "Are you sure—"

"Two weeks," Mac said certainly.

Colt grinned. "You got it." He took the ball and sauntered off toward the barn.

Mac let out a deep sigh. He had given himself two weeks to get back enough mobility to be able to run for a pass, when it was taking him thirty minutes to walk a mile.

He turned as he heard the screen door slam and saw Jewel. She was just out of the shower, having been second again this morning, since she had gotten a phone call the instant they came back in the door from their walk. She must have blown her hair dry, because it looked shiny and soft enough for him to want to put his hands in it.

The only time he had ever touched her hair in the past was to tousle it like an older brother or tug on her ponytail. He couldn't help wondering what it would feel like to have all that long, silky hair draped over his body.

Mac turned away. *This is Jewel. Your best friend. You'd better get laid soon, old buddy. You're starting to have really weird fantasies.*

She was wearing jeans and boots and a long-sleeved man's button-down, oxford-cloth shirt turned up at the cuffs with the tails hanging out. He wondered if the shirt had belonged to her fiancé and felt jealous of the man. Which was stupid, because Mac and Jewel had never been lovers.

Would you like to be?

He forced his mind away from that insidious thought. It would mess up everything if he made a move on his

best friend. He needed Jewel's friendship too much to
spoil things that way.

The shirt was big and blousy on her, and she wore her
hair pulled over her shoulders in front to hide whatever
there might have been left to see of her figure, which
wasn't much.

He started to say "You look great!" and bit his tongue.
It sounded too much like something a man might say to
a woman he wanted to impress. "Hi," he said instead.
"Hope you had enough hot water."

"Barely. I made it a quick shower. I'm definitely first
tomorrow." She took the seat next to him, leaned back
and inhaled a breath of flower-scented air that made her
breasts rise under the shirt. The sight took his breath
away.

Whenever he had thought about Jewel in the years
they had been apart, it was her laughter he had remembered. The way her eyes crinkled at the corners and her
lips curved, revealing even white teeth, and how the
sound would kind of bubble up out of her, as effervescent as sparkling water.

He couldn't imagine why he hadn't remembered her
breasts. He could see why a man might stare. Had they
been that large six years ago? They must have been, or
close to it, because he had joked with her about them a
lot, he remembered. And she had laughed in response,
that effervescent, sparkling laugh.

He realized he hadn't heard her laugh once since he
had arrived. She had smiled, but her eyes had never
joined her mouth. A sadness lingered, memories of more
than uncatchable balls. More like forfeited games.

"Who was that on the phone?" he asked.

"Mrs. Templeton. Her eight-year-old son, Brad, is supposed to be a camper during the first two-week session, but he was having second thoughts about coming."

"Why?"

"She's not really sure. He was excited at first when his parents suggested the camp. She wanted me to talk to him."

"Were you able to change his mind?"

Her lips curved. "Brad's an avid football fan. I mentioned you were here—"

"You shouldn't have done that," Mac said brusquely.

She looked as if he'd kicked her in the stomach. "I'm sorry," she said. "I didn't think you'd mind. You always seemed to like spending time with the kids."

He made a face. "It isn't that I mind spending time with them. It's just—" He didn't want them to see him hobbling around with a cane. He didn't want them feeling sorry for him. He didn't want to be asked a lot of questions for which he had no answers.

He would know in the next few weeks whether his leg was going to stand up to the rigors of running. He wanted time by himself to deal with his disappointment—if that was what it turned out to be. He wanted to be able to rage against fate without worrying about some sick kid's feelings.

"I'm sorry, Mac," Jewel said, reaching out to lay her hand on his forearm.

The hairs on his arms prickled at her touch, and his body responded in a way that both surprised and disturbed him. He resisted the urge to jerk his hand away. That would only hurt her again.

This is Jewel. My friend. There's nothing sexual intended by her touch.

Jewel might be his friend, but his body also recognized her as female. This sort of thing—unwanted arousal—had happened once or twice when they were teenagers, and she had touched him at an odd moment when he wasn't expecting it, but he had always attributed those incidents to randy teenage hormones. That excuse wouldn't work now.

All right, so she was an attractive woman.

That excuse wouldn't work either. Jewel wasn't pretty. Never had been. Her nose was straight and small, her chin was square, her mouth was a bit too big and her eyes were Mississippi-mud brown. Ordinary features all. She did have an extraordinary body. Her long legs, small waist and ample breasts were the stuff of male dreams. But Mac was offended on Jewel's behalf to think that any man could want her because of her body and not because of who she was inside.

So, it's her mind you find attractive?

As a teenager, he had liked her sense of humor, her enthusiasm for life and her willingness to reach out to others. He hadn't seen much of the first two traits this time around, and he wasn't sure whether it was a continued willingness to reach out to others that had made her return to Camp LittleHawk or, as he suspected, a desire to retreat from the world.

Mac had no explanation for his response to Jewel except that he had been celibate for too long. What had happened when Jewel touched him was merely the healthy response of a male animal to a female of the species. The problem would be solved when he found himself a woman and satisfied the simple physiological need that had been too long denied. Which meant he had better make a trip into town sometime soon and find a willing woman.

"Do you want me to call the Templetons back and tell them your plans have changed and you won't be here, after all?" Jewel asked.

He shook his head. "I guess it won't hurt me to be nice to one little boy."

"If you'd rather not—"

"I said I would." He slid his leg off his knee and reached for his cane. "It's not that big a deal, Jewel."

She rose and reached for his arm to help him up.

He jerked away. "I'm not an invalid. I wish you'd stop trying to help me."

He saw the hurt look on her face, but that was better than having her know the sharp sexual response her touch had provoked. That would ruin everything. Better to have her think he was in a lousy mood than find out that he wanted to suck on her breasts or put his hand between her legs and seek the damp heat there.

"I'm going in to town today," he said, realizing he'd better get away for a while and cool down.

"Perfect! I need some things from the hardware store. Could you give me a lift?"

Thank God she wasn't looking at him, or she would have known something was wrong. He opened his mouth to refuse and said, "Sure. Why not? Give me a chance to change into a shirt and jeans and some boots first."

She gave him a blazing smile that made his groin pull up tight. Hell. He'd better find himself a woman. And soon.

NO DOUBT ABOUT IT, JEWEL THOUGHT. Mac had been acting strange all day. Every errand he had run had taken him to the opposite end of town from her. Although they had made plans to meet for lunch at the Stanton Hotel Café, he hadn't arrived until she was nearly finished eating. She was sitting on one of the 1950's chrome seats at the lunch counter when he finally showed up, grabbed a cup of coffee, said he wasn't hungry, remembered something else he had to do in town and took off again.

If Jewel hadn't known better, she would have said he didn't want to be anywhere near her. But that was silly. They were best friends.

They had agreed to meet in the parking lot near the bank at four o'clock where Mac had parked his extended cab Chevy pickup and head back to Hawk's Pride. Jewel was sitting on the fender of the truck when Mac finally returned.

"You could have sat inside," he said. "It wasn't locked."

"It was too hot with the windows rolled up, and I needed a key to get them down," she said, lifting the hair at her nape to catch the late afternoon breeze. She heard him suck in a breath and had turned in his direction when a female voice distracted them both.

"Peter? Is that you?"

Jewel rose and turned at the same time as Mac to find a red-headed, green-eyed woman standing beside the bed of the pickup.

"Eve?" Mac replied in tones of astonishment that rivaled the woman's.

She ran toward him, and Jewel watched in awe as

Mac dropped his cane to surround the woman with his arms. Jewel hurried to pick it up, certain Mac would lose his balance and need it at any moment.

Only he didn't.

Either he was stronger on his feet than he had been two days ago, or the petite redhead was stronger than she looked.

"Peter. Peter," the woman said, her gaze searching his face.

"Eve. I can't believe it's you!" he replied, his eyes searching her face with equal delight.

He suddenly looked around for Jewel and reached out a hand to draw her closer. "Jewel, this is Evelyn Latham. Eve and I dated for a while in college. She's the only person I ever let get away with calling me Peter."

Eve simpered. "It's because you have such a big—"

"Yeah," Mac cut her off. "Eve, this is my friend, Jewel Whitelaw. I'm spending some time at her parents' ranch."

Jewel saw Eve take one look at her plain face and her unshapely clothes and dismiss her as no competition.

Eve then gave Mac a quick, but thorough, once-over. "You look *purrr*fectly fit to me."

Jewel cringed at the way the woman drew out the word with her Texas accent. Eve obviously appreciated Mac's assets—one of which she had apparently seen up close and personal—and the sexual invitation she extended was clear, at least to Jewel.

Mac must have heard it, too. "What are you doing with yourself these days, Eve? I haven't seen you since... when was it?"

"Graduation day from UT, two years ago."

He looked for a ring on her left hand, but didn't find one. "I thought you were going to marry Joe Bob Struthers."

"I only told you that because I was mad at you for dumping me after only three dates...just when we were getting to know each other so well."

He's probably slept with her, Jewel thought. She couldn't fault Mac's taste. The woman was gorgeous. She wore a clingy green St. John knit dress, with a fashionable gold chain draped across her flat stomach.

Mac gave Eve a look that suggested he would be happy to pick up where they had left off. "So you're not a married woman?"

"I'm free as a bird," Eve confirmed.

"I thought you were a Dallas girl, born and bred. What are you doing out here in the far reaches of northwest Texas?" Mac asked.

"My dad bought the bank here in town. I've been the assistant manager for the past year."

"I never expected any less of you," Mac said, "graduating the way you did at the top of the class."

Pretty *and* smart. That was a lethal combination, Jewel thought. Not that Jewel was competing in any way with Evelyn Latham for Mac's affection. She and Mac were just friends. But she couldn't help thinking that if Mac got involved with Eve, she would see a whole lot less of him, and she did enjoy his company.

"What are you doing here?" Eve asked Mac in return. "Aren't you supposed to be off playing football, or something like that?"

Jewel couldn't believe the woman had dated Mac

but had no idea when the football season began and ended.

"It's the off-season," Mac said with an indulgent smile. For the first time it must have occurred to him that he didn't have his cane. He looked around for it, and Jewel handed it to him. He took it and leaned on it. "I'm here visiting friends and recuperating from a football injury."

"You were hurt?" Eve asked.

Jewel rolled her eyes. Mac gave her a nudge with his hip, and she straightened up.

"You could say that," Mac said. "I guess you didn't hear about it."

Eve turned her mouth down in a delightful moue. "As you very well know I never cared much for football, only for the way you looked in those tight pants."

The sexual innuendo was even more blatant this time, and Jewel felt uncomfortable standing there listening to it. "Sorry we can't stay," she said. "Mac was just giving me ride home."

The pout that appeared on Eve's face would have looked right at home on a three-year-old. "Oh, Mac. I was hoping you'd have dinner with me."

"I still can," Mac said. "I'll take Jewel home and come back. What time and where?"

"How about eight o'clock? My house." She gave Mac an address in the newest condominium complex in town.

Mac grinned. "I'll be there."

"Don't dress up," Eve purred. "I want you to be comfortable."

"You got it," Mac said.

With Jewel standing right there, Eve went up on tiptoe and gave Mac a kiss right on the mouth. Jewel noticed Mac's arm went around her waist quick enough to draw her close, so the kiss wasn't unwelcome. It went on a long time, and from the way their mouths shifted, their tongues were involved.

Jewel stood frozen, unable to move. At last the kiss broke, and Mac shot her a quick, embarrassed look. It was too little, too late. He should have thought of her feelings before he practically made love to another woman right in front of her.

Only it shouldn't have mattered if he kissed somebody else. They were only friends.

"See you at eight," Mac said as he backed away from Eve.

"I'll be waiting," Eve said in a sultry voice.

Mac went around to his side of the truck without stopping to open Jewel's door. Not that she needed her door opened for her. She got in and sat near the edge of the seat, opening the window as soon as Mac started the truck and sticking her elbow out.

"Sorry about that," he said after a few minutes. "I shouldn't have embarrassed you like that."

"I wasn't embarrassed," Jewel said. "Kiss all the girls you want. It doesn't make any difference to me."

"All right. If that's the way you feel. Just so you don't worry, I may not be back tonight."

"Thanks for telling me," Jewel said. "I won't wait up for you."

She really didn't care. He was just a friend. He'd had another girlfriend most of the time she had known him. This was no different. Except, the whole time she had watched Mac kissing Eve the most stunning thought had been running through her head.

I wish it were me.

CHAPTER FOUR

MAC WENT TO EVELYN LATHAM'S HOUSE with one purpose in mind: to get laid. Eve opened the door wearing a clingy red velour jumpsuit that sent a wake-up call to his body. He was sure all it would take was one kiss to get the old machinery back into action. So he pulled her into his arms and kissed her and…nothing. Not a damned thing happened.

He worried about the situation all through supper and all through the glass of merlot they enjoyed by the fire he started for her in the stone fireplace. When they ended up entwined on the couch, he willed his body to react to the feel of her lips against his, to the feel of her body beneath his hands. He felt the sweat pop out on his forehead. But…nothing.

This wasn't supposed to happen. Just because he hadn't made love with a woman didn't mean that he didn't want to. He wanted to, all right. His damned body just wasn't cooperating! He made up some excuse for why he couldn't stay—his aching leg had come in handy for once—and bolted.

He drove around for two hours wondering if he was going to spend the rest of his life a virgin. What the hell had gone wrong? He hadn't been able to figure it out but had finally conceded that driving around all night wasn't going to give him any answers.

Then he remembered he had told Jewel he would probably be out all night. What was she going to think if he came back early?

That you don't take your time.

Yeah. Probably she'd just think he'd gotten his fill of Eve already. He couldn't imagine getting his fill of Jewel in bed. The thought of touching her skin, the feel of her hair against his body, the smell of her.

His body stirred in response.

It's too late, buddy. You already missed the party. You have to do that when there's a flesh-and-blood woman around.

And when it was some other woman besides Jewel. It wasn't going to do him any good getting aroused by thoughts of her, because she was the last person he could have sex with.

Hell, his leg *was* killing him. He had some exercises he was supposed to do at night that he hadn't done to relax the muscles. He needed to lay his leg flat in bed. He needed…he needed to know he could function as a man. The situation with Eve had been disturbing because it had never happened to him before. What if something was wrong with him? What if all those operations had done something to his libido?

You don't have any problem responding to Jewel.

He recalled his feelings for Jewel, the ones that had sent him off in search of another woman. They weren't as comforting as they should have been. He had felt the same sort of semi-arousal with Eve before he kissed her, but when it came time for action, his body had opted out.

Mac cut the pickup engine at the back door to the

cottage. No lights. At least he'd be spared the ignominy of Jewel seeing him sneaking in at two in the morning. He didn't want to have to make some explanation about why he was home early. He wasn't about to tell her the truth, and he hated like hell to lie.

He eased the kitchen door open—Western doors were rarely locked, even in this day and age—and slipped inside.

"Hi."

Mac nearly lost his balance and fell. "What the hell are you doing sitting here in the dark?"

He reached for the light switch, but Jewel said, "Don't."

The rough, raw sound of her voice, as though she had been crying, stayed his hand. He remained where he was, waiting for his eyes to adjust to the dark. He finally located her in the shadows. She was sitting with her elbows perched on the kitchen table, her face buried in her hands.

He limped over, scraped a chair closer and sat beside her. He felt her stiffen as he laid an arm across her shoulder. "Are you all right?

"I'm fine."

"You don't sound fine. You sound like you've been crying."

"I didn't think you'd be back tonight."

Which meant she had expected to have the privacy to cry without being disturbed. It didn't explain *why* she had been crying. She tried to rise, but he kept his arm around her and pressed her back down. "I'm here, Jewel."

"Why is that, Mac? I can't imagine any woman

throwing you out. Which means you left on your own. What happened?"

This was exactly the scene Mac had been hoping to avoid. "She...uh...we...uh..."

"Don't tell me Eve didn't make a pass."

"She did," Mac conceded reluctantly.

"Then why aren't you spending the night with her?"

"I...uh...that sort of thing can give a woman ideas."

"I see."

"You do?"

"Sure. Spend the whole night in a woman's bed, and she tends to think you might be serious about her. Everyone knows you're a love'em and leave'em kind of guy."

"I am? I mean, I suppose I am. I haven't found a woman I'd want to settle down with who'd have me." That was certainly no lie.

Eve had wanted him, all right. It should have been the easiest thing in the world to take her in his arms and make love to her. The situation had been perfect: willing woman, intelligent, not a total stranger, attractive—hell, absolutely beautiful. And it had been absolutely impossible.

Mac bit back the sound of frustration that sought voice.

"You should go to bed if you're going to get up early and walk tomorrow," Jewel said.

"I'd rather sit here with you," Mac replied.

"I'd rather be alone."

"Are you sure?"

"I'll be fine."

Mac leaned over to kiss her softly on the temple. Her

hair smelled of lilacs. It reminded him of warm, lazy summer days they had spent lying on the banks of the pond that bordered the Stonecreek Ranch. He resisted the urge to thread his fingers through her hair. It might comfort her, but it would drive him damn near crazy.

"Just know I'm here if you need me," he said. "You'd better get to bed, too, because I'm expecting you to walk with me tomorrow."

"I don't think that's a good idea. It would be better if you go alone."

He stared at her, wishing he could see the expression on her face. Moonlight filtered in through the kitchen window but left her mostly in shadow. "What's going on, Jewel? Why are you shutting me out?"

"I got along fine without you for six years, Mac. What makes you think I need you now?"

Mac was stunned as much by the virulence in her voice as by what she had said. "If you want me out of here, I'm gone."

She clutched his forearm as he rose, rubbing at her eyes with the knuckles of her other hand. "Don't leave. Don't leave."

He pulled her up and into his arms, and she grabbed him tight around his neck and sobbed against his shoulder. He rubbed her back with his open palms, aware suddenly that she was wearing a thin, sleeveless cotton nightgown and nothing else.

His body turned hard as a rock in two seconds flat.

His equipment worked all right. At the wrong time. With the wrong woman.

"Damn it all to hell," he muttered.

Jewel needed his comfort, not some male animal

lusting after her. He kept their hips apart, not wanting his physical response to frighten or distress her. "Tell me what's wrong, Jewel. Let me help," he crooned in her ear.

"It's too embarrassing," she said, her face pressed tight against the curve of his shoulder.

"Nothing's too embarrassing for us to talk about, my little carbuncle."

She hiccuped a laugh. "Carbuncle? Isn't that an ugly inflammation—"

"It's a red precious stone. I swear."

She relaxed, chuckling, and it took all the willpower he had to keep from pulling her tight against him.

"You always could make me laugh," she said. "Oh, Mac, I wish you'd come back a long time ago. I missed you."

"And I missed you. Now tell me what's so embarrassing that you don't want to talk about it?"

She sighed, and her breasts swelled against his chest, soft and warm. His heartbeat picked up. Lord, she was dangerous. Why couldn't this have happened with Eve? Why did it have to be Jewel?

Her fingers began to play in the hair at his nape. He wondered if she knew what she was doing to him and decided she couldn't possibly. She wouldn't purposely turn him on. What she wanted was comfort from a friend. And he intended to give it to her.

But he wasn't any more able to stop his body from responding than he had been capable of making it respond. All he could do was try to ignore the part of him that was insisting he do something. He focused his attention on Jewel. She needed his help.

"Tell me what's wrong," he urged.

"I wish things were different, that's all."

"Don't we all?" he said, thinking of his own situation. "But frankly, that doesn't sound embarrassing enough to keep to yourself. What is it? Got bucked off your horse? Happens to the best of us. Broke a dish? Do it all the time. If you broke a heart I might worry, but you can always buy another dish."

She laughed. The bubbly, effervescent sound he hadn't heard for six years. He pulled her close and rocked her in his arms in the old, familiar, brotherly way.

She stiffened, and he realized what he had done. His hips, with the hard bulge in front, were pressed tight against hers. There was no way she could mistake his condition.

"Damn, Jewel," he said, backing away from her, putting her at arm's length and gripping her hands tightly in his.

He smiled, but she didn't smile back.

When she pulled free, he let her go. "We can still talk," he said, wanting her to stay, wanting to confess the truth to her. She was still his best friend. But somehow things had changed. He couldn't tell her everything, not the most private things. Not anymore.

Maybe he had been wrong to expect her to confide in him. Maybe she felt the same awkwardness he did, the distance that had never been there before. A distance he had put there, because he saw her not just as a friend, but as a woman he wanted to kiss and touch.

"I'm going to bed, Mac."

"Will you walk with me tomorrow?"

"I don't think—"

"Please, Jewel. You're my best friend. I'd really like the company."

She hesitated so long, he thought she was going to refuse. "All right, Mac. I suppose I owe you that much." She turned and left without another word.

He waited until her bedroom door closed before he moved, afraid that if he did, he would go after her.

He wondered what had been troubling her. He wondered what she would have done if he had lowered his head and sucked on her breasts through the thin cotton. Blood pulsed through his rock-hard body, and he swore under his breath.

Mac went to bed, but he didn't sleep. He tossed and turned, troubled by vivid erotic fantasies of himself and Jewel Whitelaw. *Their legs entangled, their bodies entwined, his tongue deep in her mouth, his shaft deep inside her. She was calling to him, calling his name.*

Mac awoke tangled in the sheets, his body hot, hard and ready, his heart racing. And all alone.

He heard Jewel calling from outside the door. "Mac. Are you awake?" She knocked twice quietly. "It's time to walk."

Mac groaned. "I'll be with you in a minute." As soon as he was decent.

From the look of Jewel at the breakfast table, she hadn't slept any better than he had. She was wearing something even less attractive than the sweatshirt and cutoffs she had worn previously. It didn't matter. He saw her naked.

Mac shook his head to clear it. The vision of her breasts, large and luscious as peaches, and her long, slim legs wrapped around his waist, remained as vivid as ever.

"Are you all right?" Jewel asked.

"Fine. Let's go."

She chattered the whole way to the canyon, but he would have been hard-pressed to remember a word of what she had said or his own responses.

Everything was different. Something was missing. And something had been added.

He wanted their old relationship back. He was determined to quench any desire he might feel for her, so things could get back to an even footing. He figured the best way to start was to bring the subject out into the open and deal with it. On the walk back to the house, he did.

"About what happened last night… It shouldn't have happened." His comment was vague, but he knew she understood exactly what he meant when pink roses blossomed on her cheekbones.

She shrugged. "I was just a woman in a skimpy nightgown."

"Jewel, I—"

She stopped and turned to him, looking into his eyes, her gaze earnest. "Please, Mac. Can we pretend it never happened?"

He gave a relieved sigh. "That's exactly what I'd like to do. It was an accident. I never intended for it to happen. I wish I could promise it won't happen again, but—" He shot her a chagrined look. "I'll be sure you're never embarrassed again. Am I forgiven?"

"There's no need—"

"Just say yes," he said.

"Yes."

She turned abruptly and started walking again, and he followed after her.

"I'm glad that's over with," he said. "I can't afford to lose a friend as good as you, Jewel."

"And I can't afford to lose a friend like you, Mac."

Jewel's eyes were as brown and sad as a motherless calf. Mac wished she had told him why she was crying last night. He wished she had let him comfort her. If she ever gave him another chance, he was going to do it right. He wasn't going to let his hormones get in the way of their friendship.

When they got back to the house, she hurried up the back steps ahead of him. "I get the shower first!"

"We could always share," he teased. He could have bitten his tongue out. That sort of sexual innuendo had to cease.

To his relief, Jewel gave him a wide smile and said, "In your dreams, Mac! I'll try to save you a little hot water."

Then she was gone.

Mac settled on the back stoop and rubbed the calf muscles of his injured leg. It was getting easier to walk. Practice was helping. And it would get easier to treat Jewel as merely a friend. All he had needed was a little more practice at that, too.

AFTER HE HAD SHOWERED, MAC MADE a point of seeking Jewel out, determined to work on reestablishing their friendship. He found her in the barn, cleaning stalls and shoveling in new hay for the dozen or so ponies Camp

LittleHawk kept available for horseback rides. "Can I help?" he said.

"There's another pitchfork over by the door. Be my guest."

Mac noticed she didn't even look up from her work. Not a very promising sign. He grabbed the pitchfork and went to work in the stall next to the one she was working in. "I thought your mom usually hired someone to do this kind of heavy labor."

"I don't have anything better to do with my time," Jewel said.

"Why not?" Mac asked. "Pretty girl like you ought to be out enjoying herself."

Jewel stuck her pitchfork into the hay and turned to stare at him. "I enjoy my work."

"I'm sure you do," he said, throwing a pitchfork of manure into the nearby wheelbarrow. "But there's a time for work and a time for play. I don't see you doing enough playing."

"I'm a grown-up woman, Mac. Playing is for kids."

"You're never too old to play, Jewel." Mac filled his pitchfork with clean straw and threw it up over the stall so it landed on Jewel's head.

She came out of her stall sputtering and picking straw out of her mouth, mad as a peeled rattler. She confronted him, hands on hips and said, "That wasn't funny!"

He set his pitchfork against the stall and laughed. "I think you look darned cute with straw sticking out of your hair every whichaway." He headed toward her to help pull out some of the straw.

When he got close enough, she gave him a shove that sent him onto his behind. Only the straw Mac landed in wasn't clean. He gave a howl of outrage and struggled up out of the muck, glaring at the stain on the back of his jeans. "What'd you do that for?"

She grinned. "I think you look darned cute, all covered with muck."

"You know this means war."

"No, Mac. We're even now. Don't—"

He lunged toward her, caught her by the waist and threw her up over his shoulder in a fireman's carry.

"Watch out for your leg!" Jewel cried. "You're going to hurt yourself carrying me like this."

"My leg is fine," Mac growled. "Good enough to get you where I want you."

Mac headed for the short stack of hay at one end of the barn and when he got there, dropped Jewel into it. When she tried to jump free, he came down on top of her and pinned her hands on either side of her.

"Mac," she said breathlessly, laughing. "Get up."

"I want to play some more, Emerald, my dear," he said sprinkling her hair with hay.

"You're more green than I am," she taunted.

Mac took a look at the back of his jeans. "Yes, and I think you should pay a forfeit for that."

"You can have the shower first," she said with a bubbly laugh. "You need it!"

His laugh was cut off when he realized that what he really wanted was a kiss. He stared at her curving mouth, at the way her nose wrinkled when she laughed, at the teasing sparkle in her brown eyes. "I think I'll take something now."

He watched her face sober when she realized what he intended. He knew she must be able to feel his arousal, cradled as he was between her jean-clad thighs. He waited for her to tell him to let go, that the game was over. She stared up at him with luminous eyes and slicked her tongue quickly, nervously over her lips. But she didn't say get up or get off. And she didn't say no.

Friends, Mac. Not lovers. Friends.

Mac made himself kiss her eyelids closed before he kissed each cheek and then her nose and then…her forehead.

He rose abruptly and pulled her to her feet. She was dizzy, because her eyes had been closed, so he was forced to hold her in his arms until she was steady. She felt so good there, so very right. And so very wrong.

"I'm sorry, Jewel," he said. "That was totally out of line."

She took a deep breath and let it out. "Yes, I suppose it was. I think it's your turn to pay a forfeit, Mac."

He tensed. "What did you have in mind?"

She reached out, and for a moment he thought she was going to lay her hand on his chest and give him another shove. Instead, she grasped a nearby pitchfork and held it out to him. "You get to finish what I started. I'm going to get another shower and wash off all this itchy straw."

"Hey! That's not fair," he protested.

But she had already turned and stalked away.

"You and your bright ideas," Mac muttered to himself as he pitched manure into the wheelbarrow. "What were you thinking? Maybe you could throw straw around when you were kids and it was funny, but there was nothing funny about what almost happened in that haystack. What if you'd kissed her lips? How would you have felt when she got upset?

How do you know she'd have been upset?

Mac mused over that question for the next hour as he finished cleaning stalls. Actually, Jewel had seemed more upset that he hadn't kissed her lips. Could she have feelings for him that weren't merely friendly?

Don't even think about it, Macready. The woman's off-limits. She's your friend, and she needs your friendship. Concentrate on somebody else's needs for a change and forget what you want.

Mac knew why he was having all these lurid thoughts about Jewel. He probably would be having such thoughts about any woman he came in close contact with at this stage in his life. It didn't help that Jewel turned him on so hard and fast.

Get over it, Mac.

"I intend to," Mac muttered as he set the pitchfork back where it belonged and headed for the house. "Jewel is my friend. And that's the way it's going to stay."

AT THE END OF TWO WEEKS MAC was walking the mile to the canyon without the aid of a cane and doing it in seven minutes flat. Jewel had difficulty keeping up with him when he broke into a jog. His leg was getting better; hers never would. She could picture him moving away from her, going on with his life, leaving her behind. She was going to miss him. She was going to miss playing with him.

The scene in the barn hadn't been repeated. Nor had Mac teased her or taunted her or done any of the playful things he might have done when they were teenagers.

He had become a serious grown-up over the past two weeks. She hadn't realized how much she had needed him to play with her. To her surprise, she hadn't been intimidated or frightened by him in the barn. Not even when she had thought he might kiss her.

She had wanted that kiss, she realized, and been sorely disappointed when he kissed her forehead instead. Then she'd realized he had been carried away by their physical closeness, and when he'd realized it was her—his old friend, Jewel—he had backed off. He liked her, but not that way. They were just friends.

It should have been enough. But lately, Jewel was realizing she wanted more. She was going to have to control those feelings, or she would ruin everything. Mac would be leaving soon enough. She didn't want to drive him away by asking for things from him he wasn't willing to give.

"Hey," she called ahead to him. "How about taking a break at the bottom of the canyon."

"You got it." He dropped onto the warm, sandy ground with his back against the stone wall that bore the primitive Native American drawings and sifted the soil through his fingers. She sank down across from him, leaning back on her palms, her legs in front of her.

"You'll be running full out by this time next week," she said.

"I expect so."

"I won't be coming with you then."

"Why not?"

She sat up and rubbed at the sore muscles in her thigh. "I can't keep up with you, Mac." In more ways than one. He would be going places, while she stayed behind.

Mac dusted off his hands on his shorts, scooted around to her side and, as though it were the most natural thing in the world, began to massage her thigh. She hadn't let a man touch her like that since she had broken her engagement. Chill bumps rose on her skin at the feel of Mac's callused fingers on her flesh. It felt amazingly good. It dawned on her that she didn't feel the least bit afraid. But then, this was Mac. He would never hurt her.

The past two weeks of waiting for Mac to repeat his behavior in the barn had been wonderful and horrible. She loved being with Mac. And she dreaded it. Since the night he had come home early from Evelyn Latham's house, he had remained an avuncular friend. He had been a tremendous help planning activities for the children. He had made her laugh often. But with the exception of that brief, unfulfilled promise in the barn, there was nothing the least bit sexual in his behavior toward her.

She was unsure of what her feelings were for Mac, but there was no doubting her profound physical reaction to his touch. It was difficult not to look at him as a virile, attractive man, rather than merely as a friend. Even now, she couldn't keep her eyes off of him.

The Texas sun had turned him a warm bronze, but a white strip of flesh showed around the waist of his running shorts, confirming the hidden skin was lighter. She caught herself wondering what he would look like without the shorts.

"How does that feel?" he asked as he massaged her thigh. "Better?"

She nodded because she couldn't speak. *It feels wonderful.* She wanted his hands to move higher, between her legs. As though she had willed it, his fingertips moved upward on her thigh. She let him keep up the massage, because it felt good. Then stopped him because it felt too good.

"Wait." She gripped his wrist with her hand, afraid that he would read her mind and realize that the last thing she wanted him to do was stop.

"If you exercised more, maybe your limp wouldn't be so bad," he said.

She brushed his hand away from where it lingered on her flesh. "One leg is slightly shorter than the other, Mac. That isn't going to change with exercise."

"It might with surgery. They can do remarkable things these days. Have you thought about—"

"What's going on here, Mac?" she interrupted. "You never said a word to me in the past about my limp. You always told me to ignore it, to pretend it didn't exist, that it didn't keep me from being who I am. What's changed?"

Mac backed up against the wall again. His gaze was concentrated on the sand he began once more sifting through his fingers.

"Mac?" she persisted. "Answer me."

He looked up at her, his eyes searching her face. "How can you stand it—not being able to run?"

She shrugged. "I manage."

"I'd hate it if something like that happened to me."

"Something like that *has* happened to you."

He shook his head. "Uh-uh. I'm temporarily out of commission. I'm going to be as good as new."

Did he really believe that? Jewel wondered. Yes, he had made astonishing progress in two weeks, but even she could see the effort it had taken. One look at his leg—at the scar tissue on his leg—suggested there was never going to be as much muscle to work with as there had been in the past. "What if you can never run again like you used to, Mac? What if you can't get back to where you were?"

"I will."

"What if you can't?"

"I'll be playing again in the fall. Count on it."

"You're purposely avoiding my question. *What if you can't?*"

He rose, but it took obvious effort to do so without the cane. She said nothing while he accomplished the feat—a minor miracle considering the condition he'd been in two weeks ago.

"Let's go," he said gruffly, reaching down to help her to her feet.

She shoved his hand out of the way. "I'm not a cripple, either, Mac," she said. "I can manage on my own."

"Damn it, Jewel! What do you want from me?"

"Honesty," she said, rising and standing toe to toe with him, her eyes focused on his. "You never used to lie to me, Mac. Or to yourself."

"What is it you want to hear me say? I won't quit playing football! It's all I ever wanted to do."

"You wanted to be a paleontologist."

"That's what I said. But inside—" he thumped his bare chest with his fist "—all I ever dreamed about, all I ever wanted to do was run like the wind and catch footballs. It was just so impossible for so long, I never let myself hope for it too much. But I made it happen. And I'm not going to give it up!"

Jewel felt her heart skip a beat. She hadn't known. She hadn't realized. If what Mac said was true, then he was facing a much greater crisis than she had imagined.

"Avoiding reality isn't going to make it go away, Mac," she said gently. "You have to face your demons."

"Like you have?" Mac retorted.

Jewel's face blanched. She turned her back on him and headed up the trail toward the mouth of the canyon.

"Jewel, wait," Mac said as he hurried after her. He grabbed her arm to stop her. "If you're going to insist on honesty from me, how about a little from you?"

"What is it you want to know? You know everything," she said bitterly. "You're the only one who does!"

He gave her an incredulous look. "You never told anyone else? What about your fiancé?"

She shook her head violently.

"Why the hell not?"

"I couldn't tell Jerry. I just couldn't!"

In days gone by he would have put an arm around her to offer her comfort. But things had changed somehow in the two weeks since they had met again. His eyes offered emotional support, instead. "God, Jewel. That's a heavy burden to be carrying around all by yourself."

"I'm managing all right."

"What happened to Jerry What's-his-name? Why did you call off the wedding?"

"I couldn't… I wasn't able… I could never…"

She saw the dawning comprehension in his eyes. "I

don't want or need your pity!" She tried to run from him in awkward, hobbling strides, but he quickly caught up to her and pulled her into his arms.

"Don't run away," he said, his arms closing tightly around her. "It doesn't matter, Jewel. It'll get better with time."

She made a keening sound in her throat. "It's been six years. I can't forget what happened, Mac. I can't get it out of my head. Jerry was so patient, but when he tried to make love to me, I couldn't let him do it. I couldn't!" Her throat ached. A hot tear spilled onto her cheek and a sob broke free.

She grasped Mac tight around the waist and pressed her face against his bare chest, sobbing as she never had on the day she had been attacked or at any time since then. She had been too numb with shock to cry six years ago. And she had been too full of guilt when she broke up with Jerry to allow herself the release of tears.

"Shh. Shh," Mac crooned as he rocked her in his arms. "It's all right. It doesn't matter. Everything will be all right."

She felt his lips against her hair, soothing, comforting, and then his hands on either side of her face as he raised it to kiss her tear-wet eyelids. He kissed her nose and her cheeks and finally her mouth. His lips were firm, yet gentle, against her own. She yielded to the insistent pressure of his mouth, her lips soft and damp beneath his. He kissed her again, his lips brushing across hers and sending a surprising frisson of desire skittering down her spine. *Oh, Mac...*

She pressed her lips back against his and heard a

sharp intake of breath. She froze, then stepped back and stared up at him in confusion.

He opened his mouth to speak and shut it again, obviously upset and looking for a way to explain what had happened between them. She wondered if he had felt it, too, the wondrous stirring inside, the need to merge into one another. What if he did? Oh, God. It would ruin everything. She couldn't...and he would never... She took another step back from him.

"Wait, Jewel. Don't go," he said, reaching out a hand to her. "We have to talk about this."

"What is there to say?"

He took a step closer, and it took all her willpower not to run from him. She felt an equally driving need to press herself against him, which she resisted just as fiercely.

"I don't want what just happened to spoil things between us," he said, his voice anguished. "I could see you needed comfort, and I...I got a little carried away."

"All right, Mac. If that's the way you want it." She would ruin everything if she pressed for more. He obviously wanted things to stay the same between them. He wanted them to be friends. That was probably for the best. What if she tried loving him and failed, as she had with Jerry? She would lose everything. She couldn't bear that.

"What's wrong, Jewel?"

She mentally and physically squared her shoulders. "I shouldn't have fallen apart like that. I've spent a lot of time in counseling putting what happened six years ago behind me."

"Have you?"

"I'm as over it as I'm ever going to get," she conceded with a rueful twist of her mouth. "It doesn't matter, Mac, really. I have the kids at camp. I have friends. I have a full life."

"Without a man in it," he said flatly. "Or children."

She arched a brow. "Who says a woman needs a man in her life? And there are lots of children at Camp LittleHawk who need me."

He held up his hands in surrender. "You win. I'm not going to argue the point."

Jewel released a breath that became a sigh, glad the subject was closed. "We'd better get back to the house."

He looked as though he wanted to continue the discussion, but she knew that wouldn't help the situation. She decided levity was what was needed. "I hope you saved some energy, because I know for a fact Colt will be waiting for you when you get back to the house."

Mac groaned. "I forgot. He's going to throw me some passes."

"I can always send him away."

"I suppose I can catch a few passes and keep him happy."

"And keep who happy?"

Mac grinned. "So I'm looking forward to it. Think what that'll mean to you."

She gave him a quizzical look. If Mac was up to catching passes, it meant he was getting well. If he was getting well, it meant he would be leaving soon. She wanted to hear him say it. Maybe then she could stop fantasizing about him. "What will it mean to me?" she asked.

Twin dimples appeared in his cheeks. "You get the shower first."

Jewel laughed. It beat the heck out of crying.

CHAPTER FIVE

IF THERE WAS ONE THING COLT WHITELAW wanted
more than he wanted to fly jets someday, it was to have
Jennifer Wright look at him the way she looked at his
best friend, Huckleberry Duncan. Jenny didn't even care
that Huck had a stupid name. When Huck was around,
Jenny wouldn't have noticed if Colt dropped dead at her
feet. She only had eyes for Huck.

Which meant Colt got to spend a lot of time watching her when she wasn't looking. Jenny wasn't what
most guys would have called pretty. She was short and
skinny, her nose was too long and her teeth were slightly
crooked. But she had the prettiest eyes he'd ever seen.
Jenny's eyes were about the bluest blue eyes could get.

It wasn't just the color of them that he found attractive.
When he looked into Jenny's eyes he saw the pledge of
warmth, the promise of humor and depths of wisdom far
beyond what a fourteen-year-old girl ought to possess.

Jenny might be the same age as him and Huck, but
it seemed she had grown up faster—in more ways than
one. For a couple of years she'd been taller than Huck.
This past year Huck had caught up and passed her.
Colt had always been taller than Jenny. Not that she'd
noticed.

This past year something else had happened to Jenny.
She had started becoming a woman. Colt felt like wal-

loping Huck when Huck kidded her about the bumps she was sprouting up front, but when she bent over laughing and her shirt fell away, he had sneaked a peek at them. They were pure white and pink-tipped. He had turned away pretty quick because the whole time he was looking, he couldn't seem to breathe.

His body did strange things these days whenever she was around. His stomach turned upside down and his heart started to race and his body embarrassed him by doing other things that were still pretty new and felt amazingly good and grown-up. He had it bad for Jenny Wright. Not that he'd ever let her or Huck know about it. Because Huck felt about Jenny the way Jenny felt about Huck. It was true love both ways. When they got old enough, Colt figured they'd marry for sure.

He kept his feelings to himself. He liked Huck too much to give him up as a friend. And it would have killed him to stop seeing Jenny. Even if she was always going to be Huck's girl.

"Hey, Colt. I thought you were going to throw me some passes," Huck said, giving him a friendly chuck on the shoulder.

Colt watched as Jenny climbed up onto the top rail of the corral near the new counselors' cottages and shoved her long blond ponytail back over her shoulder. "You gonna be all right up there?" he asked.

She laughed. "I'm not one of your mom's campers, Colt. I'm healthy as a horse. I'll be fine."

Colt couldn't help it if he worried about her. He didn't want her to fall and get hurt. Not that she appreciated his concern. He turned the football in his hands, finding the laces and placing his hands where he knew they needed to be.

"Go long!" he shouted to Huck, who had already started to run over the uneven terrain, which was dotted with clumps of buffalo grass and an occasional prickly pear cactus.

Colt threw the ball with ease and watched it fall perfectly, gently into Huck's outstretched hands. Huck did a victory dance and spiked the ball.

"We are the greatest!" Huck shouted, holding his pointed fingers upward on either side of him in the referee's signal for a touchdown.

They made a pretty good team, Colt conceded. About the best in the state. Both of them would likely be offered athletic scholarships to college. Huck was so rich—his father was a U.S. senator from Texas—he didn't need a scholarship to pay for college. Colt's family could easily afford to send him to college, too, but he kept playing football because he had heard it might help him get into the Air Force Academy.

If Huck had wanted to go to the Academy, his dad, the senator, could write a letter and get him appointed. Colt didn't have that advantage. He would never presume on his friendship with Huck to ask for that kind of favor from Senator Duncan. So he had to find another way to make sure he got in.

Huck retrieved the ball and started walking back toward Colt and Jenny. Colt took advantage of the opportunity to have Jenny's full attention. "He's pretty good," he said, knowing Huck was the one thing Jenny was always willing to discuss.

"He is, isn't he," she said, a worried frown forming between her brows.

"Something wrong with that?" Colt asked, leaning his elbow casually on the top rail next to Jenny's thigh where her cutoffs ended and her flesh began. Casual. Right. His mouth was bone-dry.

"I don't want him to go away," she said.

He watched her face as she watched Huck. "You think football will take him away?"

"No. Huck loves football, but I think he'd be willing to attend a college somewhere close just so we could be together. Only..." Her head swiveled suddenly, and she looked him right in the eye. "You're going to take him away."

He swallowed hard, his hormones going into over-drive as she continued staring at him. He managed to say, "I am?"

She nodded solemnly. "He's going to want to follow wherever you go, Colt, and I know your plans don't include staying here in Texas. I don't want to get left behind."

Jenny was dirt-poor, and even if she could have gotten a scholarship to a college somewhere else—which, with her brains, she probably could—she had to stay at the Double D Ranch to help take care of her sick mother and four younger brothers.

"Huck would never leave you behind," Colt said seri-ously.

"He might not have any choice. Not if he went off to fly jets somewhere with you."

Colt felt angry, vulnerable and exposed. "How did you know about that? About me wanting to fly jets?"

She shrugged and slipped down off the top rail of the corral. "Huck and I don't have any secrets."

"He shouldn't have told you," Colt said, feeling his heart begin to thud at the closeness of her. He wanted her to step back so he could breathe, so he could think straight. Didn't she see what she was doing to him? "That was private information," he snapped. "It doesn't concern you."

Her fisted hands found her hips. "It does when Huck is thinking about going with you."

"I never asked him to come along," he retorted.

"Hey, you two! What're my two favorite people arguing about?" Huck said, grinning as he stepped between them and slipped an arm around each of their shoulders. Colt stood rigid beneath his arm. Huck still had the football in one hand, and Colt knocked it to the ground.

"Ask your girlfriend," he said, bending to retrieve the ball and pulling free of Huck's arm. "I've got to go find Mac Macready. I'm supposed to throw some passes to him this morning."

Huck left Jenny standing where she was and headed after Colt. "Macready's really here? I mean, I heard rumors in town he was, but I wasn't sure. You're really going to throw some balls to him?"

"I said I was, didn't I?" Colt stopped where he was and looked back over Huck's shoulder to where Jenny stood abandoned. Her expression said it all.

See what I mean? You lead. Huck follows.

It wasn't his fault. It had always been that way. If Jenny didn't like it, she didn't have to hang around. Colt turned back to Huck.

Huck's sandy hair had fallen over his brow and into

his eyes. His rarely combed hair, combined with his ski-slope nose and freckled cheeks and broad smile, gave him an affable appearance he deserved. Huck didn't make enemies. He wouldn't have hurt a fly. Colt was sure he hadn't meant to hurt Jenny's feelings. Huck just forgot to be thoughtful sometimes.

"What about Jenny?" Colt asked.

"Hey, Jenny," Huck called. "You want to hang around and meet Mac Macready?"

Jenny shook her head.

"See? She's not interested," Huck said. "But I am."

Colt sighed. "You want to stay?" he asked Huck.

"Does a cowboy wear spurs?" Huck replied with a lopsided grin.

They headed for the counselor's cottage where Mac was staying, leaving Jenny behind at the corral. Colt glanced over his shoulder at her. It looked for a moment like she might follow them. Then she turned to where her horse was tied to the corral next to Huck's, mounted up and loped the gelding in the direction of her family's ranch.

"You shouldn't ignore Jenny like that," Colt said, turning back to Huck.

Huck seemed to notice suddenly that she had left. "What did I do?" He shook his head. "Women. They're mysterious creatures, old buddy. Don't ever try to understand them. It's a waste of time."

"Why did you tell her about me wanting to fly?" Colt asked.

Huck looked chagrined. "We were talking about the future and...it just came up."

"Make sure it doesn't come up again," Colt said.

"That's my business, and I don't want the whole world knowing about it." Especially when he was afraid he wasn't going to be able to make his dream come true.

"Jenny isn't the whole world," Huck argued. "She's my girlfriend. I have to tell her things."

"Just don't tell her things about me," Colt insisted.

"That's hard to avoid when you're my best friend," Huck said. "Besides, if we're going to be jet pilots—"

"When did my plans become yours?" Colt asked.

Huck grinned and pulled an arm tight around Colt's neck in a wrestler's hold. "We're friends forever, pal. Where you go, I go. If you fly, I fly. Enough said?"

Colt wished it were that simple. He wished he could express his desire to be a jet fighter pilot and expect his parents to be happy about it. He had never said a word to them, because he knew they would hate the idea.

He might be one of eight adopted kids, but his mom and dad had made it pretty clear over the past couple of years that he was the one they expected to inherit Hawk's Pride. They already had his life planned for him. They expected him to come back home after college to manage the ranch.

He was grateful to have Zach and Rebecca Whitelaw for parents. He loved them enough to want to make them happy by fulfilling their expectations. It just wasn't what he wanted for himself. He wanted to fly.

So he made his plans surreptitiously, meanwhile letting his father teach him everything he would need to know to run the cattle and quarter horse end of the business. His father had told him his sister Jewel was taking over Camp LittleHawk, and that was fine with him. Although he kind of liked the ranching business, he wanted absolutely nothing to do with a camp for kids with cancer.

Not that he didn't have sympathy for the plight of all those sick kids. But he had learned his lesson early. He had befriended a couple of them when he was old enough to make friends. It was only later, when he asked why they hadn't returned the following summer, that he learned the awful truth. Sometimes sick people died.

It was a sobering lesson: *Illness could rob you of people you loved.* He had found a child's solution to the problem that had stood him in good stead. He stayed away from sick people. Which was why he hadn't been to Jenny's house much, even though Huck went there a lot. Her mom was dying slowly but surely of breast cancer.

Colt might have argued further with Huck, except he caught sight of Mac Macready coming around the corner of the house with his sister, Jewel.

"Hey!" Colt called. "Ready to catch a few passes?"

"You bet," Mac called back.

Colt looked for signs of reluctance or resignation on Mac's face. After all, Colt was just a kid. He didn't see anything but delight.

"Just give me a minute," Mac said with a smile and a wave. "Be right with you." He turned and said something in Jewel's ear, then headed in Colt's direction.

JEWEL HEARD THE KITCHEN SCREEN DOOR open and called, "Is that you, Mac?"

"Jewel?"

"Colt?" At the sound of her brother's frightened voice, Jewel hurried from her bedroom wearing an oversized plaid Western shirt, jeans and boots, her hair still wet from her shower. She met Colt halfway to the kitchen. "What's wrong?"

Her brother stood white-faced before her. "It's Mac. He fell."

Oh, dear God. "Should I call an ambulance?"

"I don't know," Colt said, his hands visibly trembling. "I thought maybe you ought to come and see for yourself first. It was awful, Jewel. One minute Mac was fine, and then Huck tackled him and...he didn't get up."

"Huck *tackled* him? What on earth were you boys thinking, Colt? You know Mac's recovering from surgery!"

"We thought it would be more fun—"

"Did he hit his head when he fell?"

"I don't think so. I think—"

Before Jewel could make the decision whether to call 911, Mac appeared at the kitchen door, one arm around Huck's shoulder, the other pressed against the thigh of his scarred leg.

Colt had been pale, but Mac's face was completely drained of blood. His teeth were gritted against the pain, and he was leaning heavily on Huck Duncan's shoulder and favoring his leg. It took her a second to realize it wasn't his poor, wounded and scarred left leg he was favoring, it was the other one. Now both legs were injured!

"What happened?" she asked as she crossed quickly to hold the screen door open for him. As soon as she moved, Colt seemed to wake from his shocked trance and took a place on Mac's other side. The two boys helped him keep his weight off both legs as they eased him through the kitchen and onto the sofa in the living room.

While the boys stood awkwardly at her side, Jewel dropped to her knees and eased Mac's foot up onto a rawhide stool that Grandpa Garth had given her one Christmas, a relic of bygone days at his ranch, Hawk's Way. Then she started untying the laces of Mac's athletic shoe.

"I can do that," he said, trying to brush her hands away.

"Sure you can, but let me," she insisted. She eased off the shoe and the sock beneath it and immediately saw the problem. His ankle was swelling. "Can you move it?" she asked.

Slowly, hissing in a breath, he rotated the ankle. "Doesn't feel broken," he said. "I've had enough sprains to recognize one when I see it. Damn. This is all I needed."

"I'm sorry, Mr. Macready," Huck said in an anguished voice. "I didn't mean to hurt you."

Mac looked up at the boy and said, "Call me Mac. And it wasn't your fault, Huck. Your tackle wasn't what caused the problem. I just didn't see that gopher hole soon enough."

Jewel watched him smile at the boy, pretending it was no big deal, when she knew very well it was. This was a setback, no doubt about it.

"But your leg—" Huck protested, his eyes skipping from the awful scars on Mac's left leg to the swelling on his right ankle. "How're you gonna walk now?"

"One step at a time," Mac quipped with an easy grin.

"Fortunately, I brought a cane with me. That should help matters some."

Jewel turned to Colt and said, "Wrap some ice in a towel and bring it here. You go help him, Huck."

When they were both gone, she gently moved the ankle. "Are you sure it isn't broken?"

He sighed. It was a sound of disgust. "It's a sprain, Jewel. Not even a bad one."

"I should have warned you about gopher holes," she said.

"I didn't step in a gopher hole," he said quietly, looking at the hands he held fisted against his thighs.

"Then what—" She saw the truth in the wary look he gave her. His leg—his *right* leg—must not have supported him. She reached out a hand, and he clutched it with one of his.

She didn't offer him words of comfort. She could see from the grim look on his face that words wouldn't change what had happened. She didn't point out the obvious—that his football career was over. He had to see that for himself.

But if she had thought this accident would make Mac quit, he quickly disabused her of the notion.

"This'll slow down my rehabilitation some," he said. "Will you mind if I hang around a little longer? I know camp's starting in a day or so—"

She rose to her feet, her hand coming free of his. "Of course you can stay!" she said, her voice unnaturally sharp. She didn't want him to go away. She liked having him here. But she couldn't believe he was ignoring the implications of this injury. How long was he going to go on batting his head against the wall? Couldn't he see the truth? Didn't he understand what this accident meant?

"Mac—"

He cut her off with a shake of his head. "Don't say it. Don't even suggest it."

"Suggest what?"

"This doesn't change my plans."

"But—"

His face turned hard, jaw jutting, shoulders braced in determination. She had seen that look before, but she had been too young and naive to recognize it for what it was.

"Be my friend, Jewel," he said. "Don't tell me why I can't do what I want to do. Just help me to do it."

She stared at him as though she had never seen him before. She knew now why Peter Macready had survived a form of cancer that killed most kids. Why he had become the best rookie receiver in the NFL, despite the fact he had never been the fastest athlete on the field. Mac didn't give up. Mac didn't see obstacles. He saw his goal and headed for it without worrying about whether it could be reached. And so he invariably reached it.

Jewel wished she had half his confidence. She might be a married woman now with a baby in her arms.

Maybe it wasn't too late for her. Maybe she could learn from him how it was done. Maybe she could take advantage of Mac's presence to give her the impetus to change her life. If Mac could recover from a shattered leg, why couldn't she recover from a shattered life?

The boys returned with two dish towels loaded with ice and fell all over each other arranging the cold compresses around Mac's ankle. Jewel saw Mac wince when their overenthusiasm rocked his ankle, but instead of snapping at them, he launched into a story about how he had played a whole football game with a taped-up sprained ankle, thanks to an injection of painkiller.

The teenage boys dropped to his feet in awe and admiration. Jewel started to leave, but Mac reached up and caught her hand. "Join us," he said.

"I have work—"

"Just for a few minutes."

She figured maybe he didn't want to be stuck alone with the boys. She would stay with him long enough to let them hear a story or two before shooing them away. She settled beside Mac on the worn leather couch—another donation from her grandfather's house at Hawk's Way. Mac's arm slid around her as naturally as if he did it every day.

She resisted the urge to lay her head on his shoulder. Putting his arm around her had been a friendly gesture, nothing more. But she was aware of the way his hand cupped her shoulder, massaging it as he regaled the three of them with stories of life in the pro football arena.

As she sat listening to him, an insidious idea took root.

What if she came to Mac tonight and explained her problem and asked him to help her out?

She trusted Mac not to hurt her. She trusted him to go slow, to be patient. He didn't love her, and she didn't love him, so there wouldn't be that particular pitfall complicating matters. It would be just one friend helping out another.

She could even explain to him how she had gotten the idea. That she had seen his determination to play football again and been inspired to try to solve a problem that she had thought would never be resolved.

All she wanted him to do was teach her how to arouse a man and satisfy him...and be satisfied by him.

She tried to imagine how Mac might react to such a suggestion. He was obviously an experienced man of the world. Only... What if he wasn't attracted to her that way?

Her mind flashed back to the scene in the canyon earlier that afternoon, when she had felt Mac's arousal. But he had apologized for that. Maybe when push came to shove, he wouldn't want to get involved with her.

Jewel didn't hear much of what Mac said to Colt and Huck. She wasn't even aware when he sent them away. She was lost deep in her own thoughts. And fears.

She wished the idea hadn't come to her so early in the day. Now she would be stuck thinking about it until dark, worrying it like a dog worried a bone.

All she had to do was cross the hall tonight and knock on Mac's door and... She didn't let her imagination take her any farther than that. Oh, how she wished night were here already! It was so much easier to act on impulse than to do something like this with cold calculation.

Of course, she was far from cold when she thought about Mac. Her whole body felt warm at the thought of having him touch her, having him kiss and caress her. She just wanted to get through the entire sexual act once without cringing or falling apart. That's all she wanted Mac to do for her. Just get her through the moments of panic before he did it. Get in and get out, like a quick lube job on the truck.

The absurdity of that comparison made her chuckle.

"Are you going to let me in on the joke?" Mac said.

"Maybe." If she didn't lose her nerve before night-fall.

CHAPTER SIX

MAC WAS LYING IN BED WONDERING what Jewel would do if he crossed the hall, knocked on her door and told her he wanted to make love to her. She would probably think he had lost his mind. He had to resist the urge to pursue her. Jewel didn't need a fumbling, first-time lover. He, of all people, knew how much she needed a kind, considerate, *knowledgeable* bed partner. Which, of course, he wasn't.

She needed a slow hand, an easy touch—wasn't that what the song said? He had a lot of pent-up passion, a lot of celibate years to make up for. He was afraid the first time for him was going to be fast and hard. Which might be fine for him. But not for her.

Mac wished he didn't have such vivid memories of what had happened to Jewel that day in July six years ago. Any man who had seen her after Harvey Barnes had attacked her... He made himself think the word. After Harvey Barnes had *raped* her...

He had never wanted to kill a man before or since. He had been there to come to her rescue because he had seen Harvey drinking too much and worried about her, like a brother might worry about his sister. Jewel would have pounded him flat if she'd known he had followed her and Harvey when they slipped off into the trees down by the river.

He had kept his distance, even considered turning around and heading back to the noise of the carnival rides at the picnic, which seemed a world away from the soothing rustle of leaves down by the river. He had heard her laugh and then…silence.

He figured Harvey must be kissing her. He was standing at the edge of the river skipping stones, thinking he'd been an idiot to follow her, when he heard her cry out. Even then, he hadn't been sure at first whether it was a cry of passion.

The second cry had chilled his blood and started him running toward the sound. He could remember the feeling of terror as he searched frantically for her amid the thick laurel bushes and the tangle of wild ivy at the river's edge, calling her name and getting no answer.

There were no more cries. He saw why when he finally found them. Harvey had his hand pressed tight over Jewel's mouth, and she was struggling vainly beneath him. He saw something white on the ground nearby and realized it was her underpants.

He might have killed Harvey, if Jewel hadn't stopped him. He hadn't even been aware of his hands clenched in the flesh at Harvey's throat. It was only Jewel's anguished voice in his ear, pleading with him, that made him stop before he strangled the life out of the boy.

Harvey was nearly unconscious by the time Mac finally let go and turned to Jewel. Seeing her torn, grass-stained dress and the trickle of blood coming from her lip enraged him all over again. Jewel whimpered with fear—of him, he realized suddenly—and the fight went out of him.

He started toward her to hold her, to comfort her, but

she clutched her arms tight around herself, turned her back to him and cried, "Don't touch me! Don't look at me!"

His heart was thudding loudly in his chest. "Jewel," he said. "You need to go to the hospital. Let me find your parents—"

She whirled on him and rasped, "No! Please don't tell anybody."

"But you're hurt!"

"My father will kill him," she whispered.

He could understand that. He had almost killed Harvey Barnes himself. Then she gave the reason that persuaded him to keep his silence.

"Everyone will know," she said, her brown eyes stark. "I couldn't bear it, Mac. Please. Help me."

"We'll have to say something to explain that cut on your lip," he said tersely. "And the grass stains on your dress."

"My beautiful dress." The tears welled in her eyes as she pulled the skirt around to look at the grass stains on the back of it.

He realized it wasn't the dress she was crying for, but the other beautiful thing she had lost. Her innocence.

"We'll tell your father Harvey attacked you—"

"No. Please!"

He reached out to take her shoulders, and she shrank from him. His hands dropped to his sides. He realized they were trembling and curled them into tight fists. "We'll tell them Harvey attacked you, but you fought him off," he said in an urgent voice. "Unless you tell that much of the tale, they're liable to believe the worst."

He had never seen—never hoped to see again—a look as desolate as the one she gave him.

"All right," she said. "But tell them you came in time. Tell them...nothing happened."

"What if...what if you're pregnant?" he asked.

"I don't think...I don't think..."

He realized she was in too much shock to even contemplate the possibility.

She shook her head, looking dazed and confused. "I don't think..."

He thought concealing the truth was a bad idea. She needed medical attention. She needed the comfort her mother and father could give her. "Jewel, let me tell your parents," he pleaded quietly.

She shook her head and began to shiver.

"Give me your hand, Jewel," he said, afraid to put his arms around her, afraid she might scream or faint or something equally terrifying.

She kept her arms wrapped around herself and started walking in the opposite direction from the revelers at the picnic. "Take me home, Mac," she said. "Please, just take me home."

He snatched up her underpants, stuffed them in his Levi's pocket and followed her to his truck. But it was too much to hope they would escape unnoticed. Not with Jewel's seven brothers and sisters at the picnic.

It was Rolleen who caught them before they could escape. She insisted Mac find her parents, and he'd had no choice except to go hunting for Zach and Rebecca. He had found Zach first.

The older man's eyes had turned flinty as he listened

to Mac's abbreviated—and edited—version of what had happened.

The dangerous, animal sound that erupted from Zach's throat when he saw Jewel's torn dress and her bruised face and swollen lip made Mac's neck hairs stand upright. He realized suddenly that Jewel had known her father better than he had. Zach became a lethal predator. Only the lack of a quarry contained his killing rage.

Jewel's family surrounded her protectively, unconsciously shutting him out. He was forced to stand aside as they led her away. It wasn't until he got back to his private room in the cottage he shared with a half-dozen boys aged eight to twelve and stripped off his jeans, that he realized he still had Jewel's underwear in his pocket.

The garment was white cotton, with a delicate lace trim. It was stained with blood.

A painful lump rose in his throat, and his eyes burned with tears he was too grown up to shed. He fought the sobs that bunched like a fist in his chest, afraid one of the campers would return and hear him through the wall that separated his room from theirs. He pressed his mouth against a pillow in the bedroom and held it there until the ache eased, and he thought the danger was over.

In the shower later, where no one could see or hear, he shed tears of frustration and rage and despair. He had known, even then, that Harvey Barnes had stolen something precious from him that day, as well.

Mac learned later that Zach had found Harvey Barnes and horsewhipped him within an inch of his life. And

Zach hadn't even known the full extent of Harvey's crime against his daughter. It seemed Jewel had been right not to tell her father the truth. Zach would have killed the boy for sure. Harvey's parents had sent him away, and he hadn't been seen since.

Things weren't the same between him and Jewel after that. She smiled and pretended everything was all right in front of him and her family. But the smile on her lips never reached her eyes.

The end of the summer came too soon, before they had reconciled their friendship. He went to her the night before he left, seeking somehow to mend the breach between them, to say goodbye for the summer and to ask if she was all right.

"Harvey Barnes is gone," she said. "And tomorrow you will be, too. Then I can forget about what happened."

"I'll be back next year," he reminded her.

She had been looking at her knotted hands when she said, "I hope you won't come, Mac."

Something bunched up tight inside of him. "Not come? I come every summer, Jewel."

"Don't come back. As a favor to me, Mac. Please don't come back."

"But why? You're my best friend, Jewel. I—"

"You know," she said in a brittle voice. She raised her eyes and looked at him and let him see her pain. "You know the truth. It's in your eyes every time you look at me."

He felt like crying again and forced himself to swallow back the tickle in his throat. "Jewel—"

"I want to forget, Mac," she said. "I need to forget. Please, please don't come back."

A lump of grief caught in his throat and made it impossible to say more. When he left that summer, a part of himself—the lighthearted, teasing friend—had stayed behind.

Mac had honored Jewel's wishes and stayed away for six long years. The really sad thing was, it had all been for nothing. She wasn't over what had happened. The past had not been forgotten.

He had often wondered if he'd done the wrong thing. Should he have told her parents the truth, anyway? Should he have come back the following summer? Should he have tried harder to get in touch with her over the years, to talk to her about what had happened?

A soft knock on the door forced Mac from his reverie. Before he could reply, the door opened, and Jewel stood silhouetted in the light from the hall. She was wearing a sleeveless white nightgown with a square-cut neck. The gown only covered her to mid-thigh. He could see the shape of her through the thin garment, the slender legs and slim waist and bountiful bosom.

He sat up, dragging the sheets around him to cover his nakedness and to conceal the sudden arousal caused by the enticing sight of her in his bedroom doorway. "Jewel? Is something wrong?"

She slipped inside and closed the door, so that momentarily he lost sight of her as his eyes adjusted to the dark. He heard the rustle of sheets and suddenly felt her body next to his beneath the covers.

"Jewel? What's going on?" He hoped his voice didn't sound as shocked as he felt. He didn't know what she thought she was doing, but he intended to find out before things went much farther.

He had expected an answer. He hadn't counted on her laying her palm on his bare chest. She followed that with a scattering of kisses across his chest that led her to the sensitive flesh beneath his ear. His body was trembling with desire when she finally paused to speak.

"Nothing's wrong, Mac," she murmured in his ear. "I came because..." She nibbled on his earlobe, and he groaned at the exquisite pleasure of it. "I need your help," she finished.

He put an arm around her shoulder, realized suddenly he was naked and clutched at the sheet again. "Anything, Jewel. You know I'd do anything for you. But—"

"I was hoping you'd say that. Because what I need you to do... It won't be easy."

He waited, his breath caught in his chest, for what she had to say. "Anything, Jewel," he repeated, his heart thundering so loud he figured she could probably hear it.

She pressed her breasts against his chest and said, "I want you to make love to me."

His heart pounded, and his shaft pulsed. In another moment, things would be out of hand. His eyes had adapted to the dark, and with the moonlight from the window he at last could see the feelings etched on her face. Not desire, but fear and vulnerability.

"I want to feel like a woman," she said in a halting voice. "I want to stop being afraid."

He couldn't keep the dismay from his voice. "Aw, Jewel."

A cry of despair issued from her throat, and she made a frantic lurch toward the edge of the bed and escape.

He grabbed for her, knowing she had misinterpreted his words. It wasn't that he didn't want her. He wanted her something fierce. He just wasn't the experienced bed partner she thought he was. He caught her by the wrist and pulled her back into his arms and held her tight, biting back a groan at the exquisite feel of her breasts crushed against his chest with only the sheer cloth between them.

"It's all right, Mac," she said in a brittle voice. "I made a mistake. Let me go, and we'll forget this ever happened."

She held herself stiff and unyielding in his arms. "Jewel—"

"Don't try to make me feel better. I deserve to feel like an idiot, throwing myself at you like this. I just thought…with all your experience…"

This time he did groan.

She tried to pull away, and he said, "You don't understand."

"I understand you don't find me attractive. I'm sorry for forcing myself on you like this."

"No!" *Tell her the truth, Macready. She's your friend. She'll understand.*

But the words stuck in his throat. If he hadn't cared for her, if he didn't want her so badly, if things hadn't changed between them like they had, maybe he could have confessed the truth.

"It's not that I'm not attracted to you," he said.

He saw the look on her face and realized she didn't believe him. How could she not see the truth when it was throbbing like mad beneath the thin sheet that separated them?

"Then why won't you make love to me?" she challenged.

"Because..."

He couldn't tell her the truth, and he saw she believed the worst—that she had imposed herself where she wasn't wanted, and he was rejecting her as kindly as he could.

"Aw, Jewel," he said again. His voice was tender, as gentle as he wished he could be with her.

She made a keening sound in her throat, a mournful sound that made him ache somewhere deep inside.

He realized he had no choice. He had to try to make love to her. He couldn't botch things much worse than he already had. He leaned over and pressed his mouth against hers, restraining the rush of passion he felt at the touch of her soft, damp lips.

She moaned and arched her body against his. Her mouth clung to his, and he felt her need and her desire.

Maybe it's going to be all right. Maybe I can get us both through this.

He tried to hold back, so he wouldn't scare her. Yet when his tongue slipped into her mouth it found an eager welcome. He thrust deep, mimicking the sex act, and she riposted with her tongue in his mouth.

He thought the top of his head was going to come off. He had never felt so out of control. His hands slid down her arms, feeling the goose bumps and her shiver of anticipation. She was as excited as he was. She wanted him, too.

His lips started down her slender throat, across the silky flesh that led to her breastbone and downward, giving her plenty of warning where he was headed. She could have stopped him anytime she wanted. He wasn't an animal. He had his desire on a firm leash.

She cried out when his mouth latched onto her nipple, and he sucked hard through the cotton. Mac knew it wasn't a cry of fear, because her hands grasped his hair and held him there.

Her moan of pleasure urged him on. He released her breast momentarily and kissed her mouth again, an accolade for her trust in him. "I won't hurt you, Jewel. I would never hurt you," he murmured against her lips.

"I know, Mac. I know," she replied in gasping breaths.

Their tongues dueled dangerously, inciting them both to greater passion. He clasped her shoulders, making himself go slow, telling himself *Go Slow.* He slid his hand across the damp cotton that covered her breasts all the way down to her belly, wishing the damned nightgown wasn't between his palm and her flesh, but feeling the heat of her even through the thin shift.

He grabbed the bottom edge of it, anxious to get it out of his way, and brushed her thigh with his fingertips. Just her thigh. She tensed slightly but didn't pull away. He managed not to heave a sigh of relief.

It's going to be all right. I'll be able to do this for her.

But he was overeager and excited, worried about whether he would be able to satisfy her, and a moment later his hand accidentally brushed against the soft mound between her legs.

She jerked away from him with a cry of alarm. But he still had hold of the nightgown, and the fragile material tore. He let go, but it was too late. She was already rolled up in a tight, fetal ball with her back to him.

"Jewel—"

"I can't!" she cried. "I can't."

He laid a hand on her shoulder, and she cringed away.

"Please don't touch me," she whispered.

He lay staring at her in shock. He should have known better than to try this. He should have known he didn't have the experience to do it right. "What can I do?"

She turned to him, her eyes awash in despair. "I'm sorry, Mac."

"Aw, Jewel."

"I thought it would be all right. Because it was you," she sobbed. "Because you're my friend."

He would have to confess the truth. He owed her that much. "It isn't you, Jewel, it's me," he said flatly.

"You're just saying that to make me feel better," she said.

"No. I'm not." He forced himself to continue as she stared up at him. "You mustn't be discouraged by what happened here tonight. I'm sure another man, a more experienced man, could have managed things better. I lost control and frightened you."

"But I trust you," she protested.

"All the more reason I should have kept my hands off of you." He huffed out a breath of air and shoved a hand through his hair in agitation.

"When you find a man you love," he said earnestly, "a man who loves you enough to take his time and do things right, I'm sure you'll be able to get past what happened to you."

She sat up slowly, her chin sunk to her chest, her hands knotted in front of her knees, which were clutched to her chest. She swallowed hard. "What you're saying is that you're not that man."

"No. I'm not."

"I see."

Evidently not. Evidently he hadn't hinted broadly enough at his inexperience for her to realize the truth.

Now it was too late. In the heat of the moment he might have confessed his virginity. But as his passion cooled, he felt appalled at how close he had come to exposing himself to her laughter.

And she would laugh. It would be gentle laughter, kind laughter, an effervescent bubble of disbelief. But he couldn't bear to hear it.

"If you won't do this for me, I don't know where to turn," she said at last.

"There are lots of men out there who'd be attracted to you, if you'd let them see your charms."

She shot him a twisted smile. "You mean my Enormous Endowments?"

"I wouldn't call them that," he protested with a startled laugh.

"What would you call them?" She thrust her chest out, and his mouth went dry.

He hesitated a heartbeat and said, "Astonishing Assets?"

She laughed, the bubbly, effervescent sound he remembered from long ago. "Oh, God, now I've got you doing it!" She grabbed a pillow and hugged it tight against her ribs, effectively hiding the Generous Giants.

"Look, Jewel, for a start, you're going to have to stop doing that."

"Doing what?"

"Hiding behind clothes, behind your hair, behind pillows." He tugged on the pillow, and she reluctantly gave it up. He was immediately sorry, because it was hard to keep his eyes off her. He could see her brownish-pink nipples beneath the damp cloth.

"It was my breasts that got me into trouble in the first place," she said. "Can you blame me for wanting to hide them?"

"Maybe not," he conceded. "But hiding your light behind a bushel is not the way to find your Prince Charming. You're going to have to want to attract a man to find the right one."

"I'm afraid, Mac."

He saw that in her shadowed eyes. In her drawn features. From the instinctive way she circled her arms protectively around herself. But if he couldn't help her out by making love to her, the least he could do was help her find another man to do it.

"You can start small—no pun intended—and do this in baby steps. You've got to crawl before you can walk."

"Meaning?"

"Go back to basics, to flirting, to wanting to attract a man's attention."

"I can't do that."

"Can't? Or won't?"

"Won't."

"You can start with me," he coaxed. "I'll be your lab rat."

She grinned wryly. "Hold that thought. Man as rat. I like it."

He gave her a crooked smile. "The idea is for you to start seeing men as *men*—get it?"

"All right," she conceded with a sigh. "I'll give it a try. Where do I start?"

"Wear some clothes that fit better. Something that shows off—"

"My Plentiful Peaches?"

He laughed. "Actually, yeah, that would do it."

She slid her legs over the edge of the bed and looked back over her shoulder at him. "I'm not so sure about this, Mac."

"Believe me, it'll work," he said, wrapping the sheet around his waist as he rose to follow her to the door. "You'll have the guys around here on their knees begging to take you out."

She arched a skeptical brow. "You really think so?"

"I guarantee it."

She paused at the door and put a hand on his naked chest. His heart thudded. His loins throbbed. She searched his face, and he hoped his lurid thoughts weren't apparent.

"What if I attract the wrong kind of attention?" she asked. "What if someone...some man..."

"Start here on the ranch. I'll keep an eye out for you. If any of the cowhands or counselors makes a wrong move, I'll be there. You can use me as your guinea pig."

"Hmm. Man as pig. I like that even better."

He laughed and tousled her hair. "Cut it out."

"You'll help me through this, won't you?" she asked, her heart in her eyes.

"If you want to try out your seductive wiles on someone safe, I'm your man," he volunteered. He would keep his libido in check if it killed him.

"You don't know how much that means to me, Mac. You really think this will work?"

"It's sure as hell worth a try."

"Thanks, Mac. Still friends?"

He wrapped his hand around her nape—to keep her at arm's distance—and said, "You bet. And don't worry. Anybody makes the wrong kind of move, I'll cut him off at the pass."

"My hero," she said, an impish grin forming on her lips.

"You bet." He knew he should shove her out the door and put temptation from his path, but he couldn't resist one last kiss.

He leaned down to her, keeping their bodies separated and pressed his mouth against hers with all the gentleness he could muster.

Her lips were pliant under his, soft and supple and incredibly sweet.

"Good night, Jewel. Go to bed and get some sleep."

"Good night, Mac. You, too."

He must have nodded, or grunted an assent, because she left the room and closed the door behind her. But he knew damned well he wasn't going to sleep.

Mac replayed the events of the evening in his head. If only he'd had more experience. If only his hand hadn't brushed against her and scared her. If only he'd known what to do to reassure her.

What was done was done. He'd had his chance and he'd blown it. The least he could do was help her find another guy to help her out, while keeping his own hormones in check. The last thing he wanted to do was scare her again. Which meant he'd better make sure she never found out her Beautiful Breasts turned him hard as a rock.

If she was going to start wearing clothes that fit, he'd better go shopping for some baggy jeans.

CHAPTER SEVEN

JEWEL DECIDED THE BEST WAY TO AVOID hiding behind her hair was to remove that option. She drove to the Stonecreek Ranch at the crack of dawn to have her sister Cherry whack it off. She had known Cherry would understand what she wanted to do and help her because, of all her adopted brothers and sisters, Cherry understood best what it meant to feel different.

Cherry was the last Whitelaw Brat to be adopted and had come to the family when she was fourteen, an extremely tall, redheaded, blue-eyed Irish girl—and an incorrigible juvenile delinquent. Jewel had been closest to her in age, only a year older. After a rocky start, during which Cherry did her best to break every rule—and offend every member—in the Whitelaw household, they had ended up becoming best friends.

The night Cherry was accused of spiking the punch bowl at the senior prom and expelled from high school, she had eloped with Billy Stonecreek to avoiding facing Zach and Rebecca. Cherry had become an instant mom to Billy's twin six-year-old daughters Raejean and Annie. Three years later, Cherry was six months pregnant, and as far as Jewel could tell, happy as a cat in a dairy.

Cherry had made the Stonecreek Ranch a comfortable place to live, substituting leather and wood furniture for the silks and satins bought by Billy's first wife, Laura, who had died in a car accident. Jewel was surprised, when she showed up at Cherry's back screen door unannounced, to catch her sister and brother-in-law kissing in the kitchen.

It wasn't the kiss that shocked her. It was the passion behind it. Billy's hands avidly cupped Cherry's breasts, and her hands clutched his buttocks. They were pressed together like flies on flypaper.

She cleared her throat noisily. "Excuse me."

Jewel imagined a ripping sound as they sprang apart.

"Jewel!" Cherry exclaimed, her voice revealing both relief and irritation. "What are you doing here?"

"Obviously interrupting something important," Jewel said with a teasing grin.

Her sister flushed a delightful pink, and Billy stuck his hands in his front pockets, a move that didn't do as much as he probably hoped to hide his state of arousal.

Jewel felt a little guilty for intruding, and if it hadn't been an emergency she might have turned and left. But she was afraid she would lose her nerve if she waited. She stepped into the kitchen, careful not to let the screen door slam behind her and wake the twins. "I need my hair cut. Could you do it for me?"

"Now?" Cherry asked, her brows rising practically to her hairline.

"Yes, now."

Jewel was wearing a sleeveless white knit shell and tight-fitting jeans that had been shut away in a drawer for six years. She watched as Cherry perused her attire and exchanged a look with Billy, whose eyes had opened wide with astonishment once she stepped inside. Jewel resisted the urge to cross her arms over her chest. She was going to have to get used to men looking at her.

"Hi, Billy," she said.

"Hi, Jewel." It came out as a croak. He cleared his throat and tried again. "You look…" He searched for a word and came up with, "Nice. What's the occasion?"

He was clearly curious, as she suspected her family would be, about why she was suddenly exposing assets she had kept hidden for the past six years. "No occasion," she said. "I just want to get my hair cut. Can you help me out?" she asked Cherry.

"Sure," Cherry said. She turned to Billy. "You don't mind if we postpone breakfast for half an hour, do you?"

"I've got some chores I can do in the barn. Give a holler when you want me." Billy grabbed his Stetson from the antler rack on the wall and headed out the screen door. Cherry caught it before it could slam.

"All right," Cherry said once she had scissors in hand and Jewel was settled in a kitchen chair with a towel around her shoulders. "Spill the jelly beans. What's going on?"

"Nothing much."

"For the first time in six years I can see you have breasts," Cherry retorted tartly. "Believe me, anyone seeing your breasts for the first time wouldn't say they're 'nothing much.'"

Jewel laughed. That was why she liked Cherry so much. She didn't pull her punches. Cherry said exactly what she was thinking, even if it wasn't necessarily what you wanted to hear.

"I had a talk with Mac Macready last night," Jewel said. "He convinced me it's time to come out of my shell."

"I see," Cherry said.

Jewel realized Cherry was *seeing* a great deal more than she wished or intended. "It isn't like that."

"Like what?"

"It's not Mac I'm trying to attract."

"It isn't?"

"No. Not that I don't love him dearly. I do. As a friend."

"A *friend*," Cherry repeated.

Jewel winced as nine-inch-long hanks of brown hair began falling to the kitchen floor. There was no turning back now. "A friend," she confirmed.

"And this *friend* suggested you'd look better in skin-tight jeans and short hair?"

Jewel laughed. "Not exactly. He simply said I should dress to attract a man."

"What you're wearing ought to do it," Cherry confirmed.

"You think so? It's not too...enticing?"

"You're dressed fine, Jewel. Half the young women in this country are probably wearing similar outfits this morning. You can't help it if you have big breasts."

Jewel noticed Cherry said it without the capital B's. Jewel automatically thought Big Breasts, something she was going to have to get over if she was going to have any hope of surviving this metamorphosis.

"There," Cherry said, surveying her handiwork. "A few turns with my curling iron, and I think you'll be pleased with the result."

When Cherry was done, she held a mirror in front of Jewel's face. "Take a look."

Her hair swept along her chin in a shiny bob, with soft bangs across her brow. Jewel sighed. "Oh, Cherry, you're a marvel. I look—"

"Cute," Cherry said with an irreverent laugh. "No getting around it. You're darned cute."

"I'm twenty-two. That's too old for cute. Besides, my features are too ordinary to be—"

"Cute," Cherry persisted with a grin. "Let me call Billy, and he can confirm it." She called out the door for Billy, who bounded up the back steps and into the kitchen.

He paused in the acting of pulling off his leather work gloves as he looked Jewel up and down. "Who would've believed a haircut could make such a difference?"

"Isn't she cute?" Cherry asked.

"Sexy," Billy countered. When his wife nudged him in the ribs, he amended, "Sexy and cute."

Jewel's brow furrowed. She had never been pretty, and "cute" sounded like something you said about a one-year-old with a lollipop. One glance down explained the "sexy." Jewel felt the heat start in her throat and work its way up her neck to sit like red flags on her cheeks. "Good God," she said. "Have you got an extra shirt I can borrow?" she asked Billy.

"What for?" Billy said.

"She wants to go back into hiding," Cherry said scornfully. "Well, we're not going to help you do it. You turn right around and head out that door with your head held high. You've got nothing to be ashamed of. What happened to you six years ago wasn't your fault.

It's about time you shoved Harvey Barnes out of your life and started enjoying it again."

"That's pretty much what Mac said."

"Good for Mac," Cherry said. "Am I going to have to go with you to make sure you don't cover yourself up like a nun?"

"No," Jewel conceded with a chagrined look. "I'll be all right."

"Stand up straight and enjoy the looks you get. Because you darn sure deserve them!"

"Thanks, Cherry," Jewel said, giving her sister a quick hug. "Thanks for everything."

Her brother-in-law gave her a quick hug and teased, "Definitely sexy. Go get 'em, Jewel."

Cherry and Billy stood arm in arm on the back porch waving as she drove away. They were already kissing again as the dust rose behind her pickup.

It wasn't easy resisting the urge to slip a long-sleeved shirt over the figure-exposing knit shell the instant she returned home. It would have been easier if Mac had been there waiting, and she could have gotten that first meeting over with.

But he wasn't there.

She had left a note hanging on Mac's door when she snuck out to get her hair cut. The note she found stuck on her door when she got back said that he had taped up his ankle and gone walking despite the sprain. She left a third note for Mac saying that she was eating breakfast with her family and inviting him to join them, then left the cottage before she lost her courage.

Jewel figured it couldn't hurt to have a buffer between her and Mac when he saw her for the first time in her new guise. Not that she thought he wouldn't approve. After all, it had been his idea for her to feature her assets more prominently. But after last night...

In the bright light of day, Jewel found it hard to believe she had crossed the hall to Mac's bedroom last night. Or that she had actually asked him to make love to her. Or that he had refused.

She wished he had done it before kissing her. Good Lord. Who would have thought a kiss from Mac Macready could turn her to mush like that? His lips had been soft and slightly damp, and he had tasted...like Mac. Familiar and good.

If that was all she had felt, she would never have gotten frightened the way she had. But there had also been something dark and dangerous about his kisses. A threat of leashed passion that once freed might... When Mac had accidentally touched her, that awful sense of powerlessness had returned, and the bad memories had all come crashing down on her.

She couldn't blame Mac for backing away like he had. What man wouldn't cut his losses? Mac had gently but firmly told her to find somebody else to make love to her. He wasn't available for the job.

She didn't want somebody else, she had realized. She wanted Mac. Which was why she was dressed like this. Cherry had seen right through her feeble protests. The only man she wanted to attract was Mac Macready. She would never have found the courage to shed her protective skin of clothing if she hadn't conceded this was one sure way of getting Mac's attention.

He had certainly seemed interested last night. That is, before she had gotten scared and scared him off.

Before he had accidentally touched her below the waist, everything had been wonderful. Her knee-jerk reaction had come before her rational mind could tell her it was Mac.

That had been followed by the disturbing thought that maybe even Mac couldn't make it all right. That maybe she would forever fear a man's touch in bed. She had kept herself curled up in a ball to avoid testing the truth. Because that possibility was too devastating to contemplate.

Jewel was determined to get over her fear. She was determined to give Mac another chance. And she wanted Mac to want another chance. She was understandably nervous about her next meeting with him. It made a lot of sense to diffuse the situation by including her family in the equation. Hence the unusual visit to her family's breakfast table. This morning she needed the support they had always given her. She wanted their reassurance that she looked all right, that she would not "stick out" in a crowd.

Jewel could smell biscuits and bacon through the screen door. She smiled and stepped inside, knowing she would find the warmth of hearth and home. She stopped just inside the door, enjoying the cacophony of seven voices—Rolleen was away at medical school—raised in excited chatter.

"Wow! You look different!"

Jewel smiled self-consciously at Colt as she settled into an empty chair at the breakfast table. She was tempted to slump down, but forced herself to sit up straight. This was the new and improved Jewel Whitelaw.

Her mom gave her a bright smile and said, "You look lovely today, sweetheart."

"Why'd you cut off all your—"

Nineteen-year-old Jake elbowed fifteen-year-old Rabbit to shut him up. "You look real nice, Jewel," Jake said. He exchanged a knowing look with their father at the head of the table.

Jewel felt her cheeks heating. They had noticed the difference, all right, but so far had avoided commenting directly on it. She decided to keep their attention focused on her hair. "It's been so hot lately, I decided to get a trim," she said to appease the curious looks she was getting from sixteen-year-old Frannie and twenty-year-old Avery.

"Good idea," her father said, buttering a fluffy biscuit.

"I've got some time this morning if you need any last-minute help getting ready for the first drove of campers," her mother offered, as she set a bowl of scrambled eggs and a second platter of bacon in the center of the table.

"Everything's under control, Mom," Jewel said.

"When do you go to the airport?" her father asked.

"The flight from Dallas arrives at 9:30 this morning with about a half-dozen kids," she replied. "There's another half dozen and the two counselors arriving from Houston shortly afterward. Mac has volunteered to go with me in the van to pick them up. I invited him to join us for breakfast," she said. "I hope that's all right."

"Of course it's all right," her mother replied. "It'll be nice to visit with him. We've barely seen hide or hair of either of you. What have you been doing?"

"Mac's been walking in the mornings—"

"Is his ankle better?" Colt asked.

"What's wrong with his ankle?" her father asked.

Colt got busy scooping another spoonful of eggs on his plate and sent a pleading look toward Jewel not to betray him.

"He tripped and twisted it yesterday," Jewel said. "It seems to be all right this morning."

"It's fine," Mac said as he opened the screen door and stepped into the kitchen. "How's everyone this morning?"

He was greeted with a chorus of smiles and "hellos" and "hi's."

Jewel feasted her eyes on him. His blond hair was still damp from the shower, and the rugged planes of his face were shadowed by a day's growth of beard, so he hadn't even stopped to shave. He must have been afraid of missing breakfast. He was wearing a Western shirt tucked into beltless, butter-soft jeans and cowboy boots.

She looked up at him defiantly, daring him not to like what he saw. He was the one who had wanted change. She had provided it. He had better not complain.

Jewel saw nothing in his blue eyes but admiration. That flustered her as much, and perhaps more than the opposite reaction. She hadn't been ready for the blatant male appreciation of her figure that she found on his face.

"I hope I'm not too late for breakfast," he said as he slipped into the last empty chair, which happened to be across from Jewel.

"Just in time," Zach said.

Jewel could feel Mac's eyes on her but kept her gaze lowered as she ate her scrambled eggs. It was going to take some time for her to adjust to having men look at her with sexual interest. It was all right when Mac did it, because she did not feel frightened by him. But he was right. If she wanted to get over the past, this was a start in the right direction.

She heard Mac exchange comments with her father about the cattle and cutting horse businesses that supported Hawk's Pride, listened to him discuss football with Colt, smiled along with him as he teased Rabbit about his nickname, which dated from his childhood when he had loved carrots. Mac obviously knew her family well, and they apparently liked him as much as he liked them.

Jewel felt a rush of guilt at having deprived Mac of their company all these years. Having been Mac's friend, she knew how hard it was for his own family to treat him normally. His parents and older sister, Sadie, had hovered over him long after he was well, afraid to let him try things for fear he would get hurt and end up back in the hospital.

Zach and Rebecca loved Mac like a son, but they hadn't spent years with him in a hospital setting where he was fighting for his life against a disease that killed kids. They were willing to let him do a man's work. Jewel knew Mac had needed his summers as a counselor at Camp LittleHawk as much as Zach and Rebecca had needed his help with the kids.

"Right, Jewel?"

Jewel looked up at Mac, startled to realize he was

speaking to her. "Excuse me. I wasn't listening. What was the question?"

Her family laughed.

"What's so funny?" she demanded, looking at them suspiciously.

"I said the reason the kids keep coming back year after year is that you're constantly making changes to keep things interesting," Mac said with a grin.

Jewel realized that this year she had made a huge change that was bound to be noticed—by the other counselors, if not the kids. One of the reasons she loved working with kids was that they never seemed to notice her ample bosom. "Change is good," she said, both chin and chest outthrust defiantly.

"Of course it is, darling," her mother said in a soothing voice.

"I wasn't complaining, Jewel," Mac said, his gaze staying level with hers.

She kept waiting for it to drop to her breasts. But it never did. There was nothing sexual in his gaze now. What she saw was approval and appreciation of her as a person. A thickness in her throat made it hard to speak. "We'd better get going," she said. "We don't want to be late to the airport."

"I'm ready when you are," Mac said, pushing back from the table. "Thanks for the breakfast, Rebecca. I don't know when I've enjoyed a meal so much. It's great to be back."

"It's great to have you back," Zach said, rising and putting a hand on Mac's shoulder as he walked him to the door." You're welcome anytime."

"Thanks, Zach," Mac said, shaking hands with the older man.

Jewel felt exposed once she and Mac emerged from the throng of hugging and backslapping brothers and sisters and parents and headed across the backyard toward the van.

She felt Mac's gaze trained on her again, intense, disturbing, because this time he was obviously looking at more than her face. She paused as soon as they were hidden by a large bougainvillea and turned to confront him.

She propped her balled hands on her hips, thrust her shoulders back and held her chin high. "All right, Mac. You were the one who asked for this. Look your fill and get it over with."

His lips curved. His eyes surveyed her intently. His voice turned whiskey rough as he said, "You could stand there till doomsday, and I wouldn't get my fill of looking at you."

Jewel would have scoffed, but the sound got caught in her throat. "Mac…"

He stepped close enough to put them toe to toe.

She struggled not to give ground. "Say what you think. Spit it out. I can take it."

His thumb caressed the faint scars on her bared cheek, then edged into her hair. "Your hair's so soft. So shiny. So sleek." His hand slid through her hair to capture her nape and hold her still as he lowered his head. "I find you irresistible, Jewel."

Jewel felt her heart thudding, had trouble catching her breath, then stopped breathing altogether as his mouth closed over hers.

He kept their bodies separated, touching her only with his mouth. The searing kiss was enough to curl her toes inside her boots.

He lifted his head and said, "Welcome back, Jewel. I missed the old you."

"Oh, Mac—" She was on the verge of blurting out her strong feelings for him—the same feelings his kiss had suggested he had for her—when he interrupted.

"I don't think you're going to have any trouble at all attracting the man of your dreams." He smile ruefully. "You're going to have to remind me to keep my distance. I don't want any good prospects to think I have any kind of claim on you except as a friend."

Jewel stared at him with stunned eyes, but quickly recovered her composure. "No sweat, Mac," she said, turning and heading for the van. "I'll make sure any men I meet know exactly where you stand."

She owed Mac too much to make him feel uncomfortable by revealing her new feelings for him before he was ready to hear them. But if kissing her like this only reinforced the bonds of *friendship,* she had her work cut out for her. The changes in her hair and wardrobe had been useful in helping Mac to see her as a desirable female. All she had to do now was figure out how to make him fall in love with her.

CHAPTER EIGHT

MAC STARED OUT THE WINDOW OF the van at the flat grassland that lined the road between Hawk's Pride and the airport, rather than at the woman behind the wheel. But he very much wanted to feast his eyes on Jewel.

He liked the bouncy new haircut that showed off the line of her chin and made her cheekbones more prominent. He liked the formfitting clothes that outlined a lush figure he yearned to hold close to his own. He was intrigued by the sparkle of wonder and delight—and unfulfilled promise—in her dark brown eyes.

Mac wished he had a Stetson to set on his lap.

He hadn't realized he would be so physically susceptible to the striking change in Jewel's appearance. A friend would have settled for giving her an approving pat on the back. His kiss had been a purely male impulse, an effort to stake his claim on an intensely desirable female.

Mac recognized his problem. He simply had no idea how to solve it. How did a man stop desiring a woman? Especially one he not only lusted after but also liked very much?

Jewel sat across from him behind the wheel not saying a word. But speaking volumes.

Tension radiated between them. Sexual tension.

He had told her to find another man, but now he

wasn't so sure. She had certainly seemed to enjoy his kiss. Maybe if he seduced her in stages... If they took it slow and easy...

Who was he kidding? When it came down to the nitty-gritty, it was still going to be the first time for him. He was still going to be guessing at what he was doing. Besides, it wasn't fair to change his mind at this late date.

Who said life was fair?

"I appreciate you coming along to help today," Jewel said, interrupting his thoughts.

"My pleasure. How many people are we picking up?"

"Twelve kids, two counselors."

"Are you still hiring college kids?"

"Patty Freeburg is still in college. Gavin Talbot is in graduate school. I should warn you, this group of kids includes Brad Templeton."

"The kid who wanted to meet me?"

Jewel nodded. "His leukemia is in its second remission. You know how that works. You're afraid to get your hopes up that this remission will last, because you've already slipped out of remission once."

"You have to keep believing you can beat the disease," Mac said.

"Most kids aren't as lucky as you were."

"You think it was luck that I beat myelocytic leukemia?" he asked.

"Statistics say the chances of a kid surviving that kind of leukemia aren't good. What else could it have been?"

"Sheer determination. Willpower. It can move mountains. Recently it put me back on my own two feet when the doctors said I would never walk again without a brace."

"Granted, willpower is important. Determination counts for a lot. But are they enough to get your leg back into shape for pro football?" Jewel asked.

Mac felt a spurt of panic. "Sure. Why not?"

"Willpower can't replace the missing muscle in your leg, Mac. Determination can't make the scars disappear."

"I can compensate."

She nodded. "For your sake, I hope so."

"Why are you being so negative about this?" Mac demanded, using anger to force back the fear that had surfaced with her doubts.

"I'm not being negative, just realistic. You learn to accept—"

"Don't accept anything that isn't exactly what you want. Don't expect anything less than the best for yourself or those sick kids, Jewel. You deserve it. And so do they."

Jewel smiled ruefully. "To tell the truth, this is an argument I don't want to win. I want to believe in happily ever after for these kids and for you. And I'm hoping desperately for it myself. I've taken the first steps toward a new me. I have to admit it feels good, even though it is a little scary."

He met her glance briefly and saw the fear, before she returned her gaze to the road in front of her. "Why scary?"

"Because I'm not sure how well I'll handle all the male attention once I have it."

"Encourage the men you're interested in, and discourage the ones you don't want."

She grunted her disgust. "You make it sound so easy. Encourage how? Discourage how?"

"Smiles. And frowns."

Jewel looked at him incredulously, then gave a bubbly laugh. "If it were only that simple!"

"It is," Mac assured her.

She eyed him doubtfully. "That's all there is to it?"

"Why not try an experiment? When this Gavin What's-his-name—"

"Talbot," Jewel provided.

"When Talbot gets off the plane, give him a 'You're the one!' smile, and see what kind of response you get."

They had arrived at the local airport just as the commuter plane from Dallas was landing. Jewel stopped the van close to the terminal and stepped out to wait for the plane door to open and the kids to come down the portable stairs to the tarmac.

The three girls and four boys on the Dallas flight all wore hats of some kind, a means of hiding the ravages of chemotherapy on their hair. Baseball caps, berets, slouch hats, straw hats, bandannas, Jewel had seen them all. Beneath the hats their eyes looked haunted, their mouths grim. Jewel looked forward to easing their worries for two weeks, to helping them forget for a short time that their lives were threatened with extinction.

A scuffle broke out between two of the boys the instant they reached the tarmac. The other kids spread out in a circle to watch.

"Hey!" Jewel cried, running to reach them.

Mac was there before her and picked up the boy who had done the shoving, leaving the other boy with no one to fight. "What's the problem?" Mac asked in a calm voice.

The boy on the tarmac was in tears. He pointed to the boy in Mac's arms. "He said I'm going to die."

"We're all going to die," Mac replied. "Could get hit by a bus tomorrow."

The other kids smiled. It was an old joke for them, but it still worked every time.

The crying boy was not amused. He pointed to the kid in Mac's arms. "He said I can't beat it. He said no one can. He said—"

Mac perused the thin, gangly boy held snug against his side. "Doesn't look like a doctor to me," he said. "Where do you suppose he got the information to make his diagnosis? You a doctor?" Mac asked the kid.

The boy clenched his teeth and said nothing.

"Guess that settles that," Mac said. "Any other questions?" he asked the crying boy.

The kid wiped his nose on the shoulder of his T-shirt and pulled his Harwell Grain and Feed cap snugly over his eyes. "Guess not."

Mac exchanged a look with Jewel, who began herding the children toward the terminal.

"Why don't you all come inside with me," she said. "We'll get a soda while we wait for the kids from Houston to arrive, along with your counselors."

As soon as they were gone, Mac set the boy down on his feet in front of him. Knowing the kid would likely run the instant he let go, Mac settled onto one knee, his hands trapping the kid's frail shoulders, and tried to see the boy's eyes under his baseball cap. The kid's chin was tucked so close to his chest, it was impossible.

"What's your name?" Mac asked.

"I want to go home."

"You sound pretty mad."

"I never wanted to come here in the first place. My mom made me!"

"Why'd you tell that boy he was going to die?"

"'Cause he is!"

"Who says?"

"He's got acute myelocytic leukemia, same as me. It kills you for sure!"

"I'm not dead."

The boy's chin jerked up, and his pale blue eyes focused on Mac's. "You're not sick."

"I was. Same as you."

The boy shook his head. "But you're—"

"I'm Mac Macready."

The blue eyes widened. "*You're* him? You look different from the picture on your trading card."

"I was younger then," Mac replied. *And twenty pounds heavier with muscle.*

"My mom said you'd be here, but I didn't believe her."

"You must be Brad Templeton." Mac let go of the kid's shoulders, rose and stuck out his hand. "Nice to meet you, Brad."

The boy stared at Mac's hand suspiciously before he laid his own tiny palm against it. Mac figured the kid for eleven or twelve, but he didn't look much more than eight or nine. The slight body, the gaunt cheeks, the hopeless look in his eyes, told how the disease had decimated him—body and soul.

"You ready to join the others?" Mac asked.

He watched as the boy looked toward the kids bunched in the front window of the terminal and made a face. "This is a waste of time."

"Why is that?"

"I mean, why bother pretending everything is all right, when it's not?"

Mac put a hand on the boy's back, and they began walking toward the terminal. "Why not pretend? Why not enjoy every moment you've got?"

The boy met his gaze, and Mac knew the answer without having to hear it. He had been through it all himself.

This was a child going through the stages that prepared him for death. The anger. The grieving. And finally, the acceptance. Brad Templeton had done it all before, when the first remission ended. Then death had given him a brief reprieve—a second remission. But having once accepted the fact he was going to die, it was awfully hard to start living all over again.

"Death doesn't always win," Mac said quietly.

Brad looked up at him. "How did you beat it?"

"Determination. Willpower."

Brad shook his head. "That isn't enough. If it was, I'd already be well."

"Don't give up."

"I have to," Brad said. "It hurts too bad to hope when you know it isn't going to make any difference."

They had reached the door to the terminal, but before going inside, Mac stooped down and turned the boy to face him. "Sometimes you have to forget about what the doctors say and believe in yourself."

Brad looked skeptical.

Mac didn't know who he was trying to convince, himself or the kid. Sometimes the doctors were right. Kids died. And football players got career-ending injuries.

He rose and said, "Come on, Brad. We can keep each other company this week and have some fun."

Brad snorted. "Fun. Yeah. Right."

Mac smiled. "If you're not smiling ear to ear when you get back on that plane in two weeks, I'll—"

"How are you two doing?" Jewel interrupted. A whoosh of cold air escaped the terminal as she joined them in the Texas heat that was already rising from the tarmac.

"I was making a bet with Brad that he would be smiling by the end of next week."

Brad grimaced.

Jewel eyed Brad, then murmured to Mac, "Looks like you have your work cut out for you."

"Come on, Brad," Mac said, giving the boy a nudge toward the door. "Let's go inside and meet the other kids."

"I've already met them," Brad said sullenly. "They all hate me."

"We'll have to work on that, too," Mac said, sending Jewel a look that said "Help!" over his shoulder.

"I'd appreciate it if you'd keep an eye on everybody while I greet the folks on the plane from Houston," she said.

Mac realized the second commuter plane had arrived, Jewel was headed back out onto the tarmac. "Don't forget," he said. "Smile."

Jewel shot him a radiant smile. "How's this?"

Mac put an exaggerated hand to his heart. "Lord have mercy, girl, that's potent stuff!"

Jewel laughed and turned away, her hips swaying seductively in the tight jeans.

Mac was glad she'd turned away when she had. His hand was still on his heart, but it was keeping the damned thing from flying out of his chest. If she kept walking like that, he wasn't going to be able to go inside anytime soon.

He felt a tug on his shirtsleeve and looked down to see Brad staring up at him.

"You got the hots for her?"

Mac stared, agog. "The *hots*?"

"You know. Sexy chick like that—"

Mac put a hand over Brad's mouth. "Where did a kid your age learn—? Don't answer that. She's Miss Whitelaw to you."

The kid reached up to uncover his mouth. "I'm twelve. I was here when I was nine and Jewel said we can call her Jewel and she's a lot prettier now."

"And you're old enough to notice, is that it?"

Brad gave Mac a man-to-man shrug. "I haven't thought too much about girls 'cause... you know."

Mac put a hand on Brad's shoulder. "Yeah, I know how that is, too."

He ushered Brad inside thinking it was going to be a very long two weeks.

JEWEL'S HEART WAS BEATING RAPIDLY. Even kidding the way he was, Mac's admiring look had been enough to take her breath away. It was easy to keep the smile on her face long enough to greet the other five campers, Patty Freeburg and Gavin Talbot.

Patty was petite and pretty, with long blond hair she wore in a youthful ponytail, blue eyes and a wonderfully open smile. "Hello," she said. "I'm glad to be back."

"Good to have you back, Patty," Jewel said. "You know the drill. Would you mind helping the kids locate their luggage inside?"

"Sure," Patty said. "Come on, you guys, hup, two, three, four!"

The two boys marched, and the three girls giggled as they followed Patty toward the terminal.

Jewel turned to greet Gavin Talbot, who was hefting a duffel bag over his shoulder. She knew Gavin's credentials backward and forward. He was twenty-six and working on a Ph.D. in child psychology. Eventually he planned to become a clinical psychologist, and work with dying kids. He was spending time at Camp Little-Hawk because it catered to children with cancer.

She knew Gavin would have to be an empathetic and caring man to choose such a career. She had not imagined he would also be stunningly handsome.

He was over six feet tall, with the sort of rangy body Jewel was used to seeing on cowhands, who led physically active lives. His sun-streaked, tobacco-brown hair suggested a lot of time out-of-doors, and the spray of tan lines around his dark brown eyes confirmed it. He was dressed in a white, oxford-cloth shirt, unbuttoned at the throat and turned up to his forearms, well-worn—though not ragged—jeans and cowboy boots.

"Hello, Miss Whitelaw," he said, reaching out to

shake her hand as they followed Patty and the kids back to the terminal.

His large, callused hand engulfed hers, offering comfort, reassurance and something else...a spark of sexual interest.

Jewel didn't think she was imagining it. She felt a small frisson of pleasure merely from his firm hand-clasp. It was probably the way he looked into her eyes, as though seeking a connection, that made her insides jump a little.

"Call me Jewel, please, Gavin," she replied.

"Jewel," he repeated, the smile broadening, becoming more relaxed. "The name fits."

Jewel only had an instant to decide whether to frown or smile, as Mac had instructed. Jewel smiled.

She had only taken two steps when Gavin put a hand under her elbow and said, "You're hurt."

"It's an old injury that causes me to limp," she said, wondering if the interest she had previously seen would diminish, now that he knew she was considerably less than perfect.

Her opinion of him went up a notch when he said, "It doesn't seem to slow you down much." She felt a spurt of anxiety when Gavin made eye contact with her again, because the sexual spark was still there. Well, she had wanted to attract him and she had. So now what did she do with him? She turned to find Mac staring at her through the terminal's front picture window.

Mac was safe. Mac was nonthreatening.

Mac also was not volunteering to help her get over the lingering fear that had kept her celibate all these years. Maybe seeing that someone else was interested in her would spur him to action.

She turned back to Gavin and forced another smile onto her face. "You look like you spend a lot of time outdoors."

"I own a cattle ranch south of Houston," he said. "I spend my weekends there when I can."

"You should be right at home here," she said. "We do a lot of trail rides in the early morning and late afternoon for the children."

"What about moonlight rides for the grown-ups?" he asked. "Ending with a romantic campfire and toasted marshmallows?"

Jewel was a little shocked at how fast Gavin had made his move. She swallowed back the knot of fear and shot him a calculated come-hither glance. "I suppose that could be arranged."

"How about tonight?"

"How about what tonight?" Mac asked.

Jewel had been so busy staring back into Gavin's brown eyes, she hadn't realized they had reached the terminal. Mac's question caught her unawares. "What?"

"Jewel and I were just setting up a moonlight ride for tonight," Gavin said.

Jewel heard the warning in Gavin's voice. *Stay clear. This one's mine. We don't want company.*

Mac ignored it. "Sounds like a fine idea," he said. "Hey, Patty, you want to go for a moonlight ride tonight?"

Patty smiled. "Sure. Who all's going?"

"Everybody," Gavin said wryly, his gaze never leaving Mac's.

At least Gavin was a good sport, Jewel thought. She was grateful that Mac had realized how uncomfortable she would have been all alone with Gavin and had invited himself and Patty. With Mac along she would feel safer flirting with Gavin. And perhaps Mac would be moved to do a little flirting himself.

Jewel was amused to see how Gavin maneuvered to be in the front seat with her on the trip back, forcing Mac into the back with Patty and the kids. Gavin wasn't the least impressed by Mac's football hero status, because he wasn't a big football fan.

"I know that sounds like blasphemy in Texas," he said. "But I'd rather spend my Saturday and Sunday afternoons at the ranch, since I'm stuck indoors reading and writing the rest of the week."

"What's the name of your ranch?" Jewel asked as she started the van and headed back toward the ranch.

"Let's not talk about me," Gavin said, avoiding an answer. "Tell me about yourself."

Jewel watched Gavin stiffen as Mac suddenly leaned forward, bracing his arms on the back of the front seat, effectively interposing himself between Jewel and the counselor. "Mind if I listen?" Mac said. "Jewel and I haven't had much time to catch up on things since the last time we were together."

Jewel heard the insinuation in Mac's voice that suggested "together" meant more than sitting on a garden swing next to each other.

"You two are old friends?" Gavin asked, eyeing the two of them speculatively.

"We're rooming together," Mac said. "Didn't Jewel tell you?"

Jewel turned a fiery red at the knowing look Gavin gave her, even though the situation with Mac was perfectly innocent. She was a little perturbed at Mac. He seemed to be saying everything he could to keep Gavin at a distance. She appreciated his concern, but until he volunteered to take Gavin's place, she was determined to be brave enough to pursue the relationship.

She forced a laugh and said, "Mac has been like a big brother to me for years. He gets a little protective at times."

Gavin's brows rose, and the smile returned. "I see. Don't worry, Mac," he said, patting Mac's arm. "I'll take good care of her."

Mac grunted and shifted back into the back seat, his arms crossed over his chest.

Jewel shivered as she made brief eye contact with Gavin. It looked like she was going to get a chance to try out her feminine wiles tonight. Mac would be there, so she wouldn't have to worry about things getting out of hand. Toasting marshmallows over a campfire would be a marvelously romantic setting, perfect for establishing a friendly rapport with Gavin.

She wondered if Gavin would try to kiss her. She wondered if she should let him. She caught Mac's narrowed gaze in the rearview mirror and wondered, with a smile, if *Mac* would let him. She had better have a talk with Mac before the trail ride and let him know she welcomed Gavin's attentions for the practice they would provide.

Jewel shivered in anticipation. She only hoped that when the time came, and Gavin made advances, she would have the nerve to follow through.

CHAPTER NINE

MAC STARED THROUGH HIS HORSE'S EARS at Jewel, riding side by side with Gavin on the moonlit trail ahead of him. Patty had decided to stay at the ranch, so he had no riding partner. Mac watched Jewel lean close to hear what Gavin was saying. A trilling burble of laughter floated back to him on the wind. His neck hairs rose, and he gritted his teeth in frustration.

That could have been him riding beside Jewel. That could have been him making her laugh. Instead, he was reduced to the role of chaperon. And not enjoying it one bit.

Mac turned to see who was coming as another horse cantered up beside him bearing one of the three late additions to their trail ride. "Hey, Colt. What's new?"

"You know anything about that Gavin guy?" Colt asked, aiming his chin toward the couple ahead of them.

Mac stared at Gavin. "He's as comfortable on a horse as any cowboy I've ever seen, he's educated, friendly, courteous and he appears to be interested in Jewel."

"You think he'll try to hurt her?"

Mac saw the worry on Colt's young face. Six years ago the kid had been only eight, but obviously Jewel's trauma had left a lasting impression on her family.

"There's not much Gavin can do with me along," Mac reassured the teenager.

Colt heaved a sigh of relief. "Thanks, Mac. Jewel is… well, she's pretty special."

"I know."

Colt glanced over his shoulder, frowned, then looked straight ahead again. "I thought I might get to see a little more of Jenny if we came along tonight. I should have known she'd stick like glue to Huck."

Mac arched a brow. "You have feelings for her yourself?"

Colt readjusted his Western straw hat, setting it lower over his eyes to hide his expression. "She's Huck's girl."

"You didn't answer my question."

"So what if I like her?" Colt retorted. "Nothing's gonna come of it. They'll probably get married as soon as Huck finishes college."

"College is a long way off. Maybe Huck will change his mind. Or Jenny will."

Colt snorted. "What difference would that make? She doesn't know I'm alive."

Mac wasn't sure what to say. He hadn't been too fortunate in the romance department himself. But he knew what he would do if he loved a woman. "Mind if I offer you some advice?"

Colt shrugged.

"If you get a chance to make Jenny your girl, grab it with both hands." He grinned at Colt. "It's awful hard for a woman to resist a man who loves her, heart and soul."

Colt eyed him sideways. "If you say so."

They had reached the ring of stones Camp LittleHawk used as a campfire site for barbecues. Mac watched as Gavin lifted Jewel from her horse, sliding her down the front of him as he settled her feet on the ground. He saw the stunned look on Jewel's face as she gazed up at Gavin. Was it fear or wonder she had felt at the intimate contact?

He kneed his horse into a lope to catch up to them. He was out of the saddle and at her side seconds later. "Hey, Jewel," he said, putting a hand on her shoulder. "Let's get the fire going for those marshmallows."

When she looked at him, he saw dazed pleasure in her eyes. Damn. She was definitely aroused. A quick glance at the front of her—at the pebbled nipples that showed through the knit top—confirmed his diagnosis.

So what was he supposed to do now? Disappear, so Gavin could get on with his seduction?

The hell he would.

He grabbed Jewel's hand. "Come on, Jewel. Let's get some firewood."

Jewel glanced at him in surprise, smiled and followed him to the box of firewood that was kept nearby. He loaded her arms with kindling and picked up a few logs to carry back himself. By the time they returned to the fire, Colt had unpacked the wire clothes hangers they had brought along and was unbending them to make marshmallow roasting sticks.

Mac and Jewel knelt together before the ring of stones that Jenny and Huck were straightening and began arranging the kindling and logs. Gavin arrived moments later with the bag of marshmallows, a thermos of hot chocolate and some paper cups from his saddlebag and a couple of blankets that had been tied behind Jewel's saddle.

"Up, you two," he said to Mac and Jewel. "Let me get this down under you."

Mac and Jewel scooted to the side, and Gavin spread the gray wool blanket where they had been, settling himself on the opposite side of Jewel from Mac and leaning close to whisper, "I think you've already started my fire."

Mac couldn't help overhearing. Or seeing Jewel stiffen slightly before she managed a smile and replied, "Give me a match, and I'll show you a real blaze."

Gavin, damn him, laughed and handed her a box of matches. Instead of letting her light the match by herself, Gavin held her hand as she drew the match along the edge of the box and lit the kindling. When the fire from the match had almost reached her fingers, Gavin lifted her hand to his mouth and blew it out.

Jewel made a mewling sound that had Mac's insides clenching. His hands fisted unconsciously, and his body tensed to fight.

Until that moment, Mac had not realized the extent of his feelings for Jewel. He had always liked her and considered himself her friend. He had missed talking to her in the years they had been apart. He was more than a little attracted to her. But the instinctual need to claim her, to make her his and only his, rose unbidden from somewhere deep inside him.

He resisted the strong urge to hit Gavin Talbot in the nose and began straightening out a clothes hanger to use as a roasting stick. Fighting the metal was a better release for his tension than starting an uncivilized brawl.

It was abundantly clear to him now, as it had not been before, that he wanted to be the man Jewel gave herself to for the first time. He wanted to see her eyes when their bodies were joined, hear her sighs as she learned the pleasure to be found in loving each other.

But Gavin moved fast, and Mac wasn't sure he was going to get a second chance with Jewel if something didn't happen pretty quick to separate the two. It didn't take much of a fire to toast marshmallows, and it wasn't long before Colt opened the bag and began tossing marshmallows around. Gavin was making Jewel laugh again, putting a marshmallow on the end of her roasting stick and whispering in her ear as it toasted on the fire.

"Jewel," Mac said quietly.

To his surprise, she looked immediately at him. "Yes, Mac?"

"Your marshmallow is on fire."

Because she was looking at him, she swung the burning marshmallow in his direction. Mac caught the coat hanger far enough back not to burn himself and blew out the fire. "Hope you like it charred," he said with a smile.

He blew on it to cool it, then pulled the gooey marshmallow off the end of the wire and held it out to her between thumb and forefinger. She leaned forward, her mouth open, and grabbed Mac's wrist as she bit into it. She held on to his wrist while she chewed, waving her hand at her mouth and making noises because the gooey marshmallow was both hot and deliciously sweet.

Then, as though it were the most natural thing in the world, she leaned over and sucked the rest of the marshmallow off of his thumb, licking it clean with her tongue.

Mac stared at her with avid eyes. She could have no idea what she was doing. By the time she was done with his thumb and had started on his forefinger, his body was strung as tight as a bowstring.

Jewel looked up at him, his forefinger still in her mouth, and caught his gaze with hers. She might not have realized beforehand what effect she was having on him, but he saw she recognized immediately what she had done.

Ever so slowly, she withdrew his forefinger from her mouth, then let go of his wrist. She had to clear her throat to speak. "I forgot to bring along wet wipes," she said. "I figured that was the best way to get rid of the marsh-mallow."

Mac took the fingers that had been in her mouth and slowly licked off imaginary specks of sugar. "It seems to be all gone."

He watched Jewel swallow hard before Gavin distracted her attention.

"How about sharing this one with me?" Gavin said, putting a hand on her forearm to stake his claim and holding out a perfectly toasted marshmallow.

Mac saw the goose bumps rise on her flesh where Gavin's hand lay. Saw her tentative smile as she turned back to the other man.

"Sure, Gavin," she said. "I'd like that."

She pulled the gooey marshmallow from the wire and ate half of it before Gavin caught her wrist and, with a grin, turned the marshmallow toward himself. Mac watched in helpless fury as Gavin ate the rest of the marshmallow from her hand and licked her fingers clean.

When Gavin started kissing her fingertips, something inside Mac snapped. "That's it!"

"What?" Jewel said, turning bewildered eyes on him.

"Let's go, Jewel." Mac stood and grabbed Jewel's wrist to drag her to her feet. He was surprised when she resisted.

"What's wrong with you, Mac?" she said.

"I think this has gone far enough." He said the words to the counselor, who understand exactly what his problem was.

Gavin rose to his feet, his legs widespread. "I didn't hear the lady complaining about my attentions."

Gavin had a point. But Mac wasn't in a rational mood. "The lady is too polite to say anything."

Gavin raised a questioning brow and faced Jewel. "Is that true, Jewel?"

"I don't see… I mean, I think I may have encouraged… I just wanted to see…"

Gavin's lip curved wryly on one side. "Your point is taken," he said to Mac.

By then, Colt was on his feet on the other side of the fire. "You need any help, Mac?"

Jenny grabbed Colt's T-shirt where it hung out of his jeans and yanked on it. "Sit down, Colt. This doesn't concern you."

"She's my sister."

"Sit down, Colt," Jenny repeated.

Mac watched as Colt met Jenny's gaze and settled back onto the ground beside her.

By then, Jewel was up and standing nose to nose with Mac. "What's gotten into you?" she demanded in a harsh whisper. "You're the one who told me to flirt with him in the first place!"

"I didn't think it would go this far," Mac said stubbornly.

"Thanks to you," she hissed, "it's not likely to go much further!"

"That's fine by me," Mac retorted.

"I think I'll excuse myself and let you two settle this alone," Gavin said. "I can find my own way back."

"We'd better get going, too," Jenny said, rising and pulling Huck and Colt to their feet. "I don't want to be late getting home."

Within moments, everything had been picked up and repacked, and the four of them were on their way back to the ranch house, leaving Mac and Jewel to put out the fire.

"All right, Mac," Jewel said. "I want to hear from your own lips what possessed you to cause such a scene."

JEWEL WAS CONFUSED BY MAC'S STRANGE behavior. "You're the one who told me to try out my feminine wiles," she said. "The first time I do, you act like a jealous lover."

She thought Mac flushed, but it was hard to tell in the firelight.

"I thought you wanted me along to protect you," he said.

"If I needed protection. Which I did not."

Mac kicked sand over the fire, creating a cloud of smoke. "You *liked* the way he was pawing you?"

"*Pawing* me?" she said. "Gavin's attentions weren't at all unwelcome."

When Gavin had smiled at her, she had allowed herself to feel the pleasure of being attractive to—and attracted to—a handsome man. When he had blown out the match, and his warm, moist breath touched her hand, she had not cut off the frisson of awareness that skittered down her spine. When he had kissed her fingertips, she had felt her heart beat more rapidly in response.

But none of those feelings in any way compared to the shock of awareness she felt when she had met Mac's gaze and discovered he had been aroused by the way she had sucked and licked his fingers clean.

It was the difference between a pinprick and being stabbed with a knife. While she was completely aware of both, one was slight and fleeting, while the other burned deep inside. One would disappear quickly; the other would not soon be forgotten.

She wasn't about to admit her vulnerability to Mac when he was behaving like a jealous idiot. Especially when he wasn't volunteering to take Gavin's place. "I liked what Gavin did," she said.

"I didn't," Mac said flatly.

"Why not?" Jewel demanded.

"He was moving too fast. You hardly know the guy."

"He didn't do anything I didn't allow."

"That's another thing," Mac said. "Just how far were you intending to go? Would you have let him kiss you?"

"Why not?" she said tartly.

Mac made a threatening, rumbly sound in his throat. "I can kiss you as well as some stranger can. If it's kisses you want, come to me."

"Last night you said—"

"Forget about last night. It never happened. We start new, here and now. You want to practice being a woman, practice with me."

Jewel eyed Mac in astonishment. She had exactly what she had thought she wanted. All she had to do was find the courage to follow through and take Mac up on his offer. She took a deep breath, let it out and said, "All right. I'll practice with you."

Mac heaved a sigh and knelt down to stir the ashes with a stick to make certain the fire was out. "Thank God that's settled."

"I want to be kissed, Mac."

She watched his shoulders tense, saw him drop the stick, then rise to face her.

"You want to be kissed now?"

"If you hadn't scared Gavin away, he'd be kissing me now," she pointed out.

It was hard to tell what Mac was feeling. His eyes were narrowed in—anger? His lips were twisted in a moue of—frustration? And his brow was furrowed deep with—apprehension? Which showed how good she was at reading men. What did Mac Macready have to be anxious about? He must have kissed a hundred women. She was the one who needed lessons.

"Come here, Jewel," Mac said in a voice that grated like an unoiled hinge.

It only took a couple of steps for her to reach him. His

arms opened wide, and as she stepped between them, they folded around her. One hand caught at her nape, the other low on her spine, just above her buttocks. She was aware of goose bumps rising along her nape as his hand slid up and grasped a handful of her hair.

He did not pull her any closer, simply angled her head and lowered his mouth. His lips felt warm and full as he rubbed them against hers. "Are you sure about this, Jewel?" he breathed against her half-open mouth.

She made a sound in her throat which he must have taken as assent, because he kissed the left side of her mouth, then the right, before returning to the center. He slipped his tongue beneath her upper lip, then nipped at her lips with his teeth.

Jewel shivered. It was strange, standing upright, being held—but not held—in a man's arms. She leaned into the kiss, returning the gentle pressure of his mouth. She slid her tongue along the seam of his lips, and he opened for her. Jewel had never been the aggressor with a man. It felt wonderful to be able to taste and tease to her heart's content without being afraid.

Her arms roamed up Mac's back, feeling the corded sinew. One hand slid into the hair at his nape and played with it as she indulged herself kissing him, feeling the damp softness of his lips, tasting the inside of his mouth with soft, tentative thrusts that he returned. She felt him begin to tremble.

"Jewel," he murmured.

"Hmm." Her lips followed the line of his chin to a spot below his ear, and she heard him hiss in a breath.

"I think we'd better stop."

She leaned back and looked up into his hooded eyes,

at lips rigid with passion. She smiled. "If I look anything like you do, perhaps you're right."

"You look beautiful," he said fervently.

"You don't have to say that," Jewel protested. "I know what I—"

He put his mouth on hers to silence her, pouring his feelings into a kiss that had her straining to be closer to him, closing the distance between them, until they were pressed close from breast to thigh. Jewel was so entranced by what Mac was doing with his mouth that it took her a moment to realize he had widened his stance enough to fit her between his legs.

He was aroused.

She squeezed her eyes shut and tried to concentrate on the kiss. It was so lovely. It felt so good. But her body below the waist had turned to stone.

Mac broke the kiss and looked down at her, his eyes worried. "Jewel?"

"Let me go, Mac."

"I won't hurt you, Jewel." He put one hand on her buttocks to keep her where she was. He smiled tenderly. "I'd very much like to put myself inside you."

Jewel felt the heat climbing up her throat at such plain speaking. "Mac—"

"But I'm not going to do anything until you're ready," he said, leaning down to give her a gentle kiss on the lips. "We have plenty of time."

"Your recuperation is almost complete," Jewel countered. "Look how far you've come in—"

He stopped her with another kiss. "We have plenty of time for you to get used to me touching you, wanting you."

"It doesn't seem fair, Mac. I mean, for me to use you like this."

He smiled. "Believe me, I don't mind."

His eyes seemed to be promising things she knew he could not mean. She looked down and said, "In a couple of weeks you'll be leaving here, and I won't be seeing you again."

He lifted her chin until she was looking into his eyes. "You'll always be special to me, Jewel. You have no idea how special." He opened his mouth as though to say something else and closed it again. "Look, let's just take this one day at a time. You can start with simple stuff like kisses and touches. Anytime you want to practice, just let me know. How does that sound?"

"Are you sure I won't be imposing?" Jewel asked.

"It'll be my pleasure," Mac said with a grin, rocking his body against hers.

"Oh!"

His brow wrinkled in concern. "What's wrong?"

"You're still...and I'm not... It's working!" she said with delight. "I'm hardly affected at all." Except that her pulse was throbbing, and she felt the strangest urge to push back against the hardness that rested between her legs.

Mac's smile looked a little forced. "See. You're already getting used to me."

He released her, and Jewel took a step back.

"I suppose we'd better get back," she said. "Camp starts tomorrow, and I'll be getting up early."

"I can help you after my workout."

Jewel smiled. "I'd like that."

"Don't forget. Anytime you feel like you want to

practice, just let me know. There's no need to flirt with that Gavin character."

"I thought I might try my wings—"

"Try your wings on me!" He swung her back into his arms, kissed her hard on the lips, then stomped off toward his horse, leaving her standing there.

It took a minute for Jewel to catch her breath and steady her racing pulse. "I was just teasing!" she called after him, as she hurried to catch up.

Mac made a growling sound in his throat. "Let's go. It's late."

She stomped right over and stood in front of him. "For heaven's sake! Where's your sense of humor?"

He grabbed her hand and placed it on the bulge in his jeans. "Right there. I'm not feeling too damn funny at the moment."

Even though he had immediately let go of her hand, Jewel was too shocked to jerk away. She left her hand where Mac had put it, feeling the length and hardness of him. This part of him didn't seem nearly so threatening through a layer of denim and cotton, warm and pulsing beneath her hand.

"Jewel," he said through gritted teeth. "What are you doing?"

"Learning."

He gave a choked laugh. "I think my sense of humor is—"

"In very fine shape," she said with a gamine grin. "Want to test it again?"

He caught her wrist and removed her hand. "I think I've had enough testing for one evening. Let's save this for another time."

"Anything you say, Mac," she answered cheerfully. "You're the teacher."

And Jewel was determined to be a very good pupil.

CHAPTER TEN

MAC REALIZED THE DILEMMA HE HAD put himself in. He was going to be kissing and touching Jewel over the next several weeks—and encouraging her to kiss and touch him—even though he had serious reservations about making love to her. Not because he didn't desire her, but because he was afraid if he did something wrong, he would mess things up for her even more. He decided he owed it to both of them to get some professional advice.

"Something's come up that I need to discuss with my agent," Mac said to Jewel at breakfast the next morning. "I've made reservations to fly to Dallas this afternoon."

"Couldn't you do it over the phone?" Jewel asked.

Mac shook his head and raised another spoonful of cornflakes. "Too sensitive. Requires face-to-face consultation."

"Why didn't you say something about this last night?" she asked suspiciously.

He grinned. "I was distracted last night."

Jewel blushed. Mac thought she had never looked lovelier. She was wearing a plaid Western shirt, tucked in at the waist of her jeans, that hinted at the fullness of her figure. Her brown hair looked sun kissed, and her brown eyes gleamed. As she turned toward him, the faded crisscross scars on her face took him back to a time when they were both much younger and someone had teased her about them.

Mac realized he must have cared a great deal for her even then. He could remember wiping away her tears with his thumbs, kissing her scarred cheek and saying, "These scars are as precious as any other part of you, Jewel, more facets to add texture to the diamond you are."

He had meant it then, and he could see it now.

Jewel laid her spoon in her cereal bowl and said, "I'll miss you, Mac. When will you be back?"

Mac met her troubled gaze and said, "I don't know." He had no idea how long it would take to get an appointment with the one sex therapist he knew. Dr. Timothy Douglas might be too busy to fit him in for several days.

"You're not coming back, are you?" Jewel said flatly. "You've changed your mind about wanting to teach me, and you're leaving." The glow had left her face and the sparkle had faded from her eyes.

"What do I have to do to convince you I'm not going away?"

"Kiss me," she said. "That was the deal. I could ask anytime, and I'm asking now." She crossed her arms over her chest as though she thought he might refuse.

Silly woman. He wasn't about to refuse.

Mac crossed to Jewel in two steps, tipped her chin up and slanted his mouth over hers, kissing her with all the passion he felt, hoping to convince her he meant what he said. They were both breathing hard when he lifted his head. "I'm coming back," he said. "I just have some business to do in Dallas."

Tears filled her eyes as she looked up at him. "That was goodbye. I know it."

Mac shook his head in disbelief. He stood and put his hands on his hips. "Look, Jewel. Why would I make an offer like the one I made last night and leave the next day for good?"

"Because you had second thoughts," she said.

"No, I did not."

"Because you realized I might fall in love with you or something stupid like that, if you started kissing me all the time."

"That never crossed my mind!" The thought hadn't occurred to him, but he liked the idea now that she mentioned it.

"Probably you never thought of me falling in love, because kisses don't mean much to a man like you," she said, lips pouting.

How wrong she was! Mac thought. Her kisses, at least, made him feel a great deal, though he wasn't willing to go so far as to think in terms of love. A great deal of *like*. That was what he felt for Jewel Whitelaw.

But he couldn't resist kissing her again. He slipped his tongue inside her mouth and tasted her thoroughly. When he stood again, the revealing bulge was back in his jeans. He noticed that she noticed and felt his body tighten in expectation.

"I'll be back, Jewel. Trust me."

It was a lot to ask a woman who hadn't found much about men to trust.

She blinked back the tears and said, "All right, Mac."

He kissed her again, to thank her for trusting him, but when he felt the urge to pull her up and into his arms, he stepped back. "You've got campers to see to, and I've got a few things to do before I join you."

"You're still going to help me with the campers this morning?"

"Of course. Why wouldn't I?"

"I thought you might have to pack..."

"I'm only taking a few things."

She walked back to him and put her arms around him and hugged him tight. "I'm so glad you're coming back," she said. "I'll be waiting for you. I won't even flirt with Gavin while you're gone."

She was already halfway to the door by the time he realized what she had said. She turned back, winked and laughed, then headed out the door.

Mac watched her till she was gone, realizing he had more problems to solve than just hers, if they were to have any hope of a future together. He had gotten a big signing bonus when he joined the Tornadoes, but his five-year contract had provided for a smaller salary in the first few years. He had most of the signing bonus left, but he had pretty much spent his first year's salary.

What if he didn't make it back onto the team?

Don't even think that!

Mac didn't believe in quitting or giving up or giving in. But it was time for a reality check. He had accomplished more than most men would have. He was walking—hell, he was running again—when the doctors said he'd be in a leg brace the rest of his life. He should quit while he was ahead. If he went back to playing football, chances were good he'd reinjure his leg. Maybe next time his prognosis would be even worse.

Mac called his agent's office and got Andy's secretary. "Tell Andy I'll be in his office about four o'clock this afternoon. I'll fill him in on everything when I see him."

He headed out the door dressed in a starched white oxford-cloth shirt belted into crisp new jeans and almost new ostrich cowboy boots, so he'd be ready if the media caught sight of him in Dallas. Mac wanted to look confident and ready to go back to work for the Tornadoes on the outside, even if he didn't feel quite that way inside.

He stopped at the boys' bunkhouse to check on Brad Templeton, but apparently the kids had already headed over to the cookhouse for breakfast. He was about to leave when he heard something hit the tile floor in the communal bathroom. He stepped inside. "Who's there?"

Nobody answered, but Mac knocked on the frame of the open bathroom doorway and said, "Anybody here?"

Brad Templeton stepped out of one of the four shower-curtained stalls. "How'd you know I was here?"

"I heard something drop."

He made a face. "My plastic cup."

"Why aren't you at breakfast with the other kids?" Mac asked, leaning casually against the bathroom doorway to put the kid at ease.

"I told Gavin I didn't feel well."

Mac's easy pose evaporated. He took the few steps to bring him to Brad's side, whipped off the kid's New

York Mets baseball cap and pressed his hand on Brad's forehead. It all happened so fast, Brad didn't have a chance to complain until Mac had already found out what he wanted to know. He replaced the cap. "No fever," he said.

Brad tugged the ball cap back down over his nearly bald head. "Naw. I'm okay."

Fever was one of the first—and worst—signs that a remission was over, that the leukemia was back. It wasn't something to be ignored. "Why'd you tell Gavin you were sick?" Mac asked.

Brad shrugged, the kind of kid gesture that could have meant anything, but really meant, *I couldn't tell him the truth.*

"What's on the agenda this morning?" Mac asked.

"Horseback riding," Brad mumbled.

"That sounds like fun. What's the problem?"

"I've never been on a horse before. I'd probably get bucked off and stomped to death. I don't want to die any sooner than I have to."

Mac grinned.

"That's not funny!" Brad said.

"You sound exactly like I did when I went riding the first time. Funny how being sick makes you want to live all the more, isn't it?"

Brad's brows rose almost to the brim of his ball cap. It was one thing for Mac to say he'd been sick, another for him to express a feeling that could only be had by someone who had personally faced death.

"Come on," Mac said, putting a hand on Brad's shoulder and ushering him toward the door. "Let's get you fed. I know just the pony for you. Gentle as a lamb."

"What's his name?" Brad asked.

Mac grinned. "Buttercup."

MAC PACED THE CONFINES OF Andy Dennison's office, from the bat signed by Ken Griffey, Jr., in one corner, to the football signed by Joe Montana in the other and back again. His agent had become his friend, and now he needed some friendly advice. But Andy was late.

He had too much time to think.

Andy must have leaked what time Mac was landing at Dallas/Fort Worth International Airport, because a bunch of photographers and reporters had been waiting for him when he exited the jetway. He had smiled for the cameras as he walked quickly toward the chauffeur-driven limousine waiting for him outside.

"It's great to see you walking so well, Mac," one reporter commented. "Will you be back with the Tornadoes this fall?"

"That's my plan," Mac said.

"You can walk. But can you run?" another reporter asked.

Mac smiled more broadly. "Does a Texas dog have fleas?"

Everybody laughed, but the reporter persisted. "What's your time for the forty?"

Mac's time for the forty-yard dash wasn't anywhere near the four-point-something-second range of most wide receivers, and nothing close to his own previous time. His hesitation in answering hinted at the problems he was having, and the reporters, smelling blood, attacked in earnest.

"Have you come to Dallas to announce your retirement?" one speculated.

"No," Mac said flatly.

"Are you here to see a doctor about your leg?"

"No."

"Are you negotiating with the Tornadoes to get your spot on the team back?"

"No comment."

That gave them more meat to chew on and distracted them from other lines of questioning. They asked a dozen more questions aimed at determining his exact status with the Tornadoes, before he reached the limousine and safety.

"Remind me to kill Andy when I see him," he muttered to Andy's driver.

The old man laughed. "He thought you could use the publicity."

"Why wasn't he here to keep the wolves off of me?"

"He's working on a big deal. Said he'd see you at the office at four, like you asked. You're all set up to stay at the Wyndham Hotel. I can take you there to freshen up, if you'd like."

"I need to make another stop first." Mac gave Andy's chauffeur the address of the sex therapist, who had agreed to see him today during a time someone else had canceled an appointment.

Dr. Timothy Douglas had first talked to Mac in the hospital after one of his operations, when Mac was scared to death that he would be impotent for life because nothing seemed to be working. The doctor had reassured Mac that the medication he was taking—and his state of agitation over the problem—had caused his lack of sex drive.

Douglas was not much older than Mac, but he was balding and wore spectacles, both of which made him look more distinguished. The good doctor had returned several times over the years to talk to Mac in the hospital, and it was during one of those discussions that Mac had admitted he was a virgin.

Douglas hadn't been able to control a smile. "Good for you," he'd said. "Too many men are indiscriminate these days."

"Sorry to burst your bubble, Doc, but I doubt I'd be able to say that if I'd been out of this bed more than a day at a time over the past couple of years."

Douglas patted his shoulder and said, "Wait for the right woman, Mac. You won't be sorry."

Douglas was the only person in the world who knew Mac's secret. And the only one he felt comfortable telling about Jewel's secret. Surely the good doctor could come up with some suggestions for how Mac could help Jewel without hurting her.

"This is a doctor's office," the chauffeur said when he stopped in front of the address Mac had given him.

"Sure is," Mac said. "Meet me back here in an hour."

Mac let himself out of the sleek black car and headed inside the office building.

The hour Mac spent with Timothy Douglas had been well worth the time and trouble to get there. As he paced his agent's office, Mac worked through the various suggestions Douglas had made for how he could help Jewel.

"Patience is essential," Douglas said. "Thoughtfulness. Consideration. All the things you would normally expect in a loving relationship. Only, each step of the way, you need to check with Jewel to make sure she's still with you. Understand?"

Mac understood all right. The man was supposed to control himself while he attended to the woman first. "What if I can't wait?" he blurted, his face crimson with embarrassment.

"Do you care for this woman?" Douglas asked.

"Why the hell do you think I'm so worried?" Mac shot back. "What if I lose control and make things worse?"

"Be sure you're thinking of her at the crucial moment, instead of yourself, and everything will turn out fine."

"That's all there is to it?" Mac asked skeptically.

"Sex is a natural bodily function," Douglas said. "We're supposed to procreate. Your body will know what to do, even if you don't."

Mac took comfort in that last word of advice. But as he was very well aware, knowing technically what to do, and actually doing it, sometimes turned out to be two entirely different things.

On Mac's next lap across his agent's office, the door opened and Andy Dennison stepped inside.

"Hi there, Mac. What's new?"

"I can walk. And I can run."

Andy smiled and crossed to shake Mac's hand. "Congratulations. I should have known you would do what you promised. How about a cigar to celebrate?"

"No thanks," Mac said with a smile. "I'm in training."

"You don't mind if I have one." Andy crossed to his desk, took a cigar from a box on top of it, clipped the end with a sterling silver device, sniffed it and rolled the tobacco lovingly between his fingers. That was as far as he could go. No smoking was allowed in the building.

"When can I set up an appointment with the Tornadoes?" Andy asked.

"Not so fast," Mac said, seating himself in one of the two modern chrome and black leather chairs facing the desk. "What's the last date I could show up in training camp and still have a chance to make the team?"

"Depends on how fast you can run when you show up," Andy said bluntly.

"How fast is the new kid?"

Andy gave Mac a figure for the forty that made sweat bead on Mac's forehead. It was two seconds better than Mac's best time before he was injured.

"What about his hands?"

"Misses a few. Fumbles now and again."

Mac smiled. "Then I have a chance. Being fastest isn't everything. I proved that when I played."

"Yeah. But being slow will get you cut from the team," Andy pointed out.

"How slow is too slow?" Mac asked, leaning forward, his elbows on his knees.

Andy shrugged. "Hard to say. But if you aren't within a second or two of your best time…" Andy shrugged again.

Mac sighed and sat back, crossing his good ankle over his scarred knee. "I was afraid of that."

"Look, there's been some interest in using you

as a sports commentator. Why not let me follow up and—"

"That isn't what I want to do with my life."

"What are you planning to do? I mean, if you don't make the team?"

Mac drew a complete blank. "I don't know. I haven't thought about it much."

"Maybe you should," Andy said. "Think about that sportscasting job. It's national television, lots of exposure, possibility of advertising bucks. Lot of dough in a job like that."

"Lots of travel, too," Mac said.

"Yeah, there's that."

"I want to settle down somewhere and have a family."

Andy cleared his throat. "Uh. I heard about that stop you made this afternoon. Anything I can do to help?"

Mac laughed. "It's taken care of, but thanks for the offer."

"Sure, Mac, just know I'm there if you need me. By the way, who's the girl?"

"Knowing your penchant for publicity I figure I'll keep that to myself for a while."

"Hey. Whatever you want," Andy said. "By the way, how long are you going to be in town?"

"Just overnight."

"Anxious to get back to your girl?" Andy said with a sly smile.

Mac thought about it, smiled and answered, "Yeah. I am."

"Look, I know some folks who'd like to have dinner with you. How about it?"

"Will it help you out?"

Andy grinned. "You're a great guy, Mac. I knew you'd come through. I'll have a tux delivered to your hotel room, and I'll have my limo pick you up at eight."

"A tux! What kind of shindig is this?"

"Charity ball in Forth Worth, complete with politicians and socialites. Won't hurt you to be seen there, Mac. You can use all the good press you can get. You'll be sitting at the mayor's table."

Mac shook his head. "How do I let you talk me into these things?"

Andy stuck the cigar between his teeth and grinned. "You like me?"

Instead of laughing, Mac looked Andy in the eye and said, "You stuck with me when a lot of other folks didn't. I'm not likely to forget that anytime soon." He left before Andy could form a response.

CHAPTER ELEVEN

COLT SAT ON THE SAGGING BACK PORCH of Jenny's house waiting for Huck to come back out. He tugged at the frayed knee of his jeans, making the tear worse, then glanced up at the hot, noonday sun. He couldn't get what Mac had said about Huck and Jenny out of his mind.

College is a long way off. Maybe they'll change their minds about each other.

Colt would never do anything to separate the two of them—not that he believed anything could alter Jenny's devotion to Huck—but Mac had offered him a sort of hope he hadn't allowed himself to feel in a very long time.

Lately, Colt let his eyes linger on her more. He let his heart fall more completely under her spell. Even though his head said it was a stupid thing to do.

"Hey, Colt. You ready to go?"

Colt leapt up guiltily as the kitchen screen door slammed and stuck his hands deep into his back pockets. "Yeah. Sure." *Good thing Huck couldn't read his mind.*

"You're acting awful jumpy lately. What's your problem?" Huck asked as he crossed past Colt and down the creaking steps. "Some girl finally caught your eye?" he teased.

Maybe Huck could read minds, Colt thought uncomfortably.

"Who is it? Sarah Logan? Freda Barnett? I know—Betty Lou Tucker!"

Betty Lou Tucker was the prettiest—and most curvaceous—girl in school. Huck was way off the mark. The only girl Colt ever thought about was Jenny. And Jenny wasn't beautiful, she was just…Jenny. Colt thought of Jenny looking up at him with her bluer-than-blue eyes and felt the heat rising up his throat to make visible spots on his cheeks.

"Thought so," Huck said with a laugh. "Betty Lou's been looking at a lot of guys since she broke up with Bobby Ray." Huck unlooped the reins from the tie rail in front of the Double D ranch house and mounted his horse. "You coming with me, or you gonna sit on Jenny's back porch all day?"

"I…uh…think I'll wait to talk to Jenny before I leave…about some stuff."

Huck shook his head in disgust. "Jenny's gotta feed the little ones before she can do anything. You might be waiting a while. She was asking me if I could help her out, but I've got better things to do with my time than housework. You're welcome to take my place."

"Maybe I'll do that," Colt said, his heart thumping a little harder.

"See you tonight at the movies?" Huck asked.

"Naw. My dad asked me to do some bookkeeping with him."

"When are you gonna tell him you're not gonna stay on the ranch?" Huck asked.

"Sometime," Colt said.

"Better be soon, or he'll be depending on you so much you'll never get out," Huck warned.

"I hear you," Colt said irritably.

Huck kicked his horse into a lope, raising a choking cloud of dust from the dry, sunbaked dirt around the house.

Colt stepped back and waved away the worst of it so he could breathe, then turned and stared at the screen door. All he had to do was knock and offer his help. It was bound to seem a little odd to Jenny for him to volunteer, since he'd never been in her house before.

There was a reason for that. He stayed away from sick people, and her mother had been sick nearly the whole time he'd known her. Her mother's breast cancer had gone into remission for a long time, but after the youngest child was born, it had come back.

Now Mrs. Wright was dying of cancer. Colt knew what that meant. Hair falling out from chemotherapy. Frail limbs. Eyes dead long before the body was. He had seen too much of it at Camp LittleHawk. Enough to know that it hurt desperately to like—let alone love— someone who was ill and who might or might not survive another week, another month, another year.

The only thing that could make him go inside Jenny's house right now was the knowledge that he would get to spend time alone with her. They would probably talk and maybe laugh together. That possibility was worth having to share Jenny's pain as she tended to her dying mother.

But Huck had said Jenny was feeding the little ones. Colt was the baby in his family, but he figured he could probably manage whatever Jenny asked of him.

Colt knocked on the door, said, "Jenny, I'm coming in," and let himself inside. He immediately took off his Western straw hat and stood still inside the screen door until his eyes adjusted to the darker room. When he could see, he found Jenny staring at him, her jaw hanging open.

"Colt. What are you doing in here?"

"Huck thought you might need some help." He clutched the hat against his chest feeling foolish, but said, "Here I am."

She smiled, and he knew it was going to be all right. He looked for a place to hang his hat, but didn't see anything.

"Put it on top of the refrigerator," she said. "That way Tyler and James can't get to it."

He looked at the baby sitting in the high chair before her and the older child sitting in a youth chair next to him. "They seem pretty well lassoed," he said, but he put the hat where she told him, anyway.

She gestured him toward her. "This is Randy," she said, sticking another spoonful of something gross looking in the baby's mouth, "and next to him is Sam. Tyler and James are playing in their room.

"Here. You can take my place." She rose and handed Colt the baby spoon and the open jar of baby food. "Randy loves peas."

Colt took one look at the contents of the jar and nearly gagged. "This doesn't look edible."

Jenny laughed, and he felt his whole body go still at the sound. "Don't tell Randy. He eats it like it was green ice cream."

Colt sat in the chair she had vacated and aimed a

spoon of peas in Randy's direction. When his mouth opened, Colt shoved it in, and Randy cleaned it off. "He's a human vacuum cleaner!"

"He'll probably end up as big and tall as my dad," Jenny said as she set a plate of more recognizable food in front of Sam. The music had gone out of her voice by the time she got to the end of her sentence.

"Where is your dad?"

"He left," she said, her eyes focused on Sam. "Took off when Mom got sick the second time."

"I'm sorry, Jenny. I didn't know."

She tried to make light of it. "Can't really blame him. It isn't pretty to watch someone die. He loved her very much, you know."

Colt couldn't believe how matter-of-factly she was speaking about such a tragic situation. "It must be hard for you and your mom to get along on your own."

Her chin came up, and she looked at him with her incredible blue eyes. "We manage."

He heard her message loud and clear: *Don't feel sorry for me.* He admired her gumption. But what choice did she have? She wasn't old enough to leave home and get a job. Where would she go? He realized now why she had been so worried about being left behind by Huck.

"Good thing you have so much help around the house," he said. "All those brothers, I mean."

"I'm the eldest," she said. "Tyler is ten, James is nine, Sam is five and Randy will be one in a couple of months."

"Who takes care of them when you're in school?"

"Mom has a sister who takes care of her during the

days and keeps an eye on the little ones. I pick up the slack at night and give Aunt Lenore a rest."

Colt caught her glance for a moment and saw a sort of desperation he had often felt himself. A yearning to be free to follow your own path, to see the world, to explore to your heart's content. And the knowledge that destiny—or your parents or family—had other plans for you.

He had thought Huck was the only impediment to having Jenny. He saw now what the future held for her as well as she probably saw it herself. Unless she ran away, and he did not see Jenny as the kind of person who ran away from anything, she would be tied to her family until the boys were grown.

Huck would leave her behind when she couldn't go with him, because Huck would never understand why she couldn't go. Colt understood, though. It was the same reason he might never fly jets. Because she couldn't bear to hurt her family to please herself. As he could never bear to hurt his.

Colt wanted to tell her that he understood. That he knew what she faced. That he would be there for her, even if Huck wasn't.

What if you get a chance to fly jets? an inner voice asked. *Would you stay and work at Hawk's Pride just to be near Jenny?*

Colt was glad he didn't have to make that kind of decision for four years. He would be here for her now. Even though she was Huck's girl. And might always be.

JEWEL, PATTY AND GAVIN WERE sitting in the sand at the bottom of a canyon with eleven campers, pencils and notepads in hand, sketching the primitive art etched on the stone canyon wall that rose up on one side of them.

Some of the kids were sitting cross-legged, some lay on their stomachs. Only one child had not relaxed and made himself comfortable. The twelfth camper, Brad Templeton, stood directly in front of the wall, staring up at it intently.

"How are you doing?" Jewel asked the campers as she rose and began to walk among them to see what they had produced in the half hour they had been drawing.

"Okay."

"Pretty good."

"What's that thing there?" A girl's finger pointed to a stick horse etched on the stone wall.

"What does it look like?" Jewel asked.

"It's a horse, dummy," the boy sitting next to the girl said scornfully.

"Yes, it is, Louis," Jewel said. "But you can see why Nolie might not recognize it. It could be some other animal."

"It has a long tail and pointy ears like a horse," Louis said.

"True. But some dogs have long tails and pointy ears."

"Oh," Louis said thoughtfully. "It looked like a horse to me."

"That's why we're making these drawings," Jewel explained. "And writing down what we think they mean." She put a supportive hand on Patty's shoulder as she encouraged one of the campers and exchanged a thankful look with Gavin, who had one of the youngest—and most homesick—campers sitting in his lap.

"We'll send your drawings to an archaeologist at the university who studies primitive art. She can tell us what she thinks the drawing means. When I send you her findings later this summer, you can compare your conclusions with hers."

"Does the drawing really mean something?" another little girl asked, staring at the primitive figures.

Jewel shrugged and smiled. "I don't know. Maybe someone a long time ago was just having fun drawing."

The kids laughed.

Jewel had reached Brad's side and noticed his drawing pad was blank. "Is something wrong, Brad?" she asked quietly.

He kept his eyes on the stone wall and spoke in a voice that only she could hear. "I know what it means," he said.

"You do?" Jewel turned to stare at the wall of stick figures and arrows pointing in different directions with a sun above it all. "Tell me. I've always been curious."

"What does it matter? What does anything matter?"

Jewel's brow furrowed. "You can't give up, Brad," she said.

"Why not?" he shot back. "People give up on stuff all the time. They quit hobbies and they quit school and they quit jobs."

"They don't quit living," she said.

"Some do," he said stubbornly. "They just stop doing things. You know what I mean."

Jewel felt a chill run down her spine. *People like her.*

As afraid of living as Brad was of dying. "Tell me about the drawings, Brad."

He turned to look up at the wall. "The man wants to go somewhere far away, to have an adventure. But he isn't sure which is the best way to go. So he doesn't go anywhere at all. He stays right where he is. Where it's safe."

Jewel stared at the wall. The sun shone brightly above a stick-figure man and his stick-figure horse. They were surrounded by arrows pointing in all different directions—some of them back at the man himself.

He doesn't go anywhere at all. He stays right where he is. Where it's safe.

Jewel's throat squeezed closed. Brad might have been describing her own life for the past six years. Recently she had begun to make changes, but even so, she had been relying on Mac to get her over the worst hurdles. That had to stop. She had to start thinking about moving forward on her own. Or she might end up stuck forever right where she was.

She had to stop letting the past control her present. She had to open herself to new relationships. She couldn't count on Mac to solve her problems. He wanted to be her friend, nothing more. That had become apparent when she discovered from reading the newspapers the real reason he had gone to Dallas three days ago.

She had died a little inside when she opened the Dallas newspaper the day after Mac had left and found a picture of Mac and Eve Latham smiling at each other at a Fort Worth charity function. If Eve was the woman Mac wanted, Jewel had to accept that and move on. She had to find the courage to start living again—without Mac's help.

The same way Brad had to keep on living, despite the fact he might be dying. "Do you think he ever took the trip?" Jewel asked softly.

Brad shook his head, and a tear spilled on his cheek. He knuckled it away with his fist. "He waited too late," Brad whispered.

Jewel took a step closer and enfolded Brad in her arms. Her chin quivered, and she gritted her teeth to keep from making any sound. How could she have been working here all these years and not have seen what Brad could see so clearly? How could she have let so many years go by not living life when it was so precious? How could she have given fear such a stranglehold on her future?

"It's never too late, Brad," she said fiercely. "All you have to do is take that first step, and then another, and another." She rubbed his shoulders soothingly, then pushed him back and tipped up his chin so she could see his eyes beneath the baseball cap. "Just one step, Brad. And the adventure begins."

"Everything all right here?" Gavin had brought the homesick child with him in his arms.

Jewel swallowed back the knot in her throat and turned to Gavin with a smile. "Sure. I think Brad is ready to do some drawing. Right, Brad?"

"Yeah," he mumbled.

"This one is about ready to go back," Gavin said, gesturing to the little girl with his chin. She looked happy and comfortable in Gavin's arms. He really was a great guy, Jewel thought, just not the guy for her.

"Tell you what," Jewel said. "Why don't you and Patty gather up everyone else and get them started back. I'll stay here a little while longer with Brad."

"You sure?" Gavin asked doubtfully. "It's pretty isolated out here."

Jewel laughed. "Hawk's Pride is safer than most big cities. Brad and I will be fine."

"Okay," Gavin said with a smile. "See you later."

"Thanks, Gavin."

"You're welcome, Boss," he said over his shoulder. "Come on, guys. Let's get you all mounted up," he called to the campers. "Day's wastin'."

Jewel helped Gavin and Patty make sure all the campers were comfortable for the horseback ride up out of the canyon. Then she crossed back to where Brad was industriously working on his drawing.

"That's looking pretty good," Jewel said, admiring his sketch.

"I've had a lot of time to practice," Brad said, his lips curling wryly.

"What do you want to be when you grow up?" Jewel asked.

"I wanted to be a football player," Brad said, changing it to the past tense. "Like Mac Macready."

"Let's get some practice, then," Mac said.

Jewel and Brad both jerked their heads toward the sound of Mac's voice. He dismounted from his horse, a football tucked into his elbow.

Jewel was surprised Mac had returned, especially after seeing the photo of him with his arm around Eve Latham. Her first impulse was to rail at him, but she had no claims on Mac Macready. What "business" he

did in his free time was up to him. She just wished he
hadn't lied to her about why he had gone to Dallas. That
wasn't something friends did to friends.

"What are you doing here?" Jewel said, her voice
sharp despite her wish to keep it level.

"I brought a football, figuring I'd throw a few passes
to the kids, but I passed them on the way down, headed
back for lunch. Gavin told me you'd stayed behind with
Brad, so I thought I'd join you."

"Hi, Mac," Brad said shyly.

"Hi, Brad," Mac said, tossing him the football. "I
need to talk with Jewel for a minute. Why don't you go
find us a place where you can throw me a few?"

"You want me to throw to you?"

"You want to be a football player someday, don't you?
No time like the present to start practicing."

Brad shot Jewel a questioning look. *Should I let
myself hope? Should I take him up on his offer?*

"One step, Brad," she said softly. "And the adventure
begins."

The boy smiled broadly and turned back to Mac.
"Okay, Mac. I'll go find us a good spot." He turned and
headed on the run toward a sandy stretch that extended
around a curve in the canyon wall.

Jewel compared the Mac in the newspaper photo to
the Mac standing before her. He had looked impressively
handsome in a tuxedo. But he was just as impressive
dressed in a cutoff T-shirt that showed off a washboard
midriff and rippling biceps. Cutoff jeans revealed his
scarred leg, but emphasized his height. Tennis shoes
and a Texas Rangers baseball cap with his blond hair

sticking out every whichaway made him look like one of the kids.

She was quite aware he was not.

Jewel forced herself to stand still as Mac eyed her up and down in return. She was wearing a T-shirt with the neck cut out that was also cut off at midriff, exposing her narrow waist, and very short, fringed cutoffs that showed off her long legs. She might as well have been naked. The look in his eyes made her skin feel prickly all over.

Now that he was back, his gaze seemed to say, they could pick up where they had left off, kissing and touching.

But she could not forget the possessive look in Eve's eyes, or the way Mac's arm reached snugly around her. She was very well aware of how long he had been gone and who he had been with, but she couldn't very well confront him with Brad nearby.

"I missed you," he said softly.

"From the picture in the newspaper I wouldn't have said you were too lonely."

He frowned. "What picture?"

"The one of you with your arm around Eve Latham at a charity ball."

Mac groaned. "I can explain—"

"Later," she said, turning to walk away from him. "Brad is waiting for you."

He caught her arm. "I want this cleared up now. It was nothing, Jewel. Publicity my agent set up."

"With Eve Latham?" she said, raising a doubtful brow.

"With her father, actually. He's a big fan of the Tornadoes."

"I suppose Eve just happened to be there?"

"Believe me, I didn't set that up. In fact, I'd planned to come right back the next morning, but Eve's father arranged a golf game the next morning with the manager of the Tornadoes that I couldn't very well get out of, and my agent snuck a few more appearances into the mix. Believe me, I only wanted to get back here as quickly as I could."

"Why?" she said, staring him in the eye. "So you could throw footballs to adoring campers?"

For the first time he looked angry. "You know better," he said through clenched teeth.

"Do I? I have no claim on you, Mac. If you'd rather not follow through on what you promised, all you have to do is say so. It isn't necessary to make excuses."

An instant later, he was kissing her hard on the mouth. It was as much a kiss of anger as of passion. Jewel felt both angry and passionate in return. Mac let her go abruptly, his breathing erratic, and said, "I have no intention of backing out on my promise to you. It's up to you whether you choose to take advantage of my offer."

Jewel stared at Mac, appalled at how easily he had aroused her, how easily he had made her want him. She was afraid to let Mac back in. "I thought you'd lied to me about why you went to Dallas," she admitted.

"I would never lie to you, Jewel. That's not something friends do."

She wanted to believe him. She wanted to go back to trusting him. Fear made her cautious. Fear made her reluctant to let him back into her life. Fear could keep her stuck in the same rut forever.

Jewel glanced at the etching on the stone wall. She took a deep breath and let it out. "All right, Mac. You've got yourself a deal."

She held out her hand for him to shake, and Mac raised it to his mouth, kissing it like a courtier of old. His grin reappeared, and she felt her insides flip-flop.

"Very well, my little hyacinth," he said.

"That's a flower."

"And a precious stone," he assured her. "See you in a little while." He let go of her and loped across the sand, calling out to Brad to throw him the ball.

Jewel stared at her hand where Mac had kissed it, then raised her fingertips to her recently kissed lips. Mac had plainly thrown down the gauntlet. She had a chance to grab for life with both hands. She had a chance to practice kissing and touching with him. And she had a chance to explore a relationship with him beyond the friendship they had shared for so many years. She could take it, or reject it. The choice was hers.

What she must not do was make no choice at all.

If she hadn't spent the past half hour in Brad Templeton's company, she might have chickened out. But Jewel couldn't very well demand Brad reach out for life, if she wasn't going to do it herself.

Brad threw Mac the ball and came racing back to her holding out his notepad and pencil.

Jewel exchanged a glance with Mac that was the closest she had ever come to flirting with him. It promised everything…later. She was rewarded with a look that made her body curl inside and her breasts feel achy and swollen.

Jewel felt a tug on her T-shirt and looked down at

Brad, who stood beside her again, his eyes gleaming with delight. Oh, yes. Football. And hope.

"I'll take those things," she said, reaching out for Brad's notepad and pencil.

Brad turned and trotted right back to Mac. She saw the boy swallow hard as he reached out for the football Mac was handing him. Jewel thanked Mac with her eyes and got a wink that flustered her in return.

She knew better than to tell either male not to overdo it. But Jewel was concerned as the sun rose higher and Brad continued to throw the ball and Mac continued to run for it. They were both drenched with sweat. Brad looked flushed. And Mac was starting to limp.

"Hey, you two. How about a break?"

She caught Mac's eye and gave him a warning look. He glanced at Brad and said, "I'm whipped, partner. How about a tall, cold glass? Of water, that is," he said, slapping Brad on the shoulder as they started back toward where Jewel sat in the shade of the canyon wall.

Jewel stood up with the canteens ready and handed one to each of them. She lifted Brad's hat as though to rearrange it on his head and surreptitiously checked for a fever. He seemed warm, but the sun was hot. "How are you feeling?" she asked, unable to keep the concern from her voice.

"Fantastic," Brad said, grinning for the first time since he had arrived at camp. "That was fun, Mac. Thanks."

"Tell you what I'm going to do, partner. I'm going to autograph this football to you with thanks for a strong throwing arm, so you can take it home with you."

"Wow! That would be neat," Brad said, sounding more like a kid his age every minute. He flopped down onto the sand, looking exhausted but happy.

Jewel was aware of Mac's wince as he settled onto the ground beside Brad.

"I've got some snacks that'll keep us until we can get some lunch," she said, dropping to her knees and opening what was left of the graham crackers and peanut butter and celery she had brought for the campers. "That'll also give you two a chance to cool off before we make the ride home."

As they munched, Mac and Brad talked. Jewel watched them closely. Brad had a smile on his face and talked a mile a minute, as though someone had turned up the rpms on a record. Mac listened. He didn't look at her often, but often enough to remind her that he was ready and willing whenever she wanted to take that final leap of faith. "Are you ready to head back now?" Jewel asked, when Brad had wound down a little.

"I guess," Brad said. "Can we do this again?" he asked Mac as he shoved himself to his feet.

"As often as you want before you leave," Mac said.

Jewel noticed Mac wincing again as he straightened his scarred leg.

He caught her watching him and grinned, as though he hadn't just been in pain. "Don't worry. Everything important is working just fine." He leered at her, making it clear exactly what he meant.

Jewel felt flustered and excited. And anxious. Mac looked exhausted. He was using humor—and sexual tension—to distract her and doing a pretty good job. She was also concerned about Brad. He seemed awfully red-faced even after his rest. "Are you sure you're both feeling all right?" she asked.

"I'm doing great!" Brad said.

"I'm just fine," Mac said.

Jewel pursed her lips. Typical males. Everything was fine until they keeled over. She decided to keep a close eye on both of them.

Mac was still grinning as he ushered Brad past her and headed for the horses, whispering for her ears only, "You look beautiful, Amethyst. And very, very desirable. I can't wait for…later."

Jewel's heart started to pound as she stared at Mac's back, wondering if she would have the courage to do this evening what she had been waiting six years to do. His calling her "Amethyst" reminded her that they had been friends for a very long time. That he would never hurt her. That she could trust him.

Surely Brad's admonition about postponing life had made a difference. Surely she would be able to let go of the fear and move forward with her life. All she had to do was take one step. And the adventure would begin.

CHAPTER TWELVE

BRAD WAS A DIFFERENT CHILD WHEN he entered the cookhouse for lunch—happy, talkative, showing off his football to the other kids and stuffing down a plateful of lasagna as though it was the best meal he had ever eaten. Jewel was proud of Brad for reaching out with both hands toward the future and grateful to Mac for putting an ear-to-ear smile on the boy's face.

However, Mac had not joined them for lunch, pleading the need for a shower. The entire time Jewel ate, she could not get the image of him naked in the shower out of her mind. She had the craziest urge to join him there which, of course, she did not indulge.

After lunch, when the campers took a rest break in their cottages, Jewel had no excuse to linger in the cookhouse. She drew herself up from the bench where she had been sitting and headed toward her cottage, not sure whether she wanted Mac to be out of the shower or not.

When she entered the cottage she felt disappointed not to hear the shower running. There was her answer. She had wanted an excuse to see all of Mac and had been thwarted. She headed for the bathroom anyway, thinking it would be nice to take a quick, cool shower herself while the campers were napping. The bathroom door was open on her side, so she assumed the room was empty.

It was not.

Mac sat in the tub covered with white bubbles—which she presumed had come from the glass-stoppered container of bubble bath she kept on the edge of the tub. He was leaning forward, his teeth gritted, his hands apparently gripping his scarred leg.

"Mac?"

He whipped his head around, swore, then groaned. She saw his biceps ripple as he applied tremendous pressure to his leg.

"What is it?" she asked. "What's wrong?"

"Cramp," he gritted through his teeth.

She dropped to her knees on the fluffy bath mat beside the tub, her eyes focused on his straining face. "What can I do? How can I help?"

"I can't move…can't get out of the damned tub!"

"Do you want me to help you stand up?"

He shook his head violently and groaned again.

"How long has the muscle been cramped?" she asked.

"Too long," he snapped back.

His face was blanched with pain. The sweat on his brow and above his lip, which she at first thought had to be from the heat of the water, was apparently the result of fighting the cramp. For how long? Fifteen minutes? Twenty? "I'll call 911," she said, pushing off from the tub to stand up.

"Don't! I don't want news of this getting out."

"You need help, Mac," she said, angry because she was frightened.

"Then help me, damn it!"

"How?"

"Maybe two sets of hands working on the muscle will get it to uncramp more quickly."

She hesitated only a moment before dropping back down onto the bath mat. Before she could change her mind, she stuck her hands beneath the thin layer of bubbles into the water—which was merely lukewarm—and reached for his leg. Her hands tangled with his before she moved them upward, closer to his knee.

As she worked her fingers into the tightly clenched calf muscle she asked, "Has this happened before?"

He nodded. "Never this bad." His head rolled back and she watched his jaw muscles work as he struggled to endure the pain without making a sound.

"Please let me call someone, Mac."

"No," he grated out.

"Then let me run some more hot water. Wouldn't that help?"

He met her gaze, struggled with the decision, then nodded.

She tipped the lever to empty the tub, realizing after she did so, that the bubbles were going to run out with the water, leaving Mac exposed. But she couldn't worry about his modesty—or hers—right now. She was too worried about his pain and the ramifications of Mac having such severe cramps in his leg after what would have been a very light workout if he had really been playing football.

The water drained quickly, and a slurping sound announced the tub was empty. Jewel shot the lever closed and turned on the water, making it as hot as she thought he could stand.

"Too hot?" she asked, turning to look at him for the first time since the tub had begun draining.

"No. It feels good."

Her breath caught at the sight of him covered here and there with bubbles. She quickly turned her head away, but the image of him, wet curls caught on his nape, water pearled on his shoulders, bubbles caught in the curls on his chest—and on other curls—stayed with her.

But not for long. For the first time, she took a good look at the leg she was massaging. "Mac, there's not much muscle left here. It's all scar tissue."

"I know," he said with a discouraged sigh. "That's the problem. What muscle there is left isn't enough to—" His hands gripped his ankle as an agonized cry tore from his throat. She moved her hands near his at the back of his ankle and felt the muscle spasming. The steaming hot water covered their hands as she held on tight with him for the sixty-five long seconds it took the spasm to pass. Suddenly, she felt the entire muscle ease.

Mac hissed out a breath and, after waiting to see if the tension would return, cautiously let go of his leg.

Jewel turned to look at him and saw his face was turned toward the tile wall. And that tears streamed from his eyes. "Oh, Mac."

"Go away, Jewel," he grated out.

She couldn't do that. Not with what she knew now.

Mac's football career was over. He knew it. And was grieving for it.

She didn't think about what she was doing, she just did it. Two seconds later she had her tennis shoes and socks off and had eased herself sideways into the tub on Mac's lap, her legs hanging over the side of the tub, her arms around his neck, her nose plastered against his throat. "I'm so sorry, Mac," she said, her nose burning, her eyes stinging with tears. "I'm so sorry."

At first she thought he was going to push her away, but his arms closed tight around her and he pulled her close, pressing his cheek tight against hers. She could feel him trembling, feel him struggling to hold back the sobs, until at last they broke free.

She held him close, crooning words that made no sense, offering the comfort of her arms and her love. *Oh, my God. I love him.* It was a stunning realization. A frightening one when she knew his life, now that his future was so uncertain, might very well move in a different direction than hers. But that would not stop what she felt for him. He was another part of her, a part she needed to feel whole inside.

Jewel had no idea how much time had passed when Mac's heaving body finally quieted. He seemed completely relaxed, as though he had accepted the inevitable and was now ready to move beyond it.

"You'd better turn off the water," he said in a voice that was amazingly calm.

Jewel lifted her head and realized the water had reached the rim of the tub and was threatening to spill over. She reached around and shut it off, then turned shyly back to Mac. "I should get off of you and let you finish your bath."

"I wish you wouldn't."

She laughed uncertainly. "What did you have in mind?"

In answer, he lifted her at the waist and rearranged

her so she was facing him, her knees on either side of his hips. The extra weight of her legs caused the water to lap over the side of the tub, but Jewel had more important things to think about than a little water on the bathroom floor.

"Mac, do you think we should be doing this now? I mean, what if your leg—"

"Let me worry about my leg," he said.

When she opened her mouth to protest again, he covered it with his hand and said, "I'm fine. Really. Please, Jewel, don't leave me."

She kept her eyes focused on Mac's as he reached for the bottom of her soaked T-shirt and began to lift it up over her head. She raised her arms and let him remove it.

I love him. And I trust him, she realized.

Mac dropped the T-shirt onto the already soaked bath mat and reached behind her for the clasp of her bra. She gripped his shoulders and said nervously, "This is a first for me."

It was a warning and an offering and a prayer. *Please be careful. Please let my body please you. Please let me not be afraid.* She did not ask for what she wanted most. She did not say, *Please love me.* That was something Mac would have to offer on his own.

His eyes were intent on her face as he pulled her lacy, heavy-duty bra off and her Beautiful Breasts—with wonderful big B's, because Mac looked at them that way—fell free. The bra went the way of her T-shirt, and Mac reached out gently, reverently, to cup her breasts in his hands.

"Exquisite," he said, his thumbs flicking the nipples.

Jewel had to remind herself to breathe as sensation streaked from her nipples to a drawstring somewhere deep inside her womb and pulled it up tight. Her hands threaded into the damp hair at Mac's nape as he lowered his head to kiss each breast. His mouth latched onto a nipple and he sucked, gently at first, then more strongly.

Jewel's hips arched instinctively toward him.

"Easy," he said, his hands gripping her hips atop her cutoff jeans. "Slow and easy, Jewel. We have all the time in the world."

"I don't know what to do with my hands," she said anxiously. "Tell me what to do to please you."

He smiled. "You're doing fine."

"I'm not doing anything!" she replied pertly.

He lifted his hips, and she could feel his arousal.

"Oh. Well. I see."

Mac laughed, a rumbly sound, and kissed her quickly on the lips. "I love your innocence," he said, his eyes staring intently into hers. "I want to be the first, Jewel. I am so honored to be the first."

"But—"

He put his fingertips to her lips. "The first," he repeated.

In truth, this situation was so incredibly different from what had happened to her all those years ago, that the past didn't seem real anymore. Mac made her feel innocent, made her feel the joy and excitement—and normal fear—of an untouched woman.

He teased her and touched her and tasted her until they were both wrinkled from the water. And she did the same, enjoying the pleasure of rubbing her breasts against the crisp curls on his chest and returning the favor of kissing and caressing and sucking his nipples—which turned out to be surprisingly sensitive.

"We'd better get out of here," Mac said, "or we're going to turn into prunes."

Jewel felt a little shy standing up and stepping out of the tub. As much as she was tempted to look, she turned her back on Mac as he stood and stepped out of the tub behind her. She had already reached for a towel to cover her breasts, when he took it away from her.

He aligned his body with hers from behind, put his arms around her to cup her breasts and played with her nipples until they were aching and pointy. His mouth teased her throat beneath her ear with kisses, before he latched onto a particular spot and sucked hard enough to make her moan with pleasure.

"I'm only going to touch you," he said, explaining as his hands slid down the front of her, unsnapped her jeans, spread them wide and slid his hand beneath her panties. "To let you feel my hands on you."

She held her breath, expecting the fear to return. But it didn't. She felt only the warmth of his hand against her cooling flesh and the feel of his fingertips probing gently between her thighs. Slowly, carefully, he insinuated one finger inside her.

"Are you all right?" he asked.

"Uh-huh."

She felt his mouth curve into a smile against her cheek. "I think maybe you'd better breathe," he said.

She exhaled and then gasped a breath of air as his finger slid deeper inside her. "Oh."

He paused. "Did I hurt you?"

"No. I feel..." She searched for the word. *Strange. Full. Achy.* Yes, but more than that. "I feel good," she said. "This feels so right."

"I'm glad." He used his other hand to encourage her to spread her legs, so he would have easier access to her. And slipped another finger inside her.

Her breath was coming in erratic spurts, and she reminded herself to keep breathing.

"Still okay?" he asked.

She nodded, then made a sound when his thumb found the tiny bud at the apex of her thighs and began to caress it. Her knees started to buckle, nature's way of getting her prone, and Mac compensated by putting a strong arm around her midriff and pulling her back tight against him. She could feel his arousal against her buttocks, hard and pulsing.

Instead of being afraid, she was aroused. She was sure she could make love to him this time without running away. She was ready to move forward. She wanted to feel him inside her. "Mac," she said. "I'm not afraid anymore."

"Good," he replied, his voice husky. "Just relax and let me make love to you."

Let me make love to you. It was what she had wanted for a very long time. Jewel let herself fully enjoy what Mac was doing to her—making love to her—without worrying about whether he was *in love* with her. He was as considerate a lover as she could ever have hoped for. He cared for her. That would have to be enough for now.

Mac had one hand inside her jeans, the other tantalizing her nipple, while his mouth teased the flesh at her throat. She writhed against him as her body experienced all the joy and pleasure she had not allowed herself to feel in the past.

As the tension built inside her, she reached out to the pleasure, indulged in it, delighted in it, until she felt herself losing control. "Mac," she said, the fright back in her voice. "What's happening to me?"

"Something wonderful. Let it happen, Jewel. Let me do this for you."

She trusted Mac. As he had trusted her to comfort him. More than that. She loved him.

Jewel gave her body into his hands and was rewarded moments later with a shattering climax, her body shuddering with wave after wave of intense pleasure. "Mac," she gasped. "Mac."

"I know," he said, his voice gentle, his breathing as erratic as hers. "I know."

Jewel felt totally enervated and was barely aware when Mac picked her up in his arms and carried her to her bedroom. He pulled the sheets down on her bed, stood her up long enough to strip the wet cutoffs and panties off her, then tucked her under the covers before she had time to feel embarrassed at being naked.

She expected him to join her. But the last thing she saw before her eyes slid closed was Mac's taut, untanned buttocks as he walked out of the room.

MAC KNEW THAT JEWEL HAD EXPECTED him to join her in bed, and that he would have been welcome there. He could have eased the ache in his loins and gotten them both over hurdles that had stood in their way for years. He had learned from their recent lovemaking that he had not only the self-control—but the desire—to put Jewel's feelings and needs before his own.

Several things had stopped him from staying.

Mac had realized, as he was making love to Jewel, that he loved her. And not just as a friend, but as an inseparable part of himself. He wanted to spend his life with her. He wanted to plant his seed inside her and help her raise the children they would make together. He wanted to grow old with her.

Which raised a second problem. Mac Macready was another football has-been, who had no idea what he wanted to do with the rest of his life. After the horrific episode with his scarred leg in the tub, there was no denying the truth any longer. He would never play pro football again. Mac had not beaten the odds this time. He had lost.

It was a devastating realization.

If he had not had Jewel to hang on to, he didn't know what he would have done. She had understood his pain and his loss. She had offered comfort without platitudes. She obviously cared for him—even after seeing him at his most vulnerable.

None of the reasons he had for fearing commitment with a woman existed where Jewel was concerned. With her, Mac felt safe making that leap into the unknown, certain he could trust her to be there when he landed.

Which brought him to a third problem. Mac had no idea whether Jewel loved him merely as a friend or the way he wanted to be loved. As a man. As her lover. As her future husband.

Mac had collected Jewel's clothes before he left the bedroom, wrung out all her wet things and hung them in the bathroom to dry. He had dressed himself in Levi's and a Western shirt, then laid himself down on his bed, his hands behind his head, to think.

On the way up out of the canyon at lunchtime, Jewel had encouraged Brad to tell Mac his interpretation of the primitive drawings on the canyon wall. Mac had listened attentively and heard in Brad's explanation an analogy of what life was like when it was lived in fear of reaching out for dreams. After all, dreams might never come true. You might end up disappointed, or in worse shape than if you had been satisfied with what you already had.

Mac had always believed in pursuing his dreams. He had never been indecisive. But clearly there were moments when old dreams had to be abandoned—and new dreams dreamed. Mac could no longer be a professional football player. So what else did he want to do with his life?

That wasn't an easy question to answer, because Mac had been so determined to regain the use of his scarred leg that he had refused to think about alternatives. Now he must. And he had to factor Jewel, and her commitment to Camp LittleHawk, into the equation.

The idea that rose immediately in his mind was such a simple solution—and yet so revolutionary in terms of how he had intended to spend his life—that Mac felt both excited and cautious about pursuing it. Maybe the best thing to do was to approach Jewel and see what she thought.

He was on his way back to her room when someone knocked hard and fast on the door to the cottage. He hurried to the door and opened it to find Gavin Talbot standing there.

"I think you better get Jewel and come to the boys' bunkhouse," he said. "Brad Templeton has a fever."

CHAPTER THIRTEEN

JEWEL BLAMED HERSELF FOR NOT recognizing that Brad's flushed face at lunch was caused not only by excitement but also by the fever that signaled the return of his leukemia—and the end of his second remission.

She could barely manage to keep a smile on her face as she belted Brad into the seat of the chartered plane for the short flight back to Dallas Children's Hospital, which was waiting to readmit him. Brad was gripping Mac's football tightly in the crook of one arm. His eyes were feverishly bright, and he had a smile plastered on his face as phony as the one on hers.

Jewel felt Mac's presence at her side. She saw the muscles in his scarred leg as he knelt facing Brad. Mac knew what the end of Brad's remission meant as well as she did. The boy's chances of survival were considerably less now than they had been at the beginning of the week. Mac might very well be bidding Brad Templeton goodbye for the last time.

"Hey, tiger," Mac said, tugging the brim of Brad's cap down playfully. "How's it going?"

Brad readjusted the cap and said, "It's back."

"I know," Mac said. "Remember what I said."

"Yeah. Doctors don't know everything."

Mac nodded soberly. "You keep fighting," he said, his voice low and fierce. He spoke so softly Jewel could barely hear him. "Don't give up. I expect to see you back here next summer. In fact, I expect you to be a counselor someday at a sports camp I'm thinking about starting, where lots of football players like Troy Aikman and Dan Marino and Reggie White and Jerry Rice will come and spend a little time with kids like you."

Jewel wondered where Mac had come up with the idea of a sports camp to encourage Brad. The way Brad's face had lit up, it had certainly been a good idea. She was surprised by the other message Brad had heard in Mac's speech.

"Does that mean you're not gonna play football anymore?" Brad asked.

Mac shook his head. "My leg can't tolerate it."

"So sometimes the doctors *are* right," Brad said.

Jewel watched as Mac gripped Brad's free hand in his and said, "Believe in yourself, and you'll come through fine."

"Time for takeoff, folks," the pilot announced. The nurse who was traveling with Brad was already buckled into her seat.

Mac stood, but Brad held on to his hand and pulled him back down onto his knee. "Good-bye, Mac," he said, a farewell in case he never came back. His chin wobbled and tears welled in his eyes.

"See you soon, Brad," Mac replied. He hugged the boy, who dropped the football and reached up to grab Mac tight around the neck with both hands.

"I don't want to go back to the hospital," Brad said. "Please don't make me leave."

"You have to go. You need help to get well."

"I'm not going to get well. I'm going to die!" Brad cried.

"You'd better not," Mac said severely. "I'm counting on you to come through for me."

Jewel watched as Mac pulled Brad's hands free and reached down to retrieve the football from the floor of the plane and put it back in Mac's arms. "Remember, if I made it, you can make it, too," Mac said.

A tear spilled over as Brad glanced at Jewel for confirmation of Mac's promise.

Her throat was too swollen to speak. She whispered, "Come back soon, Brad," then backed away, keeping the smile on her face as long as she could. It was gone before she reached the door.

Once off the plane, Jewel ran all the way to the van. She had freely chosen to work with kids like Brad, knowing they didn't all make it. With some of them, it was especially hard to let go. Brad's life had seemed so full of possibilities, as Mac's had been all those years ago. Now Mac had lost his dream. And Brad might lose his life.

Jewel felt Mac's arms close around her from behind. He turned her to face the runway, which she saw through a haze of tears, and lifted her arm so she was waving at Brad as the chartered plane took off. Then Mac turned her to face him and closed his arms tightly around her, offering her a comforting shoulder to lay her head on.

"I can't bear it," she said. "First to see you so unhappy, and now Brad..." She couldn't say the word *dying*.

"Brad will make it," Mac said fervently.

"How can you be so sure?" she sobbed.

"I know these things," he said. "Besides, I'm going to need him when I start my sports camp for kids with cancer."

It took a moment for what he said to sink in. When it did, Jewel backed out of his arms and stared at him in shocked disbelief. "I thought you made that up for Brad's sake."

"Nope. It's for real." He opened the door of the van and hustled her inside, then got into the driver's seat and started up the vehicle.

"Why haven't I heard about this sports camp before?" Jewel asked, wiping the tears from her eyes.

He grinned at her. "Because I just thought it up this afternoon."

"Oh."

"I wanted to talk to you about it before I went much further with the idea. What do you think about it?"

Jewel's first thought was that it would take Mac away from Hawk's Pride. That was selfish. What Mac planned to do would help a great many children. "I think what you're planning is one of the noblest, most considerate—"

The van veered to the berm and skidded to a halt. Before Jewel could say another word, Mac's arms were around her and his mouth had covered hers.

She had no time to think, only to feel. What she felt was overflowing love for this man who had so much strength, yet had let her see him when he was at his most vulnerable. She reached out to touch Mac's face tenderly, to thank him for being who he was.

He broke off the kiss abruptly, and she was caught by his gaze, which promised so much—hope, happiness and something else she was afraid to name, because she wanted it so much she feared she had merely wished it there.

"Look at me like that too long, love, and you're liable to get what you want right here and now, instead of when we get back to the cottage."

Jewel stared into Mac's blue eyes, her heart pounding. Had he really called her *love?* Had he said they were going to be making love in a few minutes? He didn't repeat himself, merely started up the van and pulled back onto the road.

Jewel suddenly realized why Mac had reached out to her physically. Making love was an act to reaffirm life in the presence of death. *We can reach out for joy. We still have our lives ahead of us, whatever those lives may bring. This offer of lovemaking has nothing to do with Mac actually loving me. It's a reaction to Brad's illness.* She couldn't disagree with Mac's motive. Or with wanting to be held close, no matter what the reason. She wasn't going to deny him, or herself, the lovemaking he had promised.

"Tell me more about the camp," she said to break the strained silence.

"There isn't any more to tell," he replied. "It's just an idea right now. Do you have any suggestions?"

"Where do you plan to locate it?"

He frowned. "That's a problem. I probably have enough money left from my signing bonus with the Tornadoes to advertise the place and hire help for the first year. But I doubt whether I have enough to buy a piece of land and build buildings. Any suggestions?"

Jewel would have offered her facilities immediately,

if she had thought he would accept. His explanation seemed to suggest he would be perfectly happy to open his camp right here.

The way he was looking at her, his heart in his eyes, gave her the courage to speak. "Camp LittleHawk belongs to my mother, but she's said it can be mine whenever I want it. I think having a sports program here—with famous football players participating on occasion—would be a welcome addition."

Mac smiled at her, and she felt her throat swell with emotion. "Thanks, Jewel. Incorporating my idea with what you've already established at Camp LittleHawk would please me very much."

They had arrived back at the cottage, and Mac quickly left the van and came around to help Jewel out. He took her hand and practically dragged her into the cottage. She realized why he was in such a hurry when, the instant they were inside with the door closed behind them, he pulled her into his arms and pressed her to him from breast to thigh. The evidence of his desire was hard to miss.

"I love you, Jewel."

The way he blurted it out seemed to surprise him as much as it surprised her. His eyes looked wary, as though he wished he hadn't spoken.

She shoved back the hurt and said, "It's all right, Mac. You don't have to say things like that."

The wary look disappeared, and his jaw firmed. "I don't *have* to say it. I *want* to say it. I love you, Jewel. I think I have for a very long time. I was afraid to do anything about it, afraid even to admit it, I think, because of all the bad things that happened when I loved someone in the past.

"What's happened to Brad made me realize I don't want to wait any longer. Life is too precious to waste a single day of it. I love you," he repeated. "And I want to make love with you."

Jewel took a deep breath and let it out. If he could find the courage to speak, so could she. "I love you, too, Mac. I've been afraid to tell you, afraid you wouldn't feel the same way. Afraid—"

She never got a chance to finish. His mouth captured hers at the same time he reached down to lift her up and carry her toward his bedroom.

MAC LAID JEWEL DOWN ON HIS bed as gently as he could and sat down beside her. He hadn't expected his courage to desert him, but it seemed for a moment that he wouldn't be able to go through with what he had planned.

It was late in the day, and the growing dusk gave everything in the room a soft, rosy glow. Jewel had never looked more beautiful to him. Or more trusting.

He had never been more nervous. Or frightened.

Think of her feelings, not your own.

"Are you all right?" he asked.

"More than all right," she said, a tender smile on her lips. "Kiss me please, Mac."

He had never been more gentle, more tender, more considerate of a woman. He brushed his mouth against hers, teased her lips, nipped at her and eased his tongue into her mouth to taste her. He felt her growing desire, her growing urgency to touch and taste in return.

He put his arms around her and pulled her close, feeling the tips of her breasts turn as pointy as pebbles when they made contact with his chest. "Would you like me to undress you?" he asked.

"I'd rather undress you," she said with a mischievous smile.

Mac was surprised, but when he thought about it, it seemed like a good idea. If he was undressed while she was still clothed, she would have the opportunity of escaping anytime she didn't feel comfortable. "Okay," he said. "Where would you like to start?"

She got off the bed and said, "Sit back on the bed, so I can take off your boots." She turned her back to him and tugged at each of his boot heels, while he gave her a shove with the opposite foot to help get the cowboy boots off. Then she pulled off his socks and said, "Stand up."

He stood barefoot on the wooden floor and watched as she slowly pulled his Western shirt out of his jeans and unsnapped the snaps, one at a time from the top downward. He wasn't wearing an undershirt, and she kissed her way down his chest. He was quivering by the time she reached the soft line of down that disappeared into his jeans.

When she ran her tongue around his navel, he nearly jumped out of his skin. "Good God," he muttered.

"You didn't like it?" she asked, looking up into his face.

He shoved both hands through his hair in agitation. "I'm about to explode because of it," he admitted.

Jewel smiled. "That's good, don't you think?"

Patience. Patience. Patience. He said it like a mantra,

hoping he could endure her innocent exploration. He bit the inside of his cheek when she undid his belt, pulled it through the loops of his jeans and let it drop to the floor.

She unbuttoned the top button of his Levi's and began to lower the zipper. Her hand brushed against his tumescence, and he grabbed her wrist to avoid disaster. He wanted desperately to tell her it was the first time for him, but the words wouldn't come out. Instead he said, "It's been a while for me, Jewel. I don't want to disappoint you."

"What about Eve?" she asked.

He had forgotten all about Eve. "Nothing happened with her," he said.

"But you were gone so long that first night. And when you met her in Dallas, I thought—"

"She never turned me on," Mac blurted. "I couldn't... I didn't... Damn it, Jewel! You know what I'm trying to say." He could feel the heat rising on his throat. He couldn't believe what he had just confessed.

He waited for the laughter, and it came—a warm, happy sound that made his heart soar.

"Oh, Mac," Jewel said, her dark brown eyes bright with joy. "If you only knew how much I've wanted to hear you say those exact words—or something very like them."

"You have?"

"I've been terribly jealous," she admitted. Jewel rubbed her cheek against the curls on his chest, then kissed him, sending goose bumps skittering across his flesh. "I'm so glad," she said. "I've wanted you all to myself." The smile returned as she said, "And now I've got you."

She pushed his shirt off his shoulders until it caught at his wrists, effectively making him a prisoner. Instead of releasing the snaps, she shot him a grin and said, "You're my captive now. I can do whatever I want with you."

He leaned down to kiss her, and she stepped back and wagged her finger at him.

"Oh, no, you don't. I'm going to be doing the kissing and touching." She reached down and cupped him with her hand.

"You're going to kill me," Mac said through gritted teeth.

"You don't like it?" she teased.

"You know I like it," he retorted. "I like it so much I'm about to burst."

"Good," she said. "Now you stand right there while I undress."

Mac's eyes went wide when Jewel began a striptease in front of him. No woman had ever removed a T-shirt, bra, jeans and panties quite so seductively.

Don't think of yourself. Think of her.

Mac's pulse was pounding in his temples—and elsewhere. His whole body quivered with excitement.

"You're so beautiful," he said when she was naked at last.

She touched the crisscrossing scars on her face and the more visible scar on her thigh, where the operations to mend her leg had been performed. "You don't mind?"

He solved the problem of the imprisoning shirt by

pulling his arms up over his head and using the shirt between his hands as a chain to encircle her and pull her close. "All I see is a beautiful, desirable woman."

She made a sound of pleasure when her breasts were finally pillowed against his naked chest. He spread his legs and urged her between them. Her hands curved around his waist and ventured up his back all the way to his nape. His blood raced as her hands caressed him.

He shuddered out a breath. *Think of her. Give her pleasure. Make it good for her. Don't think about yourself.*

He lowered his mouth to hers, sealing them together, mimicking the sex act with his tongue. The sounds she made in her throat caused his groin to tighten even more—if that was possible. He pushed against her and felt the heat of her through the denim as she rubbed her mound against him.

"I never knew it could feel so good," she whispered. "I never imagined how wonderful it would be."

He kissed her eyes and cheeks and nose before he reached her mouth again. She kissed him back eagerly, her tongue thrusting into his mouth, tasting him, dueling with him as he sought to return the favor.

Mac had forgotten about his jeans. She obviously had not. He felt her hands on the zipper again, and this time he let her lower it and reach inside.

"Okay?" she asked.

Think of her. Think of her. "Okay," he rasped.

But if she thought she was going to have it all her way, she was wrong. When Jewel reached for him, Mac got rid of his shirt and reached for her. He slipped two fingers inside her quickly, before she could protest, and settled his thumb on the tiny nub that was the source of so much delight.

"I can't...concentrate on you...when you're doing that...to me..." she panted.

His body was hard, pulsing in an agony of delight. It was a good thing she was not more experienced, although her innocence was likely to be his undoing.

He concentrated on bringing Jewel to a climax, focusing his attention on kissing her, touching her, pleasing her. Soon her hand was lax against him, her eyes closed, her jaw clenched as the pleasure overtook her. She leaned into him with her hips and arched her body toward him, making it easy for him to kiss her breasts, to suckle them and to tease them with his teeth and tongue.

Sweat beaded on his forehead, as he watched the play of expressions on her face. The rapture. The delight. The confusion as her body tightened more and more, as he pushed her higher and higher. The ecstasy as her body rippled with pleasure. And the love, as she looked up at him from hooded eyes and rose on tiptoe to find his mouth with hers and thank him with a kiss.

He picked her up, pulled down his bedcovers and laid her on the sheet. Her eyes had already slid closed before he pulled off his jeans and briefs and slid into bed beside her. He wrapped his arms around her and pulled her back into the hollow of his belly. He lay there bone hard and unsatisfied—but very pleased with himself.

He had brought Jewel to climax twice now and managed to control his own urgent need. Surely it would not be so difficult to put himself inside her and do it so she would not recognize his inexperience. She seemed to have put completely out of her mind what had happened six years ago.

He wished she were awake now. He wished he did not have to wait. If he could just make love to her this instant, he knew everything would be fine. But she seemed perfectly satisfied to lie beside him. She did not seem the least bit interested in any more touching or kissing.

Mac got the first hint of his error when he felt Jewel's hand sliding up his thigh, headed for the barely relaxed, unsatisfied part of him.

"Jewel? What's going on?"

She turned in his arms to face him. Her eyes were two shiny spots in the darkness. "I want to make love to you, Mac."

"We just—"

"I want you to put yourself inside me as deep as you can. I want to make you feel as wonderful as you've made me feel."

Mac swallowed hard. He felt like crying. "God, Jewel. Now?"

"Now." She touched him, and his body stood at rigid attention. She lay back and urged him over her.

She didn't have to urge him very hard.

For a moment she hesitated, and Mac realized she was remembering the past. This was the way he had found her with Harvey Barnes. Harvey was on top, and she was helpless beneath him. Like Harvey, Mac was stronger. He could do to her whatever he wanted.

Mac saw her rising fear and said, "It's me, Jewel."

Her whole body relaxed, and she smiled up at him

sweetly. "I know, Mac. Love me, please. And let me love you."

Patience. Patience.

Patience went out the window the instant his body reached the entrance to hers. Mac tried to go slow, but she was wet and hot, and he wanted to be inside her so bad, that it took only three brief thrusts before he was buried deep inside her.

Mac paused, his weight on his elbows, his hips cradled in hers, and looked down, ashamed of his haste and afraid of what he would see on her face. "Jewel?"

"I'm fine," she said, her eyes glowing, her fingertips caressing his cheeks. "I'm wonderful."

It was all right. She couldn't tell it was his first time… because it was also the first time for her, he realized.

It was easy then, to think of her and not himself. "I don't want to hurt you," he said.

In response, she lifted her knees on either side of him, then wrapped her legs around his buttocks, seating him even more deeply inside her.

"My God," he muttered. "Jewel, I…" He withdrew and thrust as slowly and gently as he could, but the inevitable urge to mate, to put his seed inside her, drove him to move faster. When she lifted her hips and pushed back, the friction created unbelievably exquisite sensations.

Go slow. Slow down. Wait for her.

He saw Jewel's face through a haze of desire, heard her guttural sounds of pleasure and finally felt her body, slick and wet beneath him, begin to convulse.

Her body squeezed him, wringing pleasure beyond anything he could have imagined. He arched his head backward in an agony of joy as he spilled his seed inside her. His body pulsed, emptying itself in powerful thrusts before he lowered himself to lie beside her and wrapped her in his arms.

His breathing was ragged, his blood still pumping so hard it throbbed in his veins. He could not find breath for words, and would not have known what to say if he could have spoken.

"Thank you, Mac," Jewel whispered, snuggling close. "No man could have made me feel more lovely... or more loved."

Mac kissed her on the temple, a wordless thanks for saying what he had not been able to find words to express. The pleasure of this first time for him was all the sweeter, knowing she was happy.

Mac thought of all the women he could have made love to and had not. All the sex he had turned down in those early years, which had put him in the position of making love for the first time to the very woman he hoped to marry. As far as Mac was concerned, that meant Jewel was the only woman he would ever make love with.

Maybe he should have felt deprived. He did not.

Intuitively Mac knew that sex with a stranger—or even an acquaintance, would not have been as earth-shattering, or as bone-melting, as his experience with Jewel. Without the love he felt for her—and the love she felt for him in return—the sex act would not have brought him nearly so much joy.

"What are you thinking?" Jewel murmured.

"How much I enjoyed making love to you," he replied with a smile.

She kept her eyes lowered, and she was obviously struggling to speak as she said, "Considering the experience of the other women you must have slept with, I can't imagine my first efforts were much to shout about."

"Will you marry me?"

Mac had meant to distract her from a discussion of his sexual experience, and the proposal worked. But not in the way he had hoped.

"Does that mean you were satisfied?" she said, arching a brow. "I don't want to spend my life wondering how I stack up against the competition," she said wryly.

"I'm never going to be comparing you to anyone else," he muttered.

"Why don't I believe you?"

"Believe me."

"How can I believe you?" she said, rising to her elbow and staring down at him. "Are you telling me you never found a single other woman who was more appealing to you in bed than me?"

"That's exactly what I'm saying," he retorted, sitting up abruptly. "Because there were no other women."

She sat up just as quickly to face him, and the sheet dropped to her waist, exposing her breasts. "You're kidding, right?"

The sight of her nipples, full and rosy, set his pulse to galloping. "No man would kid about something like that. Until a few minutes ago I was a virgin. Now damn it, will you or won't you marry me?"

He had known she would laugh if she ever found

out the truth. But he had never expected such gentle laughter. Such joyful laughter. Such loving laughter.

Jewel pushed him onto his back and straddled him with only the sheet between them. She leaned down, her lips close to his and said, "Oh, yes, my darling. I will most definitely marry you."

"It doesn't bother you that I don't have more experience in bed?" he demanded.

She chuckled. "Why should it? This way we can both learn exactly what pleases us. For instance, do you like it when I bite your earlobe like this?"

He shivered at the searing sensation of pleasure.

"Or would you rather I kissed this spot below your ear?"

Mac groaned. He had switched their positions and had her beneath him in two seconds flat. "I like it all," he said, nipping her earlobe and then kissing her below the ear, feeling the frisson of pleasure that rippled through her. "Just so long as I'm doing it with you."

"Well, then," she said, smiling up at him, "why don't we practice making a baby?"

Mac laughed, then cheerfully indulged the future mother of his children.

EPILOGUE

JEWEL SAT IN A ROCKER ON THE COVERED porch of the two-story Victorian house Mac had built for them. It stood on Hawk's Pride land her father had given them as a wedding present four years ago. Jewel had wanted a white house with lots of gingerbread trim with morning glories entwined in it, and that was exactly what she had.

She sighed with pleasure every time she looked around her. This was her favorite place to be these days. She was nursing her second son, while the first, blond-haired, blue-eyed, three-year-old Evan, played with a football at her feet.

"Daddy!" Evan cried, leaping up as Mac appeared around the corner of the house.

Mac opened his arms when he reached the foot of the steps that led up to the front door, and Evan launched himself into his father's arms. The two looked very much alike, down to the twin dimples in their cheeks.

"Welcome home," Jewel said with a smile.

"It's good to be home," Mac replied, settling into the rocker beside her with Evan on his lap. "How's Dustin?"

"Hungry, as always."

"I can see why he enjoys dinner so much," Mac said

with a teasing smile, as he eyed the breast that provided his son's nourishment.

Jewel blushed. Even after four years of marriage, Mac talked about her breasts as though they were the best gift he had ever been given. "How did your trip go?" she asked.

"I got two Pro-Bowl quarterbacks, a former Heisman Trophy winner and a record-setting kicker to commit to a week each at Camp LittleHawk."

"Fabulous!" Jewel said. "I knew you could do it! What about the fund-raiser?"

Jewel had been as surprised as Mac when Andy Dennison suggested they raise money for Mac's sports camp from the public. The Camp LittleHawk fund-raiser had become a highlight on the sports calendar and football players from around the league were delighted to be invited to participate.

"Everything is in place," Mac said. "Andy says he thinks we can double what we made last year."

"That'll mean we can build another couple of bunkhouses," Jewel said. "And hire the help we'll need to staff them."

Mac nodded and set his rocker to moving. "How were things around here while I was gone?"

"The high school-age summer counselors arrived yesterday for their week of training."

"Did he come?"

Jewel smiled. "He came."

Mac leaned his head back and turned his face away, but Jewel had already seen the tears that leaped to his eyes.

"He's been in remission for three years, Mac. Don't

you think it's safe now to admit how much you like the kid?"

Mac turned back to her and reached out to take her hand in his. "I suppose it is."

"I thought so. That's why I asked him over for dinner tonight."

"What?"

"You can come out now, Brad," Jewel said.

The screen door opened, and Brad Templeton stepped onto the front porch. "Hi, Mac."

Mac rose and set Evan down.

It was questionable which of the two men moved first, but the instant they met, they wrapped their arms around each other and hugged tight.

Neither of them said anything, but if they were as moved as Jewel was, they were both too emotional to speak.

Mac recovered first, pushed Brad an arm's length away and said, "Let me look at you. How old are you now?"

"Sixteen," Brad said.

"You've gotten taller."

"You look the same."

Mac pulled off the New York Mets baseball cap and tousled Brad's dark hair. "Looks like you need a trim."

Brad grabbed the ball cap and tugged it down. "Now that I've got a little hair, I'm not about to cut it off. Besides, the chicks like it like this."

Mac laughed as he put an arm around Brad's shoulder and headed back toward Jewel. "Just remember," he said, pointing his thumb at Jewel, "this one's taken."

"I thought you had the hots for her," Brad said, winking at Jewel. "Guess I was right."

Mac laughed, then sobered. "I'm so glad you made it back here," he said, his voice breaking with emotion.

"I owe it all to you. I kept on fighting, like you said. And here I am."

The screen door slammed again and Jewel's brother Colt appeared on the front porch, tossing a football from hand to hand. At eighteen, his shoulders had broadened, and he had grown a few more inches. His hair was too long, and his face held a perpetual look of defiance. "If the reunion is over, I promised to throw Brad a few passes."

"Sure," Mac said, giving Brad a nudge in Colt's direction. "Let's see what kind of speed you have, Brad."

Mac returned to the rocker and settled down, picking up Evan again and holding him in his lap.

"Football," Evan said, pointing to Colt and Brad.

"Yep. Someday you're going to be playing, sport. But right now we're going to watch your uncle Colt and my friend Brad."

As the two of them watched Brad run in a zigzagging pattern, Jewel said, "Colt finally told Dad he's been accepted to the Air Force Academy."

Mac missed seeing Colt throw the football, because his attention had switched to Jewel. "What did Zach say?"

"He was angry that Colt hadn't said anything to him before now about wanting to go into the Air Force."

"And?"

"They're not speaking at the moment."

"What did Rebecca say?" Mac asked, his eyes back on Colt.

"Mom was hurt by all the secrecy. And she's afraid for Colt, because what he wants to do will put him in the path of danger."

Mac's mouth turned up wryly. "That shouldn't surprise her. Colt has led a pretty reckless life the past four years. It's a wonder he got through high school alive."

"I can't help thinking how unhappy Colt must have been all these years, knowing he was going to disappoint Dad and hurt Mom when he finally told them the truth about what he wanted to do with his life."

"Who'd have thought it," Mac said, watching the perfect spiraling pass Colt had thrown land gently in Brad's outstretched arms. "He would have made one hell of a pro quarterback."

"Apparently he'll play football for the Air Force Academy," Jewel said. "When he's done, he plans to fly jets."

Mac brushed his thumb across Jewel's knuckles, sending a frisson of pleasure streaking up her arm. "Do you think Colt would talk to me?"

"I'm sure he could use an ear to listen," Jewel said. "I've invited him for dinner, too."

Mac smiled. "Have I told you lately how much I love you?"

"It's been twenty-four hours, at least."

"I love you, Jewel." Mac raised her hand and kissed her palm.

Jewel found herself breathless as she met his avid gaze. "It's time for another lesson in the bedroom," she said.

"Oh? What are we learning this time?"

"How to make a baby *girl*," Jewel said.

"Sounds interesting," Mac said. "When does class start?"

"Right after the dinner dishes are done," Jewel said, "and you talk to Colt and he drives Brad back to Camp LittleHawk and we get these two into bed."

"I'll be there," Mac promised with a grin. "This is a lesson I don't want to miss."

Jewel laughed. "Just get it right this time, or you're liable to find yourself with a whole football team before we're through."

"I wouldn't mind," Mac said softly. "As long as we get at least one girl who looks just like you."

Before Jewel could answer, a football came flying onto the porch, and Mac and Evan abandoned her to play football with the two teenagers.

Jewel fingered the soft curls at Dustin's nape and brushed her hand across his baby-soft cheek. She was looking forward to Mac's inventive lovemaking tonight. Knowing his determination to do everything to the best of his ability, it was bound to be a delightful adventure, full of fun and laughter.

Only this time, she would have the last laugh. Jewel's smile grew as she imagined the look on Mac's face when she told him—after the lesson, of course—that his daughter was already on the way.

* * * * *